AND BREAK THE PRETTY KINGS

AND BREAK THE PRETTY KINGS

LENA JEONG

HARPER TEEN
An Imprint of HarperCollinsPublishers

HarperTeen is an imprint of HarperCollins Publishers.

Dedicated to Emmeline
and all oldest daughters everywhere

Chapter
ONE

Summoning fire was easy. Mirae had been studying the manipulation of the four elements her whole life. Scorching the woman in front of her, however, was something she hadn't managed even once in the past three months.

Nevertheless, Mirae raised a hand to the heavens as if pulling fire from the sun. A small white-hot orb appeared in her palm; before its sharp heat could blister her skin, Mirae lobbed it with all her strength at her opponent.

Captain Jia, head of the palace guards, swatted Mirae's orb into wisps of harmless steam, then glanced down at her barely smoking wrist guard. "Have you considered a career in the sauna industry, Gongju?" she asked wryly. "You seem much more adept at making people sweat than burning them alive."

Mirae wiped her brow, careful not to pull any more hair loose. The palace women were starting to get suspicious about the "long morning walks" that kept ruining all their hard work, and with tonight's pre-coronation ceremony only hours away, they would be loath to redo her hair completely. It was a blessing that Captain Jia, at least, could be trusted to keep Mirae's morning trainings a secret. The last thing she needed was for a crowd of gawking royals to gather on the field, judging for themselves whether their crown princess was truly ready to assume her birthright—to stand between Seolla and ultimate ruin, no matter the cost. It certainly didn't help that her mother's recent illness, a generational madness that would incapacitate Seolla's queen all too soon, meant Mirae needed to prove her skills faster than any of her ancestors ever had. Tonight would determine whether all her work had paid off.

Mirae blew into her hot, red palms, willing herself to focus, but her mind wandered to thoughts of her grandmother, whom she had adored more than anything. The last time Mirae saw her, her weh-halmoni had been standing at the dragon gates to the palace, eyes turned white-hot with uncontrollable madness— the price all her ancestors paid for being gods-touched guardians against Seolla's ancient enemy.

You were not born to end up like me, she'd said. *I see your destiny, my little golden snake, and no one can take it from you. Never forget the dragons in your blood.*

Mirae raised her hands for another attack, feeling her heart-beat slow as she willed her body to stay calm and focused, the way a crown princess was supposed to be. Then Captain Jia's words registered, and Mirae snorted. "A sauna? I suppose it's good to have a backup plan in case I fail tonight. Assuming I survive."

Captain Jia waved Mirae's words away as easily as she did her fireballs. "The Gongju I know fails at nothing. When faced with dire odds, she'll succeed . . . creatively, if she must."

Mirae sighed. "You're never letting the flying turtle incident go, are you?"

"The flying turtle must never be forgotten."

"It was one time."

"Two, if you count the talking turtle you enchanted on my birthday."

"What, I thought you liked turtles!"

"You've trained with me for years, and *that's* what you choose to remember?"

Mirae had been studying Sacred Bone Magic—the ability to wield all three of Seolla's magic systems, a birthright that belonged only to Seollan queens and their heirs—her whole life, but since her mother's illness, she had postponed all her other studies while Captain Jia did her best to advance Mirae's talents in her own field of expertise: Jade Witchery, the first magic system Mirae would be tested in that night.

Thanks to Captain Jia, Mirae's skills had improved to the level of a woman with years more experience than she had. The Jade Witch prodigy was herself the youngest captain ever appointed to the Wonhwa, the palace guards, and was rumored to be on track to become general of Seolla's army. But both Mirae and the young captain sorely missed the days when sneaking off entailed hanging out with Mirae's brothers by the river, instead of attacking each other with all four elements as if the fate of the peninsula depended on it.

Of course, despite all her new skills, Mirae occasionally still needed to rely on other techniques to achieve the results everyone expected of her. She couldn't help but chuckle now at the memory Captain Jia had brought up. "Who knew turtles were so chatty?"

But Captain Jia's face had sobered. Mirae followed her gaze across the secluded training field and felt her own body fall still.

The royal palanquin was approaching from the west, a bloodred box looming over the shoulders of ten impassive servants. Not even the cheery yellow drapes or black canopy for cooling could draw Mirae's eyes away from the beaded curtain that hid the woman inside: her mother, Seolla's enchanted queen. The woman everyone expected Mirae to replace, years earlier than any other crown princess had attempted the Trial of the Gods.

Mirae turned back to the captain. "What is she doing here?"

"The physician said talking long walks would benefit Her Majesty," Captain Jia said. "It looks like she's taking a page out of your book when it comes to loose interpretations."

"She should be resting." Mirae looked nervously toward the tree line to the south. In truth, she was worried that her mother's increasingly unstable powers would tamper with her own carefully honed magic.

Today of all days needed to go uneventfully. The Sacred Bone Oracles were already in the forest's depths, setting up the mysterious Trial of the Gods.

"Do you think she needs to speak to me?" Mirae asked, careful not to glance back at the palanquin, lest she expose her nervousness.

Captain Jia shook her head. "I doubt Her Majesty will get too close. She knows what happens when your Sacred Bone powers interact."

A few weeks ago, there had been an . . . incident. Mirae's mother was found sleepwalking in the ancestral shrine, lighting paintings of past queens on fire. Mirae had been roused from bed and used a soothing Ma-eum illusion to draw her mother out, but her spell had waned too quickly, her skills in Seolla's second magic system too weak to compete with her mother's madness. Her mother's delusions ended up coming back with a vengeance that resulted in the rest of the building catching fire—nearly taking Mirae along with it.

After that, the councilmembers of the Hwabaek had decreed that Mirae's mother was no longer fit to rule and Mirae's Sangsok Ceremony would be scheduled for the next full moon, whether she was ready for it or not. It was now only hours away and Mirae could hardly call herself prepared.

"Gongju." Captain Jia pulled Mirae back into the present and gave her an encouraging nod. "Stay focused and show Her Majesty what you can do. Light me on fire."

Mirae nodded and held her palms in front of her, readying them for magic. She took a moment to study Captain Jia's defenses, trying to puzzle out a fresh plan of attack.

The captain's ensemble was the same as it always was. Over a thick red tunic that signified her status, she wore scale armor, which afforded her more mobility than Mirae liked when they were facing off. Around her waist was tied a bloodred sash embroidered with gold peonies that signaled her rank as captain of the palace guard.

The only weak spot Mirae could hope to exploit was the one she'd been trying and failing to set on fire all morning. "I don't suppose you'd be willing to stand still and make this easy for me."

Captain Jia snorted. "I'm not a campfire. Pretend I'm an enemy assassin from Josan."

Mirae held back a retort about how a Josan assassin wouldn't have magic; its use was forbidden in their land. Instead, she raised a hand to the sky, drawing heat from the sun yet again. Once it had gathered into a sphere in her palms, Mirae hurled the fireball at her opponent, realizing too late that her weary arm had aimed the attack poorly.

Captain Jia blocked the clumsy spell by simply raising her hand. Green flames sprouted out of her palm like dancing petals and easily devoured Mirae's orange ball, lobbed artlessly like a rotting persimmon.

Mirae clenched her fists, using the sharp pain of her budding blisters to drown out the fear she couldn't afford to let anyone see. Again, she reached her arm toward the sun, her mind willing her palms to re-create the heavenly orb.

As soon as the new fireball was formed, Mirae hurled it without warning. Captain Jia's warrior response kicked in; quick as a bamboo switch, she raised her palm, green with fire. Too late she realized that Mirae had released a second spell—a blast of air she'd been secretly preparing.

Mirae hadn't even had to blink; the only thing easier than summoning fire was channeling wind. Focusing on the morning-chilled tip of her nose, she had drawn that brisk feeling into her hands, cooling her skin with a sharp burst of icy air.

Then, with barely a thought, she had turned that small nip of wind into a narrow gale, strong enough to rush past the surprised captain, forcing the flames in her palm to fly backward. They slipped between her fingers, setting first her brace on fire, and then her whole arm.

Mirae smiled, knowing the captain's jade fire wouldn't harm the flesh of its maker, though the same couldn't be said for her clothes. Captain Jia calmly brushed her free hand down her burning arm, extinguishing every lick of green flame. "I suppose you're proud of that one."

"I was being creative," Mirae said. "You called it my greatest skill."

"I don't recall describing it that way."

"Well, it got you nice and toasty all the same."

Captain Jia held out her hands, inspecting them for damage. "See, this is why you should build the Sauna of Seolla. Your fire never actually hurts anyone, which is a great selling point."

Mirae grimaced. "That's a terrible name for my future business."

"You're opening a sauna?" asked a familiar voice from behind Mirae. "Then you'll need someone to manage your finances, since you tend to treat math like an elusive mystic art."

Mirae whirled around and beamed at her older brother, Minho, who must have remained hidden behind the palanquin to surprise her. She was glad he had been able to witness her fireball success. "Aren't you supposed to be keeping Father and Hongbin out of trouble?"

"An impossible task." Minho gave Mirae and Captain Jia a pained look, not bothering to hide his casualness with the captain around his sister; as his most trusted confidante, Mirae knew everything about their secret relationship. "The Josan dignitary's just arrived, and you know how annoying Father and our little brother are when they start trying to prove he's secretly a gumiho."

"At least they've moved on from dokkaebi. Hongbin's attempts to trick the dignitary into a wrestling match last year were getting disturbingly creative." Mirae patted her older brother's shoulder. "I know what you're thinking, orabeoni, but no, we can't ask the Josan dignitary to leave, even though no one's happy he's here. A representative of our sovereign state must witness the succession of a new queen and swear fealty to the throne."

"I know." Minho glanced back at their mother's palanquin, which waited several yards away in the open field like a ruby lantern containing Seolla's once brightest light. "There's just something about his face that makes me wish a gumiho *would* actually come eat him. If anyone was going to bring back Josan's history of thwarting the Trial of the Gods and trying to unleash our diabolic enemy, it would be him."

"He's no threat, Daegun daegam, I promise," Captain Jia said, then bowed before crossing her arms over her chest. With the royal palanquin nearby, she had resumed using full honorifics and making proper obeisance to her lieges, just as she did in public. "The dignitary can't even look outside his chamber without an entourage of my best guards interrogating his intentions. There will be no sabotaging of the Sangsok Ceremony tonight."

"You don't have to be so formal, Jia, as if we're under surveillance, too," Minho said with a grin. "I'm pretty sure my mother already suspects we're . . . more than friends."

Captain Jia blushed. "I'm attending to official business right now, Daegun *daegam*," she said pointedly, and returned her attention to Mirae, whom she also spoke to more respectfully. "Come, Gongju mama. Let's get back to training."

Minho exchanged a grin with Mirae at the captain's expense. It was almost too easy to fluster her. "Actually, Jia, I came here to help with the training. I thought you might appreciate a break from being Mirae's practice dummy."

"I told you last night, it's too risky." Captain Jia shook her head adamantly. "You don't have magic like us. You'll only get hurt."

"Is that so?" Minho deflected the captain's concern with a mischievous smile, a trait that Mirae knew annoyed the captain to no end. "Hongbin said I have a magical ability to know when he's got snacks in his pockets, so I've got that going for me."

"Our beloved Gunju daegam *always* has snacks," Captain Jia countered.

Minho crossed his arms proudly. "See, you and I share the same power. Let me stand in for you, Jia, while you take a break. I trust you to step in if Mirae tries to murder me."

Mirae watched the pair bickering and noticed, not for the first time, how exhausted Captain Jia looked; her high cheek-bones looked sharper than they had three months ago, and the bags under her eyes were growing more and more pronounced. Even her tall, muscular form stood a little less proudly. Minho, she knew, was just shielding his concern for the captain. Mirae felt bad that the past three months of training had kept the captain and the eldest prince apart, especially since she'd heard from both of them that the little time they did have usually ended in a fight about the same thing: the fact that Captain Jia was just as devoted to her duty as Minho was to the captain.

"We've got one element left to practice," Mirae chimed in, making a decision for the weary captain, whose leather armor was still smoking. The grass on the field around them also still leaned sharply toward the ground because of the wind Mirae had conjured earlier. "Do you think you can handle me hurling some water at you, orabeoni?"

"You can certainly try." Minho smoothed his shiny black hair the way Hongbin would do in front of good-looking men. Then he started stretching out his long, lean limbs. "They don't call me the strongest, most handsome man in the queendom for nothing."

"I thought only I called you that," Captain Jia said wryly.

Minho snorted and called for his personal servant, Siwon. Clearly disappointed that his master had remembered he was there, Siwon ran out from behind the palanquin. His smooth, youthful face sported the politest scowl Mirae had ever seen. "Yes, Daegun daegam?"

"I need you to secure my hair."

Siwon raised an eyebrow. "For running, swimming . . . or some mixture of both?"

Mirae laughed. "See, not even Siwon thinks you're going to escape my torrent."

Minho lifted his nose in pretend offense as Siwon did his best to tighten his master's top bun and hanbok strings. As soon as Siwon was done, Minho turned toward the trees and, without warning, bolted across the training field, leaving Mirae, Captain Jia, Siwon, and the palanquin in the dust. "Do your worst, Mirae!"

Mirae thought her older brother looked a lot like a rabbit, his zodiac animal, with his lithe body sprinting nimbly through the tall grass. As he ran, morning wind gathered into the scarlet silk bellies of his hanbok, filling the fabric like bloodred sails at dawn.

Mirae and Siwon shared a look. The servant shrugged. "He did say do your worst."

Mirae smiled and raised her palms, cupping them into tiny wells. Keenly aware of the eyes watching everything she did, Mirae searched for an inciting sense. Much like she'd relied on the cold tip of her nose to summon wind, Mirae needed something to ground her procurement of water.

The sweat on her brow would do.

In an instant, Mirae's palms began to glitter with tiny, clear pearls that bubbled up on her skin, multiplying rapidly to form two small ponds. She lifted her shallow wells into the air, and all it took was a nudge to give the droplets the power they needed to reunite with their misty forebears across the sky.

Mirae couldn't help but smile as the tiny pools rose obediently from her hands, greeting and melding with their unseen sisters and brothers above, thickening into a giant, watery pearl looming over her head.

The wind she'd summoned earlier still lingered in cold wisps around her. Mirae flung her arms together and used the gust to lob the translucent orb right at Minho's head.

It hit him almost instantly. The force of Mirae's orb and manipulated wind nearly knocked Minho off his feet, but he was nimble enough to remain standing—which only made it easier for the sphere of water to descend and devour him.

Mirae, Captain Jia, and Siwon all laughed as Minho twisted himself around in the giant, watery orb, cheeks puffed out from holding his breath. He placed his hands on his hips, his eyebrows frowning at Mirae the way his mouth couldn't.

Siwon waved at his master. "So glad you proved your point, Daegun daegam!"

Mirae snorted again, and Captain Jia shook her head at her lover. "That'll teach him to interrupt Sacred Bone training. Well done, Gongju mama."

Mirae smiled to see the captain and Siwon in agreement for once. She wasn't entirely sure why, but the two people Minho kept closest to him had been squabbling a lot lately, especially when it came to what Minho truly needed. Mirae hoped that once her Sangsok Ceremony was over and Captain Jia had more time to spend with her royal lover, this sudden jealousy or whatever it was would subside and all would be peaceful once more.

But first, Mirae had to make sure she didn't accidentally drown her older brother. She prepared to make a show of releasing Minho in a beautiful explosion of water, but before she could, something tugged on her magic like a bird plucking a butterfly abruptly out of the sky. She froze, staring at Minho. He was struggling in the liquid orb, thrashing and kicking the sides of his prison.

It looked like he was screaming.

"That's enough, Gongju mama," Captain Jia said sharply. "Let him go."

Mirae lowered her damp palms, bidding the elements under her control to disperse. But they didn't obey. Instead, the water roiled into a whirlpool of rage barely contained within the orb.

As the droplets churned each other into a storm of chaos, Minho became nothing more than a flailing blur, fast running out of air.

"Gongju mama, I said that's enough!" Captain Jia shouted.

"He learned his lesson," Siwon said anxiously.

"I can't make it stop." All Mirae could do was stare in horror alongside Captain Jia and Siwon. Water had no mind of its own. No element did. So why was it disobeying her? That wasn't possible. Unless—

Mirae whirled toward the palanquin and saw a pale, skeletal arm reaching through the beaded curtains, stretching in Minho's direction. A second later, her mother's face pushed past the beads, her eyes white as the moon—her snarling teeth even whiter.

The madness. It had taken hold of her mother, filling her mind with delusions once again. Turning her magic against those she loved. Before Mirae could call out a warning, she felt her mother's wild power turn on her. With a grip as cold and biting as ice, it froze the magic in her palms and whisked the wind from her throat.

Mirae fell to her knees, gasping for air as her mother's magic crushed her head and neck. The roar of pressure building in her ears soon became almost as loud as the bang-bang-banging of her heart.

But what frightened Mirae most was what else she could hear—Minho's voice. Low words, strangely calm. Muddled in her mind as if they were her own thoughts.

Save me, Mirae.

She forced her eyes open and saw Siwon bolting toward Minho. She heard Captain Jia shouting as she ran toward the palanquin, but Mirae knew her mother would hurt anyone who tried to stop her. Only Sacred Bone Magic could compete with the queen's mindless power.

Mirae was Minho's only hope.

She slapped her palms to the ground, facing Minho once more, and raised a prayer to her ancestors. This time she didn't reach for water, fire, or air, focusing instead on the only element her mother hadn't manipulated yet. With one stiff, ice-cold hand, Mirae gripped the grass beneath her, digging her fingers into cold, packed dirt. The other hand she raised into a fist, ignoring everything except the words ringing through her head.

Save me.

Mirae closed her eyes and struck the ground with all the strength and air left in her body before collapsing into darkness.

Chapter

TWO

Two hands pressed down on Mirae's chest, rousing her with the soothing touch of the elements. The warmth of fire was massaged into Mirae's muscles, loosening them. Refreshing, clean air was pushed gently into her lungs. Drips of cool water were summoned to rinse her burning eyes and throat, while the steadiness of earth raised her up on a low, grassy dais.

When Mirae opened her eyes, she half expected to see her grandmother smiling down at her, her weh-halmoni's hands ever gentle until her own madness had forced her into exile. But it was Captain Jia who crouched over Mirae now. "Gongju, are you all right?"

Mirae turned her aching neck slowly toward the tree line where she'd last seen Minho. The earth there was now a giant hollow.

"Minho . . . ," Mirae croaked, her throat burning. "Is he—"

"I'm here, Mirae. I'm fine." Minho crouched above her, exhausted and soaked but unharmed. Her magic had worked. Mirae saw that the ground around her bruised fist had fissured into cracks of sunken lightning, signs that the earth had heeded her command to rip itself apart. Minho had fallen into the crevasse below, safely drawn out of the bubble of water and the grip of the queen's misguided magic. Siwon knelt behind his master, massaging Minho's shoulders ferociously.

"Where's Mother?" Mirae looked to where the palanquin had been, turning her neck too quickly. Something popped loudly.

"She was taken back to her chambers," Captain Jia said. She touched Mirae's neck and sent more soothing heat through it, whispers of fire emanating from her fingertips. "Her magic retreated as soon as you intervened."

"It's getting worse." Mirae swallowed, sending sharp pains down her swollen throat. "She's never done anything like this before."

"Tell that to the shrine she burned to a crisp," Siwon muttered. "I was up till the crack of dawn with the palace women sweeping up the charred remains of priceless, beautiful art." Ignoring Captain Jia's glare at his disrespectful tone, he switched from massaging Minho's shoulders to mourning his master's matted hair.

"It ends tonight. That's all that matters," Minho said, swatting away Siwon's meddling hands so he could help Mirae sit up. "Once you take over for Mother, her mind can finally rest. I know this is all happening sooner than anyone expected, but maybe because of your willingness, Mother stands a chance of healing before she loses her mind completely."

"You mean before she becomes like Halmoni," Mirae said quietly.

You were not born to end up like me.

"We are in an auspicious year," Captain Jia said encouragingly. "Maybe all this turmoil is a sign that the gods are stirring up the winds of change. You, Gongju, might be the one to finally unite the peninsula, as foretold by the High Daughters of the Sacred Bone."

"And lead Seolla into its golden future," Minho and Siwon recited together.

Mirae did her best to smile at everyone's reassuringing words as she rose laboriously to her feet, but her heart was heavy with the part of the well-known prophecy that they'd purposefully left out. The High Daughters of the Sacred Bone—the mightiest Ma-eum Mage, Jade Witch, and Horomancer to have ever lived—had indeed foretold of a Seollan queen who would unite the peninsula, but not until she destroyed the queendom's greatest enemy, an ancient evil whose name Mirae wasn't allowed to utter.

He was the reason for her mother's fractured mind, for the madness that fell upon all queens of Seolla. The task of keeping his evil locked away eventually led to the dissolution of their sanity.

If Mirae was the queen destined to unite the peninsula, she would also be the queen to destroy their greatest foe . . . otherwise, her mind would fall just as her mother's and her mother's mother's had.

Mirae shook off all these dark thoughts as she swayed on her feet, suddenly dizzy. She couldn't afford to be distracted by anything other than passing the Trial of the Gods that night. The fate of the peninsula would have to wait. "I think I've had enough training for the day, if you don't mind, Captain. I should go check on my mother."

Captain Jia reached out to steady Mirae. "I'd say your training is complete. You just proved that your mastery of the four elements is stronger than Her Majesty's madness. That's what Seolla needs from you. You're ready to fulfill your birthright."

Mirae glanced back toward the trees where the Sacred Bone Oracles had almost finished setting up the tests that would determine her fate—*Seolla's* fate. "I can do this, right? You all really believe in me?"

Siwon raised his hand. "I believe in you, Gongju mama."

"I do too." Captain Jia placed a hand over her heart. "After all, I trained you."

"You're powerful and benevolent," Minho said. "Of course, you save lives as dramatically as possible, but no one can say you're unfit to protect Seolla. Mother least of all."

Mirae smiled and accepted her brother's arm as they walked back toward the palace proper. Captain Jia stayed behind in the training field to clean up the mess Mirae had made. As a Jade Witch, she was proficient in the manipulation of wind, water, and fire, but earth magic was her specialty. As she walked back toward the palace, Mirae heard the sound of the grass rustling as it righted itself and the ground rumbling as it stitched itself back together. It wouldn't be long before the field looked exactly as it had before, heeding the will of a powerful Jade Witch.

Mirae didn't know what she would be asked to do during the gods' test of *her* Jade Witchery, but she hoped it would include earth magic—the manipulation of everything both on and below the surface of the earth, including grass, gems, and even magma. Even though her mother had always been tight-lipped about her own Trial of the Gods, Mirae's grandmother had proudly shown her the dagger she'd forged the night of her test, one that Mirae now kept displayed on the wall of her chamber.

As Mirae's grandmother told it, when asked to create a weapon that sundered both the sky and the earth, she had manipulated the winds and the water in the heavens to stir up a storm, until a single streak of lightning struck the sandy path at her feet, creating an instantaneous sculpture of wild glass. Though the sand's true nature had been burned away by that lightning strike, it had become something new and volatile. Still, Mirae's grandmother had fearlessly willed it to take the shape of a dagger, white and horned as a coral fossil with all the stinging might of its lightning-conjuring maker.

Mirae had long dreamed of the kind of wonder she might create at the behest of the gods when it was her turn to walk in her grandmother's footsteps. Never had she imagined that she would enter the gods' trial barely trained, a princess who couldn't even light her teacher on fire.

"Here, Gongju mama, you look like you could use a little relaxing." Siwon, who had been treating Minho's back with massage-like jabs to improve his circulation, shifted to prodding Mirae's back instead, only stopping when she threatened to muss Minho's hair for the second time that day.

Just before they reached the palace gardens, Minho came to a sudden stop, letting out a dramatic gasp.

"I've got it," he said. "Your future sauna: Mirae's Magic Monsoon. That's a winner right there. I can't wait to tell Jia!"

He and Siwon celebrated his stroke of genius while Mirae rolled her eyes.

Mirae and her companions maintained a leisurely pace for their "morning walk," just in case anyone suspected that the crown princess was still in basic training on the day of her Sangsok Ceremony. Mirae, as usual, enjoyed her slow stroll home over red moon bridges dusted with maehwa, the blossoms pale as snow. She even took a few moments to gaze into the stone-lined ponds below, heavy with lily pads and bright, sunset-colored koi.

If her younger brother, Hongbin, had been there, he would have cheerfully picked flowers—for Minho, the long yellow finger-shaped buds of golden bell trees; for Mirae, he would have chosen mugunghwa. In his honor, Mirae plucked one of the blossoms, admiring its petals, splayed like a pink hand with a dark ombré eye at its center. Knowing the flower would only last until the end of the day, she stuck it ceremoniously in her hair.

Soon enough, despite their lazy pace, the inner walls of the palace came into view. Mirae nodded at the Wonhwa standing guard, who were ordered by their captain to keep her comings and goings to the training ground a secret. They admitted Mirae, Minho, and Siwon without a word.

Mirae breathed a long sigh as she stepped onto the pale sand of the courtyard and rejoined the busyness of the palace. The front-facing buildings around her—halls and offices with thick red pillars, carved green supports, blue-tiled roofs that curved like her father's mustache, and bright gables with gold trim—hid her return from the private training session. Easily seen over every roof was a magnificent three-tiered pagoda where soon, if all went well, Mirae would be crowned Seolla's next enchanted queen.

If all goes well. Mirae's blistered palms began to sweat at the thought of the ceremony, salting the open sores. To mask her pain, she bid the late-morning breeze to condense on her skin and soothe the lingering burn. She would have to come up with a story to explain her wounds—and her carelessness right before the trial—when she visited the royal physician later.

Her hands had barely cooled when someone clamped down on Mirae's shoulders from behind and whirled her around—scaring the ever-loving gods out of her. Thankfully, she saw the faces of the two men who'd dared touch her, before she sent them flying.

"Your face!" her father hooted. "I wish you could see it!"

"We got her so good," Hongbin cackled. "Look how mad she is!"

Once her heart no longer felt like it was trying to hurtle out of her chest—for the second time that morning—Mirae crossed her arms and glared at the men before her, slapping their knees like self-congratulating fools. "Aren't you supposed to be hosting the Josan dignitary?"

"Bah." Her father swatted the air. "If we were needed, the palace women would have found us. There's no escaping the shrewd, especially if your mother hired them."

Mirae turned to the Wonhwa guards. They had to have known that the youngest prince and the queen's consort were hiding just around the corner, but hadn't warned her. Instead of meeting Mirae's glare, the guards looked up at the sky as if they couldn't quite figure out what color it was.

"We have some important news," Hongbin said, leaning in to whisper. As usual, both his hair and his bright blue hanbok were immaculate, belying the trouble he was always getting into, even as a full-fledged prince only two years younger than Mirae. "The Josan dignitary is not, in fact, a gumiho. Probably."

Mirae sighed. "Do I want to know how you came to this conclusion?"

Her father shook his head. "I assure you, you do not."

Mirae appreciated what her father and younger brother were trying to do; if anyone knew how to get her out of her own head during a stressful time, it was them. But she was not in the mood for joviality, not with what she'd had to deal with that morning.

"Mother's ill again," Minho said quietly, interrupting the revelry on Mirae's behalf. "She almost killed me on the training field. Mirae barely stopped her in time."

Silence fell like a heavy cocoon around the group. Their father and Hongbin looked at Mirae, who nodded, confirming Minho's story. After taking a moment to compose himself, their father took Mirae's hand and patted it. "Well, I'm glad you were there. You're always right where we need you, the protector of this family."

He was doing his best to smile reassuringly, but recently, the signs of aging on his face were more pronounced than usual—a toll taken by his wife's premature illness. At least the changes suited him; gray hairs sparkled on his head, and the wrinkles around his eyes and mouth made it look as if his entire face was carved by laughter, even when he was hearing dire news.

Hongbin recovered more convincingly, hiding his worry with a mischievous smile. "You're going to be a great queen, noonim. Powerful, fair, and utterly committed to betrothing me to the perfect man, whom I may or may not have met this morning. The best part is, he's one of the Josan dignitary's entourage, so our match will bring peace between two feuding nations!"

"Men from Josan are very handsome," Siwon said with mock grandiosity, "if I do say so myself."

Mirae rolled her eyes at the servant, who was proudly Josan-born and kept his hair loosely flowing in the tradition of his country. "Why do you encourage him, Siwon? Do you enjoy hurting my and Minho's ears?"

"Oh, he does." Minho sighed dramatically. "I can vouch for that personally."

Hongbin laughed and put an arm around Siwon, leading them both away as he sang an impromptu song about Mirae being Seolla's greatest matchmaking queen. Their father shook his head as he stared after his son. "I better make sure he doesn't get into any more ssireum matches with the Josan delegates—or rather, with one of them in particular."

As their father wandered off, Minho turned to Mirae. "I'll make sure they *all* behave."

Mirae nodded her thanks. As Minho trotted off after the others, Mirae steeled herself for visiting her mother. She didn't have to walk far; the queen's chambers, built at the rear of the palace, were already in sight. The palace women outside bowed as Mirae approached.

Remembering the facade of regal confidence she was expected to maintain, Mirae lifted her chin, walking resolutely toward the woman whose duties would soon be hers. As Mirae prepared to enter her mother's chambers, the haetae statues on either side of the queen's residence seemed to grin down at her. She hoped to someday be like these protectors of stone, even as her heart beat as wildly as her mother's fits of madness.

To steady herself, Mirae pulled the mugunghwa from her hair and smelled it. Its aroma was strong, perfect for grounding Mirae's senses. Sweetly herbaceous. Heady and calming at the same time. Mirae inhaled until she could almost taste the essence of her favorite flower. Once she was certain the smell was caught in her nostrils, filling her with its almost tangible sweetness, Mirae laid the flower at her feet and headed into the queen's chambers.

Mirae bowed at the foot of her mother's silk sleeping mat, her face only inches from the floor. "You wished to speak with me?"

"Sit comfortably, daughter."

Mirae straightened her back and pooled her chima neatly beneath her to be more relaxed as she sat. She studied her mother's face, wondering if Minho was right—that Mirae's untimely ascension to the throne meant there was a chance to preserve what remained of their mother's fleeting mind.

The woman before her barely resembled the mother who had taught Mirae to be proud of the gods-given magic in her blood, powerful enough to protect their queendom from anything, and to be honored by the trust of her people. Now that same woman sat before Mirae like a dragon that had lost its pearl. Her mother's cheeks had sunken into jaundiced hollows, and her proud neck had faded into a waning crescent that could barely hold up her head. It was a wonder that the thick braided wig framing her face like a dark halo didn't prove too much to bear.

Mirae's mother seemed to be studying Mirae's face as well. After a moment, she gestured toward the glittering collection of ddeoljam spread before her on a red silk cloth. "Which of these should I wear tonight?"

As Mirae examined her options, she kept her expression even, hoping this random request was a simple assessment of her fashion sense and not a sign that her mother's earlier confusion was lingering.

Each hairpin in the collection was stunning, designed to adorn a queen's head. Mirae's eyes immediately went to her longtime favorites: blooming gold lotus flowers set against a blue opal base, her favorite imported gemstone. Pearls rested like milky bees on the curled petals of the gleaming flowers. But Mirae didn't point at the glittering pair. Instead she reached for a different set of pins—palm-size golden mirrors flashing beneath a dome of polished amethysts.

Her mother raised an eyebrow. "You don't think I should wear my prettiest ornaments for such an important night?"

Mirae shook her head. "We have a distinguished guest. Although the council's rules dictate that the Josan dignitary is not to come within two sword lengths of any Daughters of the Sacred Bone, you and I should still try to set him at ease when he is in our presence. After all, he must swear fealty to me when I pass the Trial of the Gods."

Mirae's mother smoothed her red chima with her pale, bony hands, making the gold embroidered dragons dance at the hem. "And what do these pins have to do with any of that?"

Mirae knew this was a test of her diplomacy, something she was well trained in. She raised her chin with confidence. "Although it has been over a century since Seolla conquered Josan with its magical army, the people of Josan still detest magic and forbid its use within their borders. It seems prudent to avoid wearing enchanted ornaments tonight, when the Josan dignitary is unhappily surrounded by magic. The pins I have chosen do not contain any spells, and they display Josan's royal colors. Hopefully this will help to set the dignitary at ease around his high queen."

Mirae's mother smiled. "A thoughtful response. Well done."

Mirae finally relaxed. If there was one thing she was good at, it was keeping straight the complex history between her queendom and its sovereign state, Josan. While relations were perennially chilly, their current accord—that Josan could maintain its monarchy as long as it submitted to the high queen of Seolla—more or less kept the peace between the two bordering nations. Mirae knew she would do well not to incite the generational rage inside the dignitary and his entourage on the night she became their high queen.

When Mirae's mother gestured for assistance with putting in the pins, Mirae shifted to sit behind her, carefully holding the extra halo of hair steady while her mother fastened the amethyst pins beside each ear. "You surprised me today, Mirae. I hadn't expected your Jade Witchery to have grown so . . . impressively under Jia's watch."

Mirae smiled at the back of her mother's head. "She pushes me hard. But this morning, she said I am ready to face the first trial."

"Excellent." Mirae's mother patted the amethyst pins, now securely fastened. "And what of your proficiency with Ma-eum Magic for the second trial?"

"You tell me," Mirae said, feeling her smile grow as she scooted to face her mother. "How do I smell?"

Mirae watched her mother pause, frown, and then smile. She sniffed the air, taking in the last vestiges of Mirae's mugunghwa illusion. "I thought you seemed a little too fresh after spending all morning on the training fields. I should have known your perfume was an illusion."

Mirae bowed humbly, but of course she'd anticipated a last-minute training session with her mother. Captain Jia was hardly her most secret, or dedicated, tutor. "It was a simple but effective spell, Mother. I'm glad you're pleased."

More important, Mirae was glad that her illusion had worked. The successful use of Ma-eum Magic—the ability to trick an opponent into sensing something that wasn't actually there—relied on the wielder's ability to convince their own mind that what they were projecting was real. That took practice, and hours of memorizing exact details to be recalled without prompting: texture, color, temperature, weight, and shape. In Mirae's case, she'd chosen something she was familiar with, and she'd only attempted to trick one of her mother's senses: smell, the easiest and most subtle. But it had worked.

Mirae braced for her mother's inevitable command to perform another illusion, this one less sneaky, but instead, she took Mirae's hands, warming them with her own. "Well done *again*. I'm proud of you."

Mirae bowed a second time, hiding a blush as she helped her mother secure her wonsam with a red silk ribbon. Her mother grabbed one final accessory, a rainbow of tassels to be draped down her front, and asked, "Are you nervous, Mirae . . . about tonight?"

Mirae arranged the tassels dangling from her mother's chest, feeling strangely calm as she worked. "I'm a little nervous about the final test, since there's no way to prepare for it."

Her mother nodded. "Tell me what you know about the third trial."

Mirae bowed acquiescently. "The final Trial of the Gods will test my aptitude for the third magic system—Horomancy, which I cannot learn without the gods' blessing. Once I earn the gods' approval and am considered fit to be queen, I will be eligible to learn how to ply the rules of time."

Of the three magic systems, which exemplified the virtues of cunning, craftsmanship, and foresight, Horomancy was the most enigmatic power. Mirae had never even seen it used outside of her sunbae getting a few small premonitions, though she knew that was for good reason. The rules of time were rigid, dangerous things to manipulate, and Mirae was grateful that she didn't have to learn anything about them before the ceremony.

Still, it was the part that came *after* she passed the trials that worried her.

As if reading her thoughts, Mirae's mother grabbed Mirae's hands with her pale ones. "Go on, tell me what happens next. After that, I'll give you a gift to lift your spirits."

Mirae nodded bravely, intrigued by her mother's promise. "My first task as the next gods-ordained queen of Seolla will be to take over your duty as warden of the Deep—the dark cage where my ancestors locked away an ancient evil—by fortifying its seal."

Mirae's mother nodded for her to continue. Mirae took a deep breath. "It will be my duty to hold this great evil at bay until I die . . . or the toll of my obligation fractures my mind."

Mirae could barely get those last words out, choking at the memory of her beloved grandmother standing at the gates with white-hot eyes, forced into exile, and thoughts of her own mother's mind splintering right in front of her.

Mirae's mother pulled her into a hug, merging her frailty with Mirae's warmth in an attempt to comfort her. "You're forgetting one thing, Mirae. The gods promised an end to the suffering of Seolla's queens with the birth of the one who will defeat our great enemy once and for all. We do what we must to keep our queendom safe until then. As hard as all this feels right now, remember that we will be rewarded for our courage."

Mirae rested her head on her mother's shoulder. "I know. I just wish we knew when all this would end. The queen who will save us may not be born for hundreds of years."

"Or she may have been born sixteen years ago, under an auspicious new moon." Mirae's mother pulled away and offered

Mirae a smile that only sharpened the shadows on her gaunt face. "I may be looking at her right now."

Mirae shook her head but offered a small smile of her own. "If I were the chosen queen, surely the gods would have made me talented like Captain Jia, or resilient like you."

Mirae's mother cupped her face with her pale, skeletal hands. "I may be the youngest queen to fall ill, and you the youngest crown princess to take the throne, but I know all this is happening for a reason. Whenever Daughters of the Sacred Bone suffer for the good of the queendom, the gods fly to their aid. Remember that."

Mirae nodded and wiped away a tear, doing her best to smile bravely. "Can I have my gift now?"

Mirae's mother chuckled as she gestured toward the glittering pins on the floor. "Pick something for tonight. Whatever you want."

Mirae took her seat before the ddeoljam, letting their beauty lift her spirits, just as her mother had promised. She scanned the pins carefully before reaching for a pair that caught her eye. They were simple—ebony discs piled with bone-white pearls—but exuded a sublimity that required no magic.

As soon as she touched them, something crossed her mother's face. After a second, the fleeting shadow passed and her mother nodded. "Those were made in Josan. I think the dignitary will approve."

Her mother knelt to help Mirae put the pins in her hair, and Mirae closed her eyes, enjoying the feeling of her mother's hands working on either side of her face. When she was done, Mirae's mother said, "I have one more gift for you. Would you like to see it?"

Mirae opened her eyes wide and nodded. She watched her mother walk over to a lacquered jewelry box with a mother-of-pearl inlay featuring opalescent dragons soaring across a rich mahogany sky, exhibiting the magnificent craftsmanship that Josan artists were famous for. Mirae's mother opened the lid and pulled out a small silk pouch—similar to one Mirae had seen around her father's neck once, before he'd tucked it back under his clothes. The queen gestured for Mirae to stand beside her and then handed her the gift.

Mirae accepted the pouch and eagerly opened it, expecting a jade necklace or bracelet for luck. Instead, a fistful of various animal-shaped beads poured into her hand. When she looked up with confusion, her mother smiled.

"These are zodiac beads. Each one has a different power, according to the animal it exemplifies." Mirae's mother reached into her palm, pulling out a small ox forged from iron. "This one, for example, will triple your strength. All you have to do is place it on your tongue."

"So, these will give me powers?" Mirae stared down at the beads with wonder. "What does the opal dragon do?"

"It enhances your magic, but only temporarily. None of the beads' effects last very long."

Mirae's mother returned the iron ox bead to Mirae. "I made these when I was about your age, and they've served me in ways that I never foresaw. But you must promise me one thing." She leaned in close, her face sobering. "Never use these beads until I explain the fullness and cost of their power. After the ceremony, there is much I need to tell you."

Mirae nodded and poured the zodiac beads back into the silk pouch. "Thank you, Mother. I look forward to everything you will teach me."

Her mother smiled again. "I know none of this has been easy, but trust me, you're ready to become Seolla's protector. You've always had a kind heart and a stubbornness for doing what's right. What more could Seolla ask for in a queen?"

Mirae and her mother held each other's hands, sharing the strength that had been passed down to them by generations of queens.

Their quiet moment was interrupted by the voice of a palace woman calling softly into the chamber.

"Your Majesty, the royal tailor is here to prepare Gongju mama for tonight."

Mirae's mother pulled her in for one last hug. "Go, get ready. And try to enjoy yourself—this is a big night, and you're going to do us all proud."

Mirae allowed herself to be shooed down the hall, where an entourage of palace women waited to whisk her away and slip her into trappings fit for a queen.

Chapter

THREE

As soon as she was deemed richly adorned enough to step foot outside, Mirae headed back toward the palace garden, where the guests were gathering. As difficult as her morning had been, Mirae considered her ability to remain upright under all the precariously weighted accessories in her hair, tassels, and chima her greatest achievement of the day.

As she neared the back gate, Mirae saw three familiar figures approaching the palace garden ahead of her, and her heart lifted despite the weight of silk and jewels on her body. She hadn't seen her friends Areum, Jisoo, and Yoonhee since she'd been pulled out of political studies to focus on her Sacred Bone training.

Areum, Jisoo, and Yoonhee were the only girls in the class who'd been unafraid to point out the crown princess's mistakes and help her do better; it wasn't long before they grew close. Now her True Bone friends, who were each blessed with the ability to wield one of Seolla's great magical powers, were preparing to either take their mothers' places on the Hwabaek or assume some other high-ranking position.

Mirae smiled fondly at her friends' predictable ensembles. Areum, as usual, had the most serene hanbok. Her soothing, sea-green jeogori cascaded down her arms like a crystal clear waterfall, while her deep blue chima, embroidered with a spiral of silver minnows, imitated the ocean's inky depths. Jisoo's dramatic outfit was the most daring; the iridescent black silks draping her body shimmered like oiled ebony, a moody backdrop against which her pale gold norigae and silver binyeo could shine.

As for Yoonhee, Mirae was unsurprised to see that she was still a walking ombré of color. Yoonhee wore layers of pink upon pink upon pink, from her cherry blossom pins to the deep magenta sunset gracing the bottom of her chima, with an ungodly number of jade accents marbling everything together.

Mirae couldn't hear what her friends were talking about, but she could see they were giggling together in a way she hadn't been able to for months. At the sound of footsteps, they turned and started at the sight of Mirae with her entourage of palace women. They stepped aside hastily, bowing to her while also clearly appraising her hanbok and jewels with wonder as she passed, almost as if they didn't recognize her beneath all the regalia.

Mirae told herself not to blame them for staring. This was, without a doubt, the most important day of her life, and the royal tailor had done everything she could to ensure the crown princess's ensemble was fittingly grand.

As Mirae was ushered quickly past her friends, doing her best not to shoot them a silly face, an early evening breeze billowed out her hanbok like the wings of a swan. The pearly ivory silk of her dangui heralded her pre-ceremony fledgling status, while her dark chima made the silver royal dragons on her sleeves and hem dance like orbiting moons.

Though Mirae would soon wear the same reds and golds as her mother—and train her neck to hold up Seolla's magnificent crown—tonight she wore a braided halo, ornamented with her mother's pearl-and-ebony pins. A jade-based cheopji straddled the parted hair on top of her head, and matching green pigment, enchanted to hold its color all night long, had been swept across her eyelids. The lotus-shaped purple gem rising out of her hairpin mirrored the bright sonjjang near her ears, which dripped cascading gold beads down the sides of Mirae's neck.

Mirae caught her friends' eyes one last time, hoping to convey the message that she'd find them later, but all thoughts left her mind as she saw the magnificent feast that had been prepared in her honor. Just as her friends had stared at her, Mirae's mouth fell open with wonder as she crossed into the palace garden.

She gaped up at the luxurious pavilion draped over low tables and silk cushions in a rainbow of colors. Lanterns in the trees shone down on silver bowls of rice, a domed moon for every invitee. It seemed to Mirae that the palace chef had ensured every kind of kimchi sat before the seated guests in an arc of fire-red flowers on bright gold lily pad plates.

Once Mirae had taken her seat across from her mother, the queen stood. "Please, everyone, enjoy this meal prepared in my daughter's honor."

As soon as everyone bowed their thanks and picked up their chopsticks to eat, palace women walked around the tables, bending low to offer slabs of kalbi—dripping with soy sauce and honey—on sizzling bronze platters, as well as strips of slow-roasted chicken leg and tender fish that still steamed. With large silver spoons, other servants carefully ladled gomtang that certainly smelled like it had been stewing all day out of ornate bronze vessels into gold soup bowls placed at the right hand of every guest. A few servants stood ready to collect bones on clean silver trays, refill depleted side dishes, and keep the wine flowing into pedestaled cups pierced with dangling gold mirrors.

Mirae wanted to settle into the overstuffed cushions and devour everything in sight. She wished her junior-ranking friends had been allowed to join this feast with their mothers, until she noticed that the crowd was watching her keenly—her mother, political figures, the Josan dignitary, and Hwabaek council-women who were, per the will of the gods, True Bone royals not in line for the throne. They were all skilled Jade Witches and Ma-eum Mages in their own right, and Mirae couldn't help but wonder if behind many of their smiles and well wishes was concern over whether this untested princess was ready to replace their seasoned queen.

But Mirae couldn't let her own doubts get to her. Not tonight. Instead, she put on a smile and ate with enough gusto to be considered hale and grateful, but not so quickly as to seem young and impetuous. As she began her meal, Mirae stole a look at the Josan dignitary.

Dignitary Yi's sharp, imposing features paired well with the steel-gray hair at his temples. He pretended like he wasn't enjoying the food, even though the spicy sea bass and soy sauce salmon dishes were made with Josan's finest catches. It probably didn't help that no servants who were born in Josan were allowed near the royal family or their guests that night, either. The traditions surrounding the Sangsok Ceremony were strict for a reason.

After all, rebels from Josan had been known to try to sabotage this important night, when the cage of Seolla's great enemy would be temporarily weakened by a transfer of power from queen to crown princess. None of these plots to release the evil bent on destroying Seolla had succeeded, thanks to the rules in place, but that didn't keep the dignitary from souring at the implication that he and his companions were the biggest threat that night.

After about an hour of feasting, Mirae's mother rose to her feet, signaling that the banquet was over. She towered over the seated guests like a crimson mountain forested with gold and jade. After exchanging a small smile with Mirae, she left the table and led the way back into the palace proper. Mirae and the other guests hurried after her, following her as she passed majestic pagodas and halls. She stopped at the main courtyard, just inside the dragon gates, which had been decorated with lanterns and waist-high tables piled with tteok and summer fruit.

The sunset's honey-yellow beams, beaded with pink, gleamed off every surface of the courtyard. Rays of warm light turned the pillars and sinuous dragon carvings into gold and ruby statues. Even stepping onto the pale, familiar sand felt like walking on the moon; the ground practically glowed with sunlight, cratered with the imprints of a hundred busy feet.

Warm from food and the beauty around her, Mirae could almost forget the trial she would face that night. Instead, she found herself smiling at every cousin and Hwabaek council-member who stopped to exchange pleasantries. In particular, she warmly greeted Sangsin Bada, head of the council, who would officiate the second test of the trials, per tradition.

"Gongju mama." The old woman bowed. Her slight figure, robed in the brilliant green silks customary for her rank, still managed to look particularly imposing, given all the ways she'd ornamented herself with bloodred ribbons. "How are you feeling?"

Mirae had been warned by her mother that Sangsin Bada was highly adept at spreading rumors that couldn't be traced back to her. It was always unwise to say more than necessary around her. Mirae chose her words carefully. "I feel . . . ready. I have worked hard to impress you and the rest of the council tonight."

"I'm sure your achievements will be remembered for generations," Sangsin Bada said, just as the sound of drums announced that the ceremony would soon begin. Mirae bowed along with everyone else as her mother reappeared at the far side of the courtyard, surrounded by palace women and Wonhwa guards. All could see their proud queen richly robed in jeweled finery, but none were close enough to see that her face didn't need powder to look so pale.

Mirae's mother gestured for everyone to continue mingling. "The oracles will be ready momentarily."

When Sangsin Bada turned back to Mirae, it appeared that seeing Mirae's mother had sparked something inside the old woman. "Her Majesty seems unwell. Did she have another . . . incident today?"

Mirae swallowed hard but kept her face neutral, never one to divulge her family's private affairs carelessly, especially to a shrewd gossip. "If she had, I'm sure you would have heard about it."

"I do try to stay apprised of the gods' dealings with you Daughters of the Sacred Bone. After all, it's through your feats and failures that they make their will known." Sangsin Bada leaned in close, lowering her voice. "I know what's at stake tonight, Gongju mama, but rest assured that I'll be testing your Ma-eum Magic thoroughly. Only the worthy may stand before the gods."

With that, Sangsin Bada gave a parting bow and walked away. Mirae stood, stunned, as the councilwoman and her mother met each other's eyes, something unpleasant passing between them. After a moment, Sangsin Bada slipped back into the crowd without even offering her queen a parting bow, as if their exchange had never happened.

How dare she disrespect Mother and me like that? Anger at Sangsin Bada's insolence gathered like a feverish cloud in Mirae's chest, making her all the more determined to pass the second trial with flying colors. She looked around for Captain Jia, needing to talk to someone who believed in her to calm herself down.

She was so caught up in looking for the captain that she almost didn't see Areum, Jisoo, and Yoonhee standing in her path. They bowed deeply, and Mirae stopped in her tracks, relieved to see far friendlier True Bone royals.

"Gongju mama." Areum spoke Mirae's full title with the respect it deserved for the sake of all listening but smiled as she would to a friend. As usual, Mirae's older and wiser sunbae brought her back to herself without even trying.

Mirae did her best to grin convincingly under the weight of both her wig and Sangsin Bada's threat. "I was beginning to wonder if you still recognized me."

"Of course we do," Jisoo said, her winged eyeliner and smoky eye shadow making her eyes look even more catlike than usual. "We'd never forget the face of the flying turtle culprit."

Mirae sighed. "Is no one going to let me live that down?"

"Absolutely not," Yoonhee said with a laugh. "What are friends for, if not to remind you of all your greatest achievements?"

Mirae gestured at Yoonhee's ombré pink chima. "What I actually want is for you to teach me the enchantments you put on your clothes. I bet even the nomads of Baljin can see it shining from across the peninsula." Yoonhee blushed with pride, the lovely peach of her cheeks contrasting prettily with the glittery, pearl-like shine highlighting her face.

Jisoo twirled her own iridescent black chima, its deep green and purple shimmers flashing like lights across the northern sky. "Yoonhee also enchanted my clothes. I shudder to think what will happen when she finally focuses her considerable abilities on something other than fashion."

Mirae wasn't surprised to hear that her friends had collaborated on their outfits. Though Yoonhee was the youngest in their group, she had an uncanny gift for Jade Witchery, advancing frighteningly quickly to learn not just how to command the elements, but also to enhance their intrinsic properties—like making a shiny silk chima glisten with a brilliance it could never achieve on its own.

Yoonhee bowed appreciatively to Mirae and Jisoo both, sending her vibrant silks fluttering and making her jade accents jingle. "I have to say, though, that working with Jisoo was a nightmare," Yoonhee said. "She was very particular about there not being any pink in her outfit, despite that being my signature color. I'll never understand such a monster."

"I believe she's including me in that," Areum said mildly. She alone wore no makeup enchanted to illuminate her face. "I wouldn't let her douse me in pink, either."

Areum's ensemble was deceptively simple compared to the hanboks of her friends. Something about her sea-green sleeves and pearl pins intrigued Mirae, while looking at the inky dark-teal chima below both drew her in and unsettled her, like gazing into the depths of the unknown. Mirae smiled at Areum slyly. "Yoonhee wouldn't dare insult your clothes, sunbae. Unless, of course, she wants you to tell her the day she dies."

Yoonhee slapped her hands over her ears. "Absolutely not."

Mirae laughed with the other girls at their running joke. Of course, Areum couldn't actually predict a precise date of death, but the foresight that came with her extremely rare ability to use Horomancy had kept them out of trouble more times than Mirae could count.

Areum's gift had been unexpected. Horomancy was a deeply spiritual power that, unlike the others, was not passed down genetically. Instead, young girls born to Jade Witches or Ma-eum Mages would wake up one day with the ability to see glimpses of the future, or experience premonitions that turned out to be frighteningly accurate. These girls, chosen by the gods to divine their will, were sent to the Temple of the Sacred Bone to be trained by the oracles.

Areum, however, as a True Bone royal, was expected to finish her schooling before leaving for the temple, where she would live out the rest of her life in service to the gods.

She grabbed Mirae's hands now, her dark eyes gleaming. "Gongju mama, we're so proud of you, and we will be waiting for your glorious return. Tonight, you will remind everyone that the gods have always stood by Sacred Bone daughters for a reason."

Before Mirae could respond, a gong sounded three times across the courtyard, signaling that the countdown had begun. The time of the ceremony was nearly at hand.

Everyone was assembling in the courtyard, waiting for Mirae to be judged by the gods. Mirae's three friends bowed in unison before shooting her looks of undiminished confidence as they moved to stand beside their mothers, who had congregated with all the other Hwabaek councilmembers.

Mirae's mouth dried at the sight of the gathered True Bone royals and Josan delegates. The only thought running through her head as she stared at all the people she'd been repeatedly assured she wouldn't let down was that she needed to get something to drink, *fast*.

Before the next gong sounded, Mirae searched hastily for something to quench the dryness that was beginning to creep down her throat.

Across from her were tables of fruit being quietly fanned by palace women. The best fruit and tteok, of course, had been set apart as a heonmul for the gods, but the remaining selection still called to Mirae's dry throat. She made for the tables, smiling tightly at everyone she passed.

When Mirae reached the tables at last, a pile of glistening pale-yellow slices of chamoe practically begged to be devoured. She reached greedily for a piece of melon only to realize a half second later that she was too late.

Another hand was creeping up from underneath the table, fingers searching like antenna for the same plate of chamoe Mirae was reaching for. Once the hand found the plate, both it and the fruit quickly disappeared beneath the table.

Mirae suspected she knew who had thwarted her, and lifted the satiny blue tablecloth to peer at the culprit below.

Hongbin squatted there like a feral creature, surrounded by empty plates. He looked up at Mirae with wide eyes, his cheeks sticky and full of fruit. He chewed quickly and swallowed. "I was told these were for everybody."

Mirae motioned for her brother to scoot over, which he did, urging her to "be careful with the goods." Mirae settled under the table next to him, and as soon as she had her chima pooled neatly enough to stave off wrinkling, she smacked the back of Hongbin's head. "You're not supposed to be here."

Hongbin held out a half-eaten slice of chamoe. "My skin needs vitamins to stay this dewy, noonim. Besides, there's no way all this was going to get eaten. I'm doing everyone a favor."

Mirae was about to smack him again when she heard voices approaching. Familiar ones. Her heart raced, but her throat was so parched, it prickled with the need to cough. She snatched a piece of Hongbin's fruit and shoved it in her mouth.

The hem of the Josan dignitary's purple hanbok fluttered against the tablecloth as he came to a stop. "You really should reconsider my offer, Daegun daegam. The Josan king will value you in his court far more than those who seek only to marry you off."

"I assure you, Dignitary Yi, that I am quite content here." Minho's voice was unfailingly patient, as polite as he might be to the king of Josan himself—someone Mirae would likely never meet, as the king of Josan and the high queen of Seolla were not permitted to enter each other's lands. The history of assassinations ran too deep.

"I suppose that makes one of us." The Josan dignitary seemed to be speaking around a mouthful of fruit. "It's hard for a man to feel at ease when he's constantly surrounded by a small army of . . . enchanted women."

"It's for your own safety," Minho said. "You are a valued subject of Seolla, and we wish to protect you as one of our own."

"You could protect me yourself, Daegun daegam, if your Sacred Bone Magic hadn't been suppressed at birth."

"It was the gods' will." Mirae detected a flicker of impatience in Minho's tone.

"So say the women, I'm sure." The Josan dignitary didn't even bother to lower his voice. "I can't imagine anything more insidious than stripping a man of his gods-given power."

"Unless I'm mistaken," Minho said, "the Josan king is far more severe when it comes to suppressing magic than Seolla is."

"True, but in Josan, all are equal." The hem of the dignitary's hanbok moved slightly as he stepped closer to Minho. "We don't believe in letting women hoard all the power."

"Remind me," Minho said, an edge to his voice. "When was the last time a woman ruled Josan . . . or is that a role given only to men?"

A tense silence fell, broken only when Minho calmly redirected the conversation. "The ceremony will start any moment. We can continue this discussion at the edge of the forest while we wait for my sister to emerge."

The dignitary grunted. "And if she fails?"

"She won't." Minho didn't even hesitate. "The gods have guided Mirae all her life. She always finds a way. Josan's continued allegiance to her will be well rewarded."

"Oh, I look forward to speaking with our esteemed Gongju mama after the ceremony." Mirae imagined the bead string ornament under the dignitary's gat swinging like grinning teeth beneath his chin. "I'm certain tonight's events will be . . . memorable."

As Minho and the dignitary walked away, discussing the coming monsoon season and how it might affect Josan's fishing industry, Hongbin leaned over to whisper in Mirae's ear. "When you are queen, you should insist on only jolly grandmothers serving as dignitaries. No snobby, semi-traitorous men."

"If Josan even has any other sort of person, I'd be surprised." Mirae clutched her chima tightly, imagining it was the dignitary's fingers she was crushing. It felt good to target her rage for once. "If that man is any indication of the sentiment of his nation, then maybe it's just filled to the brim with bitter, sexist, disloyal—"

"Gumiho," Hongbin said, nodding knowingly.

A gong sounded again from across the courtyard, two peals this time, indicating that the ceremony was about to begin and Mirae had better present herself. She and Hongbin scrambled out from underneath the table and smoothed each other's hanboks while everyone's attention was still on their mother. The queen stood in front of the dragon gates with her husband. Stretched out behind them was a line of elite Wonhwa guards—Jade Witches whose blades burned hot and Ma-eum Mages who stood with their hands clasped behind their backs, the very air around them making it clear they didn't need to move to protect their queen; they had magic enough where they stood.

"The oracles are ready," Mirae's mother declared, her eyes falling on Mirae.

Mirae couldn't help but gaze back at her mother with awe—a picture of pure majesty. The queen of Seolla stood at the head of the crowd, looking like one of the gods themselves. Though the layers of flowing silk were impressive on their own, the strings of beaded gold streaming off her mother seemed to hold the light of the rising moon, and each shimmering drop glittered like a mountain dragon's scales.

Of course, every stitch of her finery paled in comparison to the final piece of her ensemble—the crown of Seolla. It had been placed on her head just before the second gong sounded and now sat circling her brow. Finely hammered sheets of gold rose from its sun-round base, forming tall branches. Tiny silver mirrors and bean-shaped curls of jade dangled in the hundreds off every surface. Even more of these charms for good fortune and health hung from the sides of the crown in strings like glinting braids reaching just past the queen's shoulders. At the rear, two golden antlers curved off the queen's head, symbolizing the gods' promise that the legendary kirin would appear when a great ruler was born.

Although by comparison Mirae was simply adorned, she met her mother's eyes proudly, taking in the breathtaking sight of everything she was destined to become.

"Come, Mirae." Her mother's voice rang as loudly and commandingly as the gong that had gathered everyone together. "It is time for you to walk with the gods."

In a move that felt almost rehearsed, the crowd turned to Mirae and parted.

Mirae kept her head held high as she walked down the middle of the staring throng. Her eyes never left her mother, and in that moment it seemed as though nothing could ever penetrate the Sacred Bone connection between them—the gods' irrevocable blessing on a line of women exclusively ordained to rule. As Mirae approached her parents, all she could think about was how much of a relief it would be to reverse the gauntness in her mother's face and slow the worry silvering her father's hair.

A lot was at stake. A birthright. A duty. A dream Mirae had carried since she was a child, inherited from her mother and her grandmother. She couldn't afford to let anything get in her way. Minho and Captain Jia were right—she would find a way to succeed. She always did.

Mirae walked past her parents, who didn't say a word as she exited through the dragon gates, following a starlit path that led to the forest rustling darkly at the bottom of the hill.

Chapter

FOUR

Two rows of Sacred Bone Oracles lined the path into the woods, their blue robes swaying in the wind even as they stood still as monuments. They bowed, one by one, as Mirae approached, and every pale, shaved head gleamed—a sea of moons guiding her through the darkness.

Mirae searched their faces, seeing both old and young in their ranks and imagining Areum among them, which made her smile.

Halfway down the hill, she was met by the Kun Sunim. The oldest of the Sacred Bone Oracles, she stood tall, her face lit by the glowing silver sash around her waist. "Are you ready to walk among the gods, Daughter of the Sacred Bone?"

Mirae bowed deeply to the holy woman. The Kun Sunim didn't bow back. Tonight, she spoke for the Samsin, the three grandmother goddesses who were both the peninsula's progenitors and patrons of Seolla's magic. "I'm ready."

"Then we will meet again at the end, where all things begin." The Kun Sunim led Mirae the rest of the way down the hill. There would be no more speaking between them. Mirae's heart raced as she neared the trees, tempting her to hesitate at the barrier between the deep teal hill and the leafy shadows of a ritual unknown.

Back in the courtyard, the gong sounded one last time, a single peal signaling that the ceremony had officially begun. Everything that happened next would be the gods' will. Shaking off all the doubts still lurking in her mind, Mirae crossed into the forest, conscious of the eyes watching her, both ahead and behind.

In the forest, there was no path for Mirae to follow, but she stepped confidently between the trees, avoiding trickster roots and low-hanging branches bobbing in the wind. Rather than physical markings, Mirae followed a sense, an aura. A warmth that felt pure and safe, like the chorus of a lullaby. Perhaps she was guided by her own magic, humming in the presence of the gods, or a sacred connection to all the ancestors who had walked this way before her. After all, Mirae knew where her path would end; the final trial would take place in the resting place of Seolla's queens.

Long spears of blue light indicated a clearing up ahead. Mirae strode toward the misty break in the trees, letting the encouragements of her friends and the sereneness of the oracles calm her. Whatever tests lay in the forest, she would find a way to pass them all.

When Mirae reached the clearing, moonlight illuminated the scene before her: a lone figure, sword in hand, waited for Mirae at the center. The glint of the woman's gold armor and jade weapon gave her identity away immediately.

"Captain Jia?" Mirae had known a master of Jade Witchery would officiate her first trial, but she hadn't expected it would be the same woman who'd trained her.

"Gongju mama." The captain kept her voice professional. Cold, even.

Mirae walked up to the other woman, her steps less sure than before. "Why didn't you tell me you were a part of the test?"

"I was not asked until tonight."

Mirae slowed to a stop, as did the small rise of hope that perhaps Captain Jia had been teaching her how to pass the first trial all along. Still, going face-to-face with an opponent she knew so well was certainly better than facing off with a stranger.

"I guess this is a good thing, right?" she asked.

Captain Jia didn't answer. Instead, she hefted her sword in both hands and held it out, as if offering it to the gods. "As captain of the Wonhwa guards, I serve the queen of Seolla. She is my benefactor and my superior in every way. I will protect her as she protects me—at any cost."

Mirae could feel sweat beading on her forehead. "Am I going to have to fight you?"

"No." At last, some gentleness in the captain's voice. "You are to be a queen, not a soldier. But for a bond to develop between us as queen and captain, I must ask you to prove your superiority." The green glow of Captain Jia's jade sword seemed to harden her sharp features into those of an ethereal statue. "You must make me kneel."

Mirae stared at the captain, one of the best Jade Witches in the land. Captain Jia had studied the elements and their properties all her life, mastering them to the point of assuming command of the palace guards at such a young age. Mirae, meanwhile, had been stretched thin over the past three months, trying to learn everything about all magic at once. Despite the power in her blood, Mirae was hardly expected to be able to beat the best Jade Witch in Seolla just yet.

Mirae shook away the doubts that threatened to come creeping back. She couldn't afford to tear her own confidence down. Not now. Besides, she reasoned, she'd bested the captain before, in a way. Remembering the trick of wind she'd played that morning, Mirae looked around for inspiration, knowing there was only one thing she could do better than anyone else—find a compromise between cunning and strength.

Mirae took a few steps closer to Captain Jia. She hated poking at the only weakness of the captain's she knew about, but that was what the moment required. She could not fail. Captain Jia understood that more than anyone. "How much does my mother know about you and Minho?"

"Threatening my job will not let you pass, Gongju mama."

"I'm not threatening you. I'm just wondering how you can profess to protect my mother at all costs when we both know where your heart truly lies. Tell me, Captain, what would you do if you had to choose between protecting the queen or saving the one you love?"

Mirae came close enough to see the captain's face, lit up by her sword. It was working—the captain looked less sure than before. "Put your sword down, Captain, unless you intend to strike your future queen."

Captain Jia hesitated for a moment, then swung her sword point down into the earth, keeping her hands at the ready. When she spoke, her voice was heavy with disappointment. "Gongju mama, are you threatening my future in order to advance your own? Is this how you seek to build a bond?"

Mirae stepped close enough to almost touch the entrenched jade sword beside her. "There will be no bond if I can't trust you to protect me over my brother."

Mirae raised her hands, palms coated with beads of water. The last time she'd done this, her brother, whom they both loved, had nearly died. From the look on the captain's face, she was well aware of that. She raised her hands, too, green flames ready to counter Mirae's indomitable water.

But when Mirae threw out her palm, nothing happened. It was the same trick she'd used before: a feigned spell, made of nervous sweat, in one hand; and a powerful, devastating will building up in the other. The captain, expecting the worst, had dedicated all her attention, her magic, to blocking both of Mirae's distractions. Before the other woman could catch on to her real intention, Mirae grabbed the captain's sword.

While Captain Jia watched with horror, Mirae gripped the sword tightly, pouring into it all the fear her memories of Minho nearly dying had brought back up, all the need in her soul to pass these trials, whatever the cost, and her secret wish for Captain Jia to be with Minho forever—something the captain would never fully commit to as long as she was a perfect soldier with a perfect sword.

With everything inside her, Mirae bid the jade to shatter.

The sword was expertly made, handed down for generations by Captain Jia's ancestors and deeply saturated with their magic. But no amount of generational strength could repel the will of the Sacred Bone.

To Mirae's relief, the sword didn't shatter. Instead, a loud, thunderlike crack bored into her ears. It echoed throughout the clearing as the lightest veins in that perfect slab of jade splintered up and down the length of the sword.

Cracked, but not destroyed. Mirae released the weapon and turned back to its owner, who stood stock-still. "By the rules of your order, this sword belongs to me, the one who marred it under your watch. You have been dishonored and, thus, soundly beaten. Yield to your superior."

Captain Jia stared at her sword as the reality of what had just happened sank in. She lowered herself to the earth, first one knee, then the other, scraping each across the moonlit grass. There was no lecture about Mirae manipulating the Wonhwa code of honor, battling a sword instead of a witch. She simply said, "You have passed the first trial. You may proceed."

Mirae let out a breath and looked back at the sword. It wobbled in the earth but did not crack any further. The magic poured into it for generations had made it strong. It would take Mirae years to learn how to shatter such a blade to the core. For now, she gestured toward it and said, "I return your ancestors' honor to you and bless this new bond between us."

When Captain Jia didn't respond, Mirae was tempted to put a hand on her shoulder and apologize profusely. But that would only further affirm the captain's failure, dishonoring her.

Instead, Mirae respectfully left to cross the clearing alone. She'd almost reached the trees when she heard the captain speak.

"I knew you'd find a way, Gongju mama. Whatever it took."

Mirae didn't turn around. "You taught me well. Tonight will be a victory for us both."

"Yes. A victory." The captain's voice sounded hollow. She was clearly mourning her sword, so Mirae gave her the space she needed by returning wordlessly to the invisible path between trees.

Mirae stepped into the next clearing expectantly, ready to conquer whatever lay within it—but she faltered when she saw what waited for her on the forest floor.

"Mother?"

The deep red of her mother's hanbok pooled like blood beneath her. Her face turned up toward the moon, she hummed a tuneless lullaby, swaying to music Mirae couldn't hear. Mirae could only see the back of her mother's head, but she didn't need to see the white glow of her eyes to realize that the other woman was in a trance.

At least this one wasn't violent. Yet. Mirae slowly walked along the edge of the clearing, keeping as quiet as possible. She'd made it about halfway across when she saw it—a pair of unmoving feet jutted out in front of her mother, feet that didn't belong to her, capped by a deep green chima with crimson ribbons.

Mirae stared in horror at Sangsin Bada's lower half. She willed the old woman to move, to show she was all right. When nothing happened, Mirae took a deep breath and ran toward the unconscious woman, whose head rested in her queen's lap. Thank the gods she was still breathing.

Mirae fell to her knees. "Mother, what did you do?"

Mirae saw her answer in her mother's eyes. Instead of a dark, piercing gaze, Mirae was met with two white-hot stars, the same madness she'd seen in her grandmother's eyes the day she was forced to leave Seolla forever.

Mirae reached out to touch her mother, shake her out of her trance, but it was no use. Her mother kept staring at her, continuing to hum.

Mirae didn't know what mad delusions had made her mother attack Sangsin Bada, but she was calm now. Mirae had to do something before that changed. The second trial, and the fate of the queendom, depended on it.

But what could she do? When Mirae had tried luring her mother out of a trance with a soothing Ma-eum illusion, she had failed utterly. Perhaps it was time to try something a little less reserved.

Mirae closed her eyes and listened for the familiar chatter of a nearby river she would often sneak off to with Captain Jia and her brothers. She could almost hear the night-chilled water as if it flowed next to her. Millions of dips and crests with winks of sound that fluttered away as fast as they came—a trickling fanfare of melted mountain peaks.

Most important, the river was cold. Mirae thought back to when she used to plunge into the water without hesitation, just to prove she was braver than Hongbin. Remembering the chill of the water and the way it frosted every pocket of warmth in her body, she reached out and touched her mother, transferring the memory into a numbing illusion.

Mirae's mother gave a great start as a potent douse of river chill flooded her body. This time, when she looked at Mirae, it wasn't with searing white eyes full of anger. It was with her own familiar ones.

"Mother, you're back!" Mirae practically fell into the other woman as she wrapped her in a hug, overwhelmed with relief.

Her mother returned the embrace, but asked, confused, "Where are we?"

Mirae pulled back, keeping a hand on her mother's shoulder. "This is the second trial. You got here before I did, and now . . ."

Mirae's mother followed Mirae's gaze down into her lap, where Sangsin Bada lay dead asleep. Her eyes widened with horror. "Oh no . . . what have I done?"

"It's all right, Mother. We can just wake her up to continue the second trial." Mirae reached out to touch Sangsin Bada with the same freezing Ma-eum illusion that had roused her mother, but was stopped by a hand around her wrist.

"No," her mother said. "I have broken one of the most important rules of the trial by interfering. If Sangsin Bada wakes, she will declare the ceremony forfeit. She'll say you failed."

Mirae pulled back her hand as if Sangsin Bada were poisonous to the touch. "Then what do we do?"

Instead of answering, her mother fell forward, suddenly racked with inexplicable pain. When Mirae tried to steady her, her mother pushed her away, back toward the far side of the clearing. "Don't touch me. You have to leave, *now*."

"But, Mother, I—"

"You have to continue." When Mirae's mother looked up at her now, it was with eyes like two dark inkblots. "I can't hold him back much longer. Go."

"But you said as soon as Sangsin Bada wakes, she'll—"

"By the time she rouses, it'll be too late," Mirae's mother said, doubling over with pain again. "If the Kun Sunim declares that you are the next queen of Seolla, not even Sangsin Bada can overrule the will of the gods."

Mirae looked down at her mother, straining to maintain her sanity. It wouldn't be long, they both knew, before the effort of holding back that ancient, unspeakable evil would shatter her mind forever.

"Please, Mirae. Go and pass the third trial. Assume your birthright like you were always meant to."

Mirae rose wordlessly to her feet, as if compelled. She took one last glance at Sangsin Bada's unmoving body and swallowed back the fear choking its way up her throat. "I need to hear that I've passed the second test before I can move on."

"You've passed. I declare it as high queen of Seolla." Her mother's unblinking stare made it clear that Mirae was not to argue with her anymore. "And remember, failure is not an option. Do you understand?"

Mirae nodded and stepped back toward the trees. Feeling like a star cast out of its system, Mirae exited her mother's orbit. Her feet felt heavy, as if they belonged to someone else as she stumbled toward the thrum of magic in the forest ahead.

Chapter
FIVE

Her mind still reeling from the disastrous second trial, Mirae slowed only when she had reached the Garden of Queens.

Mirae and her mother visited the Garden of Queens once a year, laden with freshly cooked rice, taro soup, and an abundance of red fruit to offer their ancestors before performing seongmyo. Usually this meant walking meditatively among the domed burial mounds, trimming the hills' grassy coverings with gentle commands to the earth. But three months ago, Mirae's mother had taken her hand and confessed a grave secret—while Mirae's grandmother had staved off the deterioration of her mind for several decades, Mirae's mother would not be so lucky.

And now here Mirae was, three months later, ready to become her mother's replacement. Though the idea still terrified her, this was her duty, and, as her mother had said minutes ago, failure was not an option.

"Gongju." The Kun Sunim's voice echoed from across the clearing where she knelt, waiting. The low table that Mirae had only seen used as a shrine was now cleared of everything but a gold silk covering and a few candles that lit the Kun Sunim's face.

Mirae avoided looking at the grassy, domed burial mounds of her ancestors—or thinking of her white-eyed mother losing her mind. Instead, she stood staring at the winding path in front of her, splitting the ranks of tombs. Its sand had been raked with swirling designs and was lined by bowing oracles, their heads low. The long, loose sleeves of their blue robes rippled with the evening wind.

The trees had even been ornamented for what was meant to be Mirae's triumphant finale. Thousands of colorful ribbons danced in the wind like flowers reaching toward a rainbow vortex. Every element, every shred of color the gods had gifted to mortals was represented in this tree-domed space where lanterns—propped on arching roots—shone brighter than the stars.

Mirae looked once more at the Kun Sunim, who was waiting for her. Mirae bowed to her ancestors, and to the woman who spoke for the Samsin. Then she took a deep breath and stepped onto the swirling, sandy path.

As soon as she did, the scene around her shifted. She stopped as the bowing oracles sat straight up and turned to face the Kun Sunim. They lowered once more into a bow, then rose again, repeating the motion of rising and falling as if worshipping the Kun Sunim the way they would the three grandmother goddesses themselves.

No, it wasn't the goddesses they were praying to. Mirae followed the oracles' gaze to the trees behind the Kun Sunim and gasped. Something shifted in the shadows, as if the darkness itself had taken a breath.

"Come, daughter. Claim your birthright." The Kun Sunim observed Mirae's every move like a challenger daring her opponent to take the cowardly way out. Mirae's eyes flickered between the Kun Sunim and the patch of darkness behind her that was slowly taking shape, forming an ebony portal made of smoke.

"Daughter." From the Kun Sunim's tone, Mirae knew this was her last chance to step forward. Even though everything inside her wanted to turn and run, she approached the Kun Sunim.

Failure was not an option.

The closer she drew to the Kun Sunim and the darkness behind her, the harder it was to ignore the eerie movements of the oracles, especially once they started chanting. Their voices were soft—Mirae had to listen carefully to make out what they were saying.

> To the first was promised might of mind.
> She buried all her kin.
> The second treasured her soul above all,
> and that has doomed us.
> The third will ride the wings of time.
> She brings either hope or desolation.
> Have we not heeded the gods?
> Surely an ancient evil will fall tonight.

Mirae reached the altar, the Kun Sunim still watching her every move with eyes as dark as the shadows behind her. Mirae was tempted to bolt for the trees, but instead fell to her knees in front of the altar.

"Are you worthy to sit before us, Daughter of the Sacred Bone?" The Kun Sunim's countenance gave off a peculiar gleam, not just from the glow of her silver sash but from a lifetime of serving and sharing secrets with the divine.

"I passed the first and second trials." Mirae swallowed down the urge to blurt out the truth of what had happened in the second clearing. She had no choice but to continue on.

"The gods see all, Daughter." The Kun Sunim's eyes glittered like they reflected distant galaxies. "And they are not satisfied with what you've done."

Mirae's stomach threatened to upend her ceremonial feast right there on the altar, until she remembered that the Kun Sunim was sticking to a script, one steeped in tradition. All were deemed unworthy of queenhood, no matter their blood, until they proved themselves. She still had the third trial to finish. She'd come too far to lose her nerve now.

Following tradition, Mirae bowed and asked, "What would you have me do?"

Mirae could have sworn she heard a titter of laughter coming from the shadows behind the Kun Sunim. But the oracle spoke again, drawing Mirae's attention back to the altar.

"Your final task is before you." The Kun Sunim reached down and lifted the gold silk covering on the table, revealing what lay hidden underneath.

Mirae leaned forward, eyes wide. She'd heard about the Sacred Bone relics, of course. Everyone had. But few had ever seen them—and none had dared touch them without express permission from the gods, at least not since the deaths of their namesakes. Anyone who did would be slain instantly. Or so it was said.

The Kun Sunim gestured for Mirae to observe the relics, which she did eagerly, taking in every beautiful and haunting detail of her ancestors' most prized possessions.

The beautiful jade dagger, first of the relics, looked like a small version of Captain Jia's sword, except it was cut of pure, veinless jade. A phenomenon only the gods could have created. The dagger's only flaw was a small nick in its tip. Mirae could sense there was a story behind the defect—an old and violent one that she longed to hear.

Next to the dagger glowed a palm-size blue stone, perfectly round. It took Mirae a second to realize that the marbled light seeping out of it came from within, shifting like a luminous cloud. Understanding which relic this was, Mirae let her eyes linger a little longer. She'd never seen a soul before, and here one was, carefully preserved until it was needed again.

When she finally found the will to tear her eyes away from the soul's milky light, she couldn't help but shudder as she gazed upon the third relic. It was by far the most mysterious, as dark as the twin voids of her mother's eyes in the second clearing.

Though it was just a small black bell, it sat like a deep-sea mountain untouched by light. The lanterns around Mirae cast no warm sheen on the relic's barrel-shaped metal, nor did the pearly starlight of the nearby blue stone give it a frosty gloss. Stubbornly cold and unlit, the bell seemed as untouchable as buried ebony—an entity that knew no comfort, only darkness and loneliness.

"Do you know what these are?" the Kun Sunim asked, bringing Mirae back to herself.

Mirae cleared her throat, recalling the texts she'd read in her studies. "These are the Sacred Bone relics, tokens of the High

Daughters who were the mightiest Jade Witch, Ma-eum Mage, or Horomancer of their time—the choicest of my ancestors. They each accomplished a feat worthy of being memorialized by the gods."

The Kun Sunim nodded. "Do you know their names?"

Mirae shook her head. "That knowledge is forbidden. Instead, the High Daughters were each given a True Name, which we are to call them until the end of time."

The Kun Sunim nodded again. "What are their True Names?"

Mirae gestured toward each of the relics in turn, using both hands out of respect. "This is the dagger of the Silver Star, whose Ma-eum trickery gave us a crucial military advantage over Josan. She laid the foundation for Seolla to move toward its golden future of uniting the peninsula.

"This is the seong-suk of the Deep Deceiver, whose Jade Witchery ended a civil war without blood. One that would have threatened Seolla's path to its golden future. It is said she wished for her soul to remain on earth so she could return when she was most needed."

Mirae took a deep breath before motioning toward the third relic. "This is the black bell of the Unnamed Dragon, whose Horomancy transcended the rules of time. She is the guardian of the past, present, and future. It is said we will never know the true extent of her power until Seolla reaches its golden future, or slips into eternal ruin."

The Kun Sunim seemed satisfied with Mirae's answers. "The next question, Daughter, is this: Which of these ancient queens have the gods chosen as the guardian of your reign?"

Though the Kun Sunim's tone didn't change, Mirae knew the final trial had officially begun with that question. She breathed the way Captain Jia had taught her to when calming her nerves as she studied the relics, each a symbol of a different kind of power and legacy that flowed through her veins. Which of these ancestors did the gods want at Mirae's side?

She considered her answer carefully, praying it wouldn't cost her the crown. "If one ancestral power was going to become more important than the other, the gods would not have seen fit to give me access to all three. *All* of the High Daughters will be with me as a wielder of Sacred Bone Magic and the rightful heir to Seolla's throne."

The Kun Sunim frowned, and the smoking darkness behind her stilled as if listening as well. "Do not think you can outwit the gods with an impertinent response. Answer the question."

Mirae's mind raced to divine what she should say, wondering if her mother or grandmother had in any way prepared her for this moment. But no matter how hard she tried, Mirae couldn't remember being taught about a regal specter aiding her mother's rule. If one existed at all, it certainly hadn't guarded her against her premature madness.

Mirae glanced up at the shadowy shape behind the Kun Sunim. It had changed while she was studying the relics and now appeared as a door-shaped void from which poured tendrils of night-dark mist. Still, the Kun Sunim did not acknowledge it, even as the oracles around her prayed to the shape, which grew and shifted like the question burning in Mirae's heart. She cast her eyes around the Garden of Queens, at the tombs that had lain silently for years, at the place where her grandmother and her mother would inevitably be laid to rest as well. Mirae looked the Kun Sunim in the eye. "Before I give my answer, tell me, who was my mother's guardian ancestor?"

The elderly oracle's frown deepened. "She chose the Deep Deceiver, quasher of civil war and master of Jade Witchery."

Mirae looked down at the pearly soul drifting silently in its blue stone. It was time to stop hedging. "Then why isn't the Deep Deceiver protecting my mother from her affliction?"

The Kun Sunim narrowed her eyes and merely repeated the terms of the trial. "Choose a relic, Daughter, or profess that you are out of your depth."

Mirae heard the Kun Sunim's unspoken command: *Ask no more questions, or the trial will be forfeit.* Mirae swallowed the rest of her questions and cast her eyes over the relics once more, keenly aware of the oracles chanting behind her, the impatient Kun Sunim sitting before her, and the nebulous, ever-growing shadows behind the oracle. All waited to see if Mirae could recognize her gods-chosen ally—if she even had one at all.

Mirae shook that dark thought out of her mind. Of course she had been delegated an ancestral guide—she was her mother's heir. A Daughter of the Sacred Bone. Besides, Mirae was starting to suspect that this whole production was, at its heart, little more than a high-stakes doljanchi, the ceremony where one-year-olds picked a symbolic object that supposedly foretold their future.

Perhaps there was no reason to overthink this. Mirae needed to follow her heart with the confidence of a crown princess who had trained all her life to become queen. Maybe the best way to do this would be to decide what kind of queen she wanted to be—like the Silver Star, whose jade dagger represented Seolla's deviousness in war? Or the Deep Deceiver, indomitable with her unparalleled command of the elements? Or perhaps the Unnamed Dragon, whose Horomantic legacy was a mystery none could know until the end of time?

Strength. Statecraft. Destiny.

Which would be Mirae's legacy?

Mirae glanced back over the relics, willing them to give her the answer the Kun Sunim was waiting for. Her eyes passed quickly over the first two relics for reasons she couldn't ignore. While the jade dagger was beautiful, Mirae had never been fascinated by the aggressive side of magic. She couldn't set Captain Jia on fire if her life depended on it. And while the blue seong-suk glowed bewitchingly like a wild eye fallen from the heavens, Mirae found no comfort in its all-knowing stare, nor in the idea of choosing a guardian whose spirit clearly found walking beside a Sacred Bone Daughter a little difficult in its current state.

The black bell was all that remained, but its presence comforted Mirae the least. Who knew what secrets it held in its lightless depths, what horrors and delights?

Mirae examined its colorless curves. Everything she'd been forced to do these past few months had been because of the unknown. Perhaps if anyone needed a guardian of time, someone who could act with surety because of their knowledge of the future, it was Mirae.

She looked up at the gathering shadows again, sensing their likeness to both the monsoon orb she'd trapped Minho in that morning and the High Horomancer's bell, almost as if the past and the future were guiding the present. Perhaps the answer to the Kun Sunim's question had been in front of Mirae all along.

Mirae gestured respectfully at the ancient relic she had chosen. "The gods wish for me to walk alongside the Unnamed Dragon, High Daughter and Horomancer of Seolla."

To Mirae's relief, the Kun Sunim nodded and mirrored Mirae's gesture. "Very well. Now, show us that you are correct. Touch the High Horomancer's bell."

Mirae glanced down at the relics, no longer protected by the silk cloth that the Kun Sunim had used to transport them. She swallowed back her fear long enough to ask, "What happens if I'm wrong?"

The Kun Sunim raised an eyebrow. "You will perish."

So it was true—there were dire consequences to touching the relics without the gods' blessing. Mirae sat paralyzed with fear as the oracles chanted louder, either to hearten Mirae or provoke her to act. There was no drowning them out. The one thing she wanted in that moment was her mother by her side, and yet it was her mother's own words that made Mirae too terrified to follow the Kun Sunim's instructions.

Failure is not an option.

"Do you wish to forfeit the trial?" the Kun Sunim asked. She spoke softly, as if privately reminding Mirae that there was a way out. She might leave without the crown, and abandon Seolla to an ancient evil, but at least she would have her life.

Mirae looked into the Kun Sunim's shrewd eyes, so like her mother's in that moment, and felt something within her stir—a deep-rooted confidence that had been growing for the past three brutal months. With it came a flare of anger, flushing Mirae's cheeks.

After everything she'd sacrificed for her queendom, why would anyone think she'd even *consider* acting selfishly? The shape of the shadowy doorway reminded Mirae of what she'd proven to everyone that morning: When the world buckled under monsoons and madness, Mirae didn't run. She looked danger in the eye and did whatever it took to save a prince. Why wouldn't she do the same to save an entire queendom?

Mirae reached out slowly, almost relishing the surprise on the Kun Sunim's face when her hand hovered over the ancient relics. As the oracles chanted ever louder and the incense around the altar muffled the rest of Mirae's senses, she closed her eyes, took a deep breath, and pressed her curved palm over the top of the High Horomancer's bell.

At first nothing happened, no instant death or otherworldly calamity. Mirae felt only the icy burn of ancient metal that had lain untouched by skin or sun for many years.

But the coolness of the black bell warmed quickly under Mirae's hand, like a pot set over a fire—one that boiled without warning, heating Mirae's palm till it mimicked the scorch of a star. Mirae tried to pull away, but it was as if her flesh had melted to the bell, and a horrific sear of pain exploded up her arm until she couldn't feel anything—except for the sensation of a scream being ripped from her throat as her body fell down, down, down into darkness, followed by the low sound of distant, godless laughter.

Chapter
SIX

As soon as the darkness had swallowed Mirae, every sensation in her body melted away—the pain, the fear, the horror. All that remained was the realization that she had failed.

And now she was dead.

Mirae opened her eyes and looked around the spirit world. Gone was the pleasant warmth of summer; the forest around her was no longer a familiar tumble of tombs. Instead, it looked as if the bell had melted and pooled at her feet—becoming a black lake framed by a forest of wintry lashes. No bugs flitted in the air. No fish lipped the water's surface. Nothing moved except a chilly wind blowing over the lake, chapping Mirae's face. With it came the vile stench of deep forest rot—wasted fruit from last year, still molding. Steaming, wet leaves. It stirred nothing else on that strange, bone-white shore.

Mirae looked down at herself. Her chima, stained and damp, was hiked up and wrapped around her left hand, as if she were about to traipse into the eerie lake itself.

Perhaps this was what the Samsin thought she deserved for her mistake—to be drowned in stagnant, lifeless water. Mirae closed her eyes and bid her mind to fall blissfully blank. She couldn't bear to think of what would happen to Seolla, to her family, now that the crown princess was dead. She would have all eternity to dwell on and mourn her mistakes, but for now, she wished only for oblivion.

Mirae stepped closer to the water's edge, ready to let the dark lake swallow her whole. She would have walked right into its depths had a familiar voice not cried out, "Stop—you can't go in there! We don't know what's inside."

Mirae's eyes flew open as she whirled around, and she was astonished to see her younger brother right behind her. *What is Hongbin doing here—and in such a state?* His favorite sky-blue hanbok was as stained and wrinkled as her own; by his standards, it was intolerably soiled. Even his usually immaculate hair was sweaty and messily tied into a bun he'd clearly secured without the help of a servant.

Worst of all was the look on his face. She'd never seen that expression on him before—like he'd battled monsters and knew that the world held many, many things to fear.

This was not the brother she'd left behind, safe within the palace walls. Perhaps her eternal punishment was worse than she realized—she'd be forced to live in a twisted nightmare that showed her what would happen to the people she'd failed to protect.

"Noonim, what are you doing?" Hongbin, or whatever this apparition was, reached out to her. "You look like you've seen another ghost."

No, not a ghost. Hongbin was very much alive. He was safely back at the palace. But if this wasn't his spirit, then—

Mirae looked again at her surroundings and realized this was not the spirit world, teeming with magical creatures, demons, and celestial beings. No, this was the realm of the living, with trees Mirae could name and a sky that distanced her from the sun.

But if she wasn't dead, then what was this place, and how did she get here?

"Noonim?" Hongbin came close enough to take her hands. "You're shaking."

Mirae's teeth chattered from the cold, but her hands trembled from something else. "Hongbin, where are we? How did we get here?"

Her brother frowned, confused. "This is Wol Sin Lake. You brought us here, remember?"

Had she? Mirae had no memory of that. And what was it he'd called this place—Wol Sin Lake? She recognized the name, but only from an old ghost story. "What about the ceremony?"

"The Sangsok Ceremony?" Hongbin shook his head. "That was two days ago."

Two days? How was that possible? Had she blacked out after touching the bell and only now regained consciousness?

Was this what it was like for her mother when she succumbed to madness?

Hongbin watched Mirae's face as she tried to process what was happening, and understanding dawned on his. "Oh, this is your first switch. You told me this would happen, and that you'd be confused."

"I was just there," Mirae said, gesturing helplessly. "At the ceremony. And now I'm here with you, and I don't remember anything that happened in between."

Hongbin squeezed her hands, grounding Mirae with his warmth. "Do you remember touching the High Horomancer's bell?"

"Yes." Mirae twisted her wrists to look at her spotless palms. "It burned me."

"It made you switch." Hongbin spoke slowly for Mirae's benefit, though she wished he would hurry up and explain everything as quickly as possible. "You've been given an amazing power. Now that it's activated, it lets you switch places with yourself in the future. You, from the past, came here, and the Mirae I was talking to went back to wherever you were."

Mirae shook her head. "Are you saying . . . this is the future?"

"Your future. Yes. You traveled here in the blink of an eye, though it'll only last for a few minutes." Hongbin looked as if he wanted to give Mirae a hug. "You're very special, noonim. You're the one who will defeat our great enemy."

"What?" Mirae took a step back, stunned. Her mind reeled from a barrage of things that made no sense. She, who'd barely even made it this far in the trial, couldn't be the chosen queen foretold for over a thousand years, and she most *certainly* couldn't have time traveled. That was preposterous. Horomancy was the divine power to receive the gods' will and catch glimpses of the future, like Areum could, nothing greater than that. At least, as far as Mirae had been told. "I need you to start from the beginning, Hongbin. Tell me everything that happened after I touched the bell."

"I wasn't there, noonim. I can only tell you what you told me. Besides, there isn't time. I need to tell you something far more important."

More important than the fact that Mirae had, allegedly, traveled from one point in time to another in a matter of seconds and was the fated queen to end the great evil plaguing her queendom? "All I did was touch the bell after the Kun Sunim told me to. I don't understand how any of this is—"

"They took Minho."

The rest of Mirae's words died in her throat. "What? Who took Minho?"

"If you're from the ceremony, then that's where you'll return"—Hongbin barely paused to breathe—"which means it hasn't happened yet. I know you said it's no use trying to change things, but I have to try. You have to stop them—you have to save Minho."

"Save him from what?"

"Just don't let them take him, noonim. Not for anything." As soon as those desperate words were out of Hongbin's mouth, it was as if he'd blown out the candle measuring what little time they had left. Before he could say anything more, Mirae's world went as black as the lake.

Instead of waking back at the ceremony, she awoke again on the shore of what she now knew to be Wol Sin Lake. This time, in the middle of night. The moon and its reflection were the only spots of light in the inky eye of the lake, which stared up at Mirae as unblinkingly as before. Now, however, its lash of trees had become plump with the fullness of spring. The smell of rot was gone. Mirae could hear the chirp and whir of tiny bugs flitting through the air.

She looked around for Hongbin, but she was alone. She

turned back toward the lake just as something began to rise out of the water, slicing through its stillness. As the rising shape raced toward her, the reflected moon rose with the sudden tide, shattering into pale, dancing shards.

Just shy of the shallows, the approaching figure lifted fully out of the water. What greeted Mirae was a man-size hand, seaweed green and warted with algae. Tightly clenched like it was guarding a secret.

Mirae backed away. She didn't know what lay behind her, or how to find her way home, but she knew with great certainty that she didn't want to see what lay in that giant green palm.

The hand began to open like a drowned, moldy flower. As trapped water gushed out between its fingers, Mirae caught a glimpse of what was inside—a slick, milky orb cupped in that deeply lined palm.

Before she could take a closer look, something else erupted out of the water, re-shattering the moon spot. She caught a glimpse of long midnight hair, barely discernible against the black water and sky.

Mirae never got a good look at the figure rising out of Wol Sin Lake, though, because the same darkness as before closed in on her, blurring every shadow together until she was surrounded by endless ink, falling into a deep well that carried her far, far away.

"Gongju, please wake up."

Mirae opened her eyes and found herself back in the Garden of Queens, the Kun Sunim's worried face hovering over her own.

"She has returned," the elderly woman announced, prompting the kneeling oracles to resume their chanting. "Are you all right, Gongju? Are you hurt?"

Mirae held up her hand, noticing her palm was still smooth and unscorched. "Something very strange just happened."

The Kun Sunim, too, was like a different woman now, respectful and attentive. She helped Mirae sit up, and even offered her some water. "Tell me what you saw."

Mirae wasn't sure how to explain it. "I saw . . . the future."

The Kun Sunim smiled. "Of course. The High Horomancer is also known as the Switcher of Seolla. While we oracles dedicate our lives to divining the gods' will, you can actually step through time and find out their will for yourself."

Mirae grabbed the proffered cup of water and downed every last drop. "So this is the High Horomancer's gift to me for choosing her as my guiding ancestor? Did my mother get a new power from the Deep Deceiver as well?"

"No, Gongju, you misunderstand. *You* are the one we've been waiting for." The Kun Sunim bowed with a humility Mirae hadn't thought her capable of. "The gods giving you this power can only mean one thing: you are the final High Daughter, the Unnamed Dragon, High Horomancer, and Switcher of Seolla."

Mirae stared at the top of the elderly oracle's bald head, her own head spinning from the confusing list of names being slapped onto her, and her grandmother's near prophetic last words: *You were not born to end up like me.* "What did you say?"

"You, Gongju, are the one who has been prophesied to end a great evil." The Kun Sunim took a deep breath. "The one known as the Inconstant Son."

Mirae balked—she had been taught to never say that name out loud. She looked around the clearing, wondering if she was truly back, or if this was just another frightening scene from her personal hell. "I need to speak with my mother." *And find Minho.* Just in case the absurdities she was experiencing were indeed real.

"Of course, Gongju. There's just one final part of the ceremony we must complete."

Mirae met the elderly oracle's eyes. "If everything you're saying is true, we have to suspend the ceremony."

The Kun Sunim bowed again, and when she spoke, her words were muffled by the ground. "Please be understanding of my impertinence, but we really must see the ceremony through. If we stop now, then you will be effectively rejecting the gods' will. Your powers and mission will be forfeit, and Seolla will be doomed to fall at the hands of the Inconstant Son. I cannot allow that."

Mirae felt all her protests die in her throat. "What is required to finish?"

"Come with me." The Kun Sunim climbed to her feet and gestured for Mirae to approach the wall of shadows, which had grown to the size of a palace gate. The darkness inside the doorway churned, the oily black shapes now reminding Mirae of the water in Wol Sin Lake.

"When the gods gave our ancestors magic," the Kun Sunim said, eyeing the shadowy door, "they also gave them one command and one warning."

Mirae recited what every child in Seolla was taught: "We are to use our magic to unite the peninsula, ushering in the golden age of Seolla. However, we must only allow women's magic to flourish, or else Seolla will fall into ruin."

"Yes. But do you know why men's magic had to be curbed?"

Mirae shook her head. She knew her brothers both had a mark tattooed at the nape of their neck, which suppressed their magic. They were not allowed to eavesdrop on Mirae's magic lessons, either. "I never really questioned it. I just trusted the gods knew what they were doing and that we should obey."

"There is more to the story, and now, as our future queen, you may be told the rest of it." The Kun Sunim gestured to the dark, misty portal. "The gods were helping us prevent a great evil from being born, the only enemy who can stop us from fulfilling our destiny as uniters of the peninsula. The Inconstant Son is a man whose Sacred Bone Magic was not repressed. By failing to honor the gods' command, we allowed the Inconstant Son to rise to power, and now he seeks to destroy everything we've worked for."

So, the Inconstant Son was more than just an ancient enemy—he was a Son of the Sacred Bone, an *ancestor*. "Why does he want to destroy his own queendom?"

"All we know is what the Samsin have told us. This is why we curb the magic of men who might join the Inconstant Son's prophesied dark army and fight against us. The Deep Deceiver managed to imprison him, but as your mother's mind weakens, so does the cage." The Kun Sunim gestured toward the dark doorway once more. "You, Gongju, are the one fated to end this once and for all. Only you, as a High Daughter, have that power."

A High Daughter—the words bounced around almost meaninglessly in Mirae's brain. "But the High Horomancer is dead. She's been gone for hundreds of years."

"No, Gongju, she first *appeared* hundreds of years ago, according to record. But as she can travel through time, no one was certain when she was actually *born*."

Mirae couldn't see her own face, but whatever expression she was making caused the Kun Sunim to grab her hand soothingly. "Don't worry, Gongju. There is only one last thing you must do, and then we'll find Her Majesty. She and I will explain everything. For now, please trust me."

Did Mirae have any other choice? "What do you need me to do, exactly?"

"It's time to reseal the cage of the Inconstant Son."

Mirae balked again at the oracle's almost casual use of a name she herself had never spoken aloud. She had been told that saying his name would forge a connection between them, strengthening his power to ultimately shatter her mind, as he was trying to shatter her mother's. But everything she knew was being challenged tonight. There was nothing she could do but press forward, trusting the Kun Sunim's words.

Mirae stared at the slick, roiling darkness, dread seeping into her like the oily tendrils of shadow before her. Her heart thrummed as if a janggu had been shoved into her chest. But it was time to do her duty, so she could leave and ensure that Minho was safe. "How do I seal the cage?"

The Kun Sunim bowed. "All you need to do is put your hands into the cage. The Deep Deceiver's spell will do the rest."

The instruction sounded surprisingly simple, and Mirae was in no mood to challenge it. There would be time for all her questions later.

She turned to face the black portal and got the strange feeling that on the other side was a pair of even darker eyes, watching her with just as much interest. She stretched out her hands, slowly pushing them into the icy mist. The black tendrils seemed drawn to her, looping their feathery chill around her fingers and wrists like jewelry.

At their touch, the chill of the mist began creeping up Mirae's arms, stiffening her elbows. Soon it spread down the rest of her body, filling her with a coldness that frosted her breath.

Mirae looked into the churning shadows, wondering how she'd know when the cage was resealed. As that thought crossed her mind, other words seemed to echo out of the cage's depths, tumbling around with her own. The same ones she'd heard when Minho was trapped in her orb.

Save me, Mirae.

Save me.

This time it wasn't a desperate plea but a command from a low voice that was nothing like Minho's; and this time, it no longer rang only in her head—it reverberated through the clearing for all to hear. As soon as the rumbling words hit her ears, Mirae felt something warm press against her hands from the other side. A human chest with a beating heart.

Hands, equally warm, grabbed her wrists and flung her backward, out of the way. Mirae stumbled into the altar, knocking it over and dumping its precious treasures onto the ground.

"No," she heard the Kun Sunim cry. "This isn't possi—"

A sudden wet sound cut off the oracle's words. Mirae watched as the old woman clutched her throat, a strange noise coming out of her mouth. When the Kun Sunim turned around, her eyes wide, there was blood seeping through her fingers and running down her neck.

Mirae could only stare, her body refusing to move, her own throat too paralyzed to even scream, as the Kun Sunim fell to her knees, still making that awful gurgling sound. Behind her, the black doorway had turned gray. A dark figure, impossibly thin, floated in the swirling mist on the other side.

The sound of the oracles gasping behind her finally brought Mirae to her senses. She whirled around, raising her voice to be heard across the clearing. "Run! Go find my mother!"

But it was too late. A gale stronger than any Mirae had ever summoned swept through the trees, extinguishing the lanterns and plunging her into darkness. She tried to scramble to her feet but tripped on a leg of the upturned altar, which sent her sprawling back onto the sandy path. Mirae lay there, unable to see anything; she tried to be silent and listen to what was happening around her instead.

First came the same low laughter that had followed her during her first switch. Then the sound of something whipping through the air, trailing a series of clacking noises behind it. Chattering teeth or guttural clicks deep in the throat. More wet slices. Chokes and gurgles. Then the screams of oracles being slaughtered.

Mirae began to creep forward, staying low, hoping the sand would mute the sound of her passing. She needed to get to her mother. Or Captain Jia. Anyone who could put a stop to this. But as the low, oily laughter grew louder and the warm sprays hitting either side of her started seeping into her hanbok, Mirae felt the strength leave her body. There was no way she was getting out of there before every one of the oracles was killed, and her along with them.

Mirae rose shakily to her knees just as everything fell quiet, except for the sounds of women choking on their own blood. She was almost to her feet when she felt something press into her back. Something sticky and warm. Slick like the inside of a peach.

Mirae wanted to blast her assailant with fire, but before she could prepare an attack, the monster behind her leaned in and nuzzled her hair.

Mirae waited for a deep slice into her neck that never came. The monster seemed to be mouthing silent words with soft lips and warm, rhythmic breaths. Gently nibbling her hair until one of Mirae's pins fell to the ground.

Her mother's pin. As if plunged into the same icy river she'd hoped to rouse Sangsin Bada with, Mirae reminded herself that oracles were dying. And there were family members and foreign delegates back at the palace who were equally in danger.

Hongbin's words from her first switch echoed back like a slap in the face. Minho was also in trouble. He needed her most of all.

Calling on the fierceness of that thought, and on the dying embers of the altar candles upended onto the forest floor, Mirae hid a lick of fire in her palm like a tiny sun. As the monster moved to caress the other side of her head, Mirae reached up and struck it in the face.

She was surprised to make contact with a lock of hair but was pleased when she saw her fire flare up with newfound fuel. The monster gave an inhuman screech; the wet bulb at Mirae's back shoved her with surprising strength, dumping her once more onto the ground.

She'd barely raised her head, preparing more fire in her palm, when a bright glow at the other end of the clearing rose in solidarity with her own. It was green like a jade star, cracked with beams of light that traced a pattern in the air. Pale scars of lightning.

Mirae knew that sword. She'd tried to shatter it not long ago. Now she was gladder than ever that she'd failed.

After Captain Jia's blade thrummed to life, so did another, and another. All different colors blazing together until they formed a rainbow circling the clearing. Last of all, a queenly figure stepped forward, wreathed in violet flames. Mirae's mother spoke: "I see you've rejected my mercy, old friend. So let us have war."

The monster shrieked. Mirae felt a burst of wind above her, blowing her already loosened hair around, as the monster threw itself at the Wonhwa army and its enchanted queen.

Knowing she needed to escape before all hell broke loose again, Mirae clutched at sand and grass, trying to pull herself to her feet. Her hand caught the edge of something tough and worn. A leather boot. Two hands reached down and gripped her arms.

"Come, Gongju mama." Captain Jia pulled Mirae to her feet. "Run with me."

Chapter
SEVEN

Mirae and Captain Jia made it only a few steps from the clearing and back into the forest before the sound and heat of an explosion rammed them from behind, sending them sprawling. Mirae's shoulder collided painfully with a tree trunk, leaving her winded on the ground as another wave of explosions passed overhead.

"What was that?" she gasped as soon as she could breathe again.

"I don't know." Captain Jia hauled Mirae back to her feet, careful with the arm she cradled. "But we have to get you to safety."

"Minho, too. We have to protect him."

"I ordered everyone back into the palace." Captain Jia used her sword to light the darkness between trees. "He'll be safe there."

Another blast rang out of the clearing behind them, followed by shouts and shrieks. Then came another sound—a voice Mirae was getting uncomfortably familiar with.

Where are you going, queenling? You really shouldn't leave your mother alone with me.

Captain Jia grabbed Mirae's wrist and pulled her deeper into the trees. "Please, Gongju. We have to hurry."

Mirae sank her heels into the ground and pulled her hand away. "Captain, I need you to listen carefully. Go to the palace and find Minho. Do not let him out of your sight."

"What?" Captain Jia looked at Mirae as if she'd lost her mind. "I'm not leaving without you. I have to keep you safe."

"He's in danger." Mirae held up her hand, silencing the captain's protests. "I'm trusting you to take care of my brother, whom we both love. I know you will not fail."

"We'll protect him together once we reach the palace." Captain Jia reached for Mirae's wrist again, but Mirae twisted her body away.

"I released the monster in there." Mirae shivered as another explosion hit the far side of the clearing, followed by more screams. "I don't know how it happened, but I cannot let anyone else die. Please, go find Minho. That's a command from your future queen."

Mirae turned and ran back into the clearing, ignoring the captain's protests, knowing full well that the other woman would never disobey a direct order. When Mirae broke through the trees, she ground to a halt and stared in horror at the scene before her.

The Garden of Queens was nothing like she'd left it. The clearing was alight with massive violet flames that scorched the burial mounds, casting an amethyst glare on the blackening domes. It was as if the moon, draped in a sheer blanket of night, had come crashing down, a gods-sent decimator of queens.

Mirae shielded her eyes from the blinding firelight and the suffocating heat of its world-burning blaze. Blinking back tears, she searched for her mother. There, standing atop the farthest dome, near the shadowy door, was a red-and-gold figure lifting its arms to the sky.

Mirae stepped carefully between the firelit tombs, over rare green patches where the violet flames had not yet spread. Soon she came across Wonhwa guards taking cover behind a few of the mounds. The rest of their sisters were huddled behind a white-hot shield planted in the middle of the path leading to the altar. The Jade Witches had pressed the tips of their enchanted swords together, fortifying the pulsing, protective barricade they'd created with their beams of multicolored light.

"Gongju mama!" one of the guards cried from the center of the blazing shield, where her blade burned as the core of that relentless, electric flower. "What are you doing here?"

Mirae didn't have time to stop and explain that she was the one who'd failed to contain the great evil attacking them. That because of her, the halls of the Temple of the Sacred Bone might become empty, these holy grounds scarred forever. She had to end the chaos before it claimed anyone else. If she really was the Unnamed Dragon, now was her chance to prove it.

Mirae focused on the altar and the doorway of shadows, hoping to catch a glimpse of the horrible flying creature that had raised the forest of flames.

But it wasn't the monster she saw standing proudly, a reckless, fire-blasting enemy with unchecked rage. Instead, Mirae's mother, stationed atop the farthest dome, had her arms raised above her head like a gold-and-scarlet tree; she wasn't facing the dark doorway, attempting to seal it. No, Mirae's mother was shooting barrages of violet fire, as aggressive and white-tinged as rushing rapids, directly into the Wonhwa shield—into the women sworn to protect her.

"Mother," Mirae shouted over the roaring flames. "What are you doing?"

Her mother's eyes, star-white with madness, settled on Mirae, and her lips stretched into a smile that suited the snarl of her words. "Ah, if it isn't our pathetic guest of honor."

Mirae stepped out from behind the Wonhwa shield, despite the panicked protests of the guards. She walked slowly down the sandy path, approaching her mother as she would a wild animal. She knew better than to underestimate the strength of her mother's hallucinations. "You don't want to do this, Mother. Don't let him control you."

Her mother laughed. "You can't trick me anymore, bane of my blood. I know what you are." Fire streamed from her mother's hands, creating a wall between Mirae and the altar. After another laugh from her mother, the fire shifted. Like a snake, it made a wide circle around Mirae, slowly tightening as if to suffocate her in its blistering-hot coils. Mirae tried to stay calm; her mother wasn't talking to her—in her delusion, she was speaking to the Sacred Bone ancestor breaking her mind.

"I can practically smell the high magic in you," her mother sneered. "Such a shame to have it wasted on someone undeserving. I don't know how you managed to get past all my traps, but now that you're here, I suppose our little secret is out. I'll just have to destroy you myself, abomination."

Mirae needed to break her mother's trance before the fiery coils of her prison closed in completely, but something told her that the blast of a cold-water illusion wasn't going to work this time. "Mother, it's me—Mirae! *Please come back.*"

It didn't seem as if her mother had heard her. Worse yet, Mirae knew that any second now, the Wonhwa guards would be forced to intervene, to leap into this death trap, swords blazing. If she didn't do something now, more women were going to die.

Mirae looked down at her hands, blood in every wrinkle of skin and silk. Oracle blood. The heat of the black bell returned to her hand like a burning scar as Mirae remembered the Kun Sunim's words.

You, Gongju, are the one fated to end this once and for all. Only you, as a High Daughter, have that power.

Mirae met her mother's white-hot eyes and held out her hand. "I command you in the name of the Samsin, as their Unnamed Dragon and High Horomancer, to leave my mother alone."

The violet flames snaked closer, mimicking the clawlike curves of her mother's hands. "You seek to command me with blasphemy? You, who should never have been born?"

Mirae looked up at her mother, too far gone to be persuaded with reason. This was the woman who had taught her gentle Ma-eum tricks that filled ordinary things with light—like turning bustling gowns into paper lanterns. Together, they'd created illusionary wonders, sending each other paddling beside pink-gilled fish in bluest of blue depths, friends to whales. Now her mother stood wreathed in flames, leering at her with uncanny, starlit eyes, bent on destroying her.

Mirae forced herself to remember the burn of the black bell and its power, power that connected her to her calling. It was the only way she could hope to be strong enough to defeat a fully trained Daughter of the Sacred Bone.

I am the Unnamed Dragon, Mirae thought, recalling the blistering pain so clearly it set her nerves on fire. *Tonight, we will earn our True Name.*

Mirae raised her other arm, her bloodied hand coated with persimmon-colored flames. Her mother laughed, but the fiery snake around Mirae withdrew, returning to its maker and coiling around her until the queen's entire body was surrounded by violet fire, streaming upward to collect in a monstrous mass above her head. "I will shatter your bones, bane of my line. Your little tricks are frogs compared to the dragons in my blood."

Mirae's mother threw her arms down, lobbing a giant violet sun at Mirae's tiny, glowing palm. But the flames never reached Mirae, because her mother was wrong about one thing—Mirae's magic was neither froglike nor about to be shattered.

Instead, her mother's fire went straight into a giant red mouth: an orb unlike any Mirae had ever made. Fierce and toothed, with a long, velvety tongue. Tendrils sprouted from its chin and brow, and its eyes were as black as the High Horomancer's bell.

Mirae's dragon rose to meet the violet fire, basking in it until its looming form grew taller than the trees. She drew inspiration from the brave warriors behind her who refused to retreat, and from the joyous ribbons secured by the slain oracles. With scales that reflected every shade in the forest, the dragon's serpentine body wound through the Garden of Queens, hind legs crouching on top of ancestral burial mounds like a slithering, rainbow sunrise.

As a creature of fire, it knew what to do with every lick of magic hurled its way, easily absorbing every shade and swelter into its belly. The endless stream of violet flames attacking it split and spread like pale, rippling wings across the dragon's back, repelled and dispersed into glittering steam. Mirae's mother screamed, casting fireball after fireball, though they never reached Mirae, devoured all by her grinning dragon.

Finally, her mother lowered her arms, exhausted. She stared up at the beast, right into a mouth that could swallow her whole. "Take what you want from me—just don't hurt my family."

"I am your family," Mirae said, her voice loud in the sudden quiet. Her mother's flames had extinguished themselves with the lowering of her arms.

"No, not *you*, abomination." Her mother's face twisted with rage, but she made no move against Mirae. Instead, she sank to her knees. Her face fell smooth, eyes blank and glistening like the jewels in her hair.

After a moment, Mirae lowered her arms and took a few steps forward, bidding her dragon to disperse. Whether her mother thought Mirae was the Inconstant Son or a High Daughter, what mattered was that she had surrendered. It was finally over.

Mirae allowed herself a breath of relief, until she realized that her dragon, instead of fading into smoke, still loomed over her, its long neck and massive, scaled head turning to look down at its master. Mirae stared back, willing the dragon to return to the elements from which she'd forged it. But just like the orb that had trapped Minho that morning, Mirae's creation refused her commands.

She is mine fairly won, queenling. The debt must be repaid.

Mirae knew that voice. Realizing that the Inconstant Son had taken over her magic yet again, she took a step back. But no more than one. Though her powers were too fledgling to compete with this practiced, ancient evil, Mirae stood blood-soaked and defiant, no more willing to bow than her wayward dragon. That was not the way of the Daughters of the Sacred Bone. "Let my mother go."

You want me to release the shrewd queen, right arm of the Deep Deceiver? The dragon lowered its head, one giant black eye looking into Mirae's. *A bold request. One I may honor if you release me from my cage. Will you, out of all the false queens, prove true?*

Mirae held her head high, belying the fear that slickened the palms of her hands. "Why would I help you, when all you want is to burn my queendom to the ground?"

Is that what I want? The dragon threw back its head and laughed, spitting her mother's pent-up fire back into the trees. *I'm starting to think that what I want is you, Mirae. You, you, you, after all this time.*

"Release my mother," Mirae said, her voice cold. "Or be destroyed here and now."

Destroyed? Oh, she doesn't know. The dragon roared, arching its sinuous back and digging its claws into the earth. *She doesn't know what I can take—or what I can do from the bottom of my lake.*

His lake? The memory of Wol Sin Lake flashed in front of Mirae's eyes. Was that his lair, hidden inside the cage built by the Deep Deceiver? Mirae's switch had shown her she'd be there in two days' time—but why? What was she doing there? And what was it that the Inconstant Son would take?

"Mirae." Her father's voice startled her, and she turned around. He stood several paces away from the Wonhwa shield that should have been protecting him. The silver in his hair reflected the gem-colored fires in the clearing with more energy than he seemed to possess in his entire body. "Come to me."

At the sight of him, Mirae's shoulders slumped, while the dragon's shook with glee. *Yes, come, my pretty king. Come and break with me.*

The dragon's searing breath made the treetops crackle anew, lit with wildfire that spat and flared in as many shades as the dragon's scales. Multicolored ash rained down from above; it dusted the top of Mirae's mother's head, but the queen didn't move, still locked inside whatever paralyzing trance the Inconstant Son had left her in.

Keeping her eyes on the dragon, Mirae backed up toward her father until she felt his arms around her. Then she spoke, with all the queenly ire of her ancestors. "If you harm my family, foul creature, then this I swear—you will never, ever find release."

For a moment, her words stilled the dragon's blistering spite and writhing spine. The creature stared down at the pair of them—father and daughter, embracing, fearless in a way that seemed to sap the dragon's will while something else took its place, a sorrow darker than those bell-black eyes.

As the monster stared, silent at last, Mirae felt her father reach up to her face, parting her lips so he could slip something small onto her tongue. Warm and salty from his hand, the small morsel of what felt like light, polished wood held no particular flavor, but still managed to fill her with the same satiety and gladness as eating her favorite fruit. Mirae felt as refreshed as if she'd taken a knee-deep plunge into a koi-swarmed pond, laughing and splashing her brothers.

Mirae knew, even without seeing the tiny carved animal, that her father had given her one of the zodiac beads made by her mother.

As Mirae's body was flooded with pure, soothing love, she wondered at the power of the bead. Her heart began to slow, and with that came the feeling of her magic curling into itself and falling into a peaceful slumber. As if realizing that its maker's magic was becoming dormant, the dragon reared up. It lurched one last time at Mirae's silent, glass-eyed mother, but before its maw could snap around her, its body burst into plumes of rainbow smoke. Gone at last.

The inexplicable magic of the bead in Mirae's mouth lingered, dampening any feeling other than love, even as her father released her, pushing her back toward the Wonhwa guards, who had likewise dispelled their shield. "Take her to safety," he said. "I'll see to my wife."

"But the cage," Mirae said, fighting the sudden drowsiness that came with the warm peace still flooding her body. "I need to—"

"The monster is free now," her father said. "Only your mother can fix this."

Still, Mirae didn't retreat. Though her eyes were getting a little blurry, she saw her mother's head snap up, wild starlight returning to her eyes. A moment later, everyone else saw it, too. Mirae's father sprinted forward, shoving something into his mouth.

With the help of the calm lingering in Mirae's body, the Wonhwa guards easily held her back, preventing her from following him. "Let His Royal Highness finish this, Gongju mama. You've done enough," one of them said.

Mirae hated that she didn't have the heart to protest while her mind and body were still under the peaceful fog of the bead her father had given her. But as the bead's temporary power began to soften, her mind cleared enough to remember what Hongbin had told her in the future. Recalling his dire warning, Mirae quit resisting everyone's insistence that she leave her parents and the forest behind.

"We have to get to the palace," Mirae said, letting the soldiers pull her back toward the trees. "We must find Minho *now*."

As she and the soldiers turned to run, Mirae shot one last look at her father. Her mother was sending more violet fireballs at him, which he had so far successfully dodged. Mirae watched as her father reached her mother before she could wreathe herself in flames, grabbed her face, and kissed her, just as her clawlike hands raked red lines down his back, bloodying his blue robe like a smear of sunset against a perfectly calm sky.

The violence of that image stayed with Mirae, reddening her vision of the trees and the sky, as she turned and trailed after the Wonhwa guards back toward the palace. The dragon's final words rang in her head as everything else in the forest fell silent.

Come, my pretty king. Come and break with me.

When they finally escaped the trees, Mirae refused to slow, even as they raced up the steep hill at the foot of the palace. She itched to summon a magical gale to propel her toward Minho even faster, but she didn't dare risk it, not after seeing how easily the Inconstant Son could usurp her magic. She wasn't even sure her powers *would* work with her father's bead stifling her. This time, she had to thwart evil on her own.

Mirae and the guards rushed wordlessly past the oracles who had survived the assault, though they wailed and bowed like swooning moons as they raised desperate prayers to the heavens. True Bone royals stood on the hill as well, a scattering of stiff, midnight jewels looking up at the fire-capped forest with horror.

Though her heart was in her throat as she ran, Mirae told herself it would be all right, she'd find Minho safe with Captain Jia. But when she reached the top of the hill, she found the dragon gates being thrown wide open and Wonhwa guards rushing out of them. In their midst was Captain Jia, shouting at the top of her lungs.

"He's not inside the palace. Find Daegun daegam *now!*"

Captain Jia saw Mirae rushing up to the gates and fell to her knees. "Gongju mama, I failed you, but I swear I'll make it right."

"Where's Minho?" Mirae barely had enough breath left to utter those desperate words.

"When I got here, he and the Josan dignitary were nowhere to be found." Captain Jia lowered her head, exposing her neck as she would to an executioner. "The flying monster got here before me. There were so many wounded . . . I had to help them. By the time I could look for Daegun daegam . . . I'm sorry, Gongju mama."

"No, he can't be gone." Mirae licked her chapped lips, salty from the warmth trickling out of her eyes. But as she looked past the dragon gates and into the palace, she saw a courtyard strewn with bodies, their blood darkening the sand. Several buildings were on fire, ignited by torches dropped by the dead. Mirae clenched her fists, even though every fiber within her still called for her to remain calm. "I'll find Minho and annihilate the one who did this."

"We will find Daegun daegam," Captain Jia promised. She looked up at Mirae, eyes filled with the pain of someone who had done the unforgivable. "But you must stay here. It is your duty."

A circle of white-hot light formed around Mirae, shocking her into silence. The searing radiance quickly formed tall petals that met at the tips, encasing Mirae in a lotus prison.

"I'm sorry, Gongju mama," Captain Jia said again as Mirae struggled in the magic cage, "but if we suffer any treachery from Josan, we are to seize all members of the royal family and defend them inside the palace walls. It's the law."

Mirae's hands were already above her head, summoning Sacred Bone Magic to decimate the prison the Wonhwa captain had dared to surround her with, but her body was resistant. Before she could force the magic within her to rouse, someone behind her yanked her arms back down in an embrace tighter than any cage.

Hongbin, whose hair and clothes were as disheveled as they'd been in her vision of the future, was pinning her from behind, confident in the knowledge that she would never harm him, would never use her magic against him. Without magic or the ability to struggle without burning Hongbin against the lotus shield, all Mirae could do was fall to the ground and scream.

Chapter

EIGHT

Mirae woke the next morning on the floor of the throne room. As soon as her eyes opened, she sat up and smoothed out her bedroll, forcing herself to keep busy; otherwise, memories from last night would replay in her mind, along with all the accusing thoughts about what she should have done to protect Minho—and everyone else.

Refusing to let herself sit with the helplessness and guilt was the only way to stay sane while trapped inside the palace.

But she wasn't confined to the throne room, so Mirae rose and headed back toward the palace courtyard, stepping carefully over the slumbering bodies around her—dozens of True Bone and Wonhwa women who had collapsed in the makeshift sleeping quarters after a long night of repairing the palace with magic, still guarding their future queen even in sleep.

Feet muffled by her pointed white socks, Mirae stole quietly to the exit of the eojwa sil, where the Hwabaek would meet later to discuss what to do about their unconscious queen and Mirae's . . . complicated path to coronation. After interrogating her last night, the highest-ranking members of the Hwabaek—including a seething Sangsin Bada—had learned that though

Mirae had technically failed to complete the ceremony, she had, allegedly, been named the long-awaited High Horomancer, the queen Seolla had been waiting for, for over a thousand years.

After breakfast, she was to meet with the councilmembers again, this time with the surviving oracles as well, to prove that this incredible claim was true—since the oracles who witnessed her first switch had been brutally murdered.

Mirae pinched herself hard, letting pain cloud her mind and block out the memory of all the horrific things that had happened in the Garden of Queens, as well as the fear over whatever fate had befallen Minho.

Mirae paused at the steps leading out of the throne room to search for her shoes, their golden gleam easily picked out from all the other embroidered leather sinbal placed on the misty steps like flowery boats descending a waterfall. Once she slipped them on, Mirae took one last look back at the dragon throne across the room as if hoping, somehow, that her mother would be sitting there, telling Mirae all this had just been a horrible dream.

But the throne was empty. The thick red pillars on either side of it stood out from the dark gray tiles on the floor like flames rising from the ash. Steps leading up to the similarly bright-red raised platform sitting between the pillars aligned perfectly with the golden throne, which itself sat majestically in front of a large tryptic backdrop carved with rows upon rows of snarling dragon medallions.

Her mother was supposed to be sitting there that morning, proudly declaring that Mirae was Seolla's next enchanted queen.

Instead, her mother and her father lay in the queen's chambers exactly as they'd been found on the forest floor—still as paintings, and pale as if eternally lit by the moon. They breathed like the living, and their hearts still beat, but there was nothing the royal physician could do to reverse whatever sacrifice Mirae's parents had made to end the queen's madness.

Mirae turned away from the throne now, and from the sweeping mural of Seolla's beautiful hills and sky that stood behind it—a representation of the birthright she no longer felt she deserved. As she stepped out onto the stairs, she was grateful for the morning mist that chilled her to the bone, distracting her from the dark thoughts threatening to shatter what little composure she had left.

A group of Wonhwa guards stood waiting for Mirae on the last step. They bowed as she approached and fell in line behind her, no more than five paces away at any time. Their orders from Captain Jia were strict—after the attack on the palace, under no circumstances were they to let Mirae wander out of their sight.

The courtyard between the throne room and the dragon gates was also draped in mist, partially obscuring the bodies lined up right where the flying, throat-slitting monster had infiltrated the palace and slaughtered everyone who came near it. Fleeing royals, unsuspecting palace women, and Wonhwa guards who'd tried to protect them all lay before Mirae, their bodies shrouded with thick white cloth.

The sand beneath the dead was freshly cleaned. The rest of the courtyard, however, was still spotted with what looked like giant scabs, wounds on the palace grounds that had yet to be erased.

The night before, Mirae had found her way out here to where the Jade Witches toiled, cleaning the courtyard with their magic. It was Yoonhee who showed Mirae how it was done, despite the protests from the other Jade Witches—True Bone and Wonhwa alike—who insisted that this was not work befitting a crown princess.

Yoonhee had demonstrated with her own hands, patiently explaining, "You are already familiar with commanding the elements by understanding their properties, but summoning blood is different from conjuring fire. The properties of blood involve carrying energies that sustain life. You manipulate it by asking it to do what it was made to do—but instead of transporting all that it holds through *veins*, ask it to deliver itself into the palms of your hands. Blood will recognize its own likeness flowing through your body and be drawn to you, obeying your command."

With a little coaching from Yoonhee and a great deal of concentration, Mirae was able to replicate her friend's success— filling her cupped hands to the brim with cold, congealed blood drawn from the sand. The only thing that kept Mirae from heaving up what remained of her dinner at the sight of all that blood touching her skin was the stony resolve of the women laboring around her. No one else balked at the task before them; instead they reverently, mournfully gathered as much as they could, transferring each handful into pots to be buried with the dead. It was slow, heartbreaking work, but no one complained.

Mirae had managed to keep her composure by reminding herself solemnly that she, more than anyone else, deserved to fill her hands with the blood of the fallen. This was the least she could do, and she owed it to her people to follow through with dignity.

Now she ran through Yoonhee's instructions again before forcing herself to focus on the task at hand and nothing else, just as she had the night before. Mirae walked toward a dried pool of blood bruising the courtyard sand, knelt beside it, and got to work.

Breakfast was a somber affair. Not even the smell of rich abalone juk could make Mirae smile as she stood in line with the other women helping to repair the palace—some tasked with cleaning the sand, others with repairing what fallen torches had burned.

No one protested at the sight of their crown princess laboring among them anymore. She'd been very clear about needing something, anything to do, and once word spread that she claimed to be the High Horomancer, no one questioned her. Instead, Mirae had to ignore the looks cast her way. Most were curious. Others were full of confusion, grief, or more than a little fear.

Thankfully, Jisoo and Yoonhee treated her as they always had. Once Mirae had her bowl of juk in hand, she walked over to her friends, who waved for her to come join them on the throne room steps. As soon as Mirae sat down, Jisoo and Yoonhee began fussing over her like young mothers, smoothing out the wrinkles in her chima and fishing out their own tastiest morsels of mollusk and egg to drop into her bowl.

"Eat, you need your strength," Jisoo said, as if she and Yoonhee didn't need an energizing breakfast just as much as Mirae did. But Mirae didn't complain. She knew this was the way her friends showed their love and concern.

They ate in companionable silence for several minutes before Jisoo cleared her throat and said, "My mother's taking me back to Geumju today, since there's nothing left for a Ma-eum Mage like myself to do here. She wants me to oversee my family's household while my grandmother manages the troops at the border."

Mirae nodded, but her hands seemed to freeze around her bowl. It made sense that Commander Song, Jisoo's grandmother, would rush to tighten security at the border after hearing about Minho's disappearance. Commander Song was the one who oversaw the lone entrance between Josan and Seolla, protected by an enormous gate and a magical barrier that spanned the entire length of the border between the two nations. Mirae often heard that the barrier, which incinerated any human who touched it, was credited with the grudging peace that had finally fallen between Josan's guerrilla rebels and Seolla's army of witches. Normally, Josan and Seollan citizens could pass through the singular gate fairly hassle-free, as long as they had their identification tags.

Unless, of course, the crown princess's Sangsok Ceremony went horribly wrong, and a prince disappeared the same night as the dignitary of a country notorious for sabotaging the Trial of the Gods in order to release an ancient evil bent on destroying Seolla.

Mirae felt a hand on her knee. Jisoo leaned in close, her eyes worried. "Stop locking your emotions away, Gongju. You need to talk about what happened, or all this pain will keep festering inside you. Please, Gongju. We're here to listen."

Mirae realized she'd been gripping her bowl so tightly, her knuckles were white as snow. Small, salty drops of water spilled from her eyes and into the remaining bite of juk, and her shoulders began to shake. Jisoo scooted closer to wrap her arms around Mirae, while Yoonhee gently set Mirae's bowl aside and grabbed her hands, still streaked with blood from her work that morning. "You know none of this is your fault, don't you, Gongju?"

Mirae couldn't hold back any longer. She pulled her hands away to cover her mouth, muffling her sobs. Jisoo and Yoonhee moved immediately to obscure her from view. Yoonhee hugged Mirae, sending comforting waves of heat through Mirae's shoulders. As the air in front of them began to shimmer, Mirae knew Jisoo was casting an illusion of the three friends sitting and eating their breakfasts in peace.

Jisoo and Yoonhee continued their spells until Mirae's tears trailed away and her sobs relaxed into deep, slow breaths. As soon as Mirae was more or less composed, Jisoo dropped her illusion, joining Mirae and Yoonhee's embrace.

"Do you want to talk?" Jisoo asked gently.

Mirae looked up into her friends' kind faces and realized she *did*. In fact, if she didn't speak the words filling her heart to these girls, who would never judge her for anything, she was afraid she would explode. "It's killing me to be locked inside the palace," she blurted out. "Minho could be anywhere, and I'm not doing anything to save him."

"Yes, you are." Jisoo looked every bit the commander's granddaughter she was. Her catlike eyes narrowed with determination. "There's nothing more important than showing your enemies that you will never be cowed by their evil acts. By staying safe and keeping the heart of the palace running, you're demonstrating that Seolla will never be shaken. Maintaining order is how we'll find Daegun daegam quickly and bring him home."

"Once you are queen," Yoonhee said, nodding, "you will have the full might of Seolla behind you. Whoever did this will pay dearly."

Once you are queen. Mirae swallowed down another burgeoning sob as she gestured around the courtyard. "But just look at the horrible thing I allowed to happen. What if the oracles don't believe that I'm the High Horomancer, after what I've done?"

"They will believe you, because they always see the truth," Yoonhee said. There was no doubt in her eyes. "Areum decided to start her training early, after the events of last night. She told me the oracles are saying everything that's happened is a sign from the gods that a glorious but terrifying change is coming. Seolla might be on the brink of achieving its golden future, and we must not get in the way of that."

Or perhaps Seolla is on the brink of being destroyed by the Inconstant Son, Mirae thought gloomily. He'd proven how formidable he was, breaking a queen's mind years before she was ever meant to succumb to his dark power, unleashing a monster that could slaughter an army, and stealing a prince protected by Seolla's most adept magic users. How was Mirae, the only Seollan heir to have ruined her own Sangsok Ceremony, supposed to destroy such a powerful evil?

Jisoo seemed to sense the direction of Mirae's thoughts. "Stop being hard on yourself. I don't know what that flying monster was, but it clearly wasn't Seolla's great, fabled enemy. If you'd let *him* out, we wouldn't be here. That means the cage didn't fail completely. There's still time to seal it and fix everything."

Mirae wiped her eyes, realizing that Jisoo was right. By not letting herself dwell on everything that had gone wrong, she'd also failed to acknowledge the one thing that hadn't: the flying monster had clearly come *from* the Inconstant Son, but it wasn't the Inconstant Son *himself.* As Jisoo said, the fallout of his release would have been much, much worse. The cage may have been weak enough to let the Inconstant Son seize control of Mirae's dragon, but it was still standing. For how much longer, Mirae didn't know, but Seolla had not fallen.

"After I prove that I am the High Horomancer," Mirae said slowly, blinking back tears, "I'm sure the oracles will help me seal the cage—the right way this time."

"Or teach you how to defeat Seolla's enemy once and for all, since you are the queen we've been waiting for." Yoonhee smiled at Mirae, who nodded, feeling her heart give a small thrum of hope. It was true, Mirae didn't have to do all this alone.

"He failed last night, Gongju." Jisoo squeezed Mirae's knee. "You stopped him from taking over Her Majesty completely and setting himself free. I don't think you realize how incredible that is. I don't need any more proof that you're the High Horomancer, and I know you'll make everyone else believe in you, too."

Mirae let her friends' words sink into her heart, melting away the parts of her that blamed herself for abandoning Minho when he needed her most. She'd done what she had to do for the queendom's sake. And soon, she would use all of Seolla's considerable resources to bring Minho back home. The Inconstant Son had not won and he never would.

Mirae held out her hands to her friends, who took them warmly. "I would truly be lost without you. Thank you."

"No, we would be lost without *you*," Yoonhee said. "You saved everyone last night, and I know you'll save Daegun daegam, too."

Mirae smiled for the first time since her Sangsok Ceremony. She and her friends sat in companionable silence, and they buoyed Mirae's heart with their unwavering friendship, until the peaceful moment was interrupted by a tall, familiar figure.

"Gongju mama." Captain Jia bowed deeply, her voice urgent. "I've interviewed everyone who was in the palace last night and managed to find the last person to see Daegun daegam—his servant Siwon. I think you need to hear what he has to say."

All the soldiers' bedrolls had been gathered up for the Jade Witches sleeping in the throne room, leaving the barracks open as an interrogation chamber. Mirae entered close on Captain Jia's heels, and nearly gasped when she saw Siwon.

He sat with his knees pulled up to his chest, staring at the floor. The wry smile he usually wore had smoothed into a blank look of paralyzed fear—a state explained by his wounds. Long, deep scratches ran down his arms and back as if something had clawed him with a thirty-fingered hand. Only one side of his body was lacerated, as if he'd been shielding someone.

Siwon looked up as Mirae approached, his eyes red from crying. Mirae knelt down in front of the servant, her heart aching at the sight of him. "Siwon, what happened to you?"

His eyes fell back to the floor, his hands trembling over his knees. "I failed to protect him. I'm so sorry, Gongju mama."

Mirae took Siwon's shaking hands, careful not to touch his cuts. He looked up at her with such sadness and fear that she felt connected to his pain. Surely she had worn the same look last night after being forced into a lotus cage, babbling about dragons, beads, and gardens on fire, helpless to save her brother. "It's all right, Siwon. Just tell me what happened."

Siwon took a deep breath, shutting his eyes as he recalled the horrors of the night before. "I was helping all the other servants clean the courtyard," he began. "When we heard the sound of explosions, several of us ran to the dragon gates to see what was going on. The bright lights and roaring fire coming out of the forest frightened us. I immediately ran toward the commotion, looking for Daegun daegam, but he found me on his way back to the palace."

"And the Josan dignitary was with him," Captain Jia added.

Siwon nodded and shuddered. "Yes, Daegun daegam was trying to keep him safe. He tried to lead us to the throne room, where all the royals were gathering."

"My soldiers had the building surrounded," Captain Jia explained. "They were ordered to take everyone there, should anything happen."

"But you didn't reach the throne room, did you, Siwon?" Mirae asked quietly. The Inconstant Son's taunts came back to her like reopened wounds. *She doesn't know what I can take—or what I can do from the bottom of my lake.*

Siwon shook his head. "The Josan dignitary was being surprisingly unreasonable. He thought the throne room was sure to be a trap—one blast of fire, and everyone inside would die.

He refused to go inside. He and Daegun daegam only stopped arguing when they heard the screams."

Siwon shuddered violently at the memory. Out of mercy, Captain Jia took over. "I arrived at the palace soon after that," she said softly. "The path of destruction was unspeakable. Throat-slit bodies littered the ground, and no one had a sight line on the attacker. It seemed anyone who got near enough to see the flying monster was slaughtered by it. Except for you, Gongju mama. And Siwon."

Mirae and Captain Jia both turned back to the servant, who nodded bravely and continued his story. "As soon as the Josan dignitary heard the screams, he turned and ran deeper into the palace. Daegun daegam and I followed, shouting for him to come back. We just . . . we just wanted to keep him safe."

Siwon hung his head, face racked with shame. "He stopped running just outside Her Majesty's chambers. That's where the monster found us. It—it was—"

Siwon covered his face, at a loss for words to describe what he had witnessed. Mirae touched his shoulder, trying to share her courage. She understood his pain. "Its tail is sharp and clacks with the wind," she said. "It slits throats in the dark, and slices vitals that bring seasoned soldiers to their knees. Everything about it is drenched in blood."

Siwon nodded, relieved that someone understood what he could never explain. Captain Jia gestured for Siwon to continue. "Tell her what you saw."

"I saw how quickly it slaughtered the Wonhwa who were running toward us," Siwon said, looking as if he was going to be sick. "I saw a flash of white in the darkness, and long black hair. I can't say what that thing was—all I know is, I shielded Daegun daegam as best I could, but the monster flung me off like a rag. I landed hard. When I regained my breath and looked around, Daegun daegam and the Josan dignitary were gone, and everything was silent."

The barracks fell silent as well while Mirae sat and digested Siwon's story, wishing she knew how to comfort the shaken boy in front of her.

In the year he'd served her family's household, Mirae realized she had never looked past Siwon's curly black hair, or the striking angles of his face, as crisp and elegant as the paper cranes Hongbin liked to make. She'd never noticed that his skin was lightly tanned and perfectly smooth, like the pearly beige of a nautilus shell. All attributes of people from his home nation. Aside from that, Mirae only knew that Siwon was a competent companion whom Minho wouldn't go anywhere without; and no one could fix Hongbin's hair quite like Siwon.

But now Mirae saw things that went deeper than the occasional laugh she had shared with him. As Captain Jia had said, they were the lone survivors of contact with the Inconstant Son's monster; she was a High Daughter, but who was Siwon to warrant the protection of the gods?

"I retraced Daegun daegam's steps from last night," Captain Jia said, returning Mirae to the present, "and they end exactly where Siwon said. There's no sign of Daegun daegam or the dignitary leaving the palace by foot. We can only conclude that the flying monster must have taken them both."

Mirae nodded and turned back to Siwon, remembering the dignitary's conversation with Minho about leaving Seolla for a better future in Josan. "What did you think about the dignitary's behavior? Did he seem at all like he was . . . acting suspiciously?"

Siwon frowned. "You mean like leading Daegun daegam right to the spot where he was going to be abducted?"

"Gongju mama," Captain Jia interjected, "I don't think we should talk about this in front of—"

"A servant?" Mirae asked, eyebrow raised.

Captain Jia hesitated. "In front of a Josan citizen."

Mirae fell silent at the implication that Siwon could be a traitor, part of the Inconstant Son's age-old plot. Somehow, the captain's words rankled Mirae, though she didn't know why. After all, the captain was right to be cautious, wasn't she? With everything that had happened, tradition dictated that no Josan citizen could be trusted—or allowed near the royal family—until the truth of the attack was fully uncovered.

Yet as Mirae looked back at Siwon and saw the anger in his eyes over Captain Jia's allegation, she knew in her heart that Minho's servant would never have allowed harm to come to his master. "Siwon had nothing to do with the flying monster's attack. If anything, his survival is a blessing from the gods."

"Or proof that he was in league with the enemy," Captain Jia insisted. "I don't mean to be insensitive, but we have our rules for a reason."

Mirae could practically hear the words Captain Jia didn't say: *I lost my lover last night—I refuse to be negligent and let something terrible happen to you, too.*

A loud knock interrupted the silence that had fallen in the room, followed by the sound of a Wonhwa guard's voice. "Captain, the councilmembers and oracles have assembled. They're ready for Gongju mama's demonstration."

"I'll escort her shortly," Captain Jia called back. To Mirae, she said, "We should hurry. The sooner we have a queen back on the throne, the better. Once you're crowned, we can expand our search for Daegun daegam and find him quickly."

Mirae nodded, the captain's words echoing the same sentiment as her friends' earlier that morning. They didn't doubt that Mirae would be able to convince the council that she was the High Horomancer, or that she would be able to rescue Minho once she was queen. Captain Jia seemed to share their opinion, and as Mirae looked into Siwon's eyes, she realized he also trusted her to be the kind of queen who made things right.

Maybe it was time Mirae let herself believe that, too.

"I agree that we need to meet with the council quickly," Mirae said, gathering her chima, "but first I would like for you to release Siwon."

Captain Jia's eyes widened. "I can't do that, Gongju mama. Anyone born in Josan must be kept under guard until we get to the bottom of—"

"This was the work of an ancient evil," Mirae said. She kept her voice steady. In her heart, she knew that Minho's and the dignitary's disappearances were not orchestrated by Siwon, or any of the other Josan citizens who had served her family faithfully. "If anyone's to blame for what happened to Minho, it's me.

I'm the one who released the monster. No one from Josan had anything to do with it."

"But what about the dignitary's disappearance? You implied yourself that there's a chance this treachery was the work of more than just—"

"Do you really think the Josan king was able to ally himself with an enemy locked away by Sacred Bone Magic? That he would somehow know more about our enemy than we do?"

Captain Jia hesitated. "No, that is highly unlikely."

"Then let Siwon go. Let all our Josan servants go." Mirae turned to Siwon, the haunted look on his face melting away with every word she said. "I command it as High Horomancer."

Chapter
NINE

The guards at the dragon gates bowed and allowed Mirae to pass, flanked on either side by a small army of Wonhwa and Captain Jia. Mirae walked solemnly down the now familiar trail through the forest to the Garden of Queens. Captain Jia walked beside Mirae while the armed guards trailed them wordlessly. The Jade Witches kept a hand on their blades and the Ma-eum Mages scoured the landscape with sharp eyes, ready to manipulate sudden attackers with heart-stopping illusions or make their crown princess appear to vanish before enemy eyes.

Thankfully, no such defenses were needed; Mirae and her entourage traveled without incident, swiftly reaching the devastated clearing where the ancient queens were laid to rest. Mirae paused at the edge of the sandy path that led to the altar and steeled herself for her return to the scene of a nightmare.

What was once a sacred array of royal tombs was now almost unrecognizable. Mirae cast her eyes over the devastation— balding brown grass that used to be jewel green. Charred burial mounds that stank of smoke. Patches of pink sand where oracles had been mercilessly felled.

Mirae wanted to close her eyes to it all. It was hard not to start fixing what she could of her ancestors' resting place, but

True Bone and Wonhwa witches were already poring over every pebble and burnt scrap of clothing in the garden on the council's behalf, trying to re-create and understand everything that had happened the night before. Investigating, and later repairing, what Sacred Bone Magic had destroyed would take far more than a single night. Besides, that wasn't what Mirae had come there to do.

Mirae left the witches to their work and walked toward the altar and the women kneeling around it. Resting on the low table were the Sacred Bone relics, still unwrapped and glinting in the early afternoon light. Mirae knelt before the jade dagger, blue seong-suk, and black bell, relieved that they hadn't been harmed. Taking a moment to steel her nerves, she looked up at the smoky doorway to the cage built by the Deep Deceiver, still hovering like a murky dark moon in the shadows between the trees. It was a relief to see that the Inconstant Son's cage was still standing, but the sight of it reminded Mirae of the hole that would remain in her heart until Minho came home.

Before that could happen, however, Mirae needed to stabilize her queendom. She tore her eyes away from the doorway and settled them instead on the women who knelt across from her at the altar.

Three of the highest-ranking councilwomen, along with a stony-faced Sangsin Bada, sat in front of the surviving oracles, who bowed to Mirae. The barest hint of black stubble dotted the tops of most of the oracles' bald heads, accentuating the dark hollows under their eyes and the streaks of dirt on their cheeks. Their blue robes were equally soiled and spotted with grime.

The councilwomen, however, wore a fresh change of clothes and sported immaculate hair. Sangsin Bada offered only the slightest bow of her head; from the tense set of her lips and the steeliness in her eyes, it was clear that the older woman had not forgotten that Mirae's mother had sabotaged the second trial. A stickler for tradition, Sangsin Bada was the one who most needed to be convinced that despite everything that had gone wrong at Mirae's Sangsok Ceremony, she still deserved to become queen.

Sangsin Bada spoke first, her words cutting. "Gongju mama, are you ready to begin?"

Mirae nodded as her eyes fell on a familiar face in the group. Behind the oracles sat their newest initiate—Areum. She hadn't changed out of last night's clothes, either; the darkness of her teal chima hid the wrinkles her gown had acquired, but her sea-green jeogori looked like the Cheong River choked by the ashy aftermath of battle. Several pearls were missing from her pins, tiny stars that had fallen from the midnight sky of her hair. She gave Mirae a small, brave smile.

"What we need from you is simple, Gongju mama." Sangsin Bada's eyes bored into Mirae's. "First, you must tell us everything the Kun Sunim said about your . . . new calling. If the oracles sense the truth in what you're saying, we will proceed from there."

The foremost oracle, who looked to be the most senior one there, bowed to Mirae. "Please start by telling us what you know about the evil man incarcerated by the Deep Deceiver, and your destiny concerning him—but please, remember that you must not speak his name."

Mirae nodded and took a deep, steadying breath. After another reassuring look from Areum, she began reciting the story of the Inconstant Son as her studies and the Kun Sunim had told it—starting with the appearance of magic in Seolla.

Magic first began when the Samsin, the three grandmother goddesses, rewarded the three Go daughters for their unparalleled cunning, craftsmanship, and foresight by gifting each of them with magic that complemented their talents: Ma-eum Magic, Jade Witchery, and Horomancy. But with these boons came a directive, and a warning: these new powers were to be used to foster peace and unite the peninsula under the golden age of Seolla. This could only be accomplished, however, if women alone were allowed to wield magic, for out of the ranks of men would rise the only enemy powerful enough to get in destiny's way: the Inconstant Son—whose name Mirae made sure not to speak aloud—and his ruthless dark army.

Thus it was that Sacred Bone men like Mirae's brothers, along with every other man born with magical abilities, were given a mark at the back of their necks to suppress their powers. But this law was not obeyed by all, and the Inconstant Son still managed to seize power and threaten to overthrow Seolla. Thankfully, the gods saw fit to appoint three High Daughters of the Sacred Bone to stave him off. The Silver Star and the Deep Deceiver were able to identify and contain the Inconstant Son but not destroy him. That was a task left to their final successor—the Unnamed Dragon, High Horomancer of Seolla.

Mirae paused as those words came out of her mouth—a title and a calling that had inexplicably been placed on her shoulders on the worst night of her life. The oracle addressing Mirae bowed in acknowledgment of her difficult, lofty new mission. "Thank you, Gongju mama. Now, tell us what our late Kun Sunim told you about your new calling."

Mirae glanced back up at the shadowy door behind the altar, a pitch-black void even in sunlight. This was where she'd last seen the Kun Sunim alive, clutching her bleeding throat.

You're here to avenge her death, Mirae reminded herself. *The Inconstant Son will not get away with anything he's done.*

Reassured by the confidence of her friends and Captain Jia, who stood out of earshot at the edge of the clearing with the rest of the Wonhwa guards, Mirae took a deep breath and did as the senior oracle asked.

She started by recounting how, when asked which of the High Daughters would be her spiritual guide, she had chosen the Unnamed Dragon. Upon touching the High Horomancer's bell, Mirae's new switching power had been unlocked, as well as the discovery that she was the long-awaited final High Daughter of Seolla.

"Very well, Gongju mama. Your words ring true." The senior oracle nodded appreciatively and gestured to the relics on the altar. Beside her, Sangsin Bada scowled. "Now, please touch the High Horomancer's bell to prove irrevocably that the gods have ordained you to this calling."

"And show us this new power you told us about," Sangsin Bada added, her eyes as dark as the doorway behind her. "Show us how this . . . 'switching' happens."

Mirae swallowed, her throat suddenly dry even as her hands became slick with sweat. This was it—the last step toward securing her crown. But Mirae well remembered the burning touch of the bell, and the confusing visions of Wol Sin Lake that came after. The two women who were supposed to help Mirae make sense of this new power were either dead or dying, but now was not the time to hesitate.

Bracing herself for the searing pain and an enigmatic glimpse of the future that would surely follow, Mirae reached out and touched the top of the High Horomancer's bell.

Nothing happened.

No sear, no pain, no transportation to the future.

Keenly aware of the eyes watching her with anticipation, Mirae lifted her hand and touched the bell again. Still nothing.

Don't panic, Mirae thought desperately as she racked her mind for what she was doing wrong. But she was replicating exactly what she'd done the first time she switched. Mirae's audience watched her with mixed looks on their faces. The oracles remained calm— encouraging. The councilwomen, however, looked impatient . . . Sangsin Bada most of all.

"Well?" the old woman asked, the corners of her mouth twitching. "Was that it? Did you switch?"

"No." Mirae swallowed. "But I touched a Sacred Bone relic and survived. Isn't that proof enough that I'm telling the truth?"

"It's proof that the gods do not wish for you to perish," Sangsin Bada said, "which makes sense, considering the turmoil our queendom is in with Her Majesty so ill. But we came here to ascertain your bold claim about being the last High Daughter, and therefore still worthy of your birthright despite last night's disaster. Show us your new power, and you'll be crowned immediately."

But if you fail to show us, Mirae could almost hear Sangsin Bada say, *then we will blame* you *for everything that's gone wrong.* Mirae knew as well as anyone that the gods would not hesitate to punish an unworthy crown princess who, as Sangsin Bada no doubt believed, had cheated the Trial of the Gods and tried to seal the cage unworthily.

Mirae tried one more time to activate the High Horomancer's bell by touching it, not caring that she looked desperate. She knew, and the gods knew, that she was no liar. Why weren't they helping her prove that to the women who held her fate in their hands?

The third time Mirae tried and failed to switch, Sangsin Bada shared a look with the other councilwomen, who nodded in silent agreement. When she turned back to Mirae, her eyes gleamed darkly, like a mockery of the black bell. "Well, Gongju mama, this has been very enlightening. The rest of the Hwabaek will have assembled by now. We must go to them and relay what we've seen. I expect they'll ask you to appear before them within the hour."

"No, wait—I'm telling the truth. I'll show you." Mirae gestured for the councilwomen to remain seated. "Please, just give me a little more time."

"You have until you are summoned to . . . figure out your new power," Sangsin Bada said, rising to her feet. "I'll allow one last demonstration before the entire council. I suggest you take some time to think about what you'll do when that time comes."

With that, Sangsin Bada and the other councilwomen bowed just low enough to be polite before exiting the Garden of Queens.

Mirae turned to the oracles as the councilwomen walked away, her eyes pleading. "I don't know how the switches works. Please, you have to show me how to control this power."

The senior oracle looked at Mirae with pity. "I'm sorry, Gongju mama. The High Horomancer is meant to be our leader, her powers unfathomable. It is *you* who will show *us* what to do."

"There must be something you can tell me," Mirae begged. "The Kun Sunim helped me discover my ability. What would she tell me to do to activate it again?"

The senior oracle bowed apologetically before rising to her feet, followed by the blue-robed women behind her. "Perhaps you should stay here and meditate. After all, if you are the High Horomancer, the gods will answer your prayers."

Mirae stared down at the altar, at the unfeeling black bell, as the oracles left the Garden of Queens. Soon it was empty except for the ring of Wonhwa guards on the outskirts of the clearing and the three women they encircled—Mirae, Captain Jia, and Areum, who had remained behind, looking as devastated as Mirae felt.

Numb, Mirae could only hang her head. Areum scooted closer, touching Mirae's shoulder comfortingly while Captain Jia approached to sit beside her. The three women sat in silence for several long moments, at a loss for what to say.

"I don't understand," Mirae said when she had finally gathered the will to speak. "Why did the gods abandon me? Don't they want me to fulfill my destiny?"

"Of course they do," Areum said. When Mirae looked into her friend's eyes, she saw warmth, and unshaken faith. "Someday this moment will make sense, but for now, you must try to understand what the gods want you to do. Perhaps you *should* meditate."

"What could the gods want, if not for me to be queen?"

"You will be crowned," Captain Jia said, the resolve in her eyes as strong as Areum's. She leaned forward as if struck by a sudden thought and gripped Mirae's shoulder firmly, urgently. "All you have to do is complete the ceremony by sealing the cage, and then you will be granted your birthright. Not even Sangsin Bada can argue against something the law clearly states."

Confused, Mirae looked into the captain's eyes, gleaming with determination. "The Sangsok Ceremony is over. It's too late for that."

"No, it isn't." Captain Jia's smile reminded Mirae of Minho, who was always so proud of his clever ideas. "Do you remember what signals the end of the ceremony?"

Mirae's frown melted away. "A gong at dawn."

Captain Jia turned to Areum. "Did you hear any such thing this morning?"

Areum shrugged and shook her head. "No, I did not."

Mirae appreciated what her friends were doing, but she waved away the implications of their words. "The flying monster disrupted the ceremony, which was all my fault. That's why there was no gong. The council isn't going to be moved by a technicality."

"Oh, I think they will." Captain Jia rose to her feet and offered Mirae a hand. "Only Her Majesty can make a ruling against tradition in situations like these. The council will be powerless to stop you if you follow the letter of the law. Come, Gongju, fulfill your destiny."

Mirae let the captain pull her to her feet but didn't follow her to the shadowy doorway looming several paces away. "Even if you're right, Captain, Sangsin Bada made it clear that I must prove I'm the High Horomancer. The council will not approve of crowning a deceiver—especially if they believe all this awfulness happened as punishment for my unworthiness."

"When you are queen, you will have the means and power to prove everyone wrong," Captain Jia said, extending her hand to Mirae again. "But this must come first. Claim your right to the throne. Seolla needs its enchanted queen now more than ever, and you need the power of the crown to make everything right."

To find Minho. What wouldn't Mirae be able to accomplish with an army of mages and witches at her command, and a queendom of loyal subjects who would do anything to support the High Horomancer, called forth at long last?

The choice seemed obvious. Captain Jia's logic made sense, and yet still Mirae hesitated. She turned to Areum, her dear friend with an uncanny predilection for foresight. "Is this what you think I should do, too, eonni?"

Areum shrugged again. "Captain Jia's plan will probably work," she said, her voice even as her eyes bored into Mirae's, her face inscrutable. "If that's what you think the gods are asking you to do."

The gods weren't speaking to Mirae at the moment, that much was clear. Why else would they abandon her when she needed to demonstrate the power they'd given her?

Just as Mirae had that thought, a movement at the edge of the clearing caught her eye. Turning to look, she could only raise her eyebrows at the sight of two noblewomen hurrying into the clearing wearing jangot over their heads, much to the confusion of the Wonhwa guards. At a nod from Captain Jia, they let the women pass.

Is this it? Mirae wondered, her heart thundering. Was she being summoned before the council? What should she do—try to prove once more that she was the High Horomancer, or seal the cage now, in defiance of the council?

Mirae hadn't even considered the possibility of a third option until the two cloaked women approached her. Though she couldn't see their faces, she recognized their clothes. After all, they were hers. Mirae could only stare, stunned, as the first noblewoman lowered her jacket—*Mirae's* jacket—revealing the face of a prince. Hongbin beamed. "I heard you were having a rough morning, so I asked a mutual friend to sneak me out."

Captain Jia looked as if she might faint. "Gunju . . . you can't be here. How did you—"

The captain's confusion turned to rage as the other richly dressed woman lowered her jangot as well. "What have you done, boy?"

Siwon draped Mirae's jangot neatly over his arm. "I was free to go, wasn't I? I decided to see how Gunju daegam was doing, and it turned out he was hatching a plan to cheer up Gongju mama, as he just said. I merely helped him succeed."

"You let a royal heir leave the palace *unprotected* . . . at a time like this?" Captain Jia put a hand on her jade sword, which had started to glow. Dark patches of lightning spread across the blade where the cracks from the night before had marred its surface. "Wasn't one prince being harmed on your watch enough?"

Before anyone could react to the captain's harsh words, Hongbin pointed at the shadowy portal to the Inconstant Son's cage, his eyes wide. "What is *that*?"

Mirae turned to look at the portal. Then back at Hongbin. The sight of the two of them together sparked a memory she was surprised she hadn't considered until right then—a vision of the future where she and Hongbin, less than two days from now, would stand in front of Wol Sin Lake. And here Hongbin was, brought to Mirae by the only other person the gods had protected from the flying monster. A shiver raced across Mirae's body, as if the threads of fate had tightened around her with their feather-soft touch.

"Gongju." Captain Jia had stopped glaring at Siwon only long enough to look at Mirae with concern. "It's all right. I can escort these two back to the palace before you reseal the cage. Just say the word."

But Mirae ignored the captain. She looked at Areum instead, who was watching her intently. Her knowing eyes seemed to echo the words stirring in Mirae's heart. *The gods didn't abandon me. They've been here all along, and they've already told me what I need to do.*

Mirae felt a hand on her shoulder. Captain Jia, seeing the look Mirae was giving the dark doorway, mistook Mirae's hesitancy for trepidation. "It will work this time, Gongju. You're ready for this, and everything that comes after. I know in my heart that you will bring Daegun home."

Yes, she would, but only if she trusted the gods, who had already shown her how to find him. Mirae nodded solemnly and reached down to grab the High Horomancer's black bell, gripping it tightly. Then she gestured for the captain to move aside while she approached the shadowy doorway. The dark mist twisting inside the opening seemed to beckon Mirae to enter and fulfill her destiny.

Without turning around, Mirae held a hand out behind her. "Come, Hongbin. I need you."

If Captain Jia thought Mirae's request was strange, she didn't say. A moment later, Mirae felt her brother's warm hand take her own. "I'm here, noonim. What do you need?"

"Do you want to save Minho?" she asked, quietly enough for only him to hear.

Hongbin nodded and whispered back, "Of course."

"Will you do anything, go anywhere to bring him home?"

Hongbin nodded again, without hesitation. "I'm offended you even need to ask."

Mirae smiled. Beneath her brother's boisterous persona was a man as brave and noble as any other. His best-kept secret. "Hold on tight, then, Hongbin."

He gripped her hand trustingly. "As you wish, noonim. I just ask that if you're planning to take me through that scary wall of smoke, you don't tell me until afterward, because that thing is terrifying."

Mirae heard Captain Jia inch closer. "You should hurry, Gongju. The council is waiting for you. So is Daegun. Finish this quickly."

Mirae kept her eyes on her younger brother, knowing that the captain was more right than she knew. "Ready, Hongbin?"

Instead of answering, her younger brother looked over his shoulder, where someone had joined them by grabbing his other hand. Siwon looked right into Mirae's eyes. "Ready."

Mirae nodded, knowing in her heart that the gods had prepared everyone around her to be here, in this moment. She reached out to the doorway and touched it with her bell.

"Gongju?" Captain Jia's tone had changed, slightly panicked now as she realized what Mirae was actually intending. "What are you doing?"

The captain's voice was drowned out by the sudden, loud drumming of Mirae's heart. She sank the bell into the mist and the swirling darkness reanimated at her touch, sucking her hand in hungrily.

"No, Gongju, you mustn't." Captain Jia sounded horrified, finally understanding what Mirae had chosen to do.

For a brief moment, Mirae had that same thought: *I mustn't. The council may never understand what I've chosen to do.* But she shook off that thought as she stepped through the cold, dark door, pulling Hongbin and Siwon after her. She could hear Captain Jia's heavy boots running toward them, but it was too late.

Mirae had already stepped into the Inconstant Son's cage.

Chapter
TEN

It was nighttime on the other side. Or at least the shadows were deep enough to bruise even the light of day. Mirae blinked in the darkness as Hongbin stumbled into the world beside her, followed by Siwon. The force of their entry knocked her off her feet. A second later she was crushed under the weight of Captain Jia, who also came crashing into the cage. As soon as everyone was through, the dark doorway disappeared in a puff of black smoke.

Mirae gave a small cry as she was immediately grabbed tightly around the wrist and yanked to her feet. Captain Jia pointed at the empty air where the shadowy doorway used to be. "Take us back, Gongju. Now."

"You're hurting me." Mirae pulled out of the other woman's grasp and rubbed her wrist.

Captain Jia took a step back, remembering herself. "Please, Gongju. I know you believe in your calling, and you want Daegun back, but this is not the way."

"Yes, it is," Mirae said. She took in her surroundings. There were wintry trees all around, and the sandy path of the garden continued here, leading deeper into a forest that was nothing like the one Mirae had left behind. "The gods want me here."

"They want you trapped inside this cage, another missing royal?" Captain Jia asked incredulously. "Risking your birthright and your *crown*?"

"I'm not trapped. I'm going to find Minho at Wol Sin Lake."

"Wol Sin Lake?" Captain Jia repeated the words as if they made no sense. "I've only heard that name in a fairy tale . . . the one about the haggard moon gwisin who drowns anyone she comes across. It's just a story, Gongju. The lake isn't real."

Mirae gripped the bell in her hand tightly. "All stories have a kernel of truth. I know this is my path as High Horomancer. I saw it in a switch."

"A switch." Captain Jia pinched the bridge of her nose. "And how do you know these . . . visions . . . don't come from the man inside this cage, just like Her Majesty's delusions? Have you considered that you might be giving him exactly what he wants?"

Mirae was about to ask how the captain could possibly think that about an experience that could only have come from the gods, but after one look at the other woman's face, the words stopped in Mirae's throat. The fear in Captain Jia's eyes wasn't for the cage—it was for Mirae's well-being.

Mirae suddenly understood why Captain Jia had been so insistent that she reseal the cage and claim her crown before it was too late. From the captain's perspective, everything had started going wrong as soon as Mirae passed the first trial. Not only had Mirae threatened Captain Jia's jade sword, her most prized possession, she'd then seemingly evaded the second trial altogether by passing without Sangsin Bada's consent. And, of course, the third trial was a complete disaster, culminating in Mirae's dragon setting the Garden of Queens on fire.

Worse yet, Mirae had discovered in her meeting with the councilwomen the night before that no one had heard the Inconstant Son's voice but her. The guards reporting back to Captain Jia may have even wondered if Mirae was as mad as her mother, especially since the zodiac beads her father had given them had stopped both her and her mother's errant spells. Mirae clutched the bag of beads still hanging under her clothes, remembering that there was a lot that Captain Jia hadn't witnessed, and therefore didn't know. Which only made Mirae even more grateful for Hongbin's and Siwon's unquestioning faith in her.

She turned to her other, more willing companions. Siwon looked as determined as ever—after all, he'd chosen to come along. Hongbin was looking around the sunless, lifeless forest as if it was probably full of ghosts. Still, the sureness in his proud stance made it clear he wasn't even considering going back.

"Gongju, please." Captain Jia's voice was calmer. Quiet. She gestured toward the still cold swath of air where the dark doorway had been. "Take us home before we perish. Rushing into the same danger as Daegun isn't the way to save him."

"Even if I knew how to open the dark portal," Mirae said, replicating the captain's calm, "I wouldn't do it. I've come too far to back out now."

The captain hung her head. "You have no idea how far we've come."

Siwon interjected, surprising both women. "I think it's clear that all we can do is move forward. I doubt the cage can be opened from here with Sacred Bone Magic alone—or else it wouldn't be a cage. Not for the man inside, at least. Surely transporting us back will require something . . . complex, and impossible for Seolla's great enemy to replicate."

"You're probably right about that," Captain Jia said. If she'd been angry at Siwon before, she was clearly furious now. "And so am I, for wondering how a Josan-born boy, who just so happened to be present when Daegun was kidnapped, also knows so much about ancient, complicated magic."

"I've been surrounded by magic users for a year," Siwon said coolly. "It doesn't take a genius to understand how things work around here."

Mirae lifted her hand for silence as something on the ground caught her eye. The sand was beginning to glow. It would have been a pretty sight if the extra illumination hadn't revealed what the sand was really made of. Some of it hadn't been ground finely enough.

"Is that a tooth?" Hongbin jumped to his feet, dusting off his clothes. "And that . . . that's definitely a finger."

"Gongju, we need to leave." Captain Jia reached for her sword as her eyes searched the darkness. "Now."

"I'm right where I need to be," Mirae said. She, Hongbin, and Siwon looked at each other and nodded, gaining strength from their shared conviction. "I'm not going back."

Captain Jia looked at each of them in turn as if they must be mad. She stood silently for several seconds before speaking. "Can you live with the fact that all of us may die here, including Daegun, because of your foolishness, Gongju? Will you really abandon your duty to Seolla as its future queen?"

"Believe what you want about my switches," Mirae said, "but you know *me*, Captain. You used to have faith in me. I'm asking you to find it again, and to help me save someone we both love." She held up the black bell, an act that caused her no harm, as proof that the gods clearly thought she was doing something right. "Minho's gone because I chose duty over him. I'm not going to make that mistake again, and I hope you won't, either."

Mirae could see the captain processing her words, torn between what she thought Mirae needed to do—bend tradition to her will to have the might of Seolla at her command—and the contradictory things the gods were seemingly saying: *Throw caution to the wind, risk your birthright and the stability of the queendom at the behest of a switch that may or may not have been real, then subdue the Inconstant Son and bring Minho safely home.*

Captain Jia was silent for several seconds more. Finally, she drew her sword and faced the path ahead. When she spoke, her voice was tense but resigned. "Lead the way, Gongju. I pray your confidence is truly from the gods."

"Sorry, excuse me," Hongbin interjected, raising his hand. "What are we going to do about the flying monster lurking around here?"

"We're not in any imminent danger," Siwon said reassuringly, holding Hongbin's trembling hand. "If the monster wanted us dead, we would be."

Mirae nodded in agreement with Siwon's observation, which had done very little to set Hongbin at ease. Mirae, however, felt her body fill with peace as she looked into Siwon's confident gaze, the near black color of his eyes glinting in the eerie light of the stark white sand. "Siwon said it best—the only way out of here is to move forward."

With that, Mirae steeled her shoulders and started down the path. She tried to hold her head high, ignoring the crunch of dry bones beneath her feet, snapping louder than twigs. She took comfort in the fact that like Siwon said, the Inconstant Son seemed to want her to find his lake—no throat-slashing monsters or renegade dragons barred her way. If Mirae was careful, she and her companions would reach Wol Sin Lake alive.

Or else they would be doomed to join this endless river of bones.

They traveled easily enough by the light of the sand, glowing like a gritty ribbon of moonlight stretched out in the middle of a haunted forest. In the darkness, no one knew what time it was, nor did they speak much over the next few hours. Everyone focused instead on the trees on either side, looking for the danger they could sense lurking nearby.

When they finally stopped to take a short rest, Captain Jia ordered everyone to stay on the path while she scouted ahead. "If you need me, shout my name." With that, the captain slipped silently into the trees.

Hongbin grimaced at the crushed-bone sand and sat gingerly beside Mirae, leaning his head against her shoulder almost instinctively.

Siwon sat as well but several paces away, giving the siblings space to speak in private. Mirae repositioned so that she and

Hongbin sat back-to-back, leaning against each other as they faced different ends of the road to keep watch. Once they were both settled, Hongbin groaned and rubbed his legs. "Minho owes me a two-hour massage when all this is over."

Mirae rolled her shoulders, letting her head fall back against Hongbin's so she could rest her neck. "Thank you for coming with me."

"Of course." Hongbin gently bumped his head against hers. "Just know that I'm only coming along because I'm hoping the man in this cage, whom I keep hearing about, possesses an unearthly beauty and a curse of evil, curable only with my kiss."

Mirae laughed, though it hurt to move her cold, stiff cheeks. "I assure you, he's not your type."

Hongbin must have heard the slight chatter of her teeth. He leaned forward and untied his jangot, then draped it around Mirae's shoulders. "Look, it's my duty to marry well for the queendom. You focus on your job, Your Majesty, and I'll focus on mine."

Mirae snuggled into the jacket, still warm from her brother's heat. "So, after you and Siwon stole my clothes, how did you get past the Wonhwa guards at the dragon gate? I didn't think they were letting anyone through without Captain Jia's permission."

Hongbin resettled himself so they sat back-to-back once more. "I convinced Jisoo, my usual accomplice for these types of escapades, to cast an illusion over my and Siwon's faces. I was Yoonhee, and Siwon was Areum. We managed to convince the guards that the three of us were sent to summon you before the council. Jisoo can be very commanding when she wants to be. I'm fairly certain she gets that from her grandmother."

Mirae nodded. "Why wasn't Jisoo with you when you arrived at the garden?"

"Oh, once we were through, I said something very rude that made her turn back and leave us alone on the hill."

Mirae smacked her brother's hand, meriting a small yelp. "Why on earth did you hurt Jisoo's feelings?"

"I had to send her away! Siwon said she couldn't be complicit in what we were doing. Besides, I'll make it up to her by bringing Minho safely home." Mirae felt Hongbin's shoulders shrug. "She's been madly in love with him since she was, like, six years old."

"That's why she'll be furious when she finds out you went after him without her."

"Honestly, who *isn't* going to be furious with me?" Hongbin muttered.

Mirae snorted. "Well, just out of curiosity, are you more afraid of what Mother, Captain Jia, or Jisoo will do to you when we get back?"

"Jisoo," Hongbin said. "Definitely Jisoo."

A second later, his shoulders stiffened. Mirae chuckled. "Don't worry, I won't let Jisoo do anything to you that I wouldn't do." When Hongbin didn't respond, Mirae tapped the back of his hand. "Hey, it's not like she followed us here. You have nothing to worry about."

"Noonim, what if I gravely underestimated how bereft Jisoo would be over being left behind, to the point where she ended up drowning herself and came back to haunt me?"

"Well, that would be . . . a very specific turn of events." Mirae scooted herself around to see what had prompted Hongbin's sudden gloomy surmising. The first thing that caught her eye was a rush of silver mist spilling out of the dark tree line, creating a dense blanket of fog.

The second thing she saw was a woman standing in the haze, her hair dark and long enough to blend in with the spaces between trees. There was a starry paleness to her sleeveless knee-length dress, which wasn't long enough to hide the fact that she didn't have any legs—nor did she have a face. Yet it seemed as if she was staring at Mirae from the framework of trees, her dress as bright against the forest's darkness as a white sliver of moon in the sky.

"That's not Jisoo," Mirae whispered, remembering the ghost Captain Jia had mentioned in the story about Wol Sin Lake. "I think it's the haggard moon gwisin."

"I thought she was just a myth," Hongbin whispered back. He stared at the faceless woman in white and shuddered. "What do we do? We can't follow her. She drowns anyone who tries to help her."

If Mirae hadn't suspected that the stories about the haggard moon gwisin might be true, especially in this gods-forsaken place, she might have been tempted to follow the forlorn ghost back into the trees. Gwisin lingered because they, or someone they loved, had been wronged. It wasn't uncommon to hear stories about gwisin leading sympathetic mortals to their un-buried bones, or to the person who murdered them.

But according to legend, the haggard moon gwisin behaved differently. Having been abandoned by a friend, left to die alone and in pain, she drowned anyone who showed her any kindness, before they had a chance to betray her, too.

Just then, the gwisin moved closer, approaching the bone path. She stopped just shy of it, prompting Mirae and Hongbin to rise to their feet as the mysterious mist that followed in her wake swept over their resting spot. Its thick, cold tendrils rose to Mirae's waist as she and Hongbin backed away.

"Wait," Hongbin said nervously, "where's Siwon?"

"I don't know. I don't see him," Mirae said quietly. It felt wrong to do more than whisper in the presence of a gwisin who'd been forever silenced. "What about Captain Jia?"

Out of the corner of her eye, Mirae saw Hongbin shake his head. "Should I call for her?"

Before Mirae could answer, the gwisin crossed the final gap between them. Mirae and Hongbin backed up. Mirae made sure to keep the crunch of broken bones beneath her feet to ensure she didn't stray off the path. As Hongbin reached for Mirae's hand, she said softly, "What is it you want from us, pitiable spirit?"

The gwisin didn't answer. Her mist grew thicker, almost dense enough to put pressure around Mirae's waist. Instead of coming closer, the gwisin craned her neck to one side until her dark curtain of hair hung like a rippling shadow. She craned her neck farther still, slowly bending herself in half sideways, her head and hair sinking into the mist. The curve of her white dress and her spine—impossibly flexible for anyone but the boneless—created a milky fogbow following after itself like a long silver dragon slinking through low clouds.

Before the gwisin's body could become one with the mist, Siwon called out from somewhere near the tree line, "Leave them alone. I will follow you."

The gwisin slowly righted herself and turned to stare at Siwon, who was nothing more than a dark figure against the trees. Without hesitation, the gwisin accepted Siwon's offer, surging with inhuman speed back into the forest as if sucked there by a whirlwind. Siwon, true to his word, slipped into the forest behind her.

"Siwon, no!" Mirae's feet had barely brushed the edge of the bone path when Hongbin grabbed her arm.

"We can't leave the road, noonim. Anything could be in there waiting for us."

"As opposed to the monster who is in there now, and is going to drown our friend?"

"Then let's call for Captain Jia."

Mirae yanked her arm free. "She'll just insist that it's too dangerous—that we should leave Siwon behind. I have to go after him. You stay here and guide me back to the path with your voice. If Captain Jia returns before I do, you must tell her where I've gone. Please, Hongbin, be my anchor."

"Noonim." Hongbin grabbed her arm again. "If you think I'm going to let you go out there alone—"

Mirae raised her palm. "Don't make me root you in place."

Hongbin was not at all deterred. "I'm not going to let that gwisin drown you, too."

Mirae grabbed Hongbin's wrist, looking him dead in the eye. "You and I are getting out of here alive—I've seen it in a vision. But I can't say the same for Siwon. We who are guaranteed to survive need to look out for those whose futures are uncertain."

Mirae's voice softened, and the stubbornness on Hongbin's face finally melted away. "I'll be fine, Hongbin. Just stay where Captain Jia can find you, and if I'm not back soon, come look for me together."

Mirae wasn't sure what Hongbin saw on her face or in her eyes, but he clenched his jaw and nodded. "I'll guide you back with a story. Do not stray farther than the sound of my voice."

Mirae returned his nod. "I won't go too far. I promise."

Hongbin cleared his throat. As he raised his eyes to the mist-draped heavens, his voice transformed from its usual cheery timbre to one throatier and slower, his words resounding through the trees.

"Once upon a time, there was a particularly odious yet cunning man named Lee Byung-hee who wormed his way into considerable power, becoming a prominent judge in his province. He was quick to side with whoever could expand his wealth, but he had suspiciously bad luck when it came to his wives. In fact, the villagers in his province soon became tired of their precious daughters marrying into a life of luxury only to fall deathly ill, or be murdered by bandits who were never caught.

"Everything changed, however, when one day he set his sights on the Go family, who were rumored to have daughters as beautiful as the sun, the moon, and the stars. This is the story of how three sisters—Jeong-min, Hae-ju, and Han-bit—conspired to turn their misfortune into a chance to save their province from the evils of a would-be suitor. And how their cunning, craftsmanship, and foresight inspired the Samsin to give Seolla a priceless gift: three forms of divine magic. . . ."

Mirae listened to the introduction of the familiar story until she was sure Hongbin was completely caught up in entertaining ghosts. She took a step off the path, now clear of the gwisin's mist, leaving Hongbin to deliver his tale alone atop a pile of broken bones.

Chapter
ELEVEN

Mirae moved as quickly as she could to catch up to Siwon. Thankfully, it wasn't long before she caught a glimpse of the pink hanbok he wore parting the mist ahead, trailing the gwisin, who'd slowed her pace for Siwon's sake.

Mirae didn't want to alert the gwisin to her presence, so she walked carefully. The eerie light emanating from the haggard moon gwisin's stark white dress guided Mirae down the unmarked path leading deeper into the woods. Hongbin's voice had grown weak by the time Mirae found herself in a clearing not unlike the ones she'd entered for her trials. In this open space, the mist thinned enough for Mirae to glimpse what lay ahead.

At the center of the clearing lay a small, silvery pond overflowing with pale flowers. They rested like frail cups on slick lily pad heads, sprawling across the water in a wild constellation of drifting, petaled stars. The haggard moon gwisin circled the water, floating over it like a giant white swan. In the middle of the pond, a rocky outcropping rose like a stone finger. Balanced on top of it was a pearly white orb.

Mirae was distracted by the strange familiarity of the moonlike apparition for a moment before she was able to tear her eyes away and look for Siwon. She spotted him kneeling at the edge of the pond, eyes fixed on the gwisin. Mirae crouched low and crept over to him, moving only when she was sure she wouldn't be noticed.

"Siwon," Mirae whispered when she was close enough to touch him. "We have to get you out of here. Follow me."

But Siwon made no effort to move. Staring straight ahead, he said, "We need to get that pearl."

"What are you talking about? We need to leave *now*," Mirae hissed.

"Not without that. It's the only way to help them."

Siwon's eyes were glazed over, as if he were in a trance. He stared at the gwisin, still floating like a moon-caught moth over the silvery pond, as if he'd never seen anything more terrifying— or more beautiful. Mirae looked at the spirit dubiously. "Did the gwisin tell you that?"

"In a way." Siwon swallowed. "She doesn't exactly talk."

"But she does drown people." Mirae grabbed Siwon's hand. "I need you to snap out of it and come with me."

Siwon shook his hand from her grip and untied his jangot, draping it on the ground. "I'm not leaving without that pearl. These poor souls need our help."

Mirae studied Siwon's face in the surrounding darkness. With the gwisin's ghostly glow reflecting in his eyes and the unhealed gashes running down his cheeks, she realized it wasn't madness or a trance influencing him, only steely determination, a feeling Mirae knew well in her own heart.

But Siwon was no High Daughter, or even a Seollan man with repressed magic. He was a Josan servant who was going to get himself killed. Just as Mirae understood his determination as well as she did her own, she also knew how to break it.

Fire pooled in Mirae's palm, shining out of her hand and lighting the thinly misted clearing until it glowed like the Deep Deceiver's seong-suk. She rose to face the haggard moon gwisin across the water. The ghost in white stared back at Mirae, her face blank and pale.

"Rescind your request of my friend," Mirae said, raising her voice to reach across the pond. "Or I will hurl you, eternally burning, into the spirit world."

"Gongju mama, don't—"

Siwon's warning came too late. The curious silvery water of the pond began to shiver. When Mirae raised her glowing palm high enough to look into its depths, she froze.

Where the flowers had once been, dozens of pale heads now sprouted across the water instead. Black hair floated like seaweed over half-submerged faces. The eyes of these tormented, restless dead stared at Mirae with menacing glares that flickered cruelly in the fiery sheen of her palm light.

Mirae stared back, paralyzed with terror, until the haggard moon gwisin, master of the water ghosts, lifted her arms, bidding the horde of mul gwisin to advance.

Mirae felt someone yank her away from the water's edge as the mul gwisin's arms burst out of the water, swiping at the spot of sand she had been standing on. Their limbs were disturbingly long, as if they'd been anchored by something heavy enough to stretch out their water-softened bones—a torture they would endure until justice could be theirs.

Mirae cowered on the shore, just out of reach of the bloated arms, her palm fire exposing the extent of their rot. Their fingernails were torn and cracked, like they'd clawed through stone. Their skin was pale with blood loss, mutilated where something had gouged past muscle, puckering the stretched-out remaining flesh like a bite of sticky tteok. On the parts that remained, bruises spread from limb to limb, and veins were swollen, full of an ink that bulged and spread like dark lightning.

Mirae could only stare, speechless, at the mul gwisin, who, grasp as they might, thankfully remained confined to the pool they had died in. Siwon, on the other hand, seemed to still have his wits about him.

"You shouldn't have angered them," he said, pulling away from Mirae now that she was safe. "They've suffered enough at the hands of Sacred Bone Magic."

"What are you talking about?" Mirae asked, voice shaking.

Siwon's dark eyes gleamed with lucidity. "The gwisin came for you and Gunju daegam, not me. Clearly they have no love for your kind. Me, however, I think they want to help, because they trust me to return the favor. All I need is to get that pearl."

"No, this is a death trap." Mirae rose shakily to her knees. "How could that pearl possibly help them?"

"She told me that whoever wields it will be the one to set them free and be their arm of vengeance."

Mirae shivered. "How do you know they won't just drown you?"

Siwon touched Mirae's arm, soft as a feather. "It'll be all right, Gongju mama. The stories about the haggard moon gwisin are exaggerated. She doesn't want to hurt anyone. She just wants to find peace for herself and her companions. You'll see."

Mirae looked up with disbelief at the servant, who was far braver with the dead than she was. Why was he being so stubborn? She cast her eyes across the lake at the haggard moon gwisin, who'd somehow convinced Siwon to risk his life. Her faceless stare and arms raised to take flight made it clear that she was not going to let Siwon leave until he did as she asked.

"Please, Gongju mama." Siwon looked down at the mul gwisin with sorrow. "Show these poor souls that the Sacred Bone man who hurt them is nothing like you."

The Inconstant Son. Yes, he had to be the one behind whatever unspeakable tragedy had occurred here, creating this gwisin nightmare. Mirae was a little ashamed that Siwon had arrived at the most likely truth faster than she had. Despite how trusting he was of ghosts, Siwon seemed to be in possession of a clearer head than Mirae.

She gazed up at the pearl again, trying to see its value through Siwon's eyes. That's when the memory resurfaced: she had seen the pearl before, in her switch. It had rested like a tiny moon in the wet, deeply lined palm of Wol Sin Lake's giant green hand. She was to be the pearl's wielder, it seemed—the arm of justice for the restless dead. Which mean Siwon was right—the gwisin's pearl was supposed to come into her possession.

Mirae shook her head and sighed. "Fine, we'll get the pearl. Just know that at the first sign of trouble, I'm lighting this whole place on fire. The gwisin get one chance to prove they're not a bunch of heartless monsters."

"As do you." There was no malice in Siwon's words. In fact, when he looked at Mirae, he smiled with gratitude at her sufferance. As her own fear began melting away under the warmth of his courage, Mirae realize it was the first time she'd ever seen Siwon look completely at peace.

"I'll be back soon. Wait here, and don't taunt the ghosts." Siwon began untying the ribbon of his jeogori and the strings that held his chima up around his chest. He handed Mirae the clothes—*her* clothes—and began removing the servant's garb he wore underneath.

Mirae's cheeks burned as Siwon stripped down to his sokgot, but she couldn't allow herself to look away. She'd promised to watch over and protect him—clothed or not—but thankfully, he stopped at his undergarments.

The mul gwisin made no move against Siwon as he walked toward the silvery pond, instead drifting aside so he could enter the water unhindered. He stepped in confidently, not at all disgusted by the grotesque spirits who shared the space with him. Without hesitation, Siwon lowered his body into the water and swam for the finger-shaped rock in the middle of the pond.

He was an excellent swimmer, reaching the center in only a few long strokes. He grabbed the protruding stone and shimmied up it just far enough to reach out and grab the pearl. It came away easily, fitting perfectly into his palm. He clutched it to his chest with one arm as he dove back into the water and made his way to shore again. Through it all, neither the mul gwisin nor the haggard moon gwisin made any move to stop him.

Siwon wiped water from his brow once he'd emerged, and grinned. "It's your turn, Gongju mama. Show them you're like me, a friend with a good heart whom they can trust."

"How am I supposed to do—" Mirae gasped in midsentence as Siwon tossed her the pearl. She caught it, but not without a little nervous fumbling.

As soon as her hands touched the smooth surface of the pearl, however, the clearing began to change. The dense covering of darkness around Mirae thinned just enough to let in a swath of warm, blushing light. Amber beams parted the mist, accompanied by lines of gold that revealed the setting sun like a hand shielding a candle atop the misty, tree-lined horizon.

Speechless at the sudden changes around her, Mirae looked back at the pond, where the mul gwisin were retreating into the water. They dragged their arms across the sand, leaving inky streaks in their wake. Only the haggard moon gwisin floated closer, this time trailing a warm, sunbathed cloud behind her instead of thick, icy mist.

As the silver water turned rosy with sunlight, the last mul gwisin disappeared, as if it couldn't bear to be touched by something made for the living. The haggard moon gwisin, however, rushed over to Mirae, stopping only a few feet away.

Mirae would have turned and run had Siwon not held her arm. Instead of bolting, she watched the haggard moon gwisin as intently as Siwon was.

The gwisin's smooth face, uninterrupted by lips, lashes, or cheekbones, moved like she was speaking, her once threatening silhouette now bent as if pleading. Mirae couldn't understand what the haggard moon gwisin was trying to say, but she still paid close attention, trying to absorb every detail. The gwisin finally stopped trying to speak and instead held up her hand. On her palm was a word formed by scars. A name.

Suhee.

As the red eye of the dying sun bled its hot light over the clearing, the haggard moon gwisin turned her head to the heavens. In that instant, the sun seemed to crash fully into the clearing, shrinking the mist and darkness between trees in a burst of light. Mirae shielded her eyes until the brightness subsided. When she looked back around the clearing, the haggard moon gwisin was gone, and the misty darkness had returned.

Mirae stared down at the pearl in her hands, a palm-size moon with rainbow glints and winks of warmth—a sphere of pure beauty that filled her with awe.

"You see, Gongju mama?" Siwon said, reverence making his voice soft. "We were meant to come here and help the unfortunate find peace." He was staring down at the pearl with her as if they were admiring a newborn child.

Mirae nodded. "You were right. This pearl is going to be important—I know it."

"Exactly." Siwon met Mirae's eyes. "I can't explain it, I just . . . knew."

A warm hand grabbed Mirae's shoulder, startling her. She whirled around and found herself face-to-face with a wide-eyed Captain Jia.

"Gongju." Captain Jia dropped her gaze to the pearl and stared with wonder. After a moment, she shook her head, knocking her usual serious expression back into place. "Gunju told me what happened. I'm glad you're all right. Let's head back before he draws in another crowd of ghosts."

Mirae nodded and raised the palm-size moon that banished darkness like the sun, and together they picked their way solemnly back toward the bone-white road, following the echoing sound of Hongbin's voice.

His story rang through the trees, as radiant as the pearl in Mirae's hand.

"It was finally time for the odious Byung-hee to assess the Go sisters for himself. First, he examined the eldest daughter, Jeong-min. She was charming and witty, with a bright mind and a generous warmth that seemed to rival the sun. But she was too smart for Byung-hee. Too bright to look at for long. So he moved on to Hae-ju, whose classic beauty contained a softness and a fullness that rivaled the moon's pale yet ever-changing glow. Byung-hee was inflamed by her loveliness but nevertheless turned to assess the youngest sister. Han-bit's beauty was the most distant and cold, like stars surveying everything from their lofty height. There was something hypnotic about her eyes—like she had uncovered many secrets from her vantage point and knew the inner workings of all who fell under her gaze.

"It didn't take long for Byung-hee to decide which sister he wanted: Hae-ju, whom he considered the loveliest and least threatening of the sisters. She was to marry him in three days' time. After he left, the Go sisters huddled together, devastated. There was no way they were letting their sister marry such a horrible man, or die mysteriously by his hand as all his other brides had. It was time, Jeong-min decided,

to go to the forest and find the only creature who was trickier than she:
a dokkaebi. Which sounds like just the kind of thing my own sister
would—oh, there you are, noonim."

Hongbin fell quiet when he saw the look on her face and the
treasure in her hand. Mirae kept the pearl raised as she rejoined
her brother on the trail to Wol Sin Lake.

The trees seemed to scuttle back a few steps as she crunched
down the path, treading on bones that now gleamed like a starry
floor of fallen constellations. Wielding the comforting light of
the pearl, Mirae continued down the road to the monster's lair,
followed silently by the living.

Captain Jia spent most of the evening scouting ahead, leaving
Mirae to guide Hongbin and Siwon along the bone-white path.
The farther they traveled from the silver pond, the dimmer the
pearl's light grew. However, its warmth remained the same,
prompting Mirae to wrap it in her cast-off clothes so it could be
passed around and held comfortably by whoever had the coldest
hands.

For the most part, Hongbin and Siwon walked beside Mirae,
the former gradually complaining more and more about his
growling stomach, the latter seeming content to walk to the ends
of the earth silently and resolutely, if it was asked of him. She was
comforted and bolstered by Siwon's strong presence beside her,
and she couldn't help but notice how he'd changed since meeting the haggard moon gwisin and her horde, as if he'd found
renewed confidence and purpose.

Occasionally as they walked, she'd catch his profile in the
pearl's waning light. Twice now he had crossed paths with

monsters and survived; his face still bore the marks of the first encounter. Clearly the gods wanted to preserve him, and Mirae knew better than to question their will. If they wanted him by her side, then she was going to make sure that's where he stayed.

Soon, the silence of their somber travel was interrupted when Hongbin fell against Mirae with a dramatic groan. "I'm starving to death out here. Why did no one bring any food?"

"You're the one who's always hiding snacks," Mirae said. "I'm shocked you didn't think to stow anything in those voluminous chima you stole from me."

Hongbin groaned again. "Hey, I had to steal my entire person out of the palace with only a moment's notice. You just walked right out the gates, easy as can be. Instead of berating me, why not take pity and distract me with a story?"

"Well," Mirae said, "there actually is something I've been meaning to talk to you about. It has to do with last night."

Hongbin's carefully maintained mask of unflappability slipped for a moment, his usually warm brown eyes glinting with the fear Mirae knew he kept buried deep down. A second later, his wall of humor came right back up, and Hongbin waved imperiously for Mirae to continue. "Just spare me the gory details. I'm faint enough from hunger as it is."

Mirae knew Hongbin had been caught up on most of the events of the third trial—about the ceremony gone wrong and the high calling dropped unexpectedly into Mirae's lap. But Hongbin didn't know about her switch, nor did he know his part in it.

When Mirae finished describing Wol Sin Lake and how he was by her side in the future, Hongbin was silent for perhaps the longest amount of time in his entire life, head bowed deep in thought. When he finally looked up and met Mirae's eyes, he said, "So what you're saying is . . . I had a chance to convince you to save Minho, and I failed?"

It took Mirae a few seconds to recover from his darksome logic. She grabbed her brother's hand. "No, that's not at all what I'm saying. You did not fail. Trust me, I've agonized over this relentlessly, and there was nothing either of us could have done to avoid ending up right where we are. Mother needed to be stopped last night—I had no other choice but to stay in the Garden of Queens. Gods know what would have happened if I'd left."

"Or if the flying monster had been stopped from capturing Daegun daegam," Siwon chimed in quietly, no doubt remembering his own role in those events. "Who knows what even more horrific things it might have done."

Mirae could tell by the look on Hongbin's face that he was struggling to accept anything they were saying. She didn't blame him; it hadn't been easy for her, either. But she'd realized something important over the last few hours—something that would help him make peace with everything, too. "Hongbin, I don't think these visions are meant to change the past, but rather to show me the future. The path we must walk if we want the Samsin's guidance."

"It just seems like an awful lot of violence for the grandmother goddesses to condone."

"They want what we want," Mirae reassured him. "A peaceful, united peninsula. There's only one way that's going to happen, and that's by bringing me to Seolla's ancient enemy so I can end his evil once and for all. Taking Minho and leading me right to his lair will be his biggest, and last, mistake."

Hongbin didn't seem completely convinced by Mirae's words, but he nodded. "I suppose it's poetic, our enemy's pride leading to his own downfall."

"We would be wise not to make the same mistake." A voice from behind startled Mirae and her companions into whirling around.

Hongbin clutched his heart. "Where did you come from?"

Captain Jia had light scratches on her hands and face from scouting around in the woods. She eyed Mirae and her companions shrewdly. "I'm glad the only thing that's snuck up on you so far is me. You all need to pay better attention to your surroundings."

"Isn't that what you're for?" Hongbin quipped.

Captain Jia ignored him. "We should try to sleep for a few hours. We don't know what tomorrow may bring."

The captain was right. Mirae could feel the drain of walking all day and confronting semi-hostile ghosts. No matter her calling, she wouldn't be any use to Minho if she were to come across him or the Inconstant Son now.

Captain Jia wordlessly helped everyone arrange a campsite on the empty road. Using Mirae's extra clothes—pulled from Hongbin as well, who had thought to wear his own hanbok underneath—they created thin beds for everyone except Captain Jia, who insisted on keeping watch. At the center of their ring of bodies, Mirae placed the gwisin's pearl to keep them warm.

Its heat was welcome in the barren, chilly forest, especially since there wasn't enough fabric between Mirae and her companions to create a proper blanket.

Mirae was surprised at how easily her mind and body reached toward sleep as soon as she lay down. Though she rested on a path of ground-up bones, there was peace in the pearl's warmth and the sight of Hongbin's stomach rising and falling as he slept. Mirae thought of the mark at the nape of his neck, protecting him and Minho from the Inconstant Son's influence. She thought of Siwon, too, born magicless in Josan. It was small comfort, but it helped Mirae close her eyes, praying that the gods would continue keeping them all, and Minho especially, safe from evil.

Chapter
TWELVE

Mirae woke to something soft prodding the tip of her nose. She opened her eyes, blurry from sleep, and blinked at the finger rudely tapping her face.

"Oh good, you're awake." Hongbin scooted out of reach before she could swat him. "You stopped snoring, so I figured you were rousing."

Mirae groaned and sat up. Siwon was still sleeping, but their group's Jade Witch was missing. "Where's Captain Jia? Why are you keeping watch?"

Hongbin shrugged. "Because I have the loudest voice, apparently. Captain Jia walked ahead a bit, scouting for trouble."

"How long has she been gone?"

"Based on how bored I am, ten years. But in actuality, about fifteen minutes."

Mirae nodded tiredly. "I hope she'll stop resenting me for all this once we find Minho."

"Of course she will." Hongbin yawned. "She may be unhappy with our methods for rescuing our dear older brother, but I know deep down she's glad she came along."

Mirae met her younger brother's gaze and was surprised at the complete sincerity in his eyes—a rare sight. As if uncomfortable with Mirae reading anything else on his face, Hongbin cleared his throat and resumed his air of fake arrogance. "All I'm saying is, stop worrying. After all, I'm here now, and we both have our strengths. You have magic, and I have everything else."

Mirae leaned her head against Hongbin's shoulder, and he rested his head on hers. They sat that way in comfortable silence until Captain Jia's familiar form reappeared.

"We're close," she said. Mirae didn't have to ask the captain what she had seen that made her so certain. There was no mistaking the lake for anything other than the landmark of evil that it was.

Mirae and Hongbin folded their makeshift beds while Captain Jia nudged Siwon awake with her foot. He roused quickly from his surprisingly peaceful slumber and set about helping Mirae and Hongbin clear the camp. When everyone was ready, Mirae wrapped the pearl once more in her extra clothes and they pushed on toward the lake. She walked quickly, the bones beneath her feet crunching loudly enough to drown out the growling of Hongbin's stomach and the remaining doubts in her head that his kindness would always melt away.

The trees were thinning on both sides of the path. They were almost there. Mirae increased her pace until she reached the point where the trees abruptly ended.

There it was—Wol Sin Lake.

It was Mirae's third time seeing it, but she stood and stared as Hongbin did, afraid that even her footsteps would shatter the black mirror of water lined by a shore of white pebbles. By now, Mirae had gotten used to the smell of the place, but not to the unblinking, inky eye of the lake or the lightless hollow it seemed to rest on.

They'd made it. Here was the lair of the Inconstant Son, abductor of Minho and enemy of Seolla. Mirae took a deep breath, ready to step onto the white-pebbled lakeshore, when Siwon stopped her with an arm across her path. "Wait, Gongju mama. Look."

Mirae saw what he was referring to immediately. The air in front of her shimmered with a haze of green so sheer, she hadn't differentiated between it and the shadows of the trees. But it was clearly some kind of magical barrier, a cage within a cage.

Mirae nodded her thanks to Siwon before reaching down and taking a handful of bone dust from the road and tossing it at the barrier. When the yellowing grit hit the shimmering haze, it disintegrated into jade-colored dust.

"You almost walked into that," Hongbin said with a gulp.

"It's a good thing Siwon is so eagle-eyed," Captain Jia said. It was clear from her tone that she didn't mean that as a compliment.

Mirae studied the barrier. Sacred Bone Daughters had created this prison—and only they could operate it. If what Mirae suspected was true, she'd never been in any danger at all.

Mirae reached up and plucked a hair from her head. Her companions watched as she approached the barrier and tossed a single black strand into it. Her hair twirled in the air, crossing over unharmed. Before anyone could stop her, Mirae stuck her hand through the barrier and was unsurprised to find that nothing happened. No disintegration. The magic that bound the monster in its cage recognized the Sacred Bone blood that had made it.

Captain Jia grabbed Mirae's elbow. "What if that hadn't worked, Gongju? You need to stop being so reckless."

Mirae pulled her arm away. "Or maybe you need to start trusting me."

"I trust you, noonim." Hongbin plucked one of his own hairs and flung it at the barrier. "See, I can do it, too!"

His silky black hair floated by unharmed. Soon, so did Hongbin, passing through the barrier without hesitation. "I'm so magical."

"Gunju!" Captain Jia pressed a palm to her forehead. "Why are the two of you so intent on leaving Seolla with no royals to continue your bloodline?"

"On the contrary, we're going to make sure every royal is safe once more." Hongbin pranced about on the other side. "I mean, it was obvious that I'd be fine to cross. Mirae and I have the same blood. Also, how do you think the monster was planning on getting Minho to the lake?"

For a moment, Mirae took pity at the look of helplessness that crossed over Captain Jia's face. It couldn't be easy feeling the weight of protecting two Sacred Bone royals with rare, inimitable traits in their blood and an inability to do as they're told. "It's going to be all right, Captain. Hongbin and I are keeping our wits about us, even if it doesn't look like it."

"Yes, you've always been very proud of your cleverness." Captain Jia bit back the rest of whatever she was going to say.

Mirae reminded herself to be patient. She wouldn't be here at all if it weren't for the captain. "There's nothing wrong with cleverness. It's gotten me this far, hasn't it?"

Captain Jia shook her head. "Perhaps you have accomplished much through wit alone, Gongju. But remember that someday everyone meets their match, and the last thing you want is an enemy who's smarter than you."

At that, the captain stepped aside, reluctance weighing on her every move. "I hope you're right about all this. I do. Please be careful in there and return in one piece."

Mirae nodded solemnly and stepped over the barrier.

The transition was brief. The barrier cast a distinctly green sheen on the world, turning gravel, sky, and even Mirae's own skin various shades of jade while the wrapped pearl in her hands grew uncomfortably warm. Breaking through to the other side was like taking a drink of cold boricha—the world becoming soothing and natural once more. The gwisin's pearl grew cool to the touch, like a sudden shift to sitting in the shade.

Hongbin waited for her on the other side. "So, what happens next? Please tell me there aren't any real live gumiho around here. My heart is big and sweet, so I know they'll find me particularly delicious."

"Don't worry, I'll protect your heart at all costs." Mirae took her brother's arm and pulled him toward the lake. The switch was bound to happen soon. They needed to be closer to the water, just as they'd been in her vision. Mirae and Hongbin approached the lidless eye of the lake cautiously, as if worried it might see them coming. But all was still and quiet within the barrier. Wol Sin Lake was nothing but a calm black mirror against a pebbled white shore.

And yet the closer they got to the lake, the more Hongbin began to fidget. Especially when Mirae hiked up her chima and stepped toward the water. "Whoa, what are you doing? I don't remember the monster inviting us over for a swim party."

Mirae looked back at her brother. "What did you think we were going to do when we got here?"

"I don't know—honestly, I thought we'd just find Minho sitting around looking super bored." Hongbin glanced uneasily at the lake. "Maybe even discover a handsome sorcerer begging for a kiss to break his curse."

Mirae reached into her chima and pulled out the High Horomancer's bell. "It's going to be all right, Hongbin. Just wait for me to get back."

Mirae took another step toward the water, ignoring Hongbin's protests. The color of the thick, oily water filled her vision with a darkness that threatened to sweep her away, back to the day she and the lake had first met. The bell in her hand, however, reminded her of something else entirely—the punishing sear that had ripped through her hand like being plunged into the fiery breath of the Unnamed Dragon. A pain that heralded Horomantic powers Mirae couldn't summon on her own.

This time she didn't have to. Mirae looked down at her palm as the burning pain returned, leaving her too breathless to scream until the darkness took her.

Silence. The chill of night. That was what Mirae woke to on the other side.

A familiar face looked down at her, a visage that was sure to haunt Mirae's nightmares—a woman she'd had to watch die. Mirae looked up at the elderly blue-robed oracle, whose smooth bald head glinted in the light of the lanterns like the haggard moon gwisin's pearl.

The Kun Sunim. Alive again. Mirae could only stare up at her, the words coming out of the oracle's mouth slowly finding her ears.

"Did you see him, Gongju? The Inconstant Son? Do you know what you must do?"

Mirae couldn't take her eyes off the Kun Sunim, even as a dry heat fevered her chest and stung her eyes. "I . . . I made it to the lake."

"Good." The Kun Sunim nodded, her dark eyes gleaming as if she'd seen exactly what Mirae had seen. "Wol Sin Lake is the place that ties everything together. There you will find answers, and there you will find lies. To end this evil, you must figure out which is which."

Mirae grabbed the Kun Sunim's wrists, startling the older woman. "I need to tell you something important. After you tell me who I am and what I must do, I accidentally—"

The Kun Sunim snatched back her hands with a ferocity that stunned Mirae into silence. "No, Gongju. You must not tell me anything else."

"But this is—"

"I said no." The Kun Sunim leaned closer, the gravity in her voice and eyes stopping the words in Mirae's throat. "Remember this, Gongju, above all else. You must change *nothing* except the rise of the Inconstant Son."

Mirae looked wildly around the clearing—at a garden still green and oracles still chanting. "Doesn't that include the horrible things that happen because of him?"

"Not always." The Kun Sunim seemed to take pity on Mirae and the tears pooling in her eyes. "I know this is difficult to hear, but you were not given your power to change the past. To do so would break the rules of the goddess of time, patron of your powers. These switches are only to be used to navigate the future, the path you must walk if you are to follow the gods' guidance and end this evil. If you use these switches for anything else, your power, along with all hope of destroying the Inconstant Son, will be ripped away."

Tears began leaking out of Mirae's eyes as she listened to the oracles chanting excitedly behind her, unaware of their impending slaughter. "So I am not to prevent any horrors, or deaths in the past? I can change nothing about what has already happened, even if it breaks my heart?"

"That is correct." The Kun Sunim gripped Mirae's hands, her face reassuring even as her voice was laced with a warning. "You must not fail like those who came before, or you will be the ruin of the peninsula, not its savior. Change nothing but the Inconstant Son. Promise me."

"I promise," Mirae whispered, her throat thick with tears. From what the Kun Sunim was saying, there was no other choice. Even more unthinkable than the massacre at the ceremony was the idea that Mirae's meddling could mean the death of everyone she loved. She held the Kun Sunim's hands tightly, afraid to let go. "I thought my switches would help me bring peace to Seolla.

Now I see that foresight will only bring me pain. This is a curse, not a blessing from the gods."

The Kun Sunim looked at Mirae sadly. "The future you want requires your suffering, but that is the fault of evil, not the gods. Remember your promise, or you will be the one to bring this queendom more pain than it has ever known."

The Kun Sunim held Mirae's hands until the darkness began to take root once more. She looked into Mirae's blurring eyes. "Thank you, daughter, for everything you'll give, and everything they'll take. Be strong, and remember who you are. No one can take your truth from you."

Mirae felt her mind go reeling back into darkness, to the lake of buried truths and ancient lies where her road to suffering was only just beginning.

Mirae caught the tail end of Hongbin's desperate plea. "If you don't change what happened, noonim, we'll lose—"

"Minho," Mirae said quietly. "I know."

She looked down at her hands. Though her skin remained smooth, unmarred, her palms burned as if covered with angry, open blisters. A price, it seemed, that she would pay every time she broke the rules of time. "We can't stop it, Hongbin. There are things that must be, and to interfere with them would be a terrible mistake."

"What things? What are you talking about?" Hongbin asked.

Mirae looked out at the lake, that evil, lidless eye. Maybe she couldn't change the past, but that wasn't the point of this switching power. The future lay ahead, completely open, and it was ripe for the changing. Mirae secured her hiked-up chima, pearl in hand. "What's done is done, but I decide the future. The cycle of violence ends with me."

"You mean with *us*," Hongbin said.

"No. I don't mean that at all." Mirae whirled around and gave Hongbin a shove he couldn't recover from while she held her arms out by her sides, swinging them together until they almost touched. Almost.

Hongbin knew what was coming, but there was nothing he could do against the gale that swept him up like a kite, throwing him back toward the path of bones and into the waiting arms of Captain Jia.

Mirae turned back to the lake, heedless of her brother's pleas. She understood now that she needed to be far more careful with the information she got from her new power, or else the unthinkable could happen to her brothers, to the entire peninsula. Now was not the time to lead her brother into battles he wasn't equipped to fight, however brave he was.

She walked up to the lake and took her first step into the water. It was just as cold as she had expected, but she hated that she couldn't see where her feet were going—into the shallows or into an abyss. She shivered as she forged onward.

Once she was knee-deep in the lake, Mirae closed her eyes and steeled herself for whatever was coming by remembering what had brought her here. She thought about Minho, throat-slitting monsters, and gwisin missing pieces of their flesh. A name scarred into a palm. It was time for all the pain to end.

When Mirae opened her eyes, she saw a familiar hand reaching out of the water. Green as seaweed and warted with algae.

Large enough for her to sit in. The giant hand opened as before, like a moldy flower waiting for a gift.

Mirae unwrapped the pearl and placed it in the center of the giant green palm. As soon as it touched the lake water pooling in the hand's deep lines, the pearl swelled to fit the curve of the monstrous palm, beaming with the color of clouds laced with rainbows. Almost without thinking, Mirae grabbed the sides of the enormous pearl, suddenly afraid of losing it. As soon as she touched its smooth surface, the giant fingers clamped shut.

Mirae considered letting go. She heard Hongbin and Captain Jia shouting in the distance for her to do just that. But she maintained her grip, for she knew in her heart that this was the only way to reach the Inconstant Son—and Minho. Without warning, the hand yanked everything it held down into the inky water.

Mirae barely had time to gasp before she felt her arms nearly wrenched from their sockets by the giant hand's descent. That was all the air she took in before she was pulled under.

Chapter

THIRTEEN

Mirae had always thought death would be cold, and as dark as the backs of her eyelids. It would hurt, she imagined—the pressure of her soul climbing out of its lifelong haunt, untangling veins like cobwebs and parting ribs like a rusted-closed gate. But this was where all humans ended up, wasn't it? No one, no matter how clever, got out of this world alive.

Mirae clung to that thought for the small comfort it gave. It was the only way to deal with the pressure of an entire lake pressing against her temples, chest, and ankles, threatening to crush her into pieces. Soon it would all be over.

She clung tightly to the gwisin's pearl. The giant hand that clasped the other end of it sliced swiftly through the water. Mirae couldn't see anything in front of her, but she knew that if she didn't breathe soon, her lungs were going to release what little air she had and take in anything around her—water, murk, darkness—to fill the need.

Thankfully, before Mirae neared the brink of losing consciousness, the hand let her go. When it found her again, it grabbed the back of her neck and smashed her face against something that felt like cold acorn jelly, clogging her nose and blacking out her vision until her head burst through.

It wasn't bright on the other side, but there was air for the taking. Mirae was greedy for it, dropping the pearl as she devoted every muscle and limb to pushing herself closer to the underwater draft.

Once her lungs were no longer on fire, Mirae blinked the cold jelly out of her eyes and let them adjust to the dim green light of the cavern she was suspended above, stuck headfirst in slime while half her body floated behind her at the bottom of the lake. It took her a moment to see the room beneath her, shadowy and cavernous except for one bright spot, as if a ray of sunlight had punched through the barrier with her. Directly below was the only other entity in the room.

He stood in the minty-green circle of light, looking up at Mirae, neck craned and face unsmiling. The black hanbok he wore glittered like it was full of secret diamonds, and depicted a bloodred fire-hound eating the sun. The jawbone circlet around his head stood as tall as the Seollan crown but his was ebony-carved and black-plumed.

Mirae stared at the face of the Inconstant Son, for there was no one else he could be. Under the lake's darkening shade, everything in his world, including his skin, was cast in a weird green light.

He was tall. Handsome. Kingly, even, and not just because of his crown or the way he shimmered richly. There was something in the way he looked at Mirae. Like he understood power and where it belonged. The quiet rage in his eyes felt colder than the water at the bottom of the lake. "It looks like I have a visitor. How lovely of you to stop by, Mirae."

She recognized that voice. It was the same low, oily tone that had mocked her in the Garden of Queens and threatened to tear her family apart.

"You know my name," she said as coldly as he. "Now tell me yours."

His neck craned even farther, as if studying her was worth the risk of snapping his spine. "What is it you hope to accomplish with such rudeness, queenling?"

They stared at each other, High Daughter and Inconstant Son, as if waiting to see who would drop their act first. Finally, Mirae scowled and relented. "You know why I'm here. I want my brother back."

The Inconstant Son's eyes rested on the gwisin's pearl, a shrinking orb that had come to rest at his feet. He reached for it, and as he hefted it between his hands, his face softened. His voice, too, changed for the kinder. "Of course you assume he's here. You think me a clever little monster. I once thought so, too, I'll admit. But here's a lesson for you, queenling: anyone, no matter how powerful, can be betrayed."

He looked up at Mirae, his expression darkening once more. "I should have learned my lesson after dealing with your mother. Never trust a head with a crown."

"I'll keep that in mind," Mirae said pointedly, looking between the Inconstant Son's face and his jawbone circlet. "Now let me down. We have a lot to talk about."

The Inconstant Son scoffed. "You plunged gracelessly into my kingdom and now expect *me* to free *you*, all while plotting to defeat me with the very power that keeps me here. Where are your manners?"

Not daring to risk a repeat of her ceremony, Mirae did nothing to release herself—or the Inconstant Son, accidentally—from the gelatinous barrier.

Instead, Mirae glared down at her enemy, the scowl on her face the inverted mirror of his returning grin. "Tell me where Minho is and I might let you live."

"He means that much to you, does he, High Horomancer?" The Inconstant Son tsked. "What about your sacred duty from the *gods*? Aren't you supposed to kill me at all costs?"

Mirae hadn't been certain the Inconstant Son would know who she was. Him calling her bluff had answered that question. He knew her duty, as well as the fact that the man she was fated to destroy had the one thing she wanted. Mirae glared down at the Inconstant Son's smug smile. "What do you want in exchange for Minho? Be reasonable and I might see it done."

"Reasonable meaning I can't ask for freedom, or for my life, I presume," the Inconstant Son jeered. "How generous of you."

"There are many things I could do to make your life better," Mirae said, knowing that she was acting brashly, even as the words kept pouring out of her mouth. Her eyes darted around the room, looking for any sign of her brother. "Like getting you proper bedding, for starters. Or delicious food, and many other comforts you don't even know about."

"You would bribe me with food and fineries all so you can feel better about betraying me?" the Inconstant Son asked. "You and the Josan king have much in common."

The Josan king? When Mirae realized what the Inconstant Son had been trying to tell her, her hands clenched into trembling fists. "Minho . . . isn't here, is he?"

"He was supposed to be, I'll admit. But His Royal Annoyingness of Josan did something he really shouldn't have, and now here we are, quite princeless, I'm afraid."

Mirae struggled to speak. After everything she'd gone through, she was no closer to rescuing Minho than before; and the man who knew how to fix that had no reason to help her. After all, it seemed the Josan king had allegedly left his accomplice here to rot after getting what he wanted, which had been Mirae's plan, too; the man below her was well aware of that. Behaving like the dishonorable Josan king was no way to trick the Inconstant Son.

But perhaps she could appeal to his darker nature. "I see. So, you made a deal with the Josan king. You weakened my mother's magic while he prepared to wage both an emotional war and a military one. You got him a Seollan hostage to break my mother's heart with, seeking to destroy my queendom from the inside out. In return for all this, the Josan king promised to release you once he toppled Seolla. Am I missing anything?"

The Inconstant Son smiled dangerously, his teeth gleaming like a pale crown. He applauded slowly. "Very good, queenling. You know how to grasp the obvious."

"I've also grasped something else." Mirae tested the cold suction of the jelly around her, but there was no way to simply force her way through. Not without magic. "There's nothing you won't do for revenge, and only I can help you get it."

"What a careless offer." The Inconstant Son's sinister smile slid from his face. "You have no idea what I want, or why, or how many times I could kill you without even tipping my crown. Yet you presume to extort me?"

"You have no idea what I'm capable of, either." Mirae glared, hoping the Inconstant Son couldn't sense the apprehension rising within her, filling her cheeks with heat. "I've bested your magic twice before—don't think I won't do it again."

The Inconstant Son raised an eyebrow. "Is that so? Well, how about you come down here and show me your great power? I haven't got all day, and my tea is getting cold."

Mirae tried to hold back a shiver of dread at his challenge, but the frigid water around her lower half and his chilling gaze paired too well, freezing Mirae from the inside out. She had been foolish to hope that her job here would be simple: arrive at the lake, defeat her enemy, and bring Minho safely home. Without a switch to guide her, the future was as full of puzzles as the past—the least of which was her Sacred Bone ability to operate the Inconstant Son's cage without releasing him.

Mirae kept her eyes on the dark, glittering man beneath her, letting the coldness of her body settle into the features of her face, hardening them. "We both want something from each other, so do you want to talk this through, or not? I haven't got all day, either."

After a moment of studying Mirae's face in silence, the Inconstant Son relented. With a wave of his hand, the cold jelly around Mirae parted, dropping her into the green-lit cavern. With another wave of his hand, the black-clad Inconstant Son sent a gust of wind to catch Mirae in midair, allowing her to drift to the floor as he lowered his arm. "So, what's your proposal, queenling? I tell you where the Josan king is hiding your precious brother and you'll, what . . . *set me free?*"

Mirae swayed on her feet as if she'd forgotten her own weight while buried under the lake's. "Tell me where Minho is, and I'll force the Josan king to his knees for the both of us."

"Hm. I do not accept your terms." The Inconstant Son's eyes dared Mirae to punish him for his insolence. After all, here he was free to use his Sacred Bone powers, which included turning Mirae's own magic against her. Though he didn't seem able to control the dark, watery cage above them, he could manipulate everything beneath it. By the look in the Inconstant Son's eyes, he was well aware of the doubts going through Mirae's mind, and they amused him.

"Unless you want me, like the Josan king, to leave you here to rot, I suggest you find some way to help me." Mirae raised her chin defiantly. "So, what's it going to be?"

"Oh, you're not going anywhere." Before Mirae could raise her hands with fire at his threatening words, the Inconstant Son continued. "If you leave, you'll be bound to wander the entirety of Josan aimlessly, or worse yet, head straight for the king's palace and provoke a war. You have no proof of this alleged abduction, or any idea where the Josan king would hide a stolen prince. I, however, know exactly where you should go."

"And why should I believe you?"

"Because I cannot lie to you, queenling. That is one of the rules of the cage."

Mirae found that hard to believe, but there was no test she could think of that would disprove his words. Instead, she studied the man before her, an enemy she was forced to reason with, though they both had wills of steel and reason to hate each other.

The Inconstant Son's silk hanbok was so black it seemed to absorb light while still managing to shimmer. His crown, up close, was exactly what it looked like. The ebony jawbone circlet—crafted from something inhuman—was pressed into his long, loose hair, and its finger-long teeth gave him several inches of height. Stiff black plumes had been artfully wedged between the circle of bones. Creatures of the sky had to be rare in this place. His wardrobe was truly fit for a king, magnificent even by Seollan standards.

Mirae regarded the darksome king a moment longer before deciding that she couldn't afford to be intimidated by him, regardless of the monsters he'd killed for his crown. He hadn't made any moves against her yet, even knowing why she'd come. There had to be something he wanted, something she *could* be convinced to give him, if not his freedom. But what?

Mirae softened her stance, forcing herself to start over. "What is your name?"

The Inconstant Son narrowed his eyes, surprised by her question. "My people call me the Netherking."

"Your people?"

"Oh, don't worry, queenling. I'm quite alone, the last of my kind."

When the Netherking refused to say anything more, Mirae didn't press him. She didn't sense any other forms of life nearby, and if there was an ambush planned, the trap would have been sprung by now. It seemed he was telling the truth. "How long have you been imprisoned?"

"My whole life." The Netherking seemed to be studying her

as well, reading things off her face that no one, not even Mirae, could see. "My people and I were paying for the sins of an ancestor. Much like you."

Mirae raised an eyebrow. "The only person making me pay for anything is you."

"Really?" The Netherking began circling Mirae slowly, as if looking for a weakness. "So naive, easily believing the Deep Deceiver's lies and your mission of murder."

"Enough with the riddles." Mirae turned with the Netherking, keeping her back out of sight. "What is it you want from me? You know I won't release you—so why did you lure me to your cage?"

"Oh, I do have a use for you, queenling." The Netherking came to a sudden stop, grinning as if he'd won their battle of wits. "You are every bit the rash, irresponsible brat I've been told you are. Which has made you the perfect puppet for my revenge."

The Netherking raised his arms as he strode fearlessly toward Mirae, wreathed in green lightning that pulsed around his kingly black robe with sinister crackles.

"You didn't try to bring Minho here just to kill him," Mirae said, backing away. "You're smarter than that. That's why you're not going to kill me, either." Still, Mirae raised her own hands. "I'm the only Daughter of the Sacred Bone who's willing to reason with you."

"Oh, I'm not falling for that again." The Netherking cracked his lightning-capped fingers. "I've had nothing but time to imagine this moment. I will relish it, queenling. Every scream."

Something splashed beneath Mirae's feet—a trap the Nether-king had been edging her toward. Like the errant orb that had nearly drowned Minho, the puddle beneath her rose like a monsoon to devour her. Mirae watched with horror as she was covered by the same dark water that rested in the lake above, instantly dousing the fire in her palms.

Mirae realized she was wrong—the Netherking hadn't been trying to manipulate her into helping him. He was just biding his time until she foolishly wandered into a magic-sapping trap that would ensure his victory over her. He'd known to wager on her recklessness, and now he reaped his reward.

Mirae fought the watery spell surrounding her, knowing it was useless. She was nothing but a trapped fool blindsided by her need to find Minho. The Inconstant Son, however, had let nothing—not even his rage at the Josan king—get in the way of his true purpose.

The Netherking's voice was muffled through the oily mon-soon around her, but Mirae understood his mocking words. "So goes another High Daughter sent to destroy the Inconstant Son. It's always the same story, queenling, and it always ends the same way."

Mirae struggled against the watery prison, searching for any elements she could bend to her will. But nothing called back to her, heeding the power in her blood. She wasn't powerful enough to counteract the Netherking's will, or his command of the elements.

But she knew someone who was—someone he would never see coming.

Able to maneuver somewhat in the thick, oily orb that surrounded her, Mirae reached into her chima, finding the pocket that hid the black bell. As her fingers touched its cold, sleek metal, Mirae begged the gods to grant her a switch this time.

Show me the future, Mirae pleaded. *And bring back a version of me powerful enough to break this evil king.*

Mirae closed her eyes, shutting herself into voluntary darkness as she braced for the searing pain that would catapult her into the unknown . . . but again, nothing happened.

The bell stayed cool to the touch, her body still in danger of drowning.

The Inconstant Son's voice came muffled into her ears. "I may have underestimated the king of Josan, but it is no matter. With a beloved son stolen and a Sacred Bone heir tortured by an old enemy, your mother's dying power will fail her, and Seolla will finally bow to its one true king."

No. Mirae couldn't allow that. Not as long as there was breath still trapped in her lungs. Mirae lifted the bell to her chest, close to her heart, before smashing it as hard as she could against the rippling barrier between her and the Inconstant Son.

The bell didn't shatter the orb, but it did ring out with a startlingly loud sound that sent vibrations rocking through Mirae's body. The deep, long boom of the bell pulsed through the water, making even the Netherking stumble back as it rumbled through the under-lake cavern.

As soon as she rang the bell, the apparent secret to unlocking its power, the slow, skin-scorching agony that Mirae remembered well rushed up her arm. Just as before, the heat of the bell seemed to melt her very flesh, as if she were holding a tendril of the sun. Mirae's head tipped back as her mouth opened into a scream, flooding her throat with oily water.

Her chokes and screams consumed by the darkness of the black bell, Mirae was ripped her away from the Netherking's reach.

Right into the grasp of someone far more furious.

Instead of an orb of dark water, hands now squeezed Mirae's throat—harder than the cold green fingers of Wol Sin Lake. As she tried to wrench out of her assailant's grasp, she got a look at the man she was struggling against. He was old, with white hair slipping past his broad shoulders. His furrowed brows were slashed with gray, just like her father's.

"Why are you *really* here, manyeo? For once in your life, deal honestly with me."

There was no possibility of choking out an answer, but Mirae could feel that her magic had returned. Her free hand grasped for something, anything to manipulate, and landed on rock, a boulder coated with a fistful of fresh-fallen snow.

She cultivated the feeling of frost on her fingers, making it freeze her to the bone before sending an illusion of that sudden burn of ice through her assailant's body. The man yelped and stumbled back, allowing them both to move warily out of each other's reach.

"Stay where you are," Mirae rasped. She raised one hand defensively and held up her domed bell with the other, clasped tightly in her fist even now, in the future.

The man seemed to know exactly what the bell was and what it could do. He stared at it as if all its concavities and curves could incinerate him with only a touch.

While her attacker seethed at a distance, Mirae scoured the wintry landscape around her, looking for shelter from the man trying to murder her. The Inconstant Son's cage was leagues and seasons away from the unfamiliar mountaintop on which Mirae now stood. Several middling peaks, all of them snowcapped, interrupted the view below.

Seeing no immediate means of escape, Mirae turned her attention back to the man before her. His face was as weathered as the rocks around them. He looked darkly at Mirae's High Horomancer bell, glimmering like inky ice in her grasp. "Go ahead. Kill me. I always knew you weren't a woman of your word."

Then he turned and walked away. Mirae stared at the man's retreating back. The heavy wool durumagi he wore, protecting him from the cold, swayed behind him, as black as his hair once was. He didn't turn to see if Mirae had bothered to follow.

"Why shouldn't I protect myself from you?" Mirae shouted, her throat sore from both the pressure of the man's hands and the ice crystals in the air. The bright fabrics and silky comforts of her usual wardrobe were fineries from a different world. Here she wore a stiff hemp hanbok covered only by a wool blanket.

The old man waved at their icy, lonely surroundings without turning around, without slowing. "I told you my conditions for traveling unfettered with me, and you agreed to them. Gods know why you want to spend your final years with the man who hates you most."

"Who are you?" The wind pushed Mirae's hair forward, and she could see it was as white as his. She looked at the back of her hands, at wrinkles and age spots. "And when am I?"

At last the old man stopped and turned around. He stared at Mirae, regarding her silently as if deciding whether she was playing a trick. "Do you really think I'll fall for that? You said your ability to switch was taken from you long ago."

Taken from her? How, and by whom? The Inconstant Son? Had she failed to conquer him after all? Mirae shivered from more than the cold. "I guess I was wrong."

The old man was still watching her, an odd look on his face. "How old are you?"

"Sixteen." Mirae huddled into her ragged coat, missing the heated floors and bone-warming soups at her palace more than ever.

"So young," the old man said, looking down at the ground thoughtfully. "Young enough that we haven't even met."

Mirae studied the man's face again. Indeed, there was nothing beneath the white hair and wrinkles that she recognized. So she asked again, softer this time, "Who are you?"

The old man looked out over the mountain's edge, at its snowcapped neighbors. "A man willing to do whatever it takes to make things right—as they should be. I intend to create a world you can't ruin, even with the gods' help."

Mirae took a step closer, a small gesture of trust. She didn't know how long she had in this switch, but she wanted to learn everything she could from this glimpse of the future while her other self, the one who belonged here, brought the Inconstant Son to his knees. "What do you mean, a world I can't ruin? Why would I do something like that?"

The old man shook his head. "That's just who you are—you and every other High Daughter who's failed to break me."

Mirae took another step closer, studying the old man's face intently for any signs of the Netherking's features, changed with age. Still, she found nothing. "Tell me your name."

"Kimoon." He seemed to regret the word as soon as it came out of his mouth. "That's what you call me, anyway."

"And what does everyone else call you?" Mirae asked, suddenly dreading what he might say.

This time Kimoon hesitated as he glanced at the black bell. "An Inconstant Son."

No, that wasn't possible. There was nothing of the Netherking in Kimoon's face, and no hint of corrupted Sacred Bone Magic lingering in the crisp, cold air. He had to be mistaken. "You cannot be the Inconstant Son. I was just with him."

"Who?"

"The Netherking."

"Ah, the Netherking." Kimoon smiled bitterly. "Now there's a name I never wanted to utter again. The biggest mistake of your life ended up costing me everything."

"No, you cannot be the Inconstant Son. Why would I be traveling around with you instead of—" The rest of that terrible, cruel question caught in Mirae's throat, exacerbating the soreness already there as every last bit of cautious warmth melted from Kimoon's eyes.

"Instead of murdering me where I stand?" Mirae thought Kimoon might return to strangling her, but instead of sparking with rage, the darkness in his eyes seemed to become hollow, echoing the unspeakable pain of loss.

"You tell me, Switcher." He spat out the title like a curse. "What is it with you and letting monsters like me live?"

"You're not a monster." Somehow, Mirae felt that was the truth, and couldn't stop herself from speaking it. "You're a man in pain, and I want to help."

"Help?" Kimoon asked quietly, clearly struggling with both Mirae's acknowledgment and the endless sorrow that seemed to be eating him alive. "Then perhaps you should never have betrayed what I loved most. Yes, Switcher, you did your best to obey the Samsin, right up until you had to accept that the greatest threat to the peninsula is you. *That's* why we're here. That's why I hate you, and I always will."

Mirae could feel the pull of the darkness ready to drag her back down to the Netherking's cage, making the bell grow uncomfortably warm in her hands. She closed the gap between herself and Kimoon, catching him by surprise. "If you really are the Inconstant Son, then you're the only thing I'm allowed to change. Please, tell me how to save us both."

Up close, Mirae could see that Kimoon's eyes were the color of sunlight on thick, brown honey, though the darkness within them made her feel like she was looking into a sunless abyss.

"You're no savior, Switcher. We'll meet sooner than you think, and when we do, you should kill me like you've killed everyone else who's ever loved you."

Mirae couldn't resist the switch any longer. The sear of the bell was as deep as the hatred in Kimoon's eyes, and just as injurious. Within seconds, Mirae was dragged, screaming in a flash of white-hot pain, back to the only man who could challenge Kimoon's place as both the Inconstant Son and the man who hated her more than anything else in the world.

Chapter

FOURTEEN

When she opened her eyes, Mirae expected to see the Nether-king standing in Kimoon's place, ready to strangle her with all the rage and magic in his blood. But instead, she found him kneeling in front of her, head bowed.

The cavern, too, was nothing like she'd left it. Two giant pillars of translucent stone—one deep green and the other as red as the Netherking's fire-hound crest—had risen out of the ground. Mirae realized they were chairs, broken into pieces. Though they glowed as if lit with an inner fire, the stone shards did nothing to heat the void around them.

In their midst lay a shattered, lightning-blue table, bits of it scattered across the floor like melting ice. The Netherking, it seemed, was not made to bow easily. Whatever Mirae's future self had done or said, the Netherking was a changed man, just as Mirae was a changed woman after meeting Kimoon. Where once she had been sure the gods were leading her right to the Inconstant Son, toward her chance to end him, she now realized that her mission wasn't going to be so simple.

The man before her was very much alive—made to bow and not to bleed. That could only mean her future self had refrained from sealing his fate. *Change nothing but the Inconstant Son*, the Kun Sunim had told her. If the man before her wasn't the Inconstant Son, then it wasn't her job to destroy him. The Netherking was treacherous and evil, but he was not Kimoon.

What is it with you and letting monsters like me live?

Mirae was glad for the coldness of the bell, soothing the burns it had once inflicted on her. "I have returned. Are you ready to talk?"

The Netherking jumped to his feet, black plumes bouncing. "You didn't happen to hear that last thing I said, did you?"

Mirae shook her head.

"Good." The Netherking straightened his crown, the height of it elongating his striking face, sharpening its shadows. "There's no need to waste your breath with any more threats, queenling. I will help you retrieve your brother, and ask for only one small thing in return."

Mirae should have been more surprised by this turn of events, but her last switch had knocked a lot of the headstrong wind out of her sails, too. She studied the man before her, who wore darkness like a robe—a man perhaps wrongly imprisoned. The fight between him and her future self had left his neck-plumes ruffled and wrinkled his fine silk clothes. "What is it you want?"

"A chance to tell you the sins of your mothers. When you know the truth about their cruelty, nothing will ever be the same."

An exhaustion heavier than the weight of the Netherking's words threatened to make Mirae buckle where she stood. She felt acutely that the only things she'd taken into her body over the past day were fear, lies, and regret. The Kun Sunim's words echoed back to her. *Wol Sin Lake is the place that ties everything together. There you will find answers, and there you will find lies. To end this evil, you must figure out which is which.*

Mirae had only the words of a bitter, hateful man from the future to attest that the Netherking was not her queendom's greatest enemy. Kimoon might have even convinced her future self of this, since it seemed he had her ear. The man before Mirae could be as he claimed, just a victim of her family's cruelty. Her kin, even. He had Sacred Bone Magic, after all. Or he could, as Kimoon had said, be the biggest mistake of her life.

Once again, Mirae's trip into the future had made everything even less clear than before.

As if sensing her turbulent thoughts, the Netherking pulled the haggard moon gwisin's pearl out of his robes and extended it to Mirae. A peace offering.

"I cannot lie," the Netherking reminded her. "Not to you."

That, too, could be a lie. But it wasn't up to her to decide anything just yet—determining the truth, as hard as that would be, had to come first. Perhaps that was the real reason the gods had brought her here. Mirae accepted the pearl. "I agree to your terms. I ask only that we locate Minho first. I worry for his safety."

The Netherking nodded. "As you wish." He raised his face to the muted sunspot overhead and shut his eyes. Then he pressed a hand to his heart, clutching the fabric that covered it like he was grasping forbidden knowledge. When he opened his eyes and found Mirae's again, his expression was grim, his frown deep enough to wrinkle his otherwise unlined face.

"We must hurry, queenling. I'm afraid Minho doesn't have much time."

Mirae wasn't sure why the Netherking insisted they step out of the minty-green sunspot and surround themselves with darkness, but she wasn't in the mood to argue. The Netherking's words felt like fingers stabbing the bleeding hole of worry growing in her heart. *I'm afraid Minho doesn't have much time.*

If that was true, then neither did she.

Mirae obediently followed the Netherking farther into his lightless cage—a place he called the Deep. Mirae wished he would move faster, not just for Minho's sake, but because this walk into the Netherking's abyss filled her heart with other types of fear.

She'd never even known the darkness of the Deep existed, nor did she have any words to describe it. It contained no color, smell, or sensation she had ever felt before. Every bit of it felt like Seolla's shadow—a dark imitation of everything that gave Mirae joy. The air around her felt older than the roots of her queendom, having shared no time or space with the sun since its very creation. Mirae couldn't help but think that if the stars ever burned out, the Deep wouldn't even notice. It would simply continue to exist, just as it did now, for all eternity. Longer than mountains, forests, or river bottoms—the darkness, the Deep, would patiently outlast the world. Here there was only a cage for what may have been Seolla's greatest mistake.

Here was Seolla's greatest shame.

The Netherking finally came to a stop, the ebony of his robes blending into the darkness so perfectly that Mirae ran into him. The Netherking wordlessly grabbed her shoulders and placed her in front of him before taking her hands.

"What I'm about to teach you is very basic Sacred Bone Magic that has been purposely kept from you." Though Mirae couldn't see the Netherking's face in the darkness, she could feel the lukewarm touch of his hands. They gave hers a hard, brief squeeze. "Now focus. You're going to need to concentrate as you never have before, since this is your first time. Still, this magic is already in your blood. It'll come to you quickly."

Mirae wanted to rip her hands away. "Why can't you just tell me where Minho is?"

"You need to see this for yourself." His voice softened. "There's nothing to fear. When used to connect with loved ones, our magic is beautiful."

"Then why didn't my mother teach me whatever this is?"

"Because I do not love you." The Netherking's voice became sharp, impatient. "There is a Sacred Bone connection between you and me, linked by blood. This is what I use to torment your mother. Had you learned this magic and incidentally forged a strong connection with me, you would have been vulnerable to my attacks as well. She knew that and wouldn't risk you opening yourself up to my influence."

That was why Mirae and every other Sacred Bone Magic user had been forbidden to say the Inconstant Son's name aloud— for fear that they would accidentally open a Sacred Bone link between themselves and the Netherking, who everyone assumed was Seolla's great enemy. Another misguided rule, it seemed, for the true Inconstant Son, Kimoon, did not appear capable of wielding that kind of diabolical magic, empowered by the mere mention of his name. At least, not that Mirae had been able to see.

Mirae didn't know if the Netherking could feel the warmth fleeing from her fingers, but to her, her hands felt like ice as her mind muddled through all the confusing revelations that had barraged her since entering the Deep. The Netherking, heedless of her being overwhelmed, continued his lecture. "Now, if you're ready to begin, I want you to close your eyes. Listen to your pulse, and then search for mine."

After what he'd just told her, Mirae didn't want to open a connection with the man across from her, but if it was the only way to learn how to find Minho, she didn't have any choice. She closed her eyes and, while the Netherking put light pressure on her wrists, listened for the sounds of their hearts.

She could hear their pulses clearly, as if her ear was pressed against both their chests. Mirae listened with wonder, realizing why her heart had beat loudly as a janggu the night of the monster's attack, and again when she'd lost control of her dragon. The thunderous thrumming she'd heard had been a sign of the Netherking's magic. A sign of hers.

For their heartbeats were exactly the same.

"Memorize the rhythm," the Netherking said. "This is how we soul-walk and find each other, no matter the distance. Every Sacred Bone royal, marked or free, thrums with the beat. Listen, and you will find all who do. Then follow the beat away from here, to Minho."

Mirae gripped the Netherking's wrists, finding the strongest pulse between the ridges of his tendons. Their coupled hearts thrummed in unison. There was something else beneath the rhythm, too, a familiarity as strong as the grip that had pulled Mirae down to the bottom of the lake to meet the secrets of her blood. She didn't know if she could ever go back to not hearing or feeling that swelling chorus inside her.

Mirae tried to cast her magical hearing upward, to "soul-walk" as the Netherking had called it, but as she tried to open her ears to the world, she was bombarded with sounds: The slight whistle of breathing through her nose, the groaning of the water overhead, muffled by its own enormous weight. The slaking slither of sand shifting above their heads.

Wol Sin Lake was a dense wall of muted sound. Nothing could get through its otherworldly mass. If she hadn't witnessed the Netherking's reach with her own eyes, Mirae would have thought connection was impossible from inside the Deep.

Sensing her struggle, the Netherking pressed the strongest line of pulse he could find in her wrists. "The beat is inside you. Remember that, and you'll never be able to lose it."

The extra pressure against her hands did the trick. Like magic, Mirae could hear the beat everywhere—intensified in her ears, rippling through the water, echoing from the trees surrounding Wol Sin Lake. The sound of her own heart, hers and Minho's, carried Mirae through the dark chasm of water between the Deep and the lake's dark shallows. There was Hongbin wading in the shallows, the beat lapping against his ankles, pulsing in time with hers.

"Farther," the Netherking said. "Follow your heart to the other side of the mountain."

Yes, Mirae could hear the faint echo of her heartbeat beyond the lash of wintry trees surrounding the lake. A thin, soundless forest between her and a range of nearby peaks.

On the other side of the mountains was Josan. Mirae knew it not by sight, but by its sound—which was entirely different from the magical air in Seolla. Josan had the kind of silence that could be heard, stretching in every direction. A vast, hollow space, full of nothing, that hummed nonetheless. Mirae felt like a trapped hand scraping the bottom of a narrow-necked jar.

The Netherking's voice was the only thing that interrupted Josan's silence. "The border will be tricky to soul-walk across because there isn't any Sacred Bone Magic to amplify the sound of our hearts. But that also makes things simpler, because there's only one pulse you need to find."

"It's too quiet," Mirae whispered. "I don't hear anything."

"If that were true, you'd be back here, not floating around out there. Something is tethering you to Josan. Find it."

"I'm not strong enough," Mirae said, struggling to remain in the quiet void of a place where magic came to die. "I don't think I can go any farther."

Mirae felt something against her mouth. The cold rim of a small vial. She parted her lips, letting the Netherking pour a drop of something oily and bitter onto her tongue. She nearly spat it out but forced herself to swallow; as soon as the concoction slid down her throat, she felt its burn turn into something else. A flash of power that ignited her own. The beat—there it was, louder than ever.

"I hear it," Mirae said, her tongue thick with oil.

"Very good. You're doing well."

Mirae swallowed the rest of the bitter potion. "What next?"

"Listen for a field in front of you. Soar over it and wait for me on the other side."

Empowered by the Netherking's strange concoction, Mirae could hear the green-tea trees he was referring to and their countless leaves glossy with water, greeting each other with tiny soft claps that swelled across the field in a collective sigh. She could hear farmers crunching through the mulch ditches between each row, praising their beautiful crop, urging it to grow.

Mirae could almost smell the earthy leaves, just as she could almost see the Netherking waiting for her at the top of the farmers' hill, creased with thick bushes round and long like fresh noodles for the gods.

"Come, queenling." The Netherking's silhouette was thin as a silk screen door, his clothes and crown dark as his eyes. "We still have many miles to go."

Mirae nodded. "Which way?"

He pointed into the distance, where gray peaks lay clenched on the horizon with white-capped knuckles. "Up there is where the Josan king keeps his . . . unofficial guests. Follow the river, not the road, and it will lead you to White Spine Mountain—to Minho."

Yes, she could hear her brother's heart. It was easier now that she'd caught his sound like a scent. Mirae flew toward the river, loud with trickle-chatter, and followed the beat through its whispering rushes and the calls of red-crowned cranes. She slid along the river's long blue robe, climbing its satiny sounds as she heaved herself over White Spine Mountain's granite chest to reach its crowning jewel: a fortress set in stone.

Minho's heart was loudest there, at Josan's highest height.

"Now dive," the Netherking said. "He has been pushed deep, like me—where people put their hated things."

Diving down into the fortress's gullet, deep into its cold, dark belly, Mirae drifted past clanking soldiers, the clamor of sharpening swords, sloshing bowls, and scratching pens. Down to the inner quiet of a place few were allowed to go.

There he was, in a cell, hands chained to the wall behind him. Minho, with bruises deep enough to make out in the darkness. The veins in his warmest parts, hot with pulse—neck, wrists, and heart—looked as if they were pumping thick ebony into his body, not blood. Much like the mul gwisin who'd been tormented into a horrible, restless death.

But his chest was moving, and his heart was strong.

Mirae wanted to shatter her brother's bonds, but try as she might to touch him, her body merely floated through everything—walls, water, even Minho. It was like she wasn't even in the room.

"His magic is dormant," the Netherking said. "Unless he, too, is connecting with you through Sacred Bone Magic, you can only look, not touch."

Mirae moved as close as she could without stepping into Minho's body. "I failed to protect you, orabeoni. I'm so sorry—for everything."

To her surprise, Minho looked up, but not at her. The cell door was opening. Mirae's heart quickened in time with Minho's, keeping their Sacred Bone beat in sync, as they both stared at the newcomer. The man was dressed in the traditional colors of Josan, his hair half tied up, as was the custom of Josan nobles and royals. But it was his face that made Mirae stare.

He was young—far younger than the first time Mirae had seen him. But those honey-light, ruthless eyes, coupled with the puzzling softness of his movements, hinting at an inner gentleness, were all things Mirae had encountered before. Last time, that anger, as well as that gentleness, had been directed at her. This time, it was pointed at her brother, whom Mirae had not yet caught a glimpse of in the future. A fact that made her blood run cold.

But how—how could the elusive Inconstant Son be right here in front of her? Wasn't it the Josan king who had stolen Minho? Was the Inconstant Son working with the king after all? Mirae felt helpless, seeing her brother at the mercy of the man she was supposed to destroy.

Minho's dark eyes were pools that glittered in the light of the guards' torches. He, too, seemed to recognize the man before him. "Ah, two visits from False Prince Kimoon in one day—I must have done something *really* bad. Are you mad that I complained about my soup?"

Kimoon crouched in front of Minho, neck craned lightly, as if he'd learned the art of moving just enough to get what he wanted. "Please tell me you've changed your mind. I could really use some good news right now."

"Well, have you considered my counteroffer?" Minho asked, eyes still glittering. "If you let me mysteriously escape, Mirae will be fair when doling out her vengeance. I swear it."

Kimoon's eyes, facing away from the torches, were shadowed and impassive. "I'm afraid my father has a very different definition of what should be considered fair."

"You mean something more like this?" Minho gestured, as best he could, to his dingy surroundings. "Does this look fair to you?"

Kimoon sighed. "You know I hate this. But you also know how my father is. Please tell me you've changed your mind so I can make it all stop. I want to do that for you."

Minho turned toward the shadows, his eyes becoming dark mirrors of his captor's. "I will never write or say any of those vile things. You will not use me against my family."

Kimoon put a consoling hand on Minho's knee. "I understand how you feel. I, too, will do anything, suffer infinitely, to protect my family. But as princes, we both know that sometimes our people have to come first. A reckoning is coming, Minho, but it doesn't have to be bloody."

"You're no prince." Mirae had never seen Minho sneer before. It was an ugliness that didn't belong on his face. "We both know that's the real reason I'm here. You're just a jealous little man trying to win his father's favor so he can maybe, someday, become king."

Kimoon grabbed Minho's neck with an expression that Mirae recognized; he would grip her the same way, decades in the future. "Why shouldn't you help me, Minho? Here you will be treated the way a first son deserves. Why would you remain in a *queendom* that will only marry you off? Why endure the indignity of cutting off your true potential?"

The Josan dignitary had asked Minho the same thing. For the first time, Mirae wondered if these questions were actually touching a nerve. She'd never considered how Minho felt about his lot in life—was he as troubled by Seolla's rules as these Josan men expected him to be?

"You think you have it so much better than me?" Minho choked out a laugh. "Then why are we here? Where's your respect, O bastard of Josan?"

Kimoon squeezed harder. "My father will shower you with everything I never had. More than your mother ever intended to give you. I can live with that, as long as you renounce your family of murderers. That's the only way we both get what we want."

"What I want is for Mirae to become queen," Minho gasped, "so she can destroy you."

Kimoon released Minho with a look of disgust. "I'm not afraid of that little witch. She's reckless and vain. Condemn her and save yourself a world of trouble."

"You don't know my sister." Minho smirked through the pain. "Trust me, you won't be able to manipulate her any more than you can me. You can, of course, die trying."

"We'll see about that." Kimoon dusted off his hands, grimacing at the prison grime. He stood and gestured for two guards to enter the room. "I believe it's time for the prince's bath."

"No." Minho pressed himself against the wall, his voice shifting from smug to panicked. "I'm sorry I misspoke. Forgive me."

"How many times do I have to tell you this isn't a punishment?" Kimoon said. "My mudang is trying to fix you."

"You know that's not true." Mirae could feel Minho's heart racing as quickly as hers.

"For now, we need you alive. Be grateful for that." Kimoon nodded for the guards to continue. They unlocked Minho's chains and wrestled him off the floor.

"Please." Minho fought their grip. "I can't take it anymore—I can't."

"I know you're scared," Kimoon soothed, brushing a lock of hair out of Minho's face. "Try to think of it as medicine. You don't have to like it—but it'll be good for you all the same."

Mirae stared at the bastard son of Josan. Kimoon, the furious man from the mountain. The man who called himself the Inconstant Son and hated her for taking everything from him. Mirae's hands curled into fists as she realized why Kimoon would grow to hate her so much—because she was going to stop him. He would never become a true prince, let alone a king. Mirae would make sure of that. Even if it meant spending the rest of her days under his hateful eye, she was going to take everything from him, everything he was working for.

Anything to save Minho.

The guards dragged Minho out of the room as he begged for mercy. Kimoon stayed behind, wincing every time Minho's voice broke as he shouted Kimoon's name. Mirae studied the false prince's face, determined to memorize everything about it so she would always recognize the Inconstant Son, no matter how old or young he looked, in any wardrobe or disguise.

Past his loose, shiny black hair were high, sharp cheeks that narrowed into a delicate jawline crowned with a wide, full mouth. Flat brows, tapered like distant mountain peaks, sat over lion-like eyes holding that sun-on-honey color Mirae would never forget. But she didn't stare at Kimoon's young, handsome face or his sad eyes for long. Instead she found herself eyeing the stains on his hands and wrists—as deeply purple as his royal clothes.

Kimoon remained in the cell, taking deep breaths, eyes shut, until he composed himself enough to resume his impassivity and follow his men out into the hall.

Mirae did the same, her heart beating as fast as Minho's—filled with the same dread. She followed Kimoon into a wide stone room lined with deep basins. Each was filled to the brim with black water, smaller versions of Wol Sin Lake.

The guards pulled off Minho's pants, leaving him in his sokgot as they lifted him, fighting futilely against them, into one of the tubs. They submerged all but his head, which he kept above water with all his strength. "Please, hyungnim—don't do this!"

Kimoon, struggling once again to keep his face impassive, grabbed Minho's hair and shoved his head under. "I'm sorry."

Mirae watched, horrified, as the dark water bubbled with air her brother could no longer breathe. Once the ripples stopped altogether and the black water fell still, Kimoon removed his hands, wiping them quickly. Minho floated to the surface, face-down.

"Just three more days, and then you'll do as I ask and finally be at peace."

Minho's heart was still beating. Fast. Scared. Thunderous. Then it fell silent.

When Mirae opened her eyes into the darkness of the Deep, she felt her shaking hands steadied by the Netherking's. "What are they doing to him?"

"Soaking him in black water." The Netherking's robes shifted, as if he had turned to look up at the dark lake suspended above them. "Black water amplifies whatever spell has been instilled into it. In my case, that means containment. Fortunately, I am not steeping in it raw, like Minho is. That kind of high-level exposure will change a man."

Mirae felt the Netherking wince as her grip tightened. "Change him how?"

"That depends entirely on the spell."

Mirae pulled her hands away before she twisted the Netherking's hand off. "How long does he have?"

"I'd say Kimoon is right. Three days. Judging by the state of Minho's veins, the effects have started to become permanent."

Permanent? "Will Seolla's physicians be able to cure him?"

"I doubt it." The Netherking scoffed at the thought. "They deal with pure elements, not corruption."

Mirae breathed deeply, trying to stay calm even though she was about to do something extremely reckless. "Can you help Minho if I bring him here?"

The Netherking seemed to be studying her, determining how serious she was. "Possibly."

Mirae clenched her jaw. "You mean depending on what I give you in return?"

"Yes, and no." The Netherking grabbed Mirae's hand, as firmly as before, and began leading her back toward the distant sunspot. "It's possible that I may not be able to heal Minho entirely. I've lived beneath this wealth of black water my entire life. No one understands it as well as I do. But even I haven't unlocked all its secrets."

"If anyone can figure it out, though, it's you?"

The Netherking scoffed again. "I doubt there's anything His Arrogant Highness of Josan can do with black water that I cannot puzzle out. But you'll have to bring Minho to me quickly—certainly within three days."

"How do I know you won't hurt him?" Mirae asked as they neared the growing light. "I'll do anything for my brother, unless it makes things worse."

The Netherking was silent as he and Mirae closed the gap between themselves and the minty glow from the sun above. When they could see each other again, he turned his enigmatic gaze on Mirae. "My cooperation depends entirely on you. What will you give me for my kindness?"

It would have to be something the Netherking couldn't refuse. Mirae looked him dead in the eye, already knowing what to say. "You will get your reckoning. I will make sure you tell your story to every ear in Seolla. You will no longer be a secret. Together, with our people, we will sort out what is to be done with you. If you save Minho, their estimation of the kindness you deserve will be more than you'll ever earn on your own."

The Netherking was silent for several long moments, seeming to weigh his own dark plans against the things Mirae could get for him, if he were to choose to be cooperative instead of conniving.

"Very well, queenling. Just see that you do your part. The connection between us will be strong after this. I will not shy away from using it in uniquely torturous ways."

Mirae held back a shiver. "Whatever happened between our ancestors, you and I are allies now. The hatred ends with us."

"Perhaps." The Netherking reached into his robes, drawing out a small vial of black liquid. "As a way to mark this occasion, allow me to give you a gift."

Mirae took the vial, frowning at its contents. "Is this the stuff you made me drink?"

"A sip of pure black water will make you powerful in a pinch. But save as much of it as you can. Minho is dependent on black water now, so he'll need it to survive the trip here. Oh, and one more thing. Kimoon is clearly conflicted about what he's doing. You should use that against him."

"Yes, I gathered as much myself." Mirae put the vial into the bag of beads around her neck. Then she held up the gwisin's pearl. "How do I get out of here?"

"The same way you came in. The bohoja awaits."

Mirae shuddered at the thought of once again subjecting herself to the hand of Wol Sin Lake. But her heart wasn't in the habit of growing faint when she needed to take courage. In fact, it was proving to be more powerful than she'd ever imagined.

She closed her eyes and, knowing the Netherking would not thwart her now that his fate rested in her hands, summoned her black-eyed dragon, a creature of tendrils and teeth. In the green-lit Deep, its rainbow scales glittered like a giant pile of underwater jade.

Mirae placed a hand on her dragon's massive, fire-warm body. It did not object when she climbed onto its back, wrapping her arms around its neck and pinning the pearl to it like jewelry. She looked down at the Netherking, whose dark eyes glittered with something close to jealousy. But he did not lift a hand against her. They had too much to gain, too much to lose, to risk betraying each other again.

Mirae bowed atop the dragon, as befitting the Netherking's rank as a Sacred Bone royal. Then she buried her face in her dragon's rippling, rainbow neck. "It's time, my friend."

The dragon snapped its jaws, roaring in agreement as it launched onto its hind legs. Mirae held her breath as the dragon plunged upward into Wol Sin Lake, its body bright and warm where the water was dark and icy. She clung to the dragon and the luminous pearl at its neck as the water parted like sleek black wings around them, bringing her once more into fresh Seollan air.

Chapter

FIFTEEN

When Mirae burst out of the dark eye of Wol Sin Lake, shattering its stillness, she saw Hongbin sitting on the shore, damp and shivering. Based on the ripped collar of his hanbok and the crease between his brows, it seemed that getting away from Captain Jia had been no easy task. But when he saw Mirae, his jaw dropped, wide eyes fixed on the dragon stretching its long neck to the white-pebbled shore so Mirae could dismount.

As Mirae climbed gracefully down the scaly bridge, Hongbin continued to gape at the rainbow creature beneath her, and at the pearly moon she held over her head for balance. Mirae's eyes slid past her brother to where Captain Jia and Siwon stood. They remained on the other side of the incinerating barrier, the former looking a little shocked at Mirae's entrance, and the latter, Mirae realized with a thrill, exhibiting no surprise at all. In fact, Siwon was smiling at her triumphant return.

As soon as her feet hit the shore, Mirae turned and bowed to her glorious creation. It bowed back, scales glittering like wet jewels. She could feel its ebony eyes following her as she walked up to Hongbin and pulled him, still speechless, to his feet. Together, they approached their companions.

Mirae stopped just shy of the incinerating barrier, looking back and forth between the Wonhwa captain and Siwon. "I know where my orabeoni is, but we don't have much time to rescue him. Will you come with me?"

"Yes." Siwon's answer was immediate.

"He's not here?" Captain Jia asked at the same time.

Mirae shook her head in response to the captain's question and looked her in the eye. "I will tell you everything that happened in the Deep and how I know Minho's location. There will be no secrets between us from here on out. I promise. For now, however, I ask that you trust me."

"Gongju," Captain Jia said, as if begging Mirae not to ask such a thing of her, "I know I cannot stop you from whatever it is you think you're doing, but at least let me take Gunju back to the palace. There's no sense in risking all three of Seolla's royal children."

"Excuse me," Hongbin said. "Does this 'royal child' get any say?"

"I said I know where my orabeoni is," Mirae repeated, cutting off all further protests. "The man you love. If we do not rescue him now, not only will he be lost, but there may be a war the likes of which we've never seen. We don't have time to continue questioning my choice to go save him, or who will join me. I leave your decision in your hands, and I'm only asking one more time. Who's coming with me?"

"I am," Hongbin said, raising his hand.

Siwon bowed in solidarity. "You will need a guide through Josan."

"She never said Daegun was in Josan." Captain Jia narrowed her eyes at Siwon.

Siwon gave Mirae a knowing look, the same one they'd shared at the haggard moon gwisin's pond. "The Josan dignitary vanished alongside Daegun daegam. If he isn't here, I think it's rather obvious where he was taken."

Mirae nodded. "I appreciate your offer of being my guide, and I accept."

Mirae turned to Captain Jia one last time. "When you took the oath to become captain of the Wonhwa, you swore to protect Seolla's crown, but your heart also belongs to my orabeoni. Destiny has decided that you don't need to choose between those two things. Come with me, and honor both your desires. After all, I should think that wherever Seolla's royal children are, you should be also."

Captain Jia stared at Mirae's offered hand. Mirae could read the emotions crossing over her face as if they were being spoken aloud. The captain wanted nothing more than to bring Minho home—but was this the way? Or would indulging Mirae's "visions" mean dooming the entire royal line to being captured, or worse? *Was* there truth in her visions? Truth in what she said she was? After a long, tense moment, Captain Jia sighed and took Mirae's hand. "I hope you at least have a plan for leaving this cage and reaching Daegun alive. We have no supplies or any idea where we are."

Just then, Mirae heard a disturbance in the lake behind her—not the sound of something plunging in, but of something popping out. She turned, worried that she might see the pointed tips of the Netherking's crown, but to her relief, it was just the giant warted hand once more. Its fingers slowly uncurled like a sickly green flower, revealing the Netherking's final offering in its palm.

Mirae reached back to offer Siwon her free hand before pulling both him and the captain through to the other side of the barrier, protected by her touch.

Captain Jia flinched slightly, as if half expecting to be incinerated. But Siwon walked in with nothing in his eyes but trust. Mirae let his confidence strengthen her, just as before.

She surveyed her companions once more: a Josan ally; a captain and a friend; and a brother whose destiny, she knew, was closely tied to her own.

"For Minho," she said softly. They all nodded as Mirae reentered the lake, approaching the giant green palm. The Netherking's parting gift was a shiningly white object, folded into a crisp white package. As soon as Mirae took it, the giant hand curled into a fist and sank into the water, careful not to splash either Mirae or the Netherking's gift.

Mirae waded back to the shore, holding the package high, and locked eyes with her dragon, who lay curled in a colorful coil off to the side of the stark white beach. It nodded, knowing her thoughts. After all, without the Netherking's interference, Mirae and her dragon were of the same mind and soul—both creator and creation at the same time.

Which meant they were thinking the same thing: whatever the Netherking had gifted them, it, like the vial of black water, would surely come with a price. Mirae didn't want to use either item unless she had to, yet she had a feeling that the Netherking somehow knew she would have no other choice.

"What is that?" Hongbin reached out to help Mirae to the shore. "It's shiny."

Mirae found a spot of beach that seemed suitably clean and laid out the Netherking's parting gift. It didn't take long for her to realize that she was unwrapping a hanbok. Clean, white, and stiff. An outfit reserved for the dead and those who mourned them—a gwisin's garment of choice, as Mirae well remembered.

Hongbin crouched down next to her. "Oof. Is this the monster's way of saying 'Hello there, prepare to die'?"

Captain Jia frowned down at the hanbok, giving it the same look of contempt she usually reserved for Siwon.

"I don't think this was meant as a threat," Mirae said, carefully refolding the garment.

Siwon, unsurprisingly, was on the same page as she was. "No, it's the perfect disguise."

"What are you talking about?" Captain Jia's eyes bored into him.

Mirae gestured for Siwon to continue. "When I first came to Seolla," he explained, "I was not prepared for your people's magic. It felt like walking into a swarm of tiny, invisible sensations. Some burned, some chilled, and others made it hard to breathe. I was ill for days until my body began to acclimate to the . . . magical textures in your air. Being around people with magic will create the same effect. I still feel it around you sometimes," Siwon said to Mirae, holding her gaze for a moment.

She lowered her head, hiding a flush in her cheeks, as Captain Jia interjected, "There's no way we can hide Gongju's considerable magic."

"No, hence the hanbok." Siwon crouched down beside Hong-bin, spreading his hand gently over the bright white fabric. "It's going to help her blend in."

Captain Jia frowned. "How?"

Siwon shrugged. "There is only one kind of power in Josan that feels anything like Gongju mama's. It belongs to shamans, those who mediate between us and beings from the unseen world—gods, spirits, and the dead. This is what shamans wear."

Mirae looked down at the pure-white hanbok, gleaming against the shore. A disguise not just for her, but for her magic. How had the Netherking come across such a unique item? "But I don't know anything about shamans. How can I pretend to be one?"

Siwon smiled. "Don't worry, my mother was a shaman. I am familiar with their ways."

Mirae didn't think it was possible for Captain Jia's frown to grow any deeper. "Gongju, doesn't this all feel a little too . . . convenient?"

Mirae stood and placed a hand on the captain's shoulder, startling her. "We can talk when we're in the air. I would never ask you to trust the man I just met inside Wol Sin Lake, but please trust me."

Captain Jia stiffened. "What do you mean, 'when we're in the air'?"

Mirae turned to her dragon. "The only thing that can get us out of here is Sacred Bone Magic. We need to move swiftly, while still being able to see the lay of the land."

"So we're going to . . . ride that thing?" Captain Jia, for once, was at a loss for words. Even Siwon looked appropriately terrified. Only Hongbin fixed Mirae with a joyous grin.

"You mean, I get to fly?" he crowed.

"Yes." Mirae held out her hand. "Shall we?"

"Oh, we shall," Hongbin grabbed her arm and giggled. "Forever and ever, we shall."

Mirae turned to the others. "Are you coming?"

Captain Jia nodded grimly. She sheathed her sword down her back, covering its hilt with her long black braid. Siwon appeared to be searching for a place to vomit already. Hongbin gently unwound himself from Mirae and offered Siwon his hand. "Come on, you can ride behind with me. Let's leave the stern ladies to themselves while we have all the fun."

As usual, Hongbin's confidence and charm were contagious. Siwon visibly relaxed as he accepted his prince's arm. "Maybe you can distract me with more of your stories."

Hongbin's chest seemed to swell to twice its size. "My dear boy, for you, I shall tell all the stories in the world."

While the two boys walked off, arm in arm, Captain Jia turned to Mirae. "You'll never get us past the giant barrier between Seolla and Josan. Her Majesty enchanted it to incinerate anything with human blood. The only way through is by the main gate itself."

"I know," Mirae said. "But the flying monster got Minho through somehow, so I know the gods will provide us with a way to follow. Come, Captain. We have much to discuss."

With that, Mirae followed after Hongbin and Siwon. She locked eyes with her dragon, and the magnificent beast nodded, then lowered its head so everyone could climb aboard.

Mirae settled into the crook of one shoulder while Captain Jia took the other, clutching one of the dragon's lower neck horns.

Mirae waited until Hongbin and Siwon seemed settled, both clinging to a piece of the dragon's spine, before patting her creation's glittering neck. Knowing what she wanted, the dragon reared up onto its hind legs. Mirae was a little nervous herself, having ridden her Sacred Bone beast only once, and merely the short distance out of water. Hongbin, it seemed, was the sole person excited at the thought of actually taking flight.

"Hold on tight, Siwon," Hongbin called over the dragon's preparatory roar. "And don't be afraid to scream!"

Mirae took that advice to heart as the dragon coiled its powerful body, gathering strength into its legs before launching its long, lithe form into the sky. For a moment, Mirae feared they would slide right off the dragon's back and need to be magicked safely back to the ground. By the way Captain Jia sat, with one hand clinging and the other prepared to cast a spell, Mirae wasn't the only one worried about taking a fall.

Perhaps because of this worry—or as proof that there was never anything to worry about—just as the force of the dragon's takeoff hit Mirae in the face and chest, two pure white sheets of what looked like paper-thin clouds rose up on either side of them, billowing like sails. When Mirae realized what her dragon had created, she patted its shoulder, knowing the source of its inspiration. Just as the shaman's white hanbok would be Mirae's disguise in Josan, these cloud-white coverings would keep her and her companions safe—and prevent the dragon from being noticed once they began flying over the more habitated parts of Seolla.

Mirae turned in her seat, making sure everyone was fine inside the flying palanquin. Hongbin had his arms raised, pure joy on his face, while Siwon gripped the dragon's spine so tightly, he looked as sheet-white as the shield protecting them.

Mirae turned to the Wonhwa captain at her side. "I'm glad you're here with me."

Captain Jia didn't relax her grip on the dragon's horn. "You know I'm only agreeing to this nonsense for Daegun's sake."

"See, that's why I'm glad you're here." When Captain Jia shot her a look of confusion, Mirae continued. "You never tell me what I want to hear. You don't lie, nor do you like hiding anything from me. After all the secrets I've unearthed these past few days, I'm realizing what a blessing it is to be with someone I can trust to always speak the truth."

Captain Jia nodded, though she looked uneasy. "We'll see if that still holds true when you tell me what you saw in the cage."

Well aware that Captain Jia would have plenty of opinions about Mirae's adventure in the Deep, the words came tumbling out of her mouth nonetheless. Captain Jia didn't flinch at Mirae's barrage, as careful a listener as she ever was. Once Mirae had finished recounting everything about the Netherking and what she'd learned about the Inconstant Son—a name she no longer felt bound to never speak aloud—Captain Jia let it all sink in with several seconds of silence.

"So, we were wrong in thinking the Netherking was Seolla's great nemesis," Captain Jia said slowly. "He may be a Sacred Bone royal bent on revenge, but your real enemy is a man capable of far worse things."

"So it would seem." Mirae stared down at her stained chima. "I know this is all tied together somehow, just not as simply as

I would have liked. My switches tangle the web even more, at least for now. I feel all I can do is trust my heart and try to move forward."

Captain Jia nodded solemnly. "And you trust what you saw about Daegun's location?" When Mirae nodded, the captain frowned. "But why would the Josan king do something so foolish? What is he hoping to gain by instigating a war he cannot win?"

"Maybe he's found a way to even the odds," Mirae said. "The Netherking wasn't forthcoming about what all he had contributed to this plot against Seolla. After all, I doubt the Josan king learned how to manipulate black water all by himself."

The thought of Minho being tortured with dark magic seemed to make Captain Jia clutch the dragon's horn in a grip that would have broken anything else. "Do you really intend to free that evil man, after everything he's done? The monster that took Daegun was almost certainly his creation."

"I will let our people decide," Mirae said, urging her dragon to part its paper-kite shield enough for her to peer down through the whistling gap at the land below. "I'm confident they'll make sure the Netherking reaps all that he has sown."

Miles ahead, Mirae saw the magical barrier between Seolla and Josan. For hundreds of years, Mirae's ancestors had enchanted both the stone foundation and the beaming wall of light that soared higher than even Mirae did on her dragon. The stone wall alone was impassibly thick and taller than ten men, but it was the enchantment in the sky that, up until the night of Mirae's Sangsok Ceremony, had kept Seolla's borders safe from Josan treachery.

Mirae couldn't help but stare at the curtain of light sweeping across the nations' boundary like a thin swath of opalescent clouds. If she hadn't known any better, she might have assumed it was merely a spectacle of beauty, not a human-incinerating shield that kept Seolla safe. It was hard not to be awed by the cheery, milky mist that danced with the blue of the sky, allowing winks of rainbow shimmers to arc through like jeweled stars.

Perhaps most spectacular of all were the giant, deerlike shapes of the kirin prancing through the mist like protectors with nothing else to do. Heralds of the rise and fall of great leaders, the kirin were projected onto the filmy wall in the sky for the same reason their antlers stood on the Seollan crown—as a reminder that all was well and strong in Seolla, especially its enchanted queen.

Mirae had accompanied her mother on her yearly trip to shore up the wall's magic with spells of both of beauty and impenetrability since she was a small child. This time, as she approached the mighty, stunning barrier, Mirae did not feel the pride and wonder she'd felt before. What had once reassured Mirae that her mother and her queendom were infallible and strong now seemed like an egotistical production, carefully maintained for all the world to see.

"We should land soon, Gongju," Captain Jia said, pulling Mirae from her thoughts. "The border is fast approaching and these white coverings will not keep us safe from your mother's magic."

Mirae nodded, feeling the immense weight of exhaustion hit her at the captain's words. She laid her head against the dragon's back and bid it to bring its cargo safely to land. This time the dragon didn't roar, understanding the need to be silent. As the dragon's sail-like shield parted and began to fold, Mirae looked down at her sprawling, beautiful queendom.

Enough time had passed since Mirae's venture into the Deep that the sun was slowly closing its crimson eye, casting one final warm beam onto the golden rice fields below, which reflected the sun's rays back to the heavens. Spaced out between the fields were robust villages with walled homesteads and streets dotted with pinpricks of color—people bartering for last-minute goods, perhaps, or linking arms with friends as they headed to a teahouse for some evening fun and laughter.

Ahead, Mirae also spotted the lights of Geumju, Seolla's border town—the city she would need to pass through unnoticed to get to the gate to Josan.

The dragon's landing was quick and smooth. Once its feet were firmly planted on the ground, it lowered its wings until they fell like luxurious canopies at its sides. Hongbin was the first to get up and jump into one of the billowing sheets, laughing as he slid back to earth. He whirled back around once he was on his feet, his dusk-lit eyes as golden as the rice field around him. "Come on, Siwon! It'll be fun!"

Siwon looked ready to believe anything that would get him off the flying dragon. He rose shakily to his feet, treading warily across the dragon's back until he reached the same wing Hongbin had used. Siwon's expression once he was back on firm ground was the closest thing to pure joy Mirae had ever seen on his face.

Captain Jia dismounted next, staying as close to Siwon as Siwon did to Hongbin. After Mirae slid smoothly to the ground, she walked around to face her dragon. She looked up into its night-black eyes and bowed. The dragon bowed back, scales glittering like polished jewels, before sinking back into the earth, returning to the inky blackness from whence it came.

When she turned back around, Mirae found herself face-to-face with a far different being—a beaming brother with an embrace that somehow always managed to feel magical.

"Noonim, that was the most amazing thing *ever*. I love your magic. And you. Well, both of you, because you're one and the same. I don't care what the council says—you have *got* to be queen. I will literally stand in the great hall and wail until they see reason."

"Well, you are very persuasive when you want to be." As Mirae hugged her brother back, she was struck by the realization that she couldn't have come this far without him, nor was she meant to. It was a good thing that he and his unique, irresistible power of charm were on Mirae's side, especially since she needed his help now more than ever.

"We need to reach Geumju and find an inn before they close their gates for the night," Captain Jia said, moving to parcel out their few belongings among them, "especially if news of your disappearance has spread. They must have heard rumors of Josan's treachery by now, and everyone in the border town will be on edge."

Mirae nodded. If she hoped to rescue Minho and find proof of the Josan king's traitorous actions, she had to be careful. For once she was appreciative of Captain Jia's overly cautious ways.

Chapter
SIXTEEN

"Are you certain I can't just wear my armor?" Captain Jia grumbled as they approached the lotus-shaped lanterns at the front of Geumju's gates—and the long line of people waiting to enter through the guard checkpoint before it shut down for the night. Mirae shook her head, unafraid to admit to herself that she was enjoying the captain's discomfort a little bit.

"Wonhwa armor is one thing, but you're the *captain*," Mirae said, checking once more that her simply braided hair was still perfectly in place—though she needn't have worried about Siwon's exceptional handiwork. "By now, everyone will have been told that you and I have disappeared. You'd be identified immediately, and then so would I."

"Or I can use my rank to send all the border guards scurrying while we head for the barrier," Captain Jia grumbled. "I just can't see how any of *this* is necessary."

Even though Mirae knew Captain Jia had other worries on her mind, she still thought the captain's complaints about her clothing were a little over the top, especially considering that she was still wearing her armor underneath Mirae's fineries. They'd reversed her chima to hide the royal details embroidered onto it—the inside hems were thankfully disguised by the growing darkness—and removed the royal crests that had once rested on Mirae's shoulders. Captain Jia's head was ornamented now with whatever pins Mirae hadn't lost on her journey, which honestly looked quite stunning against the captain's sun-lightened hair.

Hongbin and Siwon were also striking in Mirae's fine, colorful silks, their long hair braided in the style of young maidens. Mirae was grateful for these ready disguises, since they meant she didn't have to cast an entire outfit for each of her companions—after all, many of the border guards would be Ma-eum Mages trained to see through illusions. However, Mirae still gave Captain Jia and the boys a small brush of illusionary glamour, for noblewomen rarely walked the streets completely barefaced. They either enchanted themselves with Ma-eum magic, if they possessed it, or relied on a maidservant to keep the spells—which were temporary—going strong.

Mirae couldn't stop herself from peeking at the palpable difference a little magic made on Siwon's face. His tanned skin held the pink blush on his cheeks with a flowerlike delicateness, and the powdery glow Mirae had dusted over his skin softened the crisp origami angles of his face. The painful-looking wounds on his cheek had also been magically smoothed over, making his warm black eyes his most distinguishing feature—the sight of them made Mirae's heart feel warm, too.

Siwon turned and caught her staring. "Oh no, is my illusion slipping?"

Mirae cleared her throat. "No, I, uh, was just . . . admiring my work."

A small smile twitched at the corners of Siwon's lips. "Is that all, Gongju mama?"

"Actually—" Mirae coughed. "I wanted to talk to you about something." She hoped he would gracefully allow her to change the subject. "I wasn't sure how to bring this up, because I was worried it would stir up sad memories . . . but I was hoping you could teach me a little about shamanism while we walk, just in case any of the guards ask me questions."

Siwon's face turned serious again, and he resumed staring straight ahead. "It was kind of you to consider my feelings, though really there was no need." His voice was light. "I know my mother would be happy I'm sharing Josan's beliefs with you, Gongju mama."

"I'm happy about it, too," Mirae said, gesturing for Siwon to continue. "I want to learn more about your life in Josan."

As Mirae and her companions took their places at the back of the line of people waiting to enter Geumju, Siwon began briefly explaining the basics of shamanism.

"There are two main types of shamans in Josan—tangol are those who inherit their status from one or both parents and study shamanism their whole lives. Then there are those who are chosen by the gods to be their vessel through something called a shinbyeong, a mystic illness that can only be cured by becoming a kangsin shaman. They speak for the gods in a trancelike possession. Both types of shaman use their powers to help people placate spirits, demons, and gods who might be stirring up trouble."

Mirae nodded, remembering that though Seolla and Josan worshipped the same greater gods, like the Samsin, the people of Josan had thousands of folk gods they honored as well. "And all genders can be shamans, right?" Mirae asked, recalling the only other thing she knew about Josan's ancient beliefs. The memory of Kimoon tormenting Minho about his role as a man in the female-controlled Seolla came to mind, making her wince. Again she wondered how her brothers actually felt about their place in her queendom.

"Correct," Siwon confirmed. "Villages usually have a resident tangol who helps out with funerary rites and makes sure local deities are properly worshipped. They're also the first ones called if there are any signs of malevolent spirits or restless gwisin sightings. Through a ritual called a kut, they send these spirits on their way."

Mirae nodded again, intrigued by Josan's indigenous spiritualism, which was older than magic itself. "And what do kangsin shamans do?"

"They are typically called when it's clear that intervention from the gods is needed—either to reveal what, specifically, needs to be done for a successful kut, or to explain why *they*, the gods, are creating the problem, and how they can be appeased."

"And kangsin shamans do this through . . . being possessed by a god?"

"Yes, and it's a truly spectacular sight." Siwon glanced down at the ground. "I've seen it happen many times; my mother was a kangsin shaman."

Mirae could tell Siwon was getting lost in his thoughts. Kindly, gently, she prodded him away from his sad memories. "So, tell me about these kuts. How do they work?"

Siwon took a deep breath, remembering himself, as he explained that kuts varied greatly depending on what they were meant to accomplish, but were typically divided into four parts—the purification of the kut grounds, the invocation of the gods, the entertainment of the gods through a ballad, and then, finally, the gods' answer and sending off, which sometimes required the possession of a kangsin shaman. All kuts, regardless of their purpose, were a public performance of devotion to Josan's deities, involving music, swords, bells, fans, and even paintings of the gods.

Mirae found her eyes widening at the vast complexities of the fundamental beliefs held by her sovereign nation, and yet there was something remarkably refreshing about Josan's openness with the spiritual world, its closeness to it, even. Perhaps if Seolla hadn't isolated its oracles but instead opened communication between the people and their gods as Josan had, the Inconstant Son would never have been able to find a secret foothold all those years ago.

A guard's voice interrupted their conversation. "Who's next? Please step forward." Mirae dragged her mind back to the present, surprised to find that she and her companions had already reached the front of the line. The city guard—a Ma-eum Mage, by the look of her black-and-silver tunic—raised her eyebrows at the sight of what appeared to be a shaman deep in conversation with a noblewoman. She held her hand out to Mirae and her fellow travelors, gesturing for their identity tags. "State your business."

To Captain Jia's credit, all her discomfort over her outfit seeped away as she took the lead, confidently holding out the wooden tag she and Mirae had crafted only minutes earlier. "I am Song Jinha, here with my cousins to celebrate my birthday. We met this shaman on the road and invited her to join us."

Her words were delivered a little stiffly, but the guard was already moving on to Siwon and Hongbin, holding out her hand for their wooden tags. Once she had them all, the Ma-eum Mage ran her fingers over them, looking for any signs of forgery, illusion or otherwise. Mirae had known that the guards in Geumju would be extra vigilant, especially with the recent trouble. They'd be on high alert to detect Josan spies. Thankfully, True Bone identity tags were authenticated by a Sacred Bone seal, something Mirae had the power to create. She'd added some to the fake tags as soon as Captain Jia had finished crafting them with magic.

The Ma-eum Mage inclined her head politely as she handed Captain Jia, Hongbin, and Siwon back their identification. She turned to Mirae last. "Give me your tag, manyeo. Don't make me ask again."

Mirae's cheeks threatened to burn at the guard's rudeness, but she reminded herself that she wasn't a princess here. The only way into Josan was by making people believe she was no one. Mirae handed over the plain, unenchanted tag Siwon had helped her fashion, hoping her hands weren't trembling noticeably. As long as Siwon's year-old memory of Josan tags was accurate and nothing had changed about them since then, the guard would have to accept that Mirae was just a shaman making her way back home.

Mirae held her breath as the Ma-eum Mage studied her identification carefully, running her fingers over every inch of it. She seemed disappointed to find no fault with it and thrust it none too gently back into Mirae's chest. "There's been some trouble with your countrymen. I'm afraid I'll need to ask you a few questions before letting you pass."

Mirae kept her eyes humbly on the ground. "I assure you, I have nothing to do with whatever happened. I came here to work, nothing more."

The guard did little to hide her disapproval for whichever superstitious citizen of Seolla had hired the services of a Josan shaman. "All the same, I have my orders." She stepped aside for Captain Jia, Hongbin, and Siwon. "I hope you have a very enjoyable birthday."

"How long will your questioning take?" Captain Jia asked the guard brusquely, nodding at Mirae. When the Ma-eum Mage looked at her with confusion, the captain added, "As I said, I asked her to join my birthday celebration."

"We're women of our word. We're not going anywhere without her," Hongbin chirped while Siwon nodded in agreement, shooting Mirae a worried look.

"I knew it." The guard frowned and stepped closer to Mirae's disguised companions. "This woman has put a spell on you."

"What? No." Captain Jia scowled indignantly at the insinuation.

"You can't be too certain," the guard continued, undeterred. "Did she give you anything to eat or drink on the road? Do you feel strange in any way? Nauseated, or like your head is too fuzzy to think?"

"I feel fine," Captain Jia protested. "The only thing making me nauseous is how difficult you're being. She's a shaman, for gods' sakes, not a roadside bandit."

"Shamans are perfectly respectable," Siwon said, his eyes steely.

"And you're ruining a *birthday*," Hongbin wailed. "They only come once a year, you know! This is un*speakably* rude."

Before Mirae's companions could rile the situation further, a familiar voice rang out from the city gates.

"Ah, there you are, cousin!" A young noblewoman came running from the direction of the city, followed closely by a second True Bone royal. "You're late, as usual. And for your own birthday, no less!"

Mirae nearly forgot her disguise and jumped joyfully to see that her friends Jisoo and Yoonhee were somehow, inexplicably, *here*. Thankfully, Captain Jia was calmer, recognizing Mirae's friends and managing to keep the surprise off her own face. She embraced Jisoo and, gesturing toward the guard, said, "I would have been on time if it weren't for this bigoted scoundrel."

"Officer Hwang, causing trouble again, I see." Jisoo casually linked arms with Captain Jia, like they were the best of friends, and narrowed her catlike eyes at the Ma-eum Mage. "What did my grandmother say about hurling baseless accusations against Josan citizens?"

Officer Hwang's jaw tightened. "We've all heard about the attack in the palace. There are rumors of Josan's treachery and how they've even taken our prince. Your grandmother, Commander Song, said it's the border guards' job to not let anything else dangerous occur, and that starts with not letting anyone slip past us who shouldn't."

"If you're going to scrutinize everyone, then do so, but do not single out our Josan neighbors, especially when nothing has been confirmed," Jisoo said, eyes flashing. "I'm certain that's not what my grandmother asked you to do."

Before Officer Hwang could say anything more, a voice from just outside the gates called out, "Let them through."

Officer Hwang turned back toward the gate, where another guard, her rank indicated by the peacock feather sticking out of her hat and the thick band of beads dangling beneath her chin, stood beneath one of the lotus-shaped lanterns. It was clear from the commanding officer's well-lit face that she was all too eager to be rid of the feisty noblewomen, who'd likely been haunting the guardhouse for hours, nitpicking every decision the border guards made.

With a satisfied smirk, Jisoo led Yoonhee, who'd had her nose turned up imperiously the entire time, back toward the city gates, followed by Mirae and her companions. Mirae kept her head down as she passed into Geumju, knowing full well that her white hanbok would only draw more soldiers' eyes to her as she wandered about the city.

The sights and sounds of civilization soon drove all nervous thoughts out of her mind, however. As Mirae entered the city's boisterous main street, she heard a mixture of drunken revelry and loud, unchecked laughter. The smell of spicy rice cakes and marinated meat searing over a fire wafted between the various restaurants and stalls lining the path, reminding Mirae painfully of how long it had been since her last meal.

"This way, Gongju," Jisoo whispered in Mirae's ear, taking her hand. "We must get you to the inn and out of sight as quickly as possible."

Mirae was desperate to know how her friends had managed to find her—and how they had guessed where she was going, no less—but she didn't ask any questions now, not while she was determined to not draw attention to herself. Instead, she followed her friend into a confusing, winding labyrinth of shadowy, less-used streets, the darkness hiding their passing. After several minutes of ducking under drying laundry dangling out of windows and lumpy pearl strings of hanging garlic, Mirae felt Jisoo slow to a more natural pace as they neared what she assumed was the inn.

It was too dark to see the building in detail, and Mirae was far too tired and hungry to do more than stumble toward the cheerily lit interior, where guests were enjoying pots of tea and warm, powdered rice cakes. As soon she stepped out of the dark street, Mirae felt her companions group around her instinctively, shielding her white hanbok from sight with their boldly colored clothes. Before Mirae could say a word, they whisked her away upstairs.

Once everyone was safely inside the room that had been rented for the night, Jisoo and Yoonhee closed the door and embraced Mirae, their cheeks wet.

"We were so worried when you disappeared," Yoonhee bawled. "Everyone's looking for you, and no one knows what on earth is going on. We're so glad you're safe."

Mirae pulled away to look gratefully into the kind faces of her friends. "How did you know where to find me?"

"Areum told us," Jisoo said simply.

Mirae nodded. She should have guessed her oracle-initiate friend would use her foresight to help Mirae from afar. "How are my parents? Has there been any more trouble at the palace? Did Areum explain to the council why I left?"

Jisoo and Yoonhee looked at each other, something passing between them. When Jisoo turned back to Mirae, she sighed heavily.

"Come, there's much we need to tell you."

Yoonhee ran downstairs to bring up food for Mirae and her weary companions while Jisoo settled onto the floor. Mirae, Captain Jia, Hongbin, and Siwon followed suit, leaning in close so Jisoo wouldn't have to raise her voice and risk being overheard.

"I hardly know where to begin," Jisoo admitted, her voice low. "But I suppose I should start with the moment everyone realized you had disappeared into thin air . . . just like Daegun."

Mirae clutched the fabric of her chima. She hadn't thought her disappearance would be linked with Minho's as another tragedy, especially since Wonhwa guards had witnessed her stepping into the shadowy doorway of her own free will. But then she remembered how the events of the past few days might have looked to outsiders—as if Mirae, like her mother, was suffering from delusions caused by the Inconstant Son. The council might have assumed Mirae was no longer in her right mind when she left, effectively abducted by an ancient evil.

Realizing that the only woman left to vouch for her sanity would have been Areum, an uninitiated oracle, Mirae nervously nodded for Jisoo to continue, not daring to look over and see whatever expression was on Captain Jia's face.

"Of course there were many theories discussed in the first few hours," Jisoo said. "Areum did her best to explain that you really are the High Horomancer and you're following the gods' will. Some members of the Hwabaek believed her, but many found her involvement, as a close friend of yours, suspicious."

Yoonhee interrupted briefly as she reentered the room bearing a tray of hot, juicy meat, rice, and cucumber kimchi, surrounded by a bed of lettuce for making wraps. She placed the tray down, then settled beside Jisoo as Mirae and her companions descended on the food like ravenous tigers. While they ate, the two friends continued their report.

"Of course, as soon as Areum was dismissed," Jisoo said, "the council devolved into an hours-long debate. As they do."

"We heard all about it from our mothers," Yoonhee concurred.

Jisoo shook her head sadly. "There were a lot of accusations thrown about, especially without any Sacred Bone women in the room. Some were bold enough to even suggest that you may have been allied with the Josan king in a plot to poison Her Majesty and take over the throne—but you were thwarted, so you ran off to the king for his protection."

"Others were less . . . fantastical in their theories," Yoonhee said, trying to be gentle after seeing the look on Mirae's face. "They seemed to think that the Josan plot ran deeper than they knew, and that all three royal children were in danger. The rest of the council, however, believed what Areum said about you taking matters into your own hands, and all this being the work of Seolla's ancient enemy. Of course, those who believed Areum were also split on their opinions."

Mirae put her food to the side, her appetite leaving her. She sat in silence for a moment, trying to let everything sink in without flying her dragon back to the palace and setting the record straight. Yes, Captain Jia had warned her that there would be political consequences to her actions, but how could the council's opinions have gone so far awry? Mirae looked down at the floor as she spoke, her voice quiet. "So, only a few members of the council believe or support me. Even when our unity and safety as a queendom is under attack."

Jisoo and Yoonhee hesitated, shooting each other another look. When Yoonhee noticed that Mirae had stopped eating, she pushed the tray of food closer.

Mirae ignored the gesture. "What did the council decide to do about . . . me?"

"There were many motions raised," Jisoo said, her voice reassuring. "But the one getting the most support asked that everything be done to wake Her Majesty before making any decisions."

"And the one with the second most support?" Mirae asked, still refusing to look Captain Jia in the eye, even though the other woman had also stopped eating and was looking right at her.

"There was a loud group of councilwomen, led by Sangsin Bada, who believed you were either a Josan turncoat or a reckless, lying fool who can't be trusted. Either way, they called for your dethronement." Jisoo rushed to say more. "*But* that appeal didn't get far."

Sangsin Bada. Of course she would raise her doubts publicly after being thwarted by the crown princess *twice*, much to her embarrassment, no doubt. With her power as head of the council, it was almost surprising that her motion hadn't passed. "What changed the council's minds?"

"They found the Josan dignitary's body," Yoonhee said quietly. Silence fell over the room. Even Hongbin lowered the lettuce wrap he was chomping on to listen more carefully.

"No one thought to search the roofs," Jisoo said, looking as if she might be sick, "until someone noticed dried blood staining the ceiling right above the council's heads. They found his body after that . . . horribly mangled. I was told that if it wasn't for his robes and tag, they wouldn't have recognized him at all."

Yoonhee shuddered. Mirae did, too, but for a different reason. She had no love for the man who'd tried to tempt Minho into running away to Josan before outright kidnapping him with the help of a monster. But she hated to think what his last moments had been like, as he was torn to shreds and dumped above the very throne room he had wanted to burn to the ground.

Brutally betrayed by a sometime ally, the dignitary's body was now a message to the Josan king, a warning of what was to come.

This is what happens to those who cross the Netherking.

"After the body was found," Jisoo continued gently, as if hoping to wipe dark thoughts from Mirae's mind with better news, "enough doubt was cast on your being a Josan traitor, or anything more than a victim of some mystifying supernatural plot, that all talks of dethroning you were abandoned. Instead, everyone is just trying to find out what happened."

"But they know what happened," Hongbin blurted out, drawing surprised glances from those who'd forgotten he was there. "You said Areum told them everything."

"And they already knew about the cage and Gongju mama's calling as High Horomancer," Siwon added, drawing even more surprise from Jisoo and Yoonhee, who hadn't expected the servant to insert himself into their conversation. "In their hearts, they must know Gongju mama is who she says she is, and why she's going after Daegun daegam. The truth is the only thing that makes sense, so why all the posturing?"

Yoonhee, taking her cues from Mirae's acceptance of Siwon's brashness, nodded at his and Hongbin's words. "It makes some sense if you consider one thing: True Bone royals have never, ever been given a chance to challenge the Daughters of the Sacred Bone, or secure the throne for their own line. My mother says this recent tragedy with Daegun is, unfortunately, being seen as an opportunity by the greedy."

Silence fell once more, heavy not just with bad tidings from the palace, but also with the weight of all Mirae had done and still had yet to do. She didn't want to consider turning back, or the idea that Captain Jia had been right all along, but it seemed that the closer she got to Minho, the more the world wanted her to doubt what the gods had put into her heart.

"Enough talk for the night," Captain Jia said, interrupting the silence. "Full bellies and clear minds will guide our next steps in the morning."

Jisoo and Yoonhee nodded and rose to their feet. Jisoo offered Mirae a bow. "Yoonhee and I must return to my grandparents' house before we raise any suspicions. We'll be back in the morning with everything you need to continue your journey."

Yoonhee bowed as well. "I'm glad we found each other, and that you are safe. Please don't let any of the council's nonsense disturb your sleep. Now that a core of corruption has been exposed in the council, you and the Samsin will be able to make things right."

With that, Mirae's friends left quietly, shutting the door behind them. Captain Jia wordlessly began sorting out the bedding, giving Mirae and Hongbin the warmest, thickest blankets to curl up in. Mirae was too overwhelmed to do much more than sit in a stunned silence. Once she laid on her sleeping mat, beside Hongbin's, she turned her back to everyone in the room and closed her eyes, hoping against hope that all the pain she was feeling could be trapped inside her like the Deep Deceiver's milky soul, held in a stony place where no one she loved would ever have to deal with it again. Heavy though her eyes were, Mirae prayed that her dear friends—both new and old—who kept her in their thoughts that night would wake up to see nothing but her strength renewed, a High Daughter to the end.

Not long after Mirae closed her eyes, she felt herself slipping into a tempestuous dream, even though sleep still felt impossibly far away.

A cold breeze ruffled the clothing at her back, causing Mirae to open her eyes. She wasn't on her sleeping mat anymore, or even in the inn. A field of darkness surrounded her, echoing with the low drum of her heartbeat, loud enough to make her ears itch with its vibrations. This time, Mirae knew the way her Sacred Bone Magic sounded and felt. Just as she had when looking for Minho, Mirae began to follow the thrumming sound toward whomever it may lead.

She'd been walking for a while when a ray of light burst through the mist. Mirae covered her eyes as she walked toward it, her feet heavy as a nightmare. As she drew closer to the beam, she realized it was an array of lanterns. Mirae recognized the wall they graced and the dragon pillars at their center.

After all, this was her home.

She slipped through the palace gates and dug her toes into the night-cooled sand of the courtyard. The green-trimmed buildings around her didn't look exactly as she remembered— everything was blushed with the ghostly golden cast of sunset, though there were only cold, distant stars and a slivered moon hanging in the sky.

Mirae didn't see any palace women or True Bone royals wandering about, just Wonhwa guards making their rounds. Though it was the dead of night, no one seemed to be paying her any mind as she walked. For the first time in her life, Mirae, crown princess of Seolla, was free to roam as she pleased.

Mirae took a few tentative steps. None of the passing guards so much as turned their heads. She didn't waste any more time, stepping quickly to the rhythm of her drumming heart in a fast courtyard dance padded by the glistening sand.

The pulsing of her heart grew louder as she reached the royal chambers at the back of the palace proper. A moment later, she reached the source of the Sacred Bone beat that was tethered to her own. There were guards at every door and window to her mother's chambers, but no one stopped Mirae from ghosting through the walls and landing lightly on the warm bamboo floor where her mother and father slept.

No, sleep wasn't the right word for it. Her parents lay still as death. A few palace women sat around them, cooling their fevered brows and combing their sweaty hair. Mirae leaned over the servants' shoulders, looking down upon her mother's unmoving form.

Unadorned with wigs and artfully placed pins, the queen's graying hair was spread out like a silver-striped halo around her head.

"Mother?" Mirae kept her voice low at first, but let it ring louder as it became clear that the palace women couldn't hear her. She was soul-walking, after all. "Mother, please wake up."

There was no answer. As Mirae knelt down, reaching for her mother's arm, she heard a soft beat rapping against the chamber walls. She fell still and listened until it came back—another Sacred Bone heartbeat, this one as lively as her own.

"Hello, queenling. It's nice to see you again."

Mirae kept her eyes on her mother, wishing she could part her mother's parched lips and bid them to speak all of Seolla's dark secrets—the things Mirae desperately needed to know to outwit the man who had appeared at her side. "Did you come here to torment my mother some more? You should leave her be. Your dealings are with me now."

"My dealings, yes." The Netherking's ghostly form, separated from his body, knelt next to Mirae's. "But my carefully planned vengeance has yet to reap its sweetest reward."

"You drove her into despair." Mirae felt the warmth of tears in her eyes, but nothing trickled down her cheeks. "Don't you think she's suffered enough?"

"No, queenling. She hasn't suffered nearly enough." The Netherking reached out to touch Mirae's father's hand, tsking sympathetically. "I do regret the collateral damage, though. Yet another sin to be added to your mother's head."

Mirae felt the bag of beads around her neck, heavy with guilt. Had she left them behind, the physicians might have been able to use them to rouse her parents; after all, she'd seen them work against the Netherking's power before, back in the Garden of Queens. But she'd been too quick to charge after Minho, without fully considering the cost to her family—or to the crown.

"Such dark thoughts rolling about in your little head," the Netherking said, clearly amused by whatever he saw on Mirae's face. "Is your body safe, queenling?"

Mirae felt another jab of guilt, salt on an already festering wound, at the thought of how Captain Jia must feel about Mirae's choices and the dire political fallout she'd tried to help Mirae avoid. "Yes. I have a protector, unlike my mother."

"Good," the Netherking said, ignoring the bitterness in Mirae's tone as he settled more comfortably, as if he and Mirae were two friends sharing a drink. "Just so you know, your body is half sleeping right now. You won't feel refreshed in the morning, but you also won't be too sleep-deprived to continue your search for Minho. I don't recommend we meet like this every night."

"Why would we?" Mirae asked, not even bothering to hide her annoyance. "I didn't ask to meet tonight."

"You made a promise. Or have you already forgotten?" The Netherking's false cheer drained from his face and voice, unsheathing the snakelike foe he really was.

Yes, she had promised to give the Netherking a chance to tell her the sins of her mothers, or at least what he believed them to be; as if anything could ever begin to justify the things he had done from the Deep, or the pain he'd caused every member of Mirae's family.

When you know the truth about their cruelty, nothing will ever be the same.

Mirae turned to look at the Netherking, who wore a haughty smile across his face like another dark, false crown. She knew what his answer would be, but she asked her question anyway: "Will you leave my mother alone after I do as you've asked? Or will you demand even more in return for that?"

"I will demand nothing, for the Liar Queen must be punished. Soon you will understand why." When Mirae merely turned away, her face hardening as she stared down at her poor parents' lifeless forms, the Netherking relented. "You're tired. It's been a long day. I will visit you again tomorrow night, and the next, until you are ready to fulfill your promise."

"So much for not meeting like this every night," Mirae muttered. "Not that I expect anything less from you. You never stop until you get your way, do you?"

"You think you're different?" The Netherking sneered. "Just look at where you are."

Mirae gripped the beads hanging against her chest, wishing more than anything that she could refute the Netherking's comparison. Rushing off to do the gods' will and rescue her brother was a far cry from the Netherking harming anyone in the way of his freedom. But the fact remained that Mirae had made mistakes, possibly terrible ones.

"Noeul's beads," the Netherking said softly, stirring Mirae from her thoughts. "You have them with you."

Mirae lowered her hand from the bag hidden beneath her clothes. "You know about my mother's beads?"

Instead of answering her question, the Netherking asked, "Have you used them? Do you even know what they are?"

Mirae shook her head, hating to reveal yet another thing he knew more about than her. "They were a gift from my mother."

"A gift?" For the first time since she'd met him, the Netherking sounded surprised. "I guess your mother has become far crueler than I realized."

Mirae refused to rise to the bait, certain the Netherking was just trying to drive a wedge between his two most powerful enemies. After all, her mother had already told her not to use the beads until she had explained their power. "I thought you said you were leaving."

"All right, queenling. Have it your way." The Netherking's voice became a whisper right beside her ear. "Though if I were you, I wouldn't touch those beads if my life depended on it."

At that, Mirae finally felt the Netherking's presence fade. She closed her eyes, searching for the Sacred Bone pulse she knew was beating tenderly on another mat, somewhere far from that room. With heavy steps, Mirae soul-walked toward the sound of Hongbin's heart and his gentle snores until the warmth of his closeness melted away the chill of night, banishing the darkness with a hand clasped trustingly in hers.

Chapter
SEVENTEEN

Mirae woke to the smell of steaming rice and beef bone soup. Despite the headache pounding behind her eyes and the unrelenting soreness of what felt like every muscle in her body, she forced herself to sit up and accept the bowl of seolleongtang Hongbin thrust into her hands. Thankfully it had cooled enough not to burn her fingers.

"Noonim, you have to try this, it's so good," Hongbin said around a mouthful of food, having devoured more than half of his own meal, as well as two small bowls of rice. "I think I'll have enough energy to walk all *month* after this."

"Just don't make yourself sick," Siwon said, enjoying his own bowl of soup. "No one but me needs to know how long you take to clear out your system."

"That was *one* time," Hongbin said, shamelessly shoving more food into his mouth. "And only because you let Minho feed me raw octopus of mysterious origin."

"He didn't expect you to actually eat it."

"I'm a goat," Hongbin said, licking his spoon like the animal of his birth year might. "Hyungnim should have known better than to challenge my ability to eat anything. I just hope the restaurants of Josan know what's coming."

Mirae appreciated how effortlessly her brother and his new friend spoke about forging ahead on a mission that felt more and more doomed with each passing moment. When Hongbin was done licking every last drop of broth off his spoon, he turned to Siwon. "I don't suppose you have a bite to spare for a poor, starving prince?"

Siwon covered his breakfast protectively. "You've already had three helpings."

Hongbin patted his belly. "Fine, but if I get hungry before lunchtime, I'm blaming you."

"What you should be blaming me for is the state of your hair," Siwon tsked. He gestured for Hongbin to turn around. "Let me fix it."

Hongbin swatted Siwon's arms aside. "Enough with the servant stuff. We're past that. I mean, we rode a *dragon* together, for gods' sakes!"

"Keep your voices down," Captain Jia said from the corner where she sat, deep in thought; her own soup was barely touched. Hongbin looked longingly at her bowl, but even he didn't dare make a grab for it.

Siwon turned to look at Mirae's breakfast, his dark eyes flitting up to hers. "You should eat before Gunju daegam gets any ideas." His tone softened. "It's a long walk to the closest Josan border town, and you'll need your energy."

Mirae obediently spooned a few bites of the savory beef soup into her mouth as Hongbin stretched out his legs between Siwon and Mirae. "So, tell us about Josan, Siwon. What should we expect, aside from charming encounters with fishers and farmers?"

Siwon set his bowl aside, scraped clean now, much to Hongbin's disappointment. "That depends on where we're going. The capital is very different from the more rural towns."

Mirae swallowed the soup in her mouth, realizing that all eyes in the room were on her, including Captain Jia's. The answer to Siwon's question lay with her—where were they going? Mirae hesitated a moment but reasoned there was no need to hide Minho's location from those who'd come to rescue him beside her. "We're heading to a fortress at the top of White Spine Mountain. That's where the Josan king is keeping Minho."

Siwon raised his eyebrows but gamely offered, "I've heard about that place. It'll be tough getting inside."

"And *reaching* it," Hongbin complained. "If it's at the *top of a mountain*."

"That's right," Siwon said, keeping his eyes on Mirae. "Assuming we want to take the quickest route, we'll have to cut across the nearest green-tea farms and continue along the river."

Mirae nodded. That was the exact path she'd taken with the Netherking when following her Sacred Bone connection to Minho. "Are you familiar with the area we'll be traversing?"

"I've traveled there a few times." Siwon looked away. "My mother helped a lot of people there."

"So, fresh fish, green-tea fields, and spiritual rituals await us in Josan," Hongbin said contentedly. "What a marvelous place. I'm actually a little happy we're going there."

"This isn't a vacation, Gunju." Captain Jia's voice, though quiet, cut through the chatter. "Not only did men from Josan conspire to kidnap your brother, but they also allied themselves with a man whose actions may have cost Gongju the crown. Josan is the most dangerous place for you to be. And don't forget that magic is illegal there—if Gongju or I slip up even a little bit, we'll all be executed without question. And that's if they *don't* discover our true identities first."

A tense silence fell over the room, broken only by a knock at the door. Captain Jia rose warily to her feet but breathed a sigh of relief after seeing Jisoo and Yoonhee standing in the doorway, bundles in their arms. She stepped aside and let them in.

Mirae's friends set down the packages they carried: lightly dyed linen and hemp tunics, and wooden poles with neatly wrapped sacks tied at the ends. Provisions and disguises for the journey ahead.

"Security at the border has tightened considerably," Yoonhee said, slightly out of breath from lugging her parcels across the city. "The guards best at identifying spies have all been stationed at the Kirin Gate to Josan, so we knew your current disguises wouldn't work. They'll spot a Ma-eum illusion or a Jade Witch guise a mile away. Dressing as Commander Song's servants is your best option."

"And we brought you new tags," Jisoo said, also out of breath. "These belonged to former servants who went on to become soldiers or scholars, which is actually very common in my grandmother's household. Anyway, they all ended up getting new tags made, so no one will miss these. When the guards see that you're a part of my grandmother's household, they shouldn't give you any trouble."

Hongbin, Siwon, and Captain Jia accepted their new clothes and identification, and set about changing while Jisoo and Yoonhee came to sit by Mirae.

"Someone didn't sleep well last night," Yoonhee said ruefully, looping a stray strand of hair behind Mirae's ear.

"I seem to be suffering from a . . . recurring nightmare of sorts." Mirae smiled bravely. "But don't worry, stubbornness runs deeper in my family than magic. I'll be fine."

"You're more than stubborn," Yoonhee said. "You're the most powerful Daughter of the Sacred Bone ever born!"

"But you are also very stubborn," Jisoo teased. "It's part of your charm."

When Mirae finally cracked a smile, her friends visibly relaxed. Jisoo took Mirae's hand. "Areum wanted us to give you something before you leave. She said you will need it."

With a nod from Jisoo, Yoonhee reached gingerly into a hidden pocket, pulling out something round wrapped in thick layers of silk. She handed it to Mirae with both hands, her arms extended in a way that made it clear she was glad to be rid of it.

Mirae knew what her friend had given her even before she unwrapped it—the Deep Deceiver's relic, boldly stolen from the palace. With each layer of silk Mirae peeled off, the seong-suk glowed more and more like a blue-and-white star on a bed of soft lotus leaves.

Mirae understood why Yoonhee was afraid of this ancient item, which could kill her with a touch. But Mirae—and Areum, it seemed—knew the relic would recognize the blood of a High Daughter. Everyone in the room gasped as Mirae grabbed the blue seong-suk with her bare hand, holding it up to the light. The soul within it swirled joyfully, like it was glad to be back where it belonged.

Mirae turned gratefully to her friends. "This was too much to ever expect," she said. "If we survive this, I will tell the council you were following my orders when you took this, so the greater punishment will fall on me."

"You will survive," Jisoo said. She and Yoonhee both raised their chins proudly. "You will come back victorious and teach the council to never doubt you again."

"We are doing what others wish they could," Yoonhee added. "Our mothers would help you in a heartbeat, if we allowed them to take such a risk. You're not alone, Gongju. The sacrifices of the people in this room speak louder than the vanities of the council."

Mirae looked around, at Hongbin and Siwon making up intricate backstories for their new identities, and Captain Jia, who looked as if neither her body nor her soul had slept in days. Still, she had stayed by Mirae's side through the night, neither betraying her to the authorities nor browbeating her into returning to the palace. Even she trusted Mirae to make up her own mind.

Mirae took one more look at the seong-suk, at the soul of an ancestor who'd given everything so Mirae could be where she was now, and took a deep breath.

"It's time to finish what we started."

As soon as Mirae stepped outside, her eyes struggled to adjust to the bombardment of light—both from the morning sun and the magical barrier rising over the city to the west. Dimmed during the night to allow Seolla's citizens to slumber peacefully, the opalescent beam and prancing kirin now brightened with the day, filling the entire horizon with a luminescence that made everything in Geumju glitter—from the beaded fineries on noblewomen's gowns to the dewy rooftops dripping crystals from their gables.

Jisoo and Yoonhee took the lead toward the Kirin Gate to Josan, followed by Hongbin, Siwon, and Captain Jia, all disguised as servants and carrying the long-poled packs of provisions. Mirae, dressed in her shaman hanbok, tailed them all closely, trying to avoid eye contact with any guards she passed. Jisoo and Yoonhee had warned her that the road to Noksan, the closest Josan border town, would be packed with merchants and buyers heading in both directions. There wouldn't be an opportunity to change clothes on the road, so although Mirae's current disguise might draw a Seollan soldier's eyes, she had to remain a false shaman if she hoped to enter Josan and not alarm its citizens with the aura of magic that surrounded her.

The citizens of Geumju, on the other hand, were bombarded with magic every day; even some of the Sacred Bone variety, like the magical barrier stretching into the heavens. No one batted an eye at the way Mirae "felt" to them. Here every woman carried magic in the puffs of cosmetic rice powder on her face or the woven threads resting against her skin.

Perhaps that was why Jisoo and Yoonhee, instead of ducking into side streets or narrow alleys like they had the night before, opted to lead Mirae and her companions through the busiest roads, where they could blend in with all the morning commerce. Even Mirae's white shaman hanbok seemed to mix seamlessly with the pale linens worn by passing servants or young scholars, sent out to buy more paper and ink.

The streets grew busier still the closer they drew to the Kirin Gate and the city's market, filled with merchants trying to entice passersby with their wares. Mirae had never been to a marketplace before. Fine silks and jewelry had always been brought into the palace for her appraisal, or given as gifts she could not refuse. As they passed through the main market square of Geumju, however, Mirae could see why this border town, one of the largest in Seolla, was called the City of Gold.

Even without the light of the barrier looming over the city, everything around Mirae vied for her attention with one of thousands of enchantments. The draped silks on display fluttered in the wind like boundless rainbows moving on the wings of myth. Golden kirin, phoenixes, and majestic cranes spiraled about on the hems and bellies of the fabrics they were embroidered onto, gilded embellishments that came to life in their dance with the morning wind.

Once Mirae was past the fluttering reaches of the market's fabric row, the silks seemed to part like a curtain to reveal the rest of the marketplace's colorful wares, everything accented with gold. Greenware ceramics of all shapes and sizes stood like jade statues on low tables—among them sat narrow-necked pots resembling cranes and playful pitchers fashioned after whimsical creatures that were half dragon, half fish. Gold and silver cups dotted these displays as well, their ornate stems complemented by geometric patterns stamped into their sides and rims.

What Mirae saw most of, however, were glittering stands of jewelry. Some of the pieces on display were made of precious stones or copious amounts of jade, while others were permanently enchanted by Jade Witches to only *look* expensive, or sported brilliantly colored glass beads instead. These items were far less expensive than their extravagant counterparts, making them the clear favorites of the non-noble maidens flocking around the stands of cheap, lovely trinkets. Meanwhile, the wealthy, who had shrewder eyes and deeper pockets, negotiated expertly over the exorbitant prices of precious metals and fine silks enchanted to shine with unparalleled beauty that was sure to make their new owners the talk of the town.

Still, regardless of their enchantments, all sparkled alike: broad chestlaces with red or blue strings of beads accented by slim gold bars; earrings with thick gold bands and tinkling chains of leaf-shaped mirrors that either grazed the jawline or dangled down to the shoulders; gold-based binyeo and other hair ornaments topped with pearls and garnet peonies. No matter where Mirae looked, magic and craftsmanship gave the world around her an unearthly glow meant to imitate the endless majesty of the heavens.

Mirae stared at everything with awe. She had been surrounded by beauty and luxury at the palace her entire life, but here, among her people, magic was less of a dutiful power and more a way of life. Mirae couldn't help but feel a pang of jealousy at how effortlessly magic was used to do nothing more than make people happy. And yet it didn't seem as if the busy world around her realized the gift it had been given—a wealth of wonder that Mirae had been born to protect. In fact, looking around, Mirae could see her demanding royal life held up as a grand ideal, based on the replicas of her and her mother's costumery that floated about: Binyeo with leaping fish at their curled ends, cleverly carved to resemble the coiled dragons only the royal family could wear. Pronged dwik-koji and fluttering ddeoljam, sometimes with red and green glass flowers embedded into them instead of garnets and jade—lotus and peony silhouettes that Mirae and her mother had worn at festivals, officiating from a distance.

It was a little unsettling, catching sight of these ornaments, tokens of adoration glittering in every corner of the marketplace, flashing and streaming off the women in the city. Although no one sported an entire royal ensemble, it was strange to see piecemeal displays of her Sacred Bone status scattered among her people.

But the most disquieting thing Mirae saw was the clear difference between the gaudily costumed nobles, mimicking her finery, and the non-royal witches and mages who treasured a few comparatively simple ornaments. The former walked unimpeded through the crowd, followed by an entourage of servants. The latter made sure to stay out of their superiors' way, bowing whenever they failed to do so. Watching all this, Mirae couldn't help but realize how easy it was for the power and worth of a person to be decided by how much magic she wore and flaunted, rather than how much she *actually* wielded, or the good she did with it.

"We're nearly there," Yoonhee whispered into Mirae's ear, pulling Mirae out of her thoughts. "Stick close enough for Jisoo to berate the guards if they give you any trouble."

Mirae nodded as Yoonhee pulled ahead quickly, so as not to draw attention to either of them. As Mirae followed her friends, moving closer and closer to the Kirin Gate to Josan, she wondered for the first time what it would be like to walk among people who rejected magic and all the status—or perceptions of power—it afforded the people of Seolla.

Those quiet musings quickly subsided, however, when Mirae and her companions finally reached the magical barrier and the massive Kirin Gate. As the crowd around them organized into makeshift lines, Mirae glanced at all the people who, like her, were waiting to enter Josan—merchants from both sides of the border, and officials waiting impatiently with an entourage of scholarly assistants. None of the Seollan travelers seemed even remotely nervous about entering Josan, a land that rejected their entire way of life.

Even the nobles who were milling about seemed unconcerned. Some rode in palanquins as if they were royalty, but Jisoo had assured Mirae that the walk to Noksan, Josan's closest border town, was one that many young noblewomen made on their own two feet to "work up an appetite" before lunch and a big day of shopping. There were enough young women linking arms and laughing together, carefree, for Mirae to see that that was true.

Mirae, on the other hand, felt sick to her stomach, knowing that if her disguise didn't work and she was caught sneaking into Josan, the Hwabaek's already low opinion of her would be the least of her worries . . . if she even survived to face their wrath.

Once she and her companions had joined what looked to be the main line leading out of the city, Mirae distracted herself from the ever-looming guard checkpoint by studying, up close,

Seolla's impressive barrier—a landmark of power that would someday be her duty to maintain.

Unlike the sun, the opalescent beam across the heavens didn't hurt the eyes when looked upon, making it easy to watch the projection of antlered kirin prancing as if on a stage, their deer-like bodies lithe and nimble as dragons even as they gazed out at the city with sage wisdom in their white-hot eyes, which could incinerate an intruder in seconds.

The line in front of Mirae was moving efficiently, and before she knew it, she was standing in front of the enormous haetae flanking the gates—statues of horned lions that shouldered the weight of Seolla's deep stone walls and its endless barrier of light. The lions grinned benevolently at those under their protection, even as their torso-size teeth dared anyone to enter or leave Seolla with thoughts of treachery in their hearts.

Or, in Mirae's case, thoughts of entering a treacherous country that had kidnapped her brother and would paint her rescue mission as an act of war if she were caught.

Ahead, Jisoo and Yoonhee had reached the front of the line, their necessary separation from the Josan shaman making them unable to see or mollify Mirae's growing agitation. Jisoo flashed her tag confidently, though the guards seemed to recognize their commander's granddaughter on sight. "I'm sending my servants to Noksan to replenish my grandmother's tea supplies."

The guards—one a Ma-eum Mage and the other a Jade Witch—bowed and glanced briefly at the tags Hongbin, Siwon, and Captain Jia held before waving them through.

"You didn't have to come down here yourself for this, Lady Jisoo," the Jade Witch said.

"Oh, I think I did," Jisoo said, her voice authoritative. "I've heard that several of your peers have been singling out Josan citizens and harassing them."

"Not on our watch," the other guard said, bowing again.

Jisoo pulled Yoonhee back, making way for Mirae. "I'll be the judge of that."

The Jade Witch guard in front of Mirae gestured for her identification, barely noting her shaman robes. When Mirae handed over her forged tag, with thankfully steady hands, the guard scanned it with shrewd eyes before giving it back. She kept her voice unfailingly polite as she recited, "Please be advised that for the next few weeks, Josan travelers will need to have documentation verifying their reasons for entering Seolla. Unless you have any questions, please go in peace."

Mirae bowed as the guards moved on to the next person in line, leaving her free to enter her sovereign state. But Mirae stopped in front of the gates, hesitant even now to break one of the biggest and only laws enacted against her as crown princess.

Mirae's fear of impending war and the mayhem that could result from the act of defiance she was about to commit subsided as two warm hands briefly grabbed and squeezed one of hers. Although Jisoo and Yoonhee didn't dare do more than that, Mirae briefly held their gazes and felt herself flooded with gratitude for their support and the sacrifices they had made to help her get this far.

Mirae took a deep breath and stepped into Josan, remembering the importance of her mission. Once she walked out past the gates, she saw Hongbin, Siwon, and Captain Jia waiting for her, and heard Jisoo calling loudly as if to her servants, "You have everything you need to retrieve our beloved . . . tea. You're the only ones who can, and we believe in you! Don't ever forget how special you are!"

Mirae turned back and saw her friends offering her enthusiastic but discreet waves before returning home. Mirae smiled despite herself, and when she reached her companions, felt the rest of the nervousness inside her melt away at the sight of them: Hongbin, looking around the Josan countryside with wonder; Captain Jia, a pillar of strength who made Mirae feel safe despite the dangerous nature of their mission; and Siwon, whose warm, dark eyes and healing wounds reminded Mirae that she was never meant to do this alone.

Once reunited, Mirae and her companions turned wordlessly toward Noksan, keeping their heads down as they walked. As they joined the throng traveling the main road, they strode alongside cheery Seollan visitors and angry Josan merchants who, just as the guards had warned, had been turned away at the border and were now muttering among themselves about suddenly needing specific documents to enter the land of their "tyrannical overlords" in order to earn their livelihoods. From the murmurs of outrage throughout the dismissed crowd, it was clear that they found this mistreatment to be an unsurprising punishment that was nevertheless grossly unfair—missing prince or no.

"Typical Seolla," one of the merchants spat. "One of their spoiled royal brats gets lost in the woods or something, and now *my* kids have to go hungry."

"For all their claims of keeping us a happy, prosperous nation," the merchant's companion agreed, "you don't have to look any further than their two-faced, ridiculous gate to know what they really think of us."

Mirae clenched her fists at the insolence she was hearing, knowing she couldn't even think about setting the record straight and risking people seeing through her disguise. Instead, she glanced back at the Kirin Gate, wondering how anyone could possibly find it appalling.

After all, the magnificent barrier had always made her feel safe—until it was breached by a prince-carrying monster whose magic knew no borders. But here on the Josan side, the wall no longer shone as a beacon of beauty and hope. Instead, the heavenly opalescent beam and kirin dancing in the light were replaced with a gray, smoky mist not unlike the tendrils of shadow at the doorway to the cage of the Inconstant Son. It was little wonder the citizens of Josan despised the barrier she had always experienced as a radiant wonder.

Mirae pulled her eyes away from the dark barrier and looked over at Siwon; she could tell he, too, was doing his best to ignore the rude comments of the disgruntled merchants. As she studied the rippling waves in his hair and the gleaming tan of his skin that made him blend in seamlessly with his countrymen, she wondered for the first time what it had been like for him, the son of a Josan shaman on this side of the Kirin Gate, to become someone who served the prince of a "tyrannical" nation. Did he once harbor resentment toward her queendom? How did he feel when he came looking for work and saw the differences between his homeland and the gaudy luxury of Seolla?

As he always seemed to do, Siwon sensed Mirae's gaze and looked over at her. She saw none of the answers to her questions in his dark eyes, but rather a face calm and determined. "We did it, Gongju mama," he said with a nod. "Daegun daegam is less than a day away. We're going to reach him in time."

Mirae nodded and smiled back at Siwon, who, whatever his past, trusted her implicitly. After all, while the people of Josan might be innocent, and thus unfairly affected by Minho's disappearance, their king had stolen something from Mirae, from Seolla, and she was going to get it back. With her friends by her side, they, like every other Seollan citizen following the path to Noksan, passed among the angry Josan crowds without saying a word.

The City of the Green Mountain was aptly named for the rolling fields that made it the largest exporter of green tea on the peninsula. While Seolla had long been the peninsula's main exporter of metals like gold and iron, and the northern nomads of Baljin were suppliers of horses and lumber, it was in the fields and rivers of Josan that grains, fruits, and fish were found aplenty, providing the peninsula with food and employing many in the profitable industries of farming and fishing.

Mirae had already witnessed some of Josan's endless glistening rows of tea trees when soul-walking to Minho's prison. The most notable thing about Josan, however, was the eerie, echoing silence of a land without magic. She felt again like she was trapped in a narrow-necked jar, unable to reach the bottom, and the sensation only grew stronger with every step she took away from the barrier.

She could tell Captain Jia felt it, too, from the way the captain kept looking around, as if the sudden stillness in the air portended the attack of a hidden enemy. Every now and then she would also tap her palms against her ears, as if there had been a change in pressure that made her head uncomfortable. Thankfully, for both the captain and Mirae, Hongbin created a welcome distraction by filling the magic-less silence with endless questions for Siwon about Josan's most eligible bachelors.

Mirae tuned out the gossip after a while, instead turning her attention to something she'd avoided thinking about ever since leaving Wol Sin Lake—her Sacred Bone connection to Minho. She'd been reluctant to soul-walk to him again, afraid that another glimpse of her brother's torture at the hands of Kimoon would enrage her and make her do something irrational, jeopardizing his rescue.

Now that she'd made it across the border, however, she didn't want to wait any longer. She needed to know if Minho was all right.

Mirae wasn't sure she could connect with Minho while she was walking, but decided to attempt it nonetheless—she didn't want to waste time by stopping for a break. Without closing her eyes, Mirae pressed a thumb against her wrist, finding the heartbeat pulsing there. Then, just as the Netherking had taught her, she listened for a heart beating like hers, the tether leading to Minho. She expected it to be difficult, since on her last attempt, she'd struggled to maintain a connection in the magic-less emptiness of Josan.

But having done it once, finding Minho again was easier. As Mirae's feet followed her companions, her spirit seemed to soar as high as her rainbow dragon, the jade-green fields of Josan and the sky-blue river spread before her like a jeweled map below. In the distance stood White Spine Mountain and the peaks that surrounded it, long teeth against the horizon, pale with sunshine.

She followed Minho's pulse to the fortress that held him captive, diving down just as she had before, nearly into the foundations of the fortress, where her brother sat in his cell.

He was awake, sitting against the wall with his knees drawn to his chest. He seemed much worse than before, looking increasingly like one of the mul gwisin. The black water in his veins had spread throughout his body, even running up his face like dark, swollen bulges of lightning. His red-shot eyes stared across the room, blank and unseeing.

Mirae sat beside him on the floor, knowing he couldn't hear, see, or feel her, but still, she wanted to be close.

She stifled a sob, trying to be brave for Minho's sake. "I'm coming, orabeoni," she whispered. "Just hold on. Stay strong. The people you love are coming to save you."

Minho gave no response, but in the corner of one puffy red eye, Mirae saw a small inky bead gather and slip down his face—a single black water tear.

"Gongju!"

Mirae's soul snapped back into her body. Dizzy and disoriented from the abrupt end to her soul flight, she looked around and realized she had stumbled, falling to her knees on the road. Captain Jia was beside her, pulling her to her feet.

"Gongju, are you all right?" Captain Jia brushed off Mirae's knees and looked her over with concern. "Are you ill?"

Siwon and Hongbin were beside Mirae in an instant, mirroring Captain Jia's worry. Mirae swayed on her feet, light-headed, as she stammered, "We need to hurry. Minho . . . he won't last much longer."

Captain Jia paled but nodded briskly, ever the soldier. "Siwon, how far are we from White Spine Mountain?"

Siwon wasted no time answering. "We should reach Noksan within the hour if we hurry. That's the fastest route to the fields, which we'll cross to reach the mountain by dawn."

"Maybe we should buy horses," Hongbin suggested, looking in the direction of the mountains, eyes wide with alarm. "We'll move a lot faster."

"Horses are expensive," Siwon said. He reached out to help Captain Jia steady Mirae. "And none of us brought any money."

"What about my dragon?" Mirae asked, lucidity returning as her nausea subsided. Minho only had two days left before the black water mutilations became permanent—and they still needed to transport him back to Wol Sin Lake. "We could go somewhere out of sight and then ride my dragon to Minho."

"No, Gongju." Captain Jia grabbed Mirae's arm, her voice firm. "We cannot use any magic in Josan. We can't risk being caught and having the entire army after us before we've even reached Daegun. We might start a war. They might move him to another location. Besides, the fortress will be heavily armed—we must be stealthy."

Mirae studied the troubled looks on her companions' faces; they depended on her to lead them, and cared about saving Minho as much as she did. She breathed deeply, composing herself for their sakes before pulling away from the captain. "Okay, we'll stick to the plan. But no more breaks if we can help it. We have to move quickly."

Once everyone nodded in agreement, faces steeled with determination, she turned and walked swiftly toward Noksan, as fast as she could without drawing every eye on the road. As she sped closer to the mountains in the distance, she thought of nothing but Minho's black water tear and his haunting, unseeing eyes.

Just as Siwon had said, Mirae could see the clay rooftops of Noksan within the hour. Soon after they came into view, the smells of the city reached Mirae's nose.

At first it was thick, smoky incense wafting through the air, smelling strongly of pine and lavender, but eventually, the smell of food and sweet desserts made the young noblewomen traveling alongside them on the road swoon with anticipation.

Their mood soon dampened, however, as they drew close enough to hear what the guards at the entrance to Noksan were shouting over the heads of the approaching crowd.

"By order of His Majesty, there is to be no use of magic within Josan. *No exceptions.* If you have any enchanted items with you, turn back now. Anyone discovered with magical objects or found to be using magic will be arrested immediately and put on trial. The punishment for these crimes is death. This is the law."

While most of the people around Mirae didn't seem fazed by the guards' announcement, having heard these threats before, the bag of her mother's zodiac beads suddenly felt heavy as river stones around Mirae's neck, and the two Sacred Bone relics on her person threatened to burn holes through the secret pockets of her hanbok. Everything about her was magic, down to her bones. She could only pray her shaman disguise was enough to mask most of it. Mirae forced herself to slow her pace to match everyone around her. With how close she was getting to Minho, she really couldn't afford to bring any attention to herself—especially not to who she was and the things she carried.

As Mirae passed the Noksan guards, who were taking turns shouting the same warning about magic over and over, she could have sworn that a few of them turned to look at her, tracking her movements. She didn't want to risk them seeing the nervousness in her eyes by returning their stares, so she strode onward as confidently as she could, facing straight ahead. Thankfully, they let her through without incident.

Mirae breathed a sigh of relief as she entered the city with her companions. Just past the entrance, a throng of people stood in their path—a bottleneck of visitors that forced Mirae to stop and take in her first Josan town.

Just as on the road, the smells hit her first. The aroma of spicy tteok and boiled eggs stirred continuously to keep from scorching reminded Mirae of her hunger—especially when mingled with hotteok frying in a pan. One of the doughy pancakes must have burst open—or perhaps the vendor had allowed it to break on purpose, because the scents of sweetly burning sugar, cinnamon, and finely chopped nuts alone were keeping people flocked around his stall.

A variety of other treats vied for Mirae's attention as she slipped through gaps in the throng—steamed buns and dumplings filled with what smelled like soy sauce–marinated beef, cabbage, and spicy pork. Mirae's stomach grumbled louder than the bamboo spoons scraping food into wooden bowls, but she forged ahead, her companions close on her heels.

Once Mirae had worked herself free of the mass of people at the entrance to Noksan, she found herself in the town's marketplace. Though it was smaller than the one in Geumju, there were more than enough stalls for visitors and Josan locals alike to crowd around and browse through excitedly.

Mirae turned to Siwon, who kept pace beside her. Sensing her unspoken question, he pointed through the already-packed street, loud with late-morning commerce. "This road cuts through the city, right to the back entrance. It's the most direct path to the fields."

Mirae nodded and forged ahead, her companions keeping close. Though she kept a steady pace, skirting groups of shoppers and merchants deftly, it was impossible not to spare some glances at the busyness around her, here in the heart of her first Josan city.

Where Seolla's market stalls had glittered shamelessly to attract customers, the merchants of Josan let their wares speak for themselves. There was no gold or fanfare anywhere; in fact, the most unassuming displays were the ones with the longest lines, as if everyone knew which vendors were the masters of their trade by word of mouth or reputation alone.

It was easy to see why so many Seollan shoppers had come to Noksan, attracted by the promise of a delicious meal and their choice of novel goods, many of which were made by inimitable craftspeople to be used, rather than put on display.

Of course Mirae spotted the lacquered chests inlaid with mother of pearl or bronze accents for which Josan was famous, but she was far more drawn to the highly textured stone and clay ceramics: perfectly round and stamped with floral, geometric, honeycomb, or ridged designs. Small covered jars for incense or cosmetics were expertly inlaid with silver plum blossoms, heralds of spring and hardships overcome.

Everything Mirae caught a glance of was designed after nature, from the carvings in pottery to the simple yet elegant embroidery on silks dyed soothing green or blushing pink. The faces and forms of lotuses, various waterfowl, fish, and even mountain ranges graced the surfaces of multitextured wares designed with purpose and heart. In fact, everything in Noksan was so naturally, subtly beautiful—including the lightly tanned, rosy-cheeked merchants with charmingly freckled skin—that the pale, powdered faces of young Seollan women, who'd had to forego their Ma-eum makeup, looked overdone and cakey compared to the clear, bare faces of the natives of Josan.

In fact, the unembellished beauty of Josan's people made Mirae wonder why she'd always felt such a need to enhance her own face, hair, and clothes in public—or even why she needed to be surrounded with enchanted items at the palace, as if magic were the only thing that made an object worthy of the crown princess's gaze. Here in Josan, where nothing was allowed to benefit from spells, life went on just the same. Different, but just as beautiful, and far less pretentious.

Mirae's heart grew heavy at the thought of the two bordering nations, who stood to learn much from each other, going to war instead of sharing the things that made them special, all because of the Josan king's treachery. Finding Minho wasn't just about saving him—but saving all the lives and the unreached potential on the peninsula.

Mirae was so distracted by her thoughts that she was forced to stop short as a group of people suddenly appeared in her path—two somber Noksan soldiers and a woman dressed just like Mirae in white shaman robes.

The woman bowed to Mirae. "Hello, I'm Noonsol, the local tangol. You have no idea how happy I am that these guards spotted you. Please come with us—we need your help."

Chapter
EIGHTEEN

Mirae just stood there, speechless, not at all sure how a shaman was supposed to act in a situation like this. Thankfully, Siwon stepped forward to speak on her behalf.

"What seems to be the matter?" he asked.

"I'm sure you've heard," Noonsol said, not batting an eye at Mirae's "servant" handling her affairs, "but there have been gwisin sightings all over the country. Here in Noksan, it's particularly bad. I've done what I can to put these poor spirits to rest, but to no avail. We need the help of a kangsin shaman."

Before Mirae could deny being one of those, Siwon quickly interjected, "We're actually on our way to another kut. Perhaps we can visit you after?"

The shaman bowed her head regretfully. "The kangsin shaman who was supposed to help us was waylaid. Please, we've been maintaining our kut for ten days without success, and I'm not sure how much longer my assistants and I can continue."

"I understand, but our other appointment needs us just as urgently—"

"We can offer you horses," one of the Noksan guards said, bowing. "We will make sure you reach your next kut on time."

"And our magistrate will pay you handsomely," the other guard said, holding out a purse that looked heavy with coins. "He would have come and requested your services in person, but ever since our kingdom's dignitary was found murdered in Seolla, all officials near the border have been asked to remain in their homes."

"As you can see, this town, this *kingdom*, needs your help," Noonsol said, holding her arms out beseechingly. "Assassinations, missing princes, and now gwisin terrorizing our citizens at night? Our people need some peace of mind. Besides, it is against our principles to turn away those in need."

Mirae could tell from the look on Siwon's face that he'd run out of ideas on how to argue his way out of the situation—at least without risking Mirae's cover. He glanced at Captain Jia and Hongbin, who looked equally stumped, before sighing and bowing resignedly. "You're right, of course. We'll gratefully accept the horses, but we have no need for any other payment. We ask instead that we are allowed to continue on our way as quickly as possible. As you said, there are many towns in need of our services."

The shaman smiled. "Thank you. We'll prepare the kut arena for you right away. Please, follow me."

As Noonsol and the guards began leading the way, Mirae leaned over to whisper into Siwon's ear, "Why didn't you tell her I was a tangol, and can't help?"

"Because you're out here traveling," Siwon whispered back, "not working in a stationary or local capacity. That means you must be a kangsin shaman. In any case, you would be obligated to help no matter what kind of shaman you are, and there's not enough time to teach you the songs or dances you're supposed to know as a tangol."

So gods-possessed shaman it was. Mirae had no other choice. "But I don't know how to act like I'm in a divine trance. What am I supposed to do?"

"Yes, what were you thinking?" Captain Jia hissed, catching up to them. "Do you know how dangerous this is?"

"It would have drawn more suspicion if we *didn't* go with them," Siwon shot back. "And we'll be getting horses out of this, which will help us make up for lost time."

Though that was true, it did little to ease the sting of Mirae's panic. As Noonsol led the way out of the city toward the fields surrounding Noksan, Mirae asked again, "How am I supposed to pull this off? I know nothing about impersonating a kangsin shaman."

"Don't worry, I've seen hundreds of possessions," Siwon said, giving Mirae a reassuring look. "I'll tell you how to fake one."

As they walked farther from Noksan proper and out into the open fields beyond it, Siwon's frantic whispering in Mirae's ear was overshadowed by the percussive sound of janggu and gongs echoing in the wind. The source of all the drumming was soon visible—a group of women dressed in shaman clothes just like Mirae's were gathered in a square section of the field, separated from the rest of the city grounds by painted gold lines filled in with sand. Around them rested a variety of musical instruments, swords, and bells. Mirae gulped as she and her companions were led right to the clearing, where desperate and hopeful-looking townsfolk had gathered to watch.

Noonsol came to stand beside Mirae once they reached the kut arena. "Thank you again for doing this. I'll tell my spirit daughters to repurify the land for your patron god, so you can begin as soon as the sun sets. How shall I announce you?"

Mirae had to clear her throat a few times to get out the words Siwon had taught her to say, and the name she had chosen for her fake identity. "I am Shaman Suhee, and I speak for the Samsin, the three grandmother goddesses."

Noonsol bowed excitedly at the news that such powerful deities—judiciously chosen by Siwon so Mirae wouldn't have to fake a high-energy possession from one of the more youth-ful gods—would be helping her solve Noksan's gwisin problem. True to her word, Noonsol quickly set about preparing the arena with her assistants.

Two of the women approached Mirae with a white durumagi and a paper kokkal for her head. While the overcoat and hat were put in place, Mirae heard the music played by the other assistants change abruptly.

While before they had been beating a steady rhythm on their janggu, now they raised their arms higher with each strike, enter-ing into a new percussive song that paired their drums' pulses with a lithe, energetic dance. Their nimble steps sent the sand within the golden arena flying like sprays of water, while the pads of their feet left half-moon imprints all over the earth, pale in the dust.

Noonsol grabbed a cluster of bells with her right hand and began jingling them to the rhythm of the hourglass drums. She closed her eyes and spoke, her voice loud: "Before the gods, ancestors, and people of this city, I declare the next stage of our kut. We invite the gods of the mountains, the rivers, and all distant places to witness our devotion. With their eyes upon us, we will purge this city of the pitiful spirits who plague it."

Caught up in her trance, Noonsol entered the gold-lined arena as the assistants around Mirae retreated back to their posts. Mirae turned immediately to her companions, who'd never left her side. "Please tell me one of you has come up with a brilliant idea to get me out of this."

"Brilliant, no," Hongbin said regretfully. "Nothing that doesn't require magic, anyway."

"Which is not an option," Captain Jia reminded them, glancing at the Noksan guards gathered to hold the crowds back at a respectful distance. If Mirae didn't prove convincing enough in her ruse, it wouldn't take the guards long to react to cries of fraud—or something worse.

Mirae looked at Siwon nervously and asked, "Are you sure this will work?"

Siwon nodded, offering Mirae a tense smile. "No one has any reason to disbelieve you. The people gathered here, *my* people, *want* to hear from the gods. Think of it as your chance to speak to their hearts as their future queen. After all, they'll be listening to every word you say."

Mirae nodded. He was right—this was a rare opportunity, and after seeing the disparities between Seolla and Josan for herself, words were already forming in her heart. As Mirae considered what to say during the kongsu, the divine message she would deliver during her fake possession, she and her companions watched the kut unfold.

From what she'd learned from Siwon, Mirae knew that the purification ritual was meant to expel any evil spirits or impurities in or near the arena, paving the way for the gods to enter both it and Mirae's body. While two assistant shamans danced to the beat of their own drums, looking like birds caught in a wind that pulsed like the tides, Noonsol chanted all the names of local demons who might have returned with each shake of her bells, commanding them to leave. The remaining two assistants ladled water mixed with salt, ash, and red pepper flakes out of a barrel, casting the purifying mixture onto the ground. Then they grabbed baskets of dried fish that rested outside the kut arena. With performative gusto, they ripped off the fish's heads and flung them far into the surrounding fields, luring away any lingering demons who refused to leave the sacred grounds until their hunger was satisfied.

Once all the fish had been torn and tossed, Noonsol seemed to snap out of her chanting trance with a jerk. The other performers stopped as well, and an almost eerie silence fell over the field. Noonsol wordlessly walked toward the gong on the far side of the gold-lined sand and rang it, letting the deep note resound.

"The land is once again pure," she announced to the crowd. "No demons or evil spirits remain to defile our work. It's time to soothe our beloved, restless dead once and for all."

According to Siwon, Noonsol would now begin an invocation to the gods who could help with this task. With a shudder, Mirae recalled her own encounter with the mul gwisin, restless spirits who'd lived in torment for many years. She promised herself that she would do everything in her power to help the haggard moon gwisin and her drowned followers finally find some peace, even if it required commissioning a kut like this one.

Noonsol waited solemnly as her assistants reset the stage for the invocation. Mirae watched, fascinated, as a bamboo mat was set before Noonsol and a large pot of water was placed on top of it. The assistant shamans then handed Noonsol a large, double-edged blade. Without warning or hesitation, Noonsol held it up to her face and licked one of the sharp edges, eliciting gasps from the crowd—and from Mirae, who wished Siwon had given her some kind of warning that invoking the gods required more than simply praying to them. While Mirae was relieved that no blood came pouring out of the shaman's mouth, that feeling was short-lived.

Again without hesitation, Noonsol hiked up her chima and pressed the blade against her leg, rocking it like a storm-tossed boat across her skin. When no blood was drawn from that motion, either, the crowd sighed with relief, clearly taking this as a sign that the gods were listening. Noonsol bowed and handed the blade back to her assistants, who immediately laid it and a second sword on their edges across the pot of water.

Mirae could hardly stand to watch as the junior shamans hoisted Noonsol up by the arms, helping her find her footing atop the twin blades. Once she was steady, one bare foot straddling each of the sharp edges, Noonsol was handed two smaller swords pierced with dangling gold leaves; she held them proudly in the air and slowly began to dance atop the blades while her assistants ensured the swords beneath her remained sharp-side up.

Mirae wanted to look away, but Siwon nudged her into facing forward again. It was important that Mirae watch, even if Noonsol bled—which, thankfully, she didn't—since Mirae was allegedly a fellow shaman with a stomach for such things. Siwon did his best to distract Mirae by explaining the meaning behind the knife dancing, which made every muscle within her wince.

This dangerous ritual, Siwon said, which only the most highly trained shamans were allowed to perform, was how the general of hell was invoked. When Mirae asked nervously what business the people of Noksan could possibly have with such an imposing deity, Siwon shrugged.

"Who better to deal with a gwisin problem than the general of the dead?"

Thankfully, the knife dance was short, and Noonsol's bloodlessness was a clear sign that she'd gotten the general of hell's attention. Now it was time to lure him, or any other gods who wished to help, away from their food and comforts through a story that honored them.

The assistant shamans cleared the stage again while Noonsol sat in the middle of the sandy gold-lined arena. The other shamans settled on either side of her, each wielding a different instrument, whether it was a janggu, a bamboo flute, a two-stringed haegeum, or a handheld cymbal. They waited patiently, solemnly, for Noonsol to begin her story.

Mirae listened, surprised to find herself enraptured as Noonsol began singing a plaintive ballad. It wasn't one she had heard before, despite her study of ancient poets and philosophers. Though the tangol didn't follow any particular rhythm, the bells in her hands moved with her words, and the other musicians complemented the jangles seamlessly.

"This is the tale of Pari, the Forsaken Princess, who became a goddess." Noonsol paused after each line, allowing her accompanists to chant the words after her. "May her pure devotion and courage inspire all who yet wander and require guidance from the conductor of the dead."

As Mirae listened to the tale of the Forsaken Princess—a royal who was cast out for being born a girl—she frowned at the thought of something like that happening in matriarchal Seolla. She found herself nonetheless drawn to the story of a princess who, like Mirae, was forced to leave home under cruel circumstances, hide her identity on a long and dangerous journey, and save her family through a fraught but successful partnership with the gods.

As the story went on, late afternoon turned into early evening, and the sun began its descent to the creased lip of the horizon like a fiery berry about to be devoured by the earth. Once Princess Pari's long, difficult quest resulted in her receiving healing water and a resurrection flower from the heavens, Siwon patted Mirae's arm.

"It's almost time, Gongju mama. You're up as soon as the story ends."

Mirae had been tracking the sun's movement across the sky, soaring toward the mountain where Minho was waiting, just as she had when soul-walking. Soon, Mirae and her companions would be heading toward him again, too. Unfortunately, one final obstacle stood in their way.

Siwon had told Mirae everything she needed to do to satisfy both the shamans and the crowd, but still she trembled at the thought of taking Noonsol's place in the sandy arena, feeling more nervous than she had at her Sangsok Ceremony just a few nights before.

And then, just like that, the story of the Forsaken Princess ended with Pari's ascension to divinity after successfully resurrecting and curing her parents, securing her role as a deified mediator for the dead. Mirae watched the shamans clear the sand one last time, its sudden emptiness to be filled with one final act—Mirae's possession by the Samsin, who would reveal whatever still needed to be done to rid Noksan of its plague of ghosts.

Mirae stared at the freshly smoothed sand, just as everyone in the crowd stared at her, eyes wide with anticipation. The guards, too, watched and waited for Mirae to begin, their sharp eyes sure to catch any un-shaman-like mistake she made. The pale durumagi and paper hat given to her sent flashes of heat from Mirae's head to her half-moon toes, prompting sweat to bubble up in every pore. She turned to Siwon, keeping her panicked voice low.

"I don't think I can do this."

"It's okay to have stage fright," Siwon said, smiling at the crowd of citizens, guards, and shamans as they waited with growing impatience for the concluding ritual, which would determine whether the days-long kut had been successful. "The gods have always been with you. Why would that change now that you're reenacting that relationship?"

Mirae knew Siwon's words were meant to be reassuring, but her mind flashed back to her Sangsok Ceremony. A night she was meant to prove that the gods were with her, and had instead unleashed a monster. She was the reason Minho was missing.

What if, by impersonating the gods to save Minho, she angered them and lost him—and her companions—forever?

Mirae felt someone grab her arm. Captain Jia, like the calm force of nature that she was, pretended to straighten Mirae's clothes with hands that, unlike Mirae's, never trembled. "Gongju, now is not the time to falter. You must go out there and fool the crowd, for all our sakes."

"I know," Mirae said. "But what if I fail, and all of you are—"

"The Gongju I know fails at nothing," Captain Jia said, echoing the words she'd spoken at Mirae's last training session. Her sharp gaze fixed on Mirae as if she could fill her with her own confidence. "Don't forget, I've seen you do the impossible, even if that means getting creative. Trust me, if those women out there can dance on dull blades and convince people of their supernatural powers, then a Sacred Bone Daughter can do that and more."

Captain Jia's dismissive words about the kut were jarring, but her confidence overshadowed Mirae's fear long enough for her to return to reason. After all, Mirae knew exactly what she needed to do. Siwon was a good teacher. Mirae closed her eyes and took a deep breath, remembering that she was a High Daughter with a mission she couldn't afford to fail.

Their lives depended on it.

Minho's life depended on it.

Mirae turned to Captain Jia. "You shouldn't belittle Siwon's mother's profession. In fact, we would do well to learn from our sovereign state how to rid Seolla of its own ghosts." She looked at Siwon next. "You're right, the gods have gotten me this far. It would be arrogant of me to think they'd abandon me now."

"Shaman Suhee," Noonsol called from across the arena. "Are you ready to begin?"

"Yes," Mirae said, turning away from Captain Jia's shocked face and Siwon's smiling one to address the hundreds of eyes resting on her, but not before meeting Hongbin's eyes for one last dose of bravery. "I am."

Mirae strode forward as she'd seen Captain Jia do many times—shoulders squared, chin raised with confidence. She crossed onto the sand and took her place at the center of the arena, accepting the ornate fan she was offered in her right hand and holding the proffered bells in her left.

Just as Siwon had instructed, Mirae raised both the fan and the bells as she softly began to sway. She closed her eyes, remembering the words Siwon had taught her as she lifted her voice to the heavens. "The gods have heard your supplication and the Samsin Halmoni wish to speak."

She heard feet shuffling—the crowd moving closer to catch every word she said. Mirae deepened her voice as low as she could as she continued to sway. "O devout children of Noksan, your prayers and trials do not go unnoticed. By the power within us, you will successfully soothe the restless dead and send them sweetly to the lotus paradise that awaits you all."

Mirae rang the bells and opened her eyes, seeing that the crowd swayed with her. "Tomorrow night, set out ten tables of food for the dead. After the gwisin are placated by the feast, we, the Samsin Halmoni, will lead them to another world."

Cheers rang out from the crowd. It was working—the city folk of Noksan smiled, harboring no doubt that Mirae was speaking the truth. While she shared their relief at how well things were going, a part of her wished her words of comfort weren't all just a lie.

Still, now came her opportunity to actually say something from the heart. Siwon had told her that after answering the supplication of the kut, the Samsin Halmoni would be expected to leave a message to inspire virtuous living and devotion. He'd given her a few suggestions on what to say when delivering this kongsu, but ultimately told Mirae that if her false possession made it this far, she could more or less say whatever she wanted as her final words.

Mirae gazed out at the crowd, smiling citizens of Josan interspersed with the curious eyes of Seollan shoppers who'd come to see the shamanistic spectacle. She looked back and forth between the tanned, bare-faced beauties of the Josan townsfolk and the powdered, ornamented heads of her own people. One treasured magic; the other reviled it as a weapon that threatened their way of life. But there was one thing binding them all together in that moment—an eagerness to hear a message from the heavens.

Mirae may not have been a kangsin shaman, a vessel for divine possession, but she was the gods' vassal nonetheless. They guided her as much as they did any shaman. With that thought, Mirae again lifted up her voice.

"All who are gathered here are precious spirits, equal before the gods." She paused, letting those words sink into her audience's hearts. "Nothing would give us greater joy than seeing every person on this peninsula, whether from Josan or Seolla, living in harmony."

She saw a few nods in the crowd. "This cannot happen, however, until you all forgive what lies in the past, and start looking for ways to enrich each other *now*. There is much to learn from your neighbors, who are loved equally by us, and we wish you could all see that you're stronger together than apart. Imagine a world where the virtues of Josan and the magic of Seolla improved life for everyone!"

Mirae was surprised to hear the ripple of murmurs in the crowd. The mood had changed; there were fewer nods now, and a growing number of frowns. She continued quickly, "Of course, the unification of the peninsula will take time. Mistakes from both sides must be—"

"Mistakes?" someone called out. "You mean like committing war crimes against our people? Murdering our delegates, who come in peace?"

"What about kidnapping Seollan princes?" someone spat in return. "Like barbarians?"

Mirae held back her rising panic; she needed to stay calm to maintain control of the situation. She held up her hands for silence. "Heed the will of the Samsin. You may not like our words, but we see all from the heavens. Seolla certainly has its sins, as does Josan. But there is nothing we cannot overcome together, for the good of all."

Instead of quelling the rising ire in her audience, Mirae realized she had fanned the flames. The people in the crowd, from Josan and Seolla alike, were turning to shout at each other, which prompted the guards to intervene. Mirae raised her arms again, but this time, no one paid her any heed. Instead, she could see Noonsol approaching the arena. Desperate for her aid, Mirae tried to make eye contact with her. But the tangol didn't say a word. Instead, she tossed the items cupped in her hands right in front of Mirae.

Chestnuts. Mirae looked down, confused, at the deep brown nuts denting the sand. Noonsol, on the other hand, studied them, seemingly very concerned with the way they landed. Then she looked up at Mirae with narrowed eyes.

Mirae shot Siwon a nervous glance, not sure what was going on. He, too, was staring down at the chestnuts in the sand, his skin noticeably paler than before.

"Only three landed right-side up," Noonsol said loudly, successfully pulling the crowd's attention back to her as she continued staring at Mirae suspiciously. "An odd number. That's strange. If the Samsin Halmoni were actually here with us, they would have revealed their presence with even numbers, as they always do."

Mirae stared at the other woman, her ability to speak momentarily taken away by the strangeness of what she was hearing. She shot Siwon another glance, but he was looking at Captain Jia, who was inching closer and closer to the sandy stage.

"The gods don't lie." Noonsol's accusing eyes never wavered. "They are telling me now that this woman . . . is an impostor."

The eyes of every guard were instantly fixed on Mirae, hands going to their weapons. The audience, who had looked on Mirae reverently minutes ago, now stared at her with anger, fear, and confusion. She had to do something, fast.

She looked to her friends for help, but Siwon was walking urgently toward Captain Jia, whose hands were raised, seconds away from committing the unpardonable sin of casting magic so that Mirae could get away. She couldn't let that happen.

No, she had to maintain this facade at all costs, but how? How could Mirae convince the people around her to doubt their own trusted tangol instead of her?

Mirae looked at her companions again, desperate for ideas. Hongbin was gesturing wildly for her attention. It was clear he was trying to tell her something; she watched, confused, as he raised a hand pointed like the head of a crane and wiggled it back and forth. Like a bird doing a silly dance.

Or a hand ringing a bell.

Mirae realized what Hongbin was suggesting, and a thrill of hope gripped her heart. If the people here needed to see a possession to believe her, then Mirae could show them one that would also summon just the woman to fix this mess.

"How dare you defile this sacred space with your shameless doubt," Mirae said, hoping that the hasty plan forming in her mind would work. She met Noonsol's gaze with all the fiery rage threatening to build in Captain Jia's palms. "Three chestnuts lay right-side up because we grandmother goddesses are a trio. A devout shaman would recognize a clear sign of divinity like that. Is it any wonder that the gwisin plague has not been handled, when a faithless tangol like yourself is the one trying to send them home?"

Noonsol's eyes widened, her hands dropping to her sides as she stared at Mirae, speechless with anger. Based on the looks shot her way, Mirae could see that while most of the Seollan citizens looked to be taking her accusations against Noonsol seriously, every Josan face was offended by her words. A few even began to shout that Mirae was just a Seollan spy, come to indoctrinate Josan so they wouldn't retaliate over the assassination of their dignitary.

Everything was spinning out of control. The guards were walking up to Mirae with their weapons drawn, and Captain Jia was en route to intercept them with fire.

There was only one thing left for Mirae to do.

"For this act of defiance," she said, reaching into her pocket, "we Samsin Halmoni rescind our offer of help, and summon another to test your faith."

Mirae tossed aside the shaman bells she'd been given, holding up instead the matte-black bell of the Unnamed Dragon. "With this, our holy bell, we summon a divine force to humble you and show you our strength."

At that, Mirae rang the High Horomancer's bell. This time, having used what she now knew to be the appropriate motion, the cold metal between her fingers obeyed her command to unleash its power. A thunderous peal resounded from its small metal frame, and a familiar sear exploded down Mirae's arm and through her body, forcing out of her throat the guttural scream of someone agonizingly possessed at the behest of the divine.

Chapter
NINETEEN

When Mirae opened her eyes, the world was bright and clear. Too bright for comfort. She looked around, squinting against the overbearing blaze, and realized she was standing in the sky— high up in the heavens at an impossible height.

Mirae looked down and saw that she stood on a bridge of swords, an infinite staggering of gleaming metal leading higher into the heavens. Unlike Noonsol's experience, however, the swords had cut through Mirae's shoes and pierced her feet; her blood dripped like sparkling garnets into the red sunrise beneath her.

"Hurry, noonim." The voice behind her was out of breath. "The sun is coming."

Mirae turned slowly, carefully pivoting on the slick, flat end of a blade to find Hongbin on the step just below her. His shoes, like hers, had been cut away by the knife-edged bridge, leaving his feet to bloody the path to the heavens as Mirae's did.

Hongbin leaned forward to tip the next blade onto its side, giving Mirae the flat end to step on. When she didn't move, he looked up at her. "What is it? Why are we stopping?"

When he spoke, Mirae noticed a few other things on her younger brother's face. A scar on his chin. Frown lines deeper than those that came from smiling. Though Hongbin looked a little older than when she'd left him, there was a pain in his eyes that seemed as ancient as the sun below.

"I just switched, Hongbin." Mirae held up her palm, placatingly. "Do you remember when I was Suhee the Shaman?"

Hongbin nodded, his face uneasy. "Take care, noonim. This switch is treacherous."

Mirae stared at the clouds below, marinating in the light of the bloodred sun. If she wasn't careful, her future self would return to a body tumbling into eternal fire. "Where are we?"

Hongbin sighed. "I know your switches are important, but we should be moving, not talking. If we lose our race with the sun, everything we've done will have been for nothing."

Mirae felt the heat of the fiery orb below, transforming the bridge of swords into branding irons. She turned to the next step and began to climb. "Can you at least tell me where we're going?"

Hongbin gently pushed Mirae forward as he pulled down the blade of the next step so she wouldn't have to walk on its edge. His fingers and palm were sliced from the task. "We're trying to find your patron goddess before you lose your powers."

"Lose my powers?" Mirae's foot slipped on a streak of blood left behind by Hongbin's finger. Thankfully, he steadied her from below. "Does the Inconstant Son . . . defeat me?"

"Oh, you never lose to anyone," Hongbin said, pushing Mirae forward a little less gently. "It's the people around you who end up paying the price. But I promised to stay by your side to the very end, so here we are."

Mirae grabbed Hongbin's hand as he reached for the next blade. "Why are you angry with me? What happened between us?"

Hongbin snatched back his hand. "We've been at this for so long. There's too much to tell."

Mirae faced him slowly. She wasn't going to move on until this was settled. "The point of these switches is to help me save the future from the Inconstant Son."

It still felt strange to say those words out loud, a name she had been told not to utter, lest it give the man inside the Deep power over her. Now that she knew the Netherking was not her ancient enemy, and had forged a connection with him by meeting him in person, she said the name without fear, as the Kun Sunim had. "The gods brought me here to you, Hongbin. There has to be a reason for that—something you're supposed to tell me."

"It doesn't matter what I tell you. You won't do it."

Mirae shook her head. "I'll do anything for you."

"Noonim." Hongbin hung his head. "I'm not the one who walked away."

Mirae's face flushed from the growing heat of the sun, and from something else—a tenderness and a rage she'd never felt before. "Hongbin, don't say that. I will never abandon you. Just tell me how to make things right and I'll do it, I swear."

"No, you won't." Hongbin kept his head bowed, refusing to let Mirae see his face. "You won't change a thing. You can't. You love him too much."

"Who?" Mirae grabbed Hongbin's shoulders. "Who do I love?"

Hongbin gripped her arms in return—not to steady her, but to lean in close, the torment on his face chilling Mirae to the bone. "You'll love him across all time and under every moon.

I understand that. But noonim, you must let him die when the time comes. You must."

Hongbin hugged Mirae desperately on that metal stair, the bloody pathway to heaven: too high, too sharp, too hot for mortals. The sun was melting the clouds. Hongbin would be next.

When he pulled away, Mirae stared into his brown eyes, taking in the way they looked at her—dark wounds on a battered soul. Slowly, while Mirae watched, those eyes filled with the deep, oily black that was becoming all too familiar, a power that carried the scorch of the rising sun and led her back to another time, before the end of everything she loved.

The first thing Mirae noticed when she came to was the touch of a cold vial in her hands, and the bitter, oily taste of black water coating her tongue.

The second thing she noticed was the sound of high-pitched humming. A droning that sent tiny vibrations through the air. When Mirae opened her eyes, she found herself sitting on the ground, which was squirming and bubbling with chirping brown insects, leaping and latching onto anything in their path. Multiplied by millions, there was precious little that wasn't peppered with the furry-legged bugs. Mirae realized that above the swarm's earsplitting chirps and drones, she could hear screams.

"Gongju!" Familiar hands hefted Mirae to her feet. Captain Jia held her close. "Now's our chance—we have to run."

Mirae let herself be pulled through the buzzing swarm, relieved that none of the billions of crickets coating the world around her seemed interested in sticking to her. Captain Jia, too, seemed immune, as she and Mirae rushed out of the arena, back toward the city of Noksan. Mirae could only hope that Siwon and Hongbin would be there waiting for them.

The swarm of crickets began to thin as Mirae and Captain Jia drew closer to the city and its buildings came into sight. The street to the marketplace appeared, and sure enough, Siwon and Hongbin stood at the entrance to the square. Mirae grabbed their hands and the four of them quickly made their way out of the city.

Though the swarm of crickets was thinnest there in the heart of the city, enough of the humming pests were still leaping about that everyone in the square was too distracted to pay attention to Mirae and her companions as they fled. They were even able to grab some spare clothes from an unmanned stall, exchanging one of Mirae's gold hairpins for the plunder. She, at the very least, was in need of a new disguise.

Down narrow streets between houses where laundry and squid were laid out to dry, side by side, and games of gonggi were left abandoned by children, they ran from the city and the cricket swarm, leaving the clay-roofed houses and buildings behind, and pushing toward the green-tea hills on the horizon, lying like cloud-veined jade heaps in the misty distance.

They didn't stop until the rooftops and blossoming lanterns from Noksan had faded completely out of sight. Once Captain Jia let go of her, Mirae bent over, hands on her knees, heaving for breath. When she could speak, she gasped, "What happened back there? Did something go wrong with my switch?"

"I don't know," Captain Jia said. She wasn't quite out of breath, though her body seemed plagued by a different kind of wildness. "But that woman who took your place—that wasn't you."

Mirae's body flashed cold. "What do you mean, she wasn't me?"

"You weren't yourself, noonim." Hongbin put a comforting, albeit sweaty, arm around Mirae's shoulders. "You started shouting about the evils of Seolla and how you were going to burn it to the ground. Then you unleashed that cricket swarm with power I've never seen."

Mirae swallowed, still tasting the oily black water on her tongue. The Netherking had said it would make her powerful in a pinch, but she was supposed to save it for Minho. Mirae reached into the bag of beads around her neck and pulled out the vial, which still looked more than halfway full.

"You only took a sip," Siwon confirmed. He, too, seemed shaken. "Just enough to give your magic a boost."

Mirae tucked the vial away with trembling hands. "I don't understand what went wrong."

"Well, what happened on your side of the switch?" Hongbin asked. "If you tell us where that other Mirae came from, maybe we can piece it all together."

Mirae didn't want to think about her switch—an encounter with a future Hongbin who resented her for things she had yet to do. A man who was walking a dangerous path to the heavens beside a woman who had apparently betrayed him utterly.

"We'll talk when it's safe," Captain Jia said, reading Mirae's expression. They were fugitives, after all, and clearly visible from the road. It was only a matter of time before crowds fleeing the swarming city arrived and spotted them.

The only traveling pack they'd managed to keep hung from Siwon's shoulder, and Captain Jia's arms were still full of the clothes she'd grabbed from the marketplace. She thrust them at Mirae now.

"Gongju, you need to change. From here on out, we stay off the road. Siwon and I will keep watch. Gunju, stick close to your sister."

Siwon nodded, rattled though he was, and Hongbin pointed out a spot behind a large bush where Mirae could change. She hurried after her brother. As soon as she was hidden, she began tearing off her shaman robes, almost angry at how cleanly white they remained even after enduring the chaos of the kut and the disgusting insect swarm that had followed.

It wasn't as if Mirae herself was untouched by either of those events—her skin still itched with the phantom crawling of invisible crickets, and Hongbin's bitter words from the future colored everything he said now.

"I just want you to know," Hongbin said from the other side of the bush, "that I personally think the whole cricket thing was amazing. It came out of *nowhere*, and the havoc was just incredible. We never would have gotten out of there in one piece if it weren't for you."

"We also wouldn't have been in any danger if it weren't for me." Mirae kicked her shaman robes into a pile on the ground, glad to be rid of them. "Now everyone knows a Seollan witch is on the loose in Josan, and it won't be long before they figure out who I am."

"Hey, the fake possession thing wasn't working," Hongbin said. "You did what you had to do to get us out of there."

Perhaps that was true, but she'd hoped to bring a message of peace to the Josan people. It hadn't worked, but still, why had her future self said vile things about *Seolla*, the queendom she was trying to protect? "What exactly did she say, the future me I switched with?"

She heard Hongbin's clothes rustle as he shrugged. "Something about the lies and evil of Seolla. I don't know, I was kind of distracted by the crickets."

"Why would I say any of that?" Mirae asked. "Even just for show?"

"I don't know, maybe you and Mother were fighting again, and you threw a tantrum."

"I don't throw tantrums," Mirae said. "Not like that. Besides, Mother wasn't in the place I switched to. It was just you and me."

Hongbin fell still on the other side of the bush. It was almost predictable now, the way he'd go silent for a few seconds, trying to come up with something silly to take her mind off things. "Well, there you go. *I* must have said something very irritating and it set you off."

Mirae pulled her new clothes on angrily. She knew her brother meant well, but she was getting tired of people making light of things, thinking it would make her feel better. "This is serious, Hongbin. In my switch, you and I were on bad terms. What if that's because someday I become an enemy to Seolla?"

"Hey." The leaves beside Mirae began to shake as Hongbin's hand slithered through to her side. "You couldn't hurt anyone if you tried. It's just not in you. Even when we were all in danger of being arrested, you sent a harmless swarm of crickets. That's just who you are."

Mirae sighed and took Hongbin's disembodied hand. "What about the horrible things I said? What if I actually meant all that?"

"Impossible." Hongbin squeezed her hand twice before returning to his side of the bush. "You've already proven you'll do anything for Seolla. You're relentless that way, which is something no one can ever take from you. They'd best just get on board, including future me."

Mirae froze, recalling a similar but twisted version of that sentiment spoken by Hongbin in the future. *Oh, you never lose to anyone. . . . It's the people around you who end up paying the price.*

"Gongju," Captain Jia called from the road. "We need to get moving."

Mirae hastily finished tying the sashes on her clothes and walked back with Hongbin toward Captain Jia and Siwon, who were scouring the distance on either side of the road for signs that they were being followed.

"If we hurry, we can make it back to the border by nightfall." Captain Jia had rebraided her hair tightly, making it easier to reach the jade sword strapped under her clothes. "There will be enough guards there to protect us from any Josan mob or cavalry. We'll be safe."

"Wait, we're going back?" Hongbin looked between Captain Jia and Mirae with confusion. "What about Minho?"

"It's too dangerous to go after him now." Captain Jia spoke firmly, but Mirae looked into the other woman's eyes and knew every word she said cut her to the core. "Gongju used Sacred Bone Magic, and now every Josan soldier will be on high alert looking for us. The king will know we're here and why we came. He'll either hide Daegun somewhere we'll never find him, or hurt him to send a message. In any case, we've failed. We have to turn back."

"We don't know that." Siwon held the traveling pack firmly on his shoulder and faced the captain with a determined look. "The Josan king probably assumes we're heading toward the capital. He'll station all his men on the main road, leaving our true path relatively free."

"You do not speak for the Josan king," Captain Jia snapped, then turned her ire, more carefully controlled, onto Mirae. "And you, Gongju, do not speak for Her Majesty, who is still queen of Seolla. If she hadn't been incapacitated at your Sangsok Ceremony, she would tell us to turn back now. You know I'm right."

Somehow, the captain's words pulled more air out of Mirae's lungs than escaping Noksan had. She stared at the captain, knowing what she said was true. But Mirae had rage of her own rising like fire in the pit of her belly as words from her switch echoed back to her like a command from the gods.

I'm not the one who walked away.

Hongbin had given her a warning. If she just gave up and took the easy road, now or in the future, the only things that awaited her were a bloody path to the heavens, the risk of losing her power, and the chance to lose Hongbin's trust forever.

She glanced at Hongbin's face now, and the look in her younger brother's eyes made it clear what he wanted them to do. No, Mirae couldn't just abandon him, or the brother they loved—not now, not ever.

"There's no point in arguing about whether we should go after Minho," Mirae said, locking eyes with Captain Jia. "You know where I stand. Besides, if I go home without proof of the Josan king's treachery, he'll make up lies about me that will allow him to start the war he's always wanted. He'll have won."

"No matter what, there will be war," Captain Jia said. "Would you rather be executed here, or go back to Seolla and fight with the fullness of our army, instead of just the four of us?"

"The council will not take my side," Mirae shot back. "They'll force me to abandon Minho to save myself, my crown. Just like you. And even *if* your plan worked, it would take too much time. Time Minho doesn't have."

"You think I don't know that?" Captain Jia said, her voice strangled with barely contained rage. "My plan is what we should have done all along, but you refused to listen. Even now, it's the only path where everyone *might* live. I cannot let you continue this foolishness if it will cost you and Daegun your lives."

"Foolishness?" Mirae clenched her fists to keep them from filling with magic. "So you don't believe in my calling, or in the gods' will? You think I'm just as mad as my mother?"

Captain Jia gestured at the land around them, bloodred with sundown. "I don't believe the gods' plan would look anything like this. It's time to stop fooling ourselves and use our brains. You know the gods gave us those, too."

"Oh, so you don't think I'm insane—just incredibly stupid." The more Mirae kept her fiery rage out of her hands, the more it filled her chest instead. "When exactly did you stop having faith in me, Captain? Was it when I broke your precious sword and humiliated you? Does your pride still smart from that?"

"You mean when you chose to be cruel instead of cunning or capable?" Captain Jia's jade sword glowed with her righteous anger, even through her clothes. "You're right, I did learn something that night—the kind of queen you will be if I don't curb your selfishness."

"How has anything I've done been selfish?" Mirae demanded. Hongbin tried to step between them, but Mirae pushed him aside; she needed to fight this fight. "Everything I do is for my queendom and my family."

"No, Gongju, everything you do, or have been asked to do, has been for yourself. To keep *your* birthright and preserve *your* family. You may get everything you've been fighting for, but only if you continue to ignore the cost."

"Well, I'm not like you," Mirae said coldly. "I don't quit when things get hard. I don't give up on the people I love."

The silence that fell after those words left Mirae's mouth was deeper, darker than the Netherking's cage. It seemed to suck all the air out of the sky, leaving the captain to stagger backward, breathless with the pain of Mirae's blow. Hongbin and Siwon, however, looked stricken, frozen in place, eyes darting back and forth between Mirae and Captain Jia.

After a long, painfully tense moment, the captain recovered her ability to speak. "What you are, Gongju," she said, her voice deathly quiet, "is a candle that doesn't realize everything around it can burn. Maybe today you feel illuminated with confidence, but the brighter you blaze, the more you will destroy. Right now, there's nothing on the peninsula more dangerous to Daegun, to all of us, than you."

Mirae stared right back at the captain without flinching. She knew the other woman was wrong—Mirae had seen the face of evil, the Inconstant Son, with her own eyes. Captain Jia had no idea what Mirae was up against—what Minho and *Seolla* were up against—or why there was no way she could allow herself to be swayed from her path. "I'm not turning back, Captain. You know me better than that. If you want, you can go home. I have others who will stay by my side."

With that, Mirae turned to Hongbin and Siwon. When they stepped closer to her, making their allegiance clear, Captain Jia closed her eyes as if she couldn't bear to look at any of them anymore. "Remember my warning when you get us all killed, Gongju."

Mirae ignored the captain. "Siwon, which way to the river?"

Siwon pointed ahead, his face smooth and confident once more as he met Mirae's eyes. "Through that green-tea field."

Mirae nodded and began walking in the direction he pointed, officially stepping off the road. Behind her, she heard Captain Jia offer one last plea to Hongbin and Siwon.

"Stop indulging this madness. We must give up this reckless quest and proceed only when we have the full might of Seolla at our back."

"We already do," Hongbin said, following after Mirae. "My noonim is everything Seolla is supposed to be. I'm not turning back for the world."

Siwon's footsteps followed Mirae as well. "I, too, believe in Gongju mama and her quest."

After a moment, Captain Jia relented and joined them. "I hope you're all willing to pay whatever price is asked of you."

"The only person who must pay is the Josan king," Mirae said, without slowing. "If he knew me as well as you do, Captain, he would run and hide. After all, like you said, I'm a candle with the power to burn down the world."

Chapter

TWENTY

Mirae had seen the green-tea fields before, each time she'd soul-walked to Minho's prison, but once she was close enough to view their jade-like shine in person, she couldn't help but stare at them with wonder, almost forgetting that she and her companions were on the run. Though the sun had all but finished its red-eyed descent, the army of small lanterns held aloft by the retreating workers lit the hilly field warmly like small yellow stars.

By the lantern light, she could see enough to make out their surroundings. Cultivated on the widest side of a short hill, the carefully trimmed bushes lined the sloping land like brushstrokes. Every so often, the wide hats of scarved workers could be seen leaving the fields as their day of work ended, like straw and silk flowers caught in the wind. Mirae stared at the slanted fields knuckling the horizon, breathing in the pungent smell of leaves in all stages of growth and decay, feeling renewed by the life around her. These quiet landmarks of her path to Minho cooled her flaring anger and growing unease.

Her final destination loomed ahead, mountains red-lined with sunset, reaching into the sky like paper-cut fingers. As

Mirae and her companions approached the green-tea field, the sun's final spark was snuffed out by the crease between Josan and the sky.

Within minutes, they reached the foot of the low green-tea hill. The dirt trails between the rows of trees were only wide enough for one person to pass at a time, so Mirae, Siwon, Hongbin, and a still seething Captain Jia snuck single file through the field once all the workers had passed out of sight.

Despite the peaceful surroundings, Mirae still expected soldiers from Noksan to burst out at any moment and capture them. And she still felt the heated words she had shared with Captain Jia stuck between them like a double-edged sword. Hongbin clearly felt the weight of all that had passed hanging over them, too, and began trying to lighten the mood. "I don't know about you folks, but I think we're in desperate need of a name for our little band of travelers."

When no one responded, Hongbin continued cheerily, apparently perfectly content with talking to himself. "I've narrowed it down to two potential names: the Seolla Rescue Squad or the Pretty Kings."

"None of us are kings, though, Gunju daegam," Siwon interjected.

"I beg to differ!" Hongbin smiled. "When my noonim and hyungnim make it back home, they'll be confined to their chambers for approximately five hundred years. That leaves me, the third-born Sacred Bone royal, to take over as regent. Naturally, I shall marry a man from Josan for the sake of peace, and my top choice is the incomparably clever and handsome

Siwon. So if you think about it, you'll find that there is indeed a pair of pretty kings walking among us."

"Do I get any say in the romance of this narrative?" Siwon asked mildly.

"Don't be silly. Everyone wants to marry me."

"Well, I suppose my sudden social climb will make quite the rags-to-riches story," Siwon said conspiratorially. "Especially with the plot twist that I'm secretly . . . a gumiho."

Hongbin gasped. "I did *not* see that coming. That's it, I'm turning this into a song."

Mirae had heard Hongbin draft enough impromptu ballads that she didn't even need to turn around to know he was strumming an invisible gayageum as he ran through rhymes and hummed to himself. She might even have helped him come up with a few verses, if it weren't for the anger still brewing in her heart and the singsongy words running through her own mind, low and chilling echoes from the Deep.

Come, my pretty king. Come and break with me.

Lost in thought, Mirae failed to notice an abandoned basket of tea leaves on the ground and tripped over it, despite the light of the waning full moon overhead.

Siwon caught her as she stumbled. "Are you all right, Gongju mama?"

"I'm fine," Mirae said as she steadied herself. "Just tired. I think we should stop to eat and rest soon. Hongbin gets extra chatty when he's tired, which is fine, but he turns grumpy when he's hungry, which we don't want to risk."

"Then stop and rest we shall, as soon as we're out of this field," Siwon said. He waited a moment before hesitantly adding, "For what it's worth, I'm glad you're not giving up on our quest. You make the rest of us brave."

When Mirae didn't respond, Siwon put a hand on her shoulder. "*Are* you all right, Gongju mama? You can talk to me about anything. Daegun daegam always said I'm a good listener."

Siwon's courage, steady as always, brushed against Mirae's skin like the gust of wind whispering through the field ahead of them, scattering flurries of valuable leaves. She glanced over her shoulder at the man she'd allowed to follow her through dark portals, pools of gwisin, and rituals gone wrong—a man tethered to her, initially, through her fears. Fear of losing Minho and fear of being the only monster-touched person on this journey.

But now, every time she looked at him, Mirae was reminded that if she was truly as brave as Siwon said, she wouldn't be growing more and more terrified with each step she took toward White Spine Mountain, or dreading what she might have to do to free Minho from the Inconstant Son.

Her failure in Noksan had cost them dearly. Set back by hours, and without horses, it seemed likely that by the time they reached Minho, he'd only have one day left before they lost him forever. That was barely enough time to get him home, especially if they were waylaid by anything else unexpected. . . .

Rather than speaking her dark thoughts aloud, or telling Siwon the difficult decision brewing privately in her heart, Mirae forced a smile. "I'm fine, Siwon. Really."

Thankfully, he didn't press her, but the pearly moon above gleamed off his eyes, making them look like a chest of black opals freshly opened. The meek but friendly servant boy Siwon had once been seemed like a stranger from a past life all but forgotten. "Is it all right if I tell you something in confidence, Gongju mama?"

"Only if you stop addressing me and Hongbin like we're stuffy monarchs. We've been through too much together to bother with all these formalities," Mirae scolded lightly. "That being said, you better not be about to tell me that you are, in fact, a gumiho."

"Trust me, if I were, Gunju would have figured that out by now," Siwon said with a smile, looking more relaxed than Mirae had ever seen him as he honored her request to treat her and her brother like friends. "No, there was actually something you said to me in your switch that I can't get out of my head."

"Oh?" Mirae asked, not sure why her cheeks were suddenly growing warm.

"It was during the thickest part of the cricket storm, so I'm not sure anyone else heard."

"I see." Mirae cleared her throat. "What did I say?"

Siwon paused, his voice revealing he was as nervous as Mirae. "Well, first you said something that implied we were . . . very close. Bonded, even, by love."

The heat in Mirae's cheeks seemed to melt her lips shut. Though she didn't speak, Siwon continued, "Then you told me to save you, but you didn't say from what."

Mirae had always known the gods wanted Siwon on this journey with her, but the idea of him playing a larger role in her future than even she had considered made her heart flutter—until she remembered Hongbin's grim warning, and the fluttering turned to lead in her stomach.

Just tell me how to make things right and I'll do it, I swear.

No, you won't. You won't change a thing. You can't. You love him too much.

Who? Who do I love?

"Gongju." Siwon's touch brought Mirae back to the present, where things had started to make even less sense than her glimpses of the future. "I just wanted you to know that I have no doubt you and I are exactly where we're supposed to be. In fact, seeing you back there as a shaman, and the way you spoke to me from the future, it gave me a lot of clarity. That's why despite the dangers we may face ahead, I'm not going anywhere."

Looking into Siwon's eyes, she saw a man at peace, whose every word and thought expressed the absolute truth. Before she could put her own feelings into words, the green-tea field came to an abrupt end, revealing the expanse of Josan in front of Mirae—a land that seemed as vast as the Samsin's mysteries. She observed the terrain in silence, weighing Siwon's words, his revelations. She didn't know how to respond to anything he had said, but he didn't seem to expect anything. Instead, they walked in a strangely comfortable silence toward a river shining like a silver ribbon, the sounds of its distant trickling overshadowed by the rest of Hongbin's warning from the future.

You'll love him across all time and under every moon. I understand that. But noonim, you must let him die when the time comes.

You must.

When they reached the river, the moon was overshadowed by clouds, making it too dark to walk any farther. Mirae remembered the long, reedy river from her first attempt at soul-walking with the Netherking. Considering her and her companions' growing hunger and exhaustion, she decided it was as good a place as any to break for the night. They settled beside the riverbank—scaring off a swoop of red-crowned cranes—to eat some of the food Jisoo and Yoonhee had provided, which, by some miracle, had survived the swarm of crickets and the tempestuousness that had followed.

Siwon parceled out the slightly mushy persimmons and dried squid before reanimating the large bowl of noodles with a bit of cold water from the river. Meanwhile, Mirae set out the carefully wrapped side dishes—steamed sprouts, roasted seaweed squares, and cucumber kimchi.

Captain Jia's silence had begun to weigh on Mirae, so she attempted a conciliatory smile as she handed the captain a bowl of noodles. The other woman only shook her head, her face tight, and looked down at the ground. Everyone else began eating wordlessly as the chill of night descended. Hongbin shuddered and set down his food so he could rub his arms.

"Noonim, can I borrow the gwisin's pearl? I could use some of its warmth right now."

Before Mirae could respond, Captain Jia lifted her head. "Absolutely not. We cannot use any more magic, for any reason."

"It's just a little heat and light—" Hongbin protested.

"We're being hunted." Captain Jia's voice was like cold steel. "Unless you want to risk giving away our position, you should listen to me, for once."

"I agree," Siwon said, surprising everyone. He scooted closer to Hongbin, as if to warm him. "We need the Josan king to believe we're heading toward the capital. They can't know we're anywhere *near* the fortress, even if that means freezing our bottoms off."

Hongbin nodded ruefully. "Do we even know Minho's still up there?"

"He is," Mirae said quietly, eyes closed as she found the Sacred Bone connection once more. "And he's alive. I can feel him."

A loud splash snapped Mirae back into her body and turned everyone's heads toward the river. Captain Jia was on her feet in an instant, sword unsheathed from her back. "Everyone stay here," she hissed, keeping her voice low. "Siwon, stand guard."

A moment later, she disappeared into the darkness, heading toward the river. Siwon positioned himself to sit between Mirae and Hongbin, and the sound Captain Jia was investigating. No one even dared to breathe until she returned a few seconds later, her sword resheathed. "It was just a crane catching dinner. We're still safe . . . for now."

Everyone breathed a sigh of relief, except Captain Jia, who kept surveying their surroundings as if something sinister waited in the darkness, ready to attack at any moment. "I'll go on patrol, make sure we weren't followed. The rest of you try to get some sleep."

With that, the captain disappeared again, melting into the darkness.

Mirae, Hongbin, and Siwon sat huddled in silence, chilled by both the air and the fear that every sound they heard was Josan guards sneaking up on them. As Mirae shifted to share warmth with Hongbin, her hand brushed the captain's untouched food. In that moment, she felt a rise of guilt for instilling so much pressure and fear in the bravest woman she knew. A loyal woman, who would do anything to protect Seolla's future queen, whether that meant repressing what she herself thought was right or, if necessary, leaving the man she loved in the hands of a torturer.

Mirae's harsh words from earlier haunted her now as she imagined Captain Jia, the woman she'd unfairly accused of being a coward, watching over her all night, weary, hungry, and scared that she would fail everyone who depended on her.

Mirae tapped Hongbin and Siwon on the shoulder. "I'm going to help Captain Jia scout the area. Lay out some blankets and get as much rest as you can."

Hongbin laid a hand on Mirae's arm. "I know this has been hard on you both, but you'll make her come around. You always find a way to get what you want, and that's the kind of strength we need right now, no matter what Captain Jia says. Remind her that Minho isn't going to die if you have anything to say about it. You won't let him."

Mirae tried to smile at her younger brother's attempt at comfort, but his words from the future, uttered on a bridge of swords in the red, brutal heavens, came echoing back to her.

You must let him die. . . . You must.

Oh, you never lose to anyone. . . . It's the people around you who end up paying the price.

Mirae patted Hongbin's hand, glad nevertheless to have him as her anchor, whether she was diving into the Deep or bleeding in the heavens. No matter what, Hongbin would never let her lose her way. In that, he and Captain Jia were of the same mind.

Mirae rose to her feet. "I think I know how to bring our resident warrior back. Wish me luck."

She grabbed what she could of Captain Jia's abandoned meal and went to look for her friend.

Mirae found the captain sitting by the river, not far from their camp. She was looking across the water's moonlit stillness the way Mirae had looked across the gwisin's pond—like danger rippled just beneath the surface. Her fingers tightened around the captain's dinner bowl, and she made sure to walk loudly enough not to startle the other woman.

This time, when Mirae offered her the supper of cold noodles, Captain Jia accepted without a word. Mirae sat beside her friend and mentor in companionable silence for a moment before saying, "I want to apologize for many things, but mostly for this—when I first asked you to come with me, I said it was because I valued your opinion. But since then, I've done nothing but disregard your feelings. I'm sorry."

The captain remained impassive, staring fixedly across the river.

"I promise that from now on, I will give your opinions equal weight with my own. I truly believe that if we are united, Minho's enemies don't stand a chance against us."

The captain still said nothing, but Mirae knew she was listening to every word. "I'm sorry for the horrible things I said, and I don't blame you at all for calling me selfish. At first, of course, I didn't understand why you would say that, since I'm doing all this for you, too. But now I know that the problem isn't with what I'm doing, but *how* I'm doing it. If saving someone requires endangering everyone else I care about, including my queendom, then what I want is more important than what's right. And there's nothing more selfish than that. I just wanted you to know that I understand why you're angry. You have every right to be, and I'm sorry. If you'll let me, I'd like to prove to you that I meant what I said before—your opinion really does mean the world to me. I don't know what I would do without you."

Mirae turned to leave, but before she had walked even a few steps back toward camp, Captain Jia's voice stopped her, gruff but relenting. "Are you just saying all that because you have no idea how to get up the mountain without me?"

Mirae smiled as the tension between them finally broke. "No, but if you have any ideas, I'm very happy to start keeping my promise to you now."

When Mirae turned back around, Captain Jia was looking at her, her face tired but gentle. "Despite what you think, I do believe the gods chose you for an important work, Gongju. It's just that ever since the Sangsok Ceremony, you've stopped being the cunning young princess I was looking forward to serving as my queen. Now you just seem so . . . recklessly devoted to a path I can't see, and that scares me, especially with Daegun's life on the line."

Mirae let the captain's words sink in without letting them rile her up. She'd made a promise to listen and try to understand. "I'm sure it seems like I've been acting senselessly, but that's because things really have changed. You haven't seen my visions of the future, or felt the invisible pull of the gods. It's scary to me, too, moving forward with faith instead of a plan. You and Mother were always so sure of what to do, so sure that I would just follow. But that road ended with disaster, and I don't think it's fair to say that that was all my fault."

"No, that isn't fair," Captain Jia admitted. "You trusted us and our honoring of tradition, even when we were wrong about so much. I can see why you want things to change."

Mirae put a hand on the captain's shoulder. "I'm still the princess you trained. I'm just asking that we trust *each other* now. Your lessons prepared me to be brave when my entire world was turned on its head, but now the Samsin are speaking through me to show us the path we must follow, even if it leads us away from what we once thought was our duty."

The captain was silent for a moment. "You're right about one thing—we're better united than we are at odds. Daegun needs both our strengths. Just promise me that you *will* try to use your head sometimes, rather than leaving that completely to me."

Mirae tapped a finger against her chin. "When you say use my head, do you mean not sending in a dragon to cool things down when my mother launches a storm of fire into the Garden of Queens? Is that the gist of it?"

"How fast she learns." It might have been a trick of shadows, which were shifting as the clouds continued to pass over the moon, but Mirae could have sworn she saw the hint of a smile on the captain's face. "Before you know it, she'll be steering clear of ghosts and saying no to strange hands that come out of the water."

"Well, when you put it like that, I sound as dumb as Hongbin's list of 'hot suitors.'"

Captain Jia shook her head. "We don't talk about the list."

They laughed quietly. In the silence that followed, they could hear the sounds of Hongbin and Siwon tidying up the campsite. "Can I ask you a personal question, Captain?"

Captain Jia nodded. "Of course."

Mirae hesitated but forced the question out of her mouth before she could back down. "When did you know that you and my orabeoni . . . were in love?"

Captain Jia narrowed her eyes. "Why do you ask?"

"No reason," Mirae said hastily, embarrassed at how defensive she sounded. "I just . . . want to be prepared in case I ever experience the same thing."

Captain Jia was gracious enough to pretend she didn't know what—or who—Mirae was talking about. Her voice softened as she recalled tender memories. "Our . . . love didn't really feel like anything at first. Daegun was the one who oversaw my entrance into the Wonhwa. After I easily defeated all the other applicants, he asked for a closer look at my sword, in case I was cheating. We talked about weapons a lot at first. And then we began meeting to talk about other things. It just grew naturally, I suppose, until we found ourselves making up excuses to be together as much as possible. That's when we knew it was becoming something more."

Mirae raised an eyebrow. "Please tell me that 'talking about weapons' is a euphemism for something way more romantic."

Captain Jia grimaced. "You need to stop hanging around with Gunju."

"Oh, it's far too late for that."

Captain Jia snorted. "Well, while we're talking about the men in our lives, which I try to do as little as possible, there is something I've been meaning to ask you—why do you trust the Josan boy so much?"

Mirae tensed as she looked over at the forms of Hongbin and Siwon farther upriver, illuminated as the clouds overhead moved to unveil the moon. *You said something that implied we were . . . very close. Bonded, even, by love.* "I trust him because he and I want the same thing. To save Minho."

"As do I."

"There's more to it," Mirae said. "He and I were the only people who saw the monster released from the Inconstant Son's cage and *survived*. I need to understand why it spared us."

"But he's hiding something," Captain Jia insisted. "Surely you've felt that. And besides, he's clearly no ordinary servant. I find it hard to believe that a man who fixes the hair of princes for a living could have worked up the muscles and the ability to run long distances that Siwon has."

The thought of glancing over Siwon's body to ascertain the validity of Captain Jia's suspicions brought a sudden heat to Mirae's face, which she hid with a smirk. "Now, what would Minho say if he heard you talking about another man's body like that?"

Captain Jia snorted again. "Daegun can work on his own muscles before telling me what to do."

Both women tried to stifle their laughter. But at the sound of their giggles, Hongbin stood and waved them back over, while Siwon gestured proudly at the blankets he'd spread on the ground. Mirae took the captain's hand and walked them both back toward the camp. "I will keep a closer eye on Siwon if you promise to give him a chance. I know he wants to reach Minho as much as we do. We can at least trust him to help us with that."

"I promise to do as you say on one condition," Captain Jia said, still holding Mirae's hand. "Remember yourself around him. I've seen the way he looks at you when you're not paying attention. You wanted to know what it's like to feel a . . . spark between you and someone else. Well, I can see it in his eyes. But this is the most important thing you need to know—feelings of love are not meant to protect you."

Mirae tried to focus on the captain's advice, to give it due consideration as promised, but she found her attention slipping away at the words: *I've seen the way he looks at you.*

"Did you hear me, Gongju?"

"Yes." Mirae squeezed the captain's hand. "And I will heed your wisdom."

Captain Jia nodded as they walked, hand in hand, back toward Hongbin and Siwon. The captain gestured for everyone to lie down and get some rest while she sat and finally ate her meal. With a heart warm from renewed friendship, and somewhat fluttery after her and Captain Jia's conversation about Siwon, Mirae curled up on one of the blankets and let herself slip into what she hoped would be a short but peaceful slumber.

Chapter
TWENTY-ONE

This time when Mirae stepped out onto the gleaming courtyard sand, she knew she wasn't dreaming. This was the half sleep the Netherking had threatened to plague her with until she fulfilled her promise to him. Still, hidden within this punishment was an opportunity to check in on her family; she wouldn't waste this chance. Instead of listening for the echoing drumbeat of her heart to chase after like before, Mirae soul-walked toward the rearmost part of the palace where her father's chambers were.

The magic-lit walls and torches around Mirae shone with small pearls of radiance, reminding her that she'd always thought the palace felt like a moon, isolated from the rest of the queendom by giant stone walls, even as it harbored Seolla's greatest light. As she followed in the wake of a Wonhwa patrol, stepping into their footprints as if they were a stream of shallow boats leading her home, Mirae vowed that if she should return and take up the mantle of queen, she would turn her sheltered moon palace into a welcoming place for all—Josan servants, shamans, and exiled royals alike. Everyone who had been wronged or enriched by her family.

Mirae would make Seolla everything it had always promised to be, for everyone under its wing. Nothing else would be worth the suffering she knew lay both ahead and behind.

Mirae stopped a few paces away from the Wonhwa patrol, who paused as a line of palace women rushed across their path. The guards resumed their march as soon as their path was clear, but Mirae broke away and ran toward her father's chambers, from which the palace women had just emerged.

In their haste, the women had left the outer doors open—not that Mirae needed them to ghost into the dimly lit room her father had been moved to. He lay motionless while the head palace woman, with one of her aides, tended to him. There was no mistaking that he had taken a turn for the worse. His breaths were labored, his face alarmingly pale, yet sweaty and feverish at the same time. Mirae dropped to her knees beside him, trying to grab the hand that the head palace woman was holding—but her fingers were as impotent in this state as they had been when she'd found Minho in his cell, grasping at nothing but air.

"At this rate, His Royal Highness won't last a week," the head palace woman said quietly, eliciting a sad shake of the head from her aide, who laid a fresh, cool towel on his feverish brow. "If only Her Majesty would wake. Surely she could do something for him."

"I'm sure she could," the other palace woman murmured. "But the only person who can wake her is off riling up barbarians in Josan. I mean, magic within their borders? What was Gongju mama thinking?"

"She was probably using her head as much as she ever has. Meanwhile, half her family wastes away in the palace she should be running, and the other half is out doing gods know what and getting themselves killed. The whole queendom is as good as dead with her in charge."

"The one time Gongju mama really needed to do as she was told." The palace woman sighed. "The people who need her are right here."

"It really is a pity," the head palace woman agreed. "Gongju mama was born under an auspicious sky. I remember the oracles saying she would either be the greatest queen we've ever known, or she would be the one to destroy us all. It seems clear which path she's choosing. I only pray it's not too late for someone to intervene, though I'm not sure anyone ever born has the power to make her listen to reason."

Mirae wasn't sure what she would have done had she been able to touch the women in the room, but she wanted to grab them by the shoulders and yell the truth into their faces. She *was* the High Horomancer, and the gods had shown her that her current path was the only way to save everyone she loved—including the rest of the queendom! None of the fallout from her obedience to the Samsin had been her fault. In fact, the tides of treachery had begun flowing long before Mirae was even born, and she was the only one who could make things right.

And yet in her heart, Mirae knew the palace women were right about one thing—her parents couldn't be revived as long as Mirae was off on her quest. Only victory would vindicate her choices now, even though it seemed that everything she did was a gamble that no one was convinced would pay off, not even those who spoke to her from the future.

You must let him die. . . . You must.

You won't change a thing. You can't. You love him too much.

Failure is not an option.

Queenling. Mirae looked up, then around the room, but found no sign of the Netherking. His voice echoed through her mind again. *Come, queenling. We have much to talk about.*

A blink was all it took for Mirae to find herself back in the Deep. Where her father's chambers should have been was a pit of darkness with only one spot of moonlight, dimmed by the black lake above, carving out a chamber-size orb of light. At the center of this pitiful glow sat the Netherking, clad in black, a hunched statue of darkness waiting for Mirae in his ancient underground prison.

He was eating dinner at his lightning-blue table, which had been made whole once more. When he looked up and saw Mirae, he set his chopsticks down. "You seem upset, queenling. Is something the matter?"

"Well, I can't say I'm happy to be back." Mirae stepped into the circle of sickly green light surrounding him like a venomous crown. The Netherking raised a hand and drew one of the stone thrones out of the earth, gesturing for Mirae to sit across from him.

As Mirae took her seat, she eyed the food on his plate, wondering who had taught him how to cook, and where he'd gotten the food. Compared to the plentiful side dishes and meats she was used to at the palace, his meal was humble and surprisingly ordinary—marinated potatoes, glazed carrots, and rib-cracked fish. All foods that could be found underground.

"Are you finally ready to fulfill your promise?" the Netherking asked, eyebrow raised.

"In part," Mirae said. "I won't be resting for long, so I'd actually like to request a particular history lesson tonight."

"Oh?" The Netherking leaned back in his seat. "And what might that be?"

Mirae had known all day that she and the Netherking would meet again like this, and that he was the only one who could help her begin to make sense of the question growing in her mind—triggered by the shaman robes he'd had on hand, and something strange he'd said. "I want to hear the story of Suhee the Haggard Moon Gwisin."

The Netherking stilled. "Where did you hear that name?"

"She's the one who gave me the pearl. I'd like to know who she is and what you did to the mul gwisin who hate Sacred Bone Magic so much."

The Netherking looked away. "You said she was a gwisin. Are you sure?"

"Yes." Mirae studied the Netherking's face. "She was important to you, wasn't she?"

"I don't see what this has to do with our deal." The Netherking smoothed out his robes, gathering himself. "It's a personal matter. None of your business."

"Oh, I think it is has everything to do with us." Mirae pressed her hands into the table until her knuckles were as white as the gwisin's pearl. "I've had a lot of time to think about the day we met. You said some things that didn't make sense at the time, but I'm starting to piece it all together."

"Are you, now?" The Netherking sneered, as if there was no reason to believe Mirae's intellect was a threat. He picked up his chopsticks and stabbed one of the glazed carrots.

Mirae took a deep breath, hoping she wasn't about to make a fool of herself.

"You said my mother betrayed you, and that she should have begged for your forgiveness. You also said that killing me would be an act of revenge—an eye for an eye. That's an interesting saying, because it implies that you've suffered a similar wrong. The loss of a loved one. I have a feeling that Suhee's story is tied to my mother's, and to everything you've done to my family. What happened between you two? What exactly did my mother do?"

The Netherking peeled off one last strip of fish before pushing the platter away. Mirae stared at the mangled body, its ribs parted open. Gutted. The Netherking watched Mirae as she peered into its hollow, greasy chest—the endgame between predator and prey. "Are you sure you want to know who your mother really is?"

Mirae looked the Netherking in the eye. "I want to know why she thought all this pain and heartache was better than letting you go. I need this—all of this—to start making sense."

The Netherking pushed the rest of his dishes away so he could rest his elbows on the table and steeple his fingers in front of his face. "Well, far be it from me to do anything that would keep the False Queen's reputation white as snow. Are you ready to hear the truth as only I can tell it?"

"Yes," Mirae said, hoping it was true that the Netherking couldn't tell a lie. Not to her.

The Netherking smiled, his teeth a bone-white crown.

To understand Suhee, you first have to imagine the world's most infuriating know-it-all. If you unearthed even a small gap in her understanding, she'd obsess over it until she was able to prove that she knew more about it than you ever did. No matter how many years you dedicated to a skill, she'd surpass you in it in a matter of weeks. Everything she saw or heard, she remembered. Anything she learned, she used to her advantage. These were all the things that drove me mad when we first met. But they were also the things I loved most about her.

As you can imagine, Suhee was a precocious child, and quickly grew academically successful enough in her Josan hometown to catch the attention of royal scholars. Back then, efforts were being made to unite the peninsula through shared education, so they invited her to the Seollan palace to study with the best. That was how she and Crown Princess Noeul met. They became fast friends. The best of friends, to the point that they began admitting their guilty pleasures to each other. Crown Princess Noeul was obsessed with crafting enchanted beads inspired by the dark powers of the nine-tailed gumiho—right under her mother's nose.

Suhee's guilty pleasure? Practicing the mysterious shamanism of Josan.

Crown Princess Noeul was intrigued and wanted to see this strange power in action. So one night, the two friends snuck out to the Garden of Queens, where Suhee could summon the royal dead for their descendant to speak with. Of course, this was all done in the name of having a good time. And it was fun, at first. Until they heard what the dead had to say.

That was the first time Crown Princess Noeul had ever heard of the Deep. And based on the way her ancestors howled about it, demanding that she destroy the abominable nether-fiends before it was too late, she'd stumbled onto a grave family secret. Had she been alone, she might have gone straight home and tried to push the horrible screams of her ancestors out of her mind. But she was with Suhee. And if Suhee was good at anything, it was being consumed with curiosity when she should be running for her life.

It wasn't long before Suhee convinced her friend to seek out these nether-fiends—for, as I said before, I wasn't always alone here—and see what all the fuss was about. The road to Wol Sin Lake and the barriers surrounding it were different back then. Following clues they'd heard in the furious words of the royal dead, they found my prison, much like you did, and trod carelessly into my domain.

I was different back then, too. For when I sensed the crown princess's magic, I didn't stop to think about what I was doing. I sent my hand out to grab the first ankle it could find.

That's how I ended up with Suhee stuck in my ceiling, while the crown princess scuttled back to safety. By the time I realized I had the wrong woman, it was too late to correct my mistake. And the crown princess wasn't keen on taking Suhee's place. I tried to reason with her, barter for her friend's life. But Suhee remained my unwitting hostage, for I had hope that Noeul would yet change her mind as she grieved for her innocent friend trapped in the Deep.

The process of Suhee's acclimation isn't something I will bore you with. The only thing you need to know is that her curiosity was far more resilient than her self-pity. She adjusted quickly, and it wasn't long before she started driving me mad with questions and insatiable nosiness. I couldn't keep anything from her for long. Thankfully, there came a time when I didn't have to, because she decided my predicament, like hers, was unjust. Freedom for herself became equal to freedom for me and my people. Our wrongs were her wrongs.

Our enemies, her enemies. And, as you probably suspect, our hearts became one.

I'll admit, Suhee changed me. Having someone who could adore me and be adored by me almost made me content with life. Perhaps living out my days in darkness would be bearable, as long as there was this small source of light. I'd never made room for love before, because my friends and family kept dying around me. But Suhee taught me what made life worth living, and then she gave me the greatest gift of all—a daughter to love as I've never loved anything before.

I was smitten, queenling. And so was Suhee. Once again I was almost convinced to bury my need for revenge. I thought I knew what I wanted for the rest of my life. I even considered myself lucky.

Everything changed the night my little girl fell ill. As it turns out, the blood of the free isn't meant to mix with the cursed blood of the caged. My paternity was doing something to her. Something that would kill her if I didn't find a cure.

That was when I resumed my pestering of your mother. I begged her to release my people before we all died. When she refused, I revealed that Suhee was still alive, and that it wasn't too late to do the right thing. I was willing to let Suhee go if my child could go with her. I begged for that much, at least—the lives of my family.

But Noeul refused. You see, there's a very, very strict rule when it comes to the cage: no one with the blood of the cursed may leave. When Suhee, doing her part to beg for Noeul's mercy, refused to leave without her child, your mother tested Suhee's resolve by giving her the pearl. It would let Suhee out, and only Suhee, because she had "pure, uncursed" blood. She had a choice, one your mother thought would *be easily made. Well, it was, queenling, because Suhee would never choose anything over her family.*

You want to know why all this is happening. You want all this to make sense. Well, the night your mother first fell ill with madness was the night my rage finally broke through the centuries-strong barriers of the Deep, because I was truly alone with nothing to lose. When my daughter died, Suhee couldn't bear it, so she did the unthinkable. I lost both my loves in one night. After that, I had nothing to live for except my rekindled all-consuming need for revenge.

And that, queenling, is why your mother will never, ever escape my rage.

"Do you see?" The Netherking looked gaunt in the green moonlight, more shadow than man. "The mul gwisin you speak of, whose story I will tell when you finally keep your promise to me, are my people. They died because your mother wouldn't free them. As such, all are bound to rot down here with hatred in their hearts. So yes, they loathe Sacred Bone Magic, but not for the reasons you think. The haggard moon gwisin only let you have the pearl because you somehow proved to her that you are the one who can finally bring an end to all this suffering."

Mirae sat in silence as the pieces explaining her mother's premature illness finally fell into place. Was it any wonder that her mother was so disapproving of Mirae's recklessness when her own had rekindled a war between Seolla and the Deep? In betraying a Josan friend, she'd also given the Josan king a powerful ally, unlike any he'd ever known. Yet none of this was ever supposed to reach Mirae's ears—she was meant to blindly lead a queendom she had never truly known. A queendom rife with corruption. A queendom drowning in secrets. With a queen and a monster at the heart of it who had caused the death of an innocent—and her child.

Mirae clenched her fists on the table. So much death at the hands of both her mother and the dark king sitting in front of her. For it was his greed that had kept Suhee here against her will.

"Every word I've said is true," the Netherking said, studying Mirae's face, "yet you look displeased. Why?"

Mirae pressed two fingers against her temples, as if that would keep them from bursting. "Because it seems like everyone trying to earn my trust also tries to manipulate me."

"If the truth is hard to hear, that's your problem, not mine," he scoffed.

"You would have me take your side and rebel against my mother," Mirae said. "But you're not just a victim in this tragedy. You held Suhee against her will. You, too, are to blame for her horrible end."

The Netherking leaned back in his seat, his face lined with disappointment. "After all this, your inclination is to find fault with me, rather than with your mother?"

"Well, why should I think you're any better, after everything you've done?" Mirae demanded. "What if Suhee hadn't grown to love you? What would you have done if she had never stopped wanting to leave?"

"I could ask you the same thing about Josan," the Netherking said, his voice cold, his eyes even more so. "You think you sit cleanly on your throne, but you have no right to judge me from up there. Not when your palace was built on the broken bones of the furiously unwilling."

The words Mirae had prepared remained bottled up in her throat. The Netherking was right. Every word, every accusation, every qualm. What the Netherking had done out of desperation was nothing compared to what Seolla had done with its insatiable need for power.

As if sensing the direction of her thoughts, the Netherking relaxed his face and voice, revealing a hint of the man he might have been when he'd had a family to love. "When I first saw you, you were a Seollan heir, through and through. The world was split between right and wrong—and Seolla, of course, was always in the right. The woman who sits before me tonight has seen the truth, and it has changed her. You are the balance between the dark and the light. The magic of your grandmothers may be in your blood, but it is I, in the Deep, who give you your spine. It is because of my truth that you will unite us all. *You* are my reckoning."

Mirae looked into the Netherking's dark eyes. They were the same as hers, twin inkblots of fury pressed into faces pale as paper. But the sheets were otherwise still blank. There was time to write a better ending for them both. Mirae leaned forward in her seat. "When I bring Minho to you, you will make him whole. And then I will do whatever I can to set you free. You have my word."

The Netherking stared back at her, the whites of his eyes like smooth, unblinking moons. "I will hold you to that promise, queenling. After all, words spoken in the Deep cannot be false."

Mirae and the Netherking sat silently across from each other, letting the promise of restitution sink between them. After a moment, the Netherking leaned forward in his seat, too. "There is one more thing I'd like to tell you, as a kindness. It's about your mother's beads."

Mirae had almost forgotten he'd mentioned them. She clutched the silk bag around her neck. "You said my mother made these . . . through the dark powers of the gumiho?"

"She was *inspired* by their magic," the Netherking corrected her. "Do you know the myth surrounding gumiho beads?"

Mirae thought back to childhood stories she'd read. "It is through transferring their beads into the mouths of humans, and then back into their own, that gumiho eat the thousand souls they need to become human."

The Netherking nodded. "Your mother's beads were enchanted to exhibit the qualities of the zodiac, as you know. But her method of empowering them was the same."

"Through eating a human soul?" Mirae asked, doubtful.

The Netherking picked up a small piece of potato from his dinner and stuck it into his mouth very deliberately. And suddenly Mirae understood.

In the Garden of Queens, her father had put a bead on Mirae's tongue to pass the power of calmness, of love, into her body. She'd assumed the bead carried that power intrinsically. But now she remembered what had happened next—her father had stuck a bead into his own mouth before transferring it to her mother through a kiss. Using his own life force first to animate the bead's ability.

Mirae felt every inch of her body tense with horror. Images flashed through her mind of her father's sudden decline in health over the past three months—exhibiting the toll of her mother's madness in more ways than Mirae knew. She stumbled over the words that came almost unbidden out of her mouth: "She tried to stave off her madness with the power of those beads—power she stole . . . from my father's soul?"

The Netherking nodded, a hint of pity, and something else, on his face. "All this begins and ends with her. Had she not abandoned her friend in the Deep, and then been so cruel to her friend's child, I would have never suffered such loss that I broke a hole in my cage, determined to make your mother pay for her sins. And, of course, had I not been forced to torture her with all my hatred, she wouldn't have used your father like this, nor set you on this course. Minho wouldn't be in Josan, needing to be saved."

There were no words left in Mirae's heart, only rage. The kind that vowed to never die. "Did my father know his wife was killing him to save herself?"

"The person sacrificed to the beads does not need to be willing," the Netherking said, "but I believe your father was. He was groomed to be that kind of man, as were his sons, who were raised to be defenseless against their queen, their Sacred Bone Magic repressed by a mark."

It was true—her father was the kind of man who would gladly trade his life for his family, for his queendom, without questioning the woman who sent him to the slaughter. Mirae squeezed the bag of beads around her neck, vowing to return them so that her father's life force could be put back where it belonged. Then she made another promise, heart blazing with fury.

She would not be like her mother. No one, however willing, was going to be sacrificed for the sake of her reign—starting with Minho.

The silence between Mirae and the Netherking was broken by a low rumble that started in the darkness behind her from which she'd emerged. She turned to look into the cavern of impenetrable shadows until she recognized the sound. It was a voice traveling from far, far away until it was close enough to echo clearly.

Wake up, noonim. Please wake up.

Mirae turned back to face the Netherking, who nodded. "Don't forget that both Minho and our deal are running out of time. Find him quickly and bring him to me."

The Netherking reached out his hand, level with Mirae's chest. And then, inches away from her racing heart, he clenched his fist and sent Mirae reeling back into her body.

Chapter

TWENTY-TWO

Mirae woke up sore from lying on the ground, unmoving. The back of her throat burned from breathing in the cold night air, and she wasn't even sure her icy toes were still attached to her feet. What she did feel acutely, however, was someone slapping the sides of her face.

"Wake up, Mirae. Please wake up."

When Mirae opened her eyes, she saw Hongbin fall backward onto the ground before whispering to someone nearby, "Okay, she's up. What do we do now?"

Mirae craned her neck to see Captain Jia standing by her head, looking out at the fields beyond. With a hand from Hongbin, Mirae sat up and followed the captain's gaze.

Their camp was surrounded. No matter where she turned, Mirae saw a wide, silent circle of men stretching across either side of the river. They stood far enough away that they would have blended in with the dark, waiting all through the night without being heard over the chortling river. But now the gray of morning had turned them into a crown of stark silhouettes.

"Josan soldiers. I'm not sure why I didn't sense them approaching," Captain Jia murmured. She held her sword in a defensive stance, ready to imbue it with lethal magic when the time came for battle.

"What do we do?" Mirae asked, eyeing the circle of soldiers.

"You and the others run. Let the river lead you back toward the border, then get across as quickly as you can. Siwon, I'm counting on your knowledge of the terrain to get them home." When Mirae began to protest, Captain Jia silenced her with a look. "It's over, Gongju. For now, the Josan king wants us alive. That's either very good or very bad—but it's almost definitely because he knows who you are. He'll never let us get close to Daegun now. You only have two options—you either flee or surrender."

"If we surrender, the Josan king will use me as proof of Seolla's treachery. He'll get his war, and we cannot allow that." Mirae rose to stand beside the captain. "There's a third option—we could fight."

"Are you prepared to kill every single soldier here who witnesses our magic? Because that's the only way we can avoid leaving proof that the crown princess of Seolla attacked people in Josan." Though the captain's face was too far away for the surrounding soldiers to see, Mirae was certain the anger there would have scared quite a few of them. "If one of us has to fight, let it be me. I will accept the death penalty if it means you get away."

"Or . . . we could just find out what they want," Siwon offered from where he sat on the ground, his traveling parcel packed and ready to go. Mirae was no longer surprised to see him looking calm in the face of danger. "If they're not here to kill us, then they're probably going to arrest us and escort us to the fortress. That's where we want to go anyway."

Mirae looked up at the mountain, gray and pink in the misty dawn. Craggy, unforgiving terrain. She'd said they could trust the river to lead them to the top, but truly the paved road was by far the safest option; perhaps Siwon was onto something.

"There's no way the Josan king will simply escort you up to the fortress and keep two valuable hostages in one place." Captain Jia shot Siwon a look. "I'm sure the entire queendom knows you're here by now, Gongju, which means the Josan king will march you to the capital and make a show of your capture. His plan has always been to bring Seolla to its knees—what better way of doing that than leaving it with one mad queen and no heirs? You have no choice, Gongju—*you must escape.*"

Mirae heard the truth in Captain Jia's words, but she'd made a promise to Minho, to everyone her mother's selfishness had hurt. She couldn't bear to run now when she was so close. There had to be another way, just as Siwon said.

By now a small group of soldiers had broken ranks and was approaching the camp. Captain Jia held out her unlit blade, pushing Mirae behind her. "Go back to the border, Gongju. I won't ask again."

But Mirae caught the other woman's arm and reversed their positions. "We didn't come all this way just to give up. I can convince them to take us to Minho without a fight."

"By letting them arrest us for using magic? They'll execute us."

"They're not going to arrest us." Mirae said. "I saw something in a switch that can help. Please trust me, Captain. I'm using my head, I promise."

Captain Jia looked into Mirae's eyes, perhaps seeing something there that she wanted to believe. After a moment, the captain lowered her sword and allowed Mirae to stand in front of her as the soldiers approached—but she did not put away her blade.

With all three of her companions by her side, Mirae stared at the approaching men; two captains with long feathers on their hats spurred their horses forward slowly.

Mirae took one last look at the men surrounding them. They stood in a perfect circle, each with one hand—the same hand—resting on their sword. Everything about them was in unison, even the way they breathed. Though the soldiers looked like they belonged in the Josan army, with their full-body bronze mail and purple tunics peeking out, there was something about the way they carried themselves that felt . . . off.

Mirae and her companions waited as the two captains came close enough to speak. "I'm Captain Keon, and this is Captain Sado. You being here, Gongju mama, is an act of war."

Mirae took a deep breath before responding. "You speak boldly, Captain, considering you know full well that what your king has done is also an act of war. I will give you one chance to return my brother so we can all go peacefully on our way."

Captain Keon waved Captain Sado back, who had started to ride closer. "Do not force my hand, Gongju mama. If you try anything, I have permission to kill you where you stand."

"But you won't," Mirae said, holding out her arm to keep Captain Jia from rushing the man who'd threatened her. "And I'm not going anywhere until you take me to Kimoon."

The impassive captain paled. "What did you say?"

Mirae walked forward, close enough to grab the reins of his horse if she wanted to. "You know who I am. A witch of my caliber can discover all manner of secrets."

"I don't care what you are—you shouldn't know that name."

"I shouldn't know what Kimoon has done, either. But I've seen my brother's chains and his black water baths. I know how Kimoon is trying to earn his place as a true prince of Josan. And I know, as you do, that he's not comfortable with the cost of reclaiming his throne—not if it means allying himself with a king who possesses Deep-seated issues."

Captain Keon was speechless. Mirae said one last thing to convince him. "I bet after everything I've just said, Kimoon will want to talk to me as much as I want to talk to him."

The captain looked back at Captain Sado, then again at Mirae. "Once you go up that mountain, Gongju mama, there is no turning back. Prince Kimoon will not let you leave."

"That's what I was told when I visited the Netherking. And yet here I am."

That name seemed to shock Captain Keon even more than the first. "All right, Gongju mama. I'll take you to the prince and let him decide what to do with you."

Captain Keon turned his horse around, consulted quietly with the other captain, and then gestured for Mirae and her companions to follow. They gathered their things and trailed after the two captains, passing right through the circle of soldiers, who remained exactly where they were.

As Mirae followed the soldiers up the steep mountain path, she couldn't imagine trying to reach the top unseen, let alone still breathing. The wear and tear on her knees and shins from the steep incline and the loose gravel, along with the dry air that made her nose burn as they neared the top, were enough to make her want to turn back.

But more than that, it made her grieve for what Minho, bruised and bullied, had endured to reach this prison. Alone with monsters.

"Noonim," Hongbin said, "please tell me my face is not as chapped as it feels. I cannot appear before a prince looking like I can't handle a little wind."

"You look fine," she said, remembering a time when his chin would be marked with a scar. "It's your destiny to be handsome forever."

"Promise?"

She lowered her voice. "I'm the Switcher of Seolla, remember? I know things."

He smiled, but not for long. "What about Minho? And the others? Will they be all right?"

"Of course. I wouldn't have come all this way just to watch them die," she said. The lie on her tongue tasted worse than the Netherking's oily black water. "None of my pretty kings will be broken today."

"Or princesses," he said. "Though in my experience, they're the ones who do all the breaking. Kimoon has no idea what's coming."

Mirae nodded, but she knew better than to be so certain about anything. As long as there was an Inconstant Son for her to kill and switches to complicate everything, the threat that Mirae posed to evil—or to the peninsula, should she fail—would never be fully known.

"So, on to lighter topics. Is Kimoon single?" Hongbin asked. "If he's handsome and woo-worthy, I'd like to think I can be of some help in that department. I might be the one who can persuade him to leave our brother alone."

Mirae bumped his shoulder with hers. "One boyfriend at a time, Hongbin. What about that member of the Josan delegation you were pursuing?"

He chuckled. "Ah, noonim, what would you know of the complicated art of love?"

Mirae snuck a glance over at Siwon, who was walking alone, shivering in the mountain air. He caught Mirae looking and shot her a comforting smile. She felt lifted by it. After all, their plan had worked, and now it was only a matter of time before they would see Minho again.

"We're almost there," Captain Keon called from atop his horse.

The road was wide enough for Mirae and her companions to walk abreast, watching for the mountain fortress. When she saw it materialize around a bend, all Mirae could do was stare.

Set in stone, massive and foreboding, it appeared all but indestructible. It would have been impossible to break into on their own. The giant front wall arced between two cloud-capped cliffs, and the only gate leading in looked as thick as the stone surrounding it—stone that was built straight out of the mountain, making walls as strong as the ageless peak beneath Mirae's feet. Farther ahead, Mirae could see the top of a three-tiered pagoda, wide and curved like a warship. The entire fortress seemed like an extension of the mountain, built by the gods.

Captains Keon and Sado stopped at the massive gate so the guards could search Mirae and her companions, confiscating their belongings. Captain Jia was forced to surrender her jade sword, Siwon his traveling pack, and Mirae the contents of her pocket—Suhee's pearl and the blue seong-suk of the Deep Deceiver. Mirae handed the latter over wrapped in its protective silk.

"Don't disturb the relic inside," Mirae said to Keon. "Whoever touches it will die."

Keon nodded at Sado, who handed over an empty rice sack for stowing the deadly relic. Then Sado patted Mirae down himself while other guards frisked her companions. He was respectful with his hands, and Mirae was glad that he didn't seem to notice the bag of beads and black water tucked under her jeogori, or the black bell she'd tied into the thickest part of her braid, hoping its lumpiness would be mistaken for an unkempt knot.

Keon and Sado led them quickly across the sandy courtyard to the three-tiered pagoda at the center of the fortress. The proud structure was made from the same stone as the mountain, but its outer facades were painted red, its roofs black and curved like bows—the kind carried by the guards stationed at every corner. They paced about on patrol, occasionally sneaking glances at the visitors who'd been allowed into their fortress.

Once inside the pagoda, Mirae gasped, totally unprepared for the lavish scale of the interior after seeing the sensible, intimidating stonework that made this place look like a prison, not a temple.

The jade-green walls, bloodred pillars, and golden accents on dozens of murals looked opulent enough to be dedicated to the gods. But what took Mirae's breath away was the golden staircase in the middle of the room, steps beginning in the very center, then leading up to the outer walls before climbing back toward the middle of the room where the entrance to the next level began. There was no support for the stairs, no giant pillars holding up the next level. An architectural masterpiece unlike anything Mirae had ever seen.

Keon and Sado didn't give Mirae long to stare before shepherding her toward the very staircase she was ogling. She and her companions walked up to the next level, this one just as luxuriously painted as the first. Several branching halls partitioned the second level into a string of private rooms. Keon and Sado led them to the largest chamber at the end of the hall, which spanned the entire back wall of the pagoda.

"No magic is permitted here," Keon said. "I must ensure you adhere to our laws."

Mirae nodded. "I will. I promise."

"Promises from Seollan royalty are not considered binding," he said, and before Mirae could even blink, Sado grabbed Hongbin tightly from behind and pressed a knife against his neck.

Mirae shot Keon a glare of rage that only the Netherking had ever seen. "Let him go, or you will be incinerated with all the magic running in my veins."

"Gongju mama," Captain Jia said warningly.

"It's all right, Gongju," Siwon said, his calm voice right beside Mirae's ear. "I'll stay with Gunju while you do what you came here to do. They have no reason to harm us yet."

"No, not *yet*." Keon pointed at Captain Jia. "But you will also be taken to the prison below."

"Why?" Mirae demanded, stepping between Keon and Captain Jia.

"Don't, Gongju mama," Captain Jia said, softer this time. "I'll be fine."

When Keon spoke next, it was with barely restrained impatience. "Magic was used in Noksan, which means someone needs to be punished. For now, I'm going to pretend that wasn't you, Gongju mama. As a kindness."

Mirae wanted more than anything to show Keon what it meant to fear Sacred Bone Magic, but at a look from Captain Jia, she let the rage within her slowly dissipate, sending it back to a place where it wouldn't risk Hongbin's life—or anyone else's.

"May I at least hug my brother goodbye?"

Keon nodded gruffly, so Mirae wrapped her arms around Hongbin, slipping a small ruby bead into his pocket as she did. Then Sado heaved Hongbin away, carting him down the hall. Captain Jia and Siwon followed wordlessly.

When they were gone, Mirae turned to Keon, not caring if he saw the blistering fury within her that had once created a dragon out of air. "You've taken something far more precious than magic, so you'd better trust me now. I won't risk my brother's life for anything."

Keon nodded. "I know, Gongju mama. I'm hoping that's why you came."

He opened the door behind him, gesturing for Mirae to enter and meet the man inside.

Mirae's eyes skimmed the room and its lavish red furniture, coming to rest on the young man sitting at a large mahogany desk inlaid with mother-of-pearl phoenixes. He didn't look up when Mirae and Keon arrived, but she didn't need to see his face to know who he was:

Kimoon.

Instead of greeting them, he continued to practice his calligraphy, transcribing what appeared to be classic Josan poems, if the examples displayed around the room were any indication. Words of a vengeful nation. Nothing like the impassivity on Kimoon's face.

He looked exactly as he had in Mirae's vision, with dark hair and honey-brown eyes that gleamed, concealing all manner of secrets. Soft skin cooled by the deep purple of his hanbok. Kimoon finished the painstaking stroke he was working on before glancing up, his long, loose hair as smooth and black as the ink he dipped his brush into. "What is it, Keon?"

"We found her." Keon bowed. "She knows much more than expected. I didn't think it prudent to let her leave until you questioned her."

Kimoon leaned back in his chair, gently wiping ink off the tips of his fingers with a white cloth, forever stained. "It was bold of you to think I'd disobey my father's orders to send her to the capital immediately, with a fanfare of shame. She must have given you quite a shock."

"She knew your name," Keon said. "And what we're doing here."

Kimoon finally looked at Mirae. "Well, I guess that makes us even, Switcher."

Looking into Kimoon's cold eyes flung her right back into that wintry landscape where a man had squeezed her neck and uttered her title with deep contempt. Was this really him—the old man on the mountain? The two men shared a name, and possibly a destiny as an enemy feared by even the gods. Was Mirae supposed to kill him right here, right now, despite what that might mean for her brothers and friends?

She knew what Captain Jia would say. Hongbin and Siwon, too. With a calming breath, Mirae lifted her chin as she faced the bastard Josan prince. "Since we don't require any introductions, let's cut to the chase. What will it take for you to give Minho back?"

Kimoon stood, straightening his deep purple hanbok as he walked to the front of his desk and leaned against it. "He's not a prisoner, Mirae. He's my patient, and I'm not letting him leave until he's better."

"That's a lie," Mirae said. "You're a greedy bastard prince, not a physician."

Keon started as if he was ready to reach over and snap her neck, but Kimoon didn't even blink. "As you said, no introductions are necessary. I know full well what you are, too." He turned to Keon. "Did she have anything on her?"

Keon handed over the rice sack with Mirae's things. The beads and the vial still hidden between her breasts felt as heavy as the bell beneath her braid as she watched Kimoon take out Suhee's pearl.

"Ah, the precious key to the Deep that I've heard so much about." A sharp smile split Kimoon's face. "It'll be nice to convene with our dear friend in person. Make sure he holds up his end of the bargain. How is the Netherking these days? Feeling especially bereft, I suppose?"

Mirae kept her face as composed as Kimoon's. "He's as insolent as ever."

Kimoon's smile melted into a sneer. "I had a feeling today would bring me good fortune. I'm glad I was right." Kimoon tucked the pearl into his pocket. "My mudang warned me that Seolla's gods would try something desperate. But they're like you, Switcher. They are nothing without their magic—and Josan is very good at destroying magic."

Mirae stepped closer to where Kimoon leaned against his desk. Keon didn't stop her, but he did follow. When she was near enough, she let her eyes skim over the poem Kimoon had been working on.

> *Only the sun god can live in eternal summer*
> *And autumn is for heaven's falling leaves, the stars*
> *I pray to sister moon for the rebirth of spring*
> *But her pale, closing eye brings only winter to my soul.*

Mirae looked up and met Kimoon's gaze, remembering what the Netherking had said just a few days ago, about the conflict they both saw on Kimoon's face.

You should use that against him.

Kimoon's sneer softened ever so slightly as he nodded at the poem. "I wrote it today. What do you think?"

Mirae read the poem again. "I think the rebirth you're waiting for is the recognition and respect you are owed as a prince. But the winter of your soul is the torment and regret you feel over how those things will become yours."

Kimoon inclined his head. "That's an interesting interpretation. Are you hoping to crack open my heart with your deep discernment and transform me?"

"I already know what's in your heart," Mirae said. "What you're doing to Minho is eating you up inside. You're hoping to find another way to get what you want."

"And you've got just the thing?" Kimoon asked mockingly. "All I have to do is trust the word of the Switcher of Seolla, and all my dreams will come true?"

The way he spat out her title yet again reminded Mirae of the man on the mountain, who hated her more than anyone else in the world. Yet Hongbin had said she wouldn't stop the Inconstant Son because she "loved him across all time and under every moon." Was it possible he was talking about Kimoon? Were the gods telling her this was the only way out of this mess where nobody had to die?

Mirae steeled herself for what she would say next. She was dutiful like Captain Jia. Devoted to peace like Hongbin. Willing to sacrifice like Minho. Resourceful like Siwon. But she was also patient like the Netherking. Calm like Kimoon. Ruthless like her mother.

Emboldened, Mirae raised her chin. "I will make you a king, Kimoon. All I'm asking is that you follow your heart when it comes to Minho. Find another way to get your rebirth, and you will get everything you want, and more."

Kimoon set his cold gaze on Mirae, studying her. After a moment, he leaned forward, close enough that Mirae could smell the ginger and honey tea on his breath. "How stupid do you think I am, Switcher? Do I seem so desperate, so naive that I would be beguiled by the way you flaunt your despotic power, just as you've beguiled everyone around you?"

Mirae pulled back as if she'd been slapped. "That's not what I—"

"You think yourself so noble, willing to sacrifice your happiness for Minho's life. And for what? You assumed I would jump for joy at the thought of being a Seollan consort instead of a Josan king?"

"The assumption is yours," Mirae said sharply. "I never said we would marry, only that I would make you a king."

"It doesn't matter how you'll go about it." Kimoon's pale skin flickered with the dancing fire of the candles on his desk. "It's your attitude that disgusts me. You thought you could just walk in here after terrifying my citizens, breaking our laws, and robbing us of our freedoms for generations and somehow convince me to ease your own suffering? Well, here's a lesson for you, Switcher. No one, least of all me, is inclined to listen to your sob story. After all, what's good for you and Seolla has never, ever been good for us."

Mirae looked into Kimoon's eyes, narrowed with rage, and yet somehow all she could see was an old man on a freezing mountain, studying her with a face weathered by pain. Mirae swallowed down everything Kimoon's vicious words woke up inside her. This was not the time to prove he was right about the selfish attitude and tactics she'd learned from Seolla.

"I'm sorry I offended you," Mirae said, softening. "You're right. The whole reason I came here was to look out for my people, not yours. It's no way for a queen to act."

Kimoon stared at her much like he had on that distant mountain, as if he couldn't decide just how little he trusted her. "Why do I feel like you're about to make me another offer?"

"Not an offer," Mirae said, amazed that her voice didn't shake. "A trade. Me for Minho. Something that isn't for you or me, but for your father."

Kimoon swung some loose hair back over his shoulder. "I already have you in custody. I'd hardly call that a trade—"

"I'm offering myself without magic," Mirae said, finally getting Kimoon to fall silent. "Escort my friends and family safely home, and I will remain here in Josan for as long as you want, abiding by the laws of your land."

Kimoon scoffed. "Oh, you just *won't use magic*? You *swear*?"

"There's a way to take away my powers," Mirae said, suddenly feeling how cold her hands and feet had become despite the room's heated floors. "A mark you can put on my flesh, which we give to magic-adept men. Only someone of Sacred Bone blood can do this to me, so I'm offering to do it to myself. I will be yours to do with as you wish, powerless, like Minho."

Kimoon leaned back against his desk, somehow both relaxing his body and making it look more threatening at the same time. He seemed lost in his own thoughts, even though his gaze remained fixed on Mirae. "I already told you that I can't let Minho go in his state. Black water is the only thing keeping him alive."

"Then we'll take some with us," Mirae said, hesitant to reveal that she'd managed to keep a vial of it with her, hanging around her neck. "You can really, truly let him go. Your torment, and his, can finally end."

There—a spark of something in Kimoon's eyes that didn't look comfortable being pulled into the light. He rubbed his face tiredly, and Mirae spotted the inky crescents beneath his nails. "I have to say I'm surprised by you, Mirae. You really know how to get under a man's skin."

"I think Minho was doing that already," Mirae said. "Deep down, you know that if any part of this nightmare is going to end, you've got to end it with me."

Kimoon was silent for a moment, studying Mirae's face like he was studying his own soul. After what felt like several minutes, he turned to Keon, who had been standing and listening silently beside them. "Prepare the courtyard, and tell the guards to execute all prisoners if our guest of honor shows even a hint of magic."

Keon nodded and exited the room quickly. Kimoon turned back to Mirae, his face as calm and collected as before. "There is a chance that my father will find your offer of a trade favorable. But before I put my neck on the line and ask him to consider shifting our plans, I need you to prove that you are a woman of your word."

Mirae nodded. "And then you'll let my friends and family go?"

"I can promise you nothing," Kimoon said. "However, having you on our side will allow us to expedite our plan, so it's possible that I'll be able to work something out. Your companions know too much to be allowed to leave, but soon, that may not matter."

Kimoon gestured to a lacquered mahogany chest on the far side of the room. "You'll find some of my extra clothes in there. Please change and come out when you're ready."

With that, Kimoon left, leaving Mirae to peel off her traveling clothes and robe herself in the purple silk of Josan—a color, she thought, that resembled the bruises blooming deep inside a traitor's heart.

Chapter
TWENTY-THREE

As soon as she was done changing, Mirae joined Kimoon outside his office. He led her wordlessly toward a balcony on the opposite side of the second level. From there, Mirae could see the thick walls of the fortress and the sandy courtyard below, where a small crowd had gathered. At least a dozen soldiers surrounded a block of wood anchoring a prisoner kneeling at their feet—Captain Jia. A man with a golden axe stood above her, posing with all the confidence of someone more than happy to continue his streak of one-swing kills.

It was clear what he'd been called there to do. The Wonhwa captain looked steadily forward, keeping her head high while it was still attached to her body, eyes dry as the courtyard sand.

Mirae whirled to face Kimoon. "What is this? What are you doing?"

"This is the test I spoke of." Kimoon gestured toward the courtyard, staged for an execution. "You said you will stay here and abide by the laws of Josan in exchange for your brothers' freedom, so let's see if you can keep your word."

Magic was illegal in Josan, punishable by death. Someone had broken the law in Noksan and needed to be made an example of. If Mirae confessed that the crime was hers, she would be executed, and all hopes of rescuing Minho gone forever.

If she let Captain Jia take the fall, however, the trade-off could go on. Mirae could remain in Josan in Minho's stead, helpless against the king's political whims; but only if she proved here and now that she could be trusted to put Josan's beliefs above her own.

"This isn't what we talked about," Mirae said, voice shaking. "I agreed to take Minho's place and suppress my magic, but only if all my friends and family are returned safely home."

"We'll return her body safely. You have my word." Kimoon at least had the decency to stare impassively down at the courtyard, rather than sneer at Mirae as he had before.

As Mirae's hands itched to form a fire she couldn't afford to release, she finally understood what it was like to face a tyrant completely in the wrong, and for the power she was born with to be precisely what made her an enemy. Condemned and helpless, Mirae felt the rage that had festered so long in the Deep fill her heart with the righteous anger of the unfairly damned. She had no choice but to make her would-be oppressor back down by any means necessary, even if that made her no better than the Netherking.

"Do you really think it wise to provoke me when I offer peace?" Mirae asked, gripping the sides of the balcony tightly. "You could have a prisoner who is contrite out of honor and loyalty to her loved ones, rather than one who hates you and will persecute you every day for the rest of her life."

"Now, now, Mirae. Neither of us really believes that you would ever be loyal to me," Kimoon said. "Not while you continue to reject the beliefs that make me who I am."

"What you are is a murderer, and a sadist. Maybe you should be the one reconsidering the things you believe."

Kimoon scoffed. "Congratulations on your narrow, elitist worldview, Mirae. You are a Seollan princess, through and through."

"Because I refuse to murder in cold blood?" Mirae fumed. Her nails dug so deeply into the balcony railing that the tips began to bend backward.

"Because you cannot even *fathom* a situation where you are unable to reclaim the upper hand." Kimoon narrowed his eyes. "If you want my cooperation, there's an important lesson you need to learn."

"And what is that?" Mirae asked, feeling the palms of her hands burn with something more than pain—a fire she wasn't sure she would be able to contain much longer.

"What it's like to be laid low." Kimoon leaned in close, his voice a mere whisper. "Will you persist in the Seollan delusion that you are above the natural order of things and all the world must bend to your will? Or will you do what no other Seollan monarch has ever done—submit to the reality of Josan, a place where people suffer so that our deranged oppressors may thrive, and those brave enough to carry ancestral rage must vow to destroy the vile powers that keep them on their knees?"

Mirae looked down at the courtyard, searching for the face of a friend who had always kept her calm when she wanted to burst. A woman who was not afraid to die, but deserved a long, honorable career alongside the love of her life. Mirae knew saving Minho at the expense of his heart wouldn't be saving him at all.

Mirae lifted her chin. "I should congratulate you as well, for being the biggest hypocrite this peninsula has ever seen." Kimoon raised an eyebrow but didn't interrupt. "I know what you're doing to Minho. And I know what I saw down by the river. Those soldiers aren't themselves anymore, are they? What did you do to them? Am I supposed to believe you haven't used any magic yourself?"

Kimoon inclined his head, his voice cool. "They have been enchanted to become perfect soldiers, as a gift for the upcoming war. We have our mutual friend to thank for that. In any case, the dark army was transformed on Seollan soil. Improved by the Netherking with black water compliance. All of that magical corruption was the Netherking's doing, not mine."

The dark army. Mirae had heard those words before—from a dead oracle who gave her life to stop the rise of the Inconstant Son and his peninsula-ending cult. So this, then, was how that dark army was to be wielded.

The Netherking had told Mirae that black water enhanced the effects of whatever spell was put into it. The image of Minho facedown in a tub flashed in Mirae's memory. Was that his future, to be transformed like the soldiers down by the river to be compliant—mindlessly obedient? As she had that thought, the memory of the rotting mul gwisin also came flying back to her, all that remained of the Netherking's final deception.

An obedient army led by a mind-controlled prince. These were the things the Netherking had promised to Josan, which would in turn pave the way for the Inconstant Son's rise to power. That had been the Netherking's plan all along, and in return, Mirae's mother would be brought to her knees, broken by an overwhelming army and a beloved son permanently transformed by the hatred of her enemy. That had been the Netherking's price for helping Josan win this war. A kingdom for a queen—one who would have no choice but to set the Netherking free.

And then, in the aftermath of that devastating war, one man would rise to the top as the true leader of the dark army— the Inconstant Son himself, whether he was the Netherking, Kimoon, Siwon, or even Minho.

You'll love him across all time and under every moon.

But . . . you must let him die when the time comes. You must.

"Minho was never meant to be like the others in the dark army," Kimoon said, staring at Mirae intently. "A piece of him was going to remain so that he might be more convincing. Like himself, but full of hatred. We needed him to break every heart that ever loved him. But with you, Mirae, we will achieve more than my father could have ever dreamed."

This was the lesson Kimoon wanted her to learn—that there was no way out. Whether she left Minho to this horrible fate so she could track down and destroy the dark army or traded Captain Jia's life for Minho and became a monster herself, every road led to the same evil end. The rise of Josan atop the broken pieces of Mirae's heart.

"So, what's it going to be?" Kimoon asked, his voice low and oily as the Netherking's. "Who will become my obedient, broken thing? Will you save yourself and your friend, and give me Minho for good? Or will you watch her die for a chance to be bent to my will instead? I am the one Minho is bound to, and I promise you the same mercies I extended to him. You will find me a far kinder master than my father would have been."

Mirae looked down at Captain Jia, who couldn't hear the conversation happening above her but gazed up at Mirae, unafraid. Although Kimoon wanted to break Mirae with an impossible decision, forcing her to join him in the ranks of those who had lost their souls in this ruthless game of kings and queens, the look on Captain Jia's face was asking her to do something very different.

The truth was written there like the torment in Kimoon's poem. This was no test—it was a show of power. Kimoon never intended to let Mirae or anyone else leave alive; he just wanted to see how low he could force Mirae to go. Well, he was forgetting one thing. Mirae knew who she was: the High Horomancer, Switcher of Seolla, and High Daughter of the Sacred Bone. She was the Unnamed Dragon, who no longer feared the taunts of those who called her selfish for saving those she loved. She was not her mother. Besides, *everyone* had deep desires for which they would stoop low. No one could save their own piece of the world from disappearing without risking it all.

And as for Kimoon, he was just as pathetic as everyone else— nothing more than a lying, angry boy playing a game he didn't understand.

He, at least, Mirae could destroy before he ever became the Inconstant Son.

Mirae released her hold on the balcony, taking strength from the captain's stony resilience. Kimoon nodded for the man with the golden axe to take his position. "Well, Mirae? What will it be? If you show me a queen I can trust, I'll let you make me a king."

Mirae felt emboldened, as very different words echoed back to her from the mouth of a prince she loved and trusted more than anyone else.

You must let him die. . . . You must.

Kimoon lifted his hand as the executioner lifted his axe, waiting for Mirae's answer.

Instead of giving him one, Mirae let her dark eyes rest on Kimoon's amber ones with the same impassivity he thought he'd so cunningly used on her. She saw the way it disarmed him, and that made her smile.

"You thought you could bring me low," Mirae said. "But don't forget that I can always force you lower."

Before Kimoon's raised hand or eyebrow could drop back into place, Mirae shoved him over the balcony.

When Mirae didn't hear Kimoon's body hit the ground, she looked over the edge, half afraid of what she would see.

He was alive, hanging by his fingertips from the rim of the sloping roof, but the distraction of Mirae's stunt was all that Captain Jia needed to slice her bonds against the axe held above her head and kick her would-be executioner where it would hurt most. Her hands free, she snatched his weapon and let her

Jade Witchery flow into its golden head, making it too hot for the other man to even try to wrest away from her.

Blazing with light, the executioner's axe was deadlier in the captain's hands—a force of pure, godlike power. The arcs of her swings were bright enough to trail after her, hanging in the air for a split second after each attack. Golden lightning seared Mirae's eyes as it brought swift justice to all who wanted Captain Jia dead.

Once all the guards around her were incapacitated by their own prisoner, Captain Jia looked up to the pagoda at Kimoon, who dangled just out of reach of both her and Mirae. "Go, Gongju. Get the others before it's too late."

Mirae hesitated. This was her chance to kill Kimoon—the self-professed Inconstant Son. But more guards were running toward Captain Jia, and it was only a matter of time before their shouts got the attention of the ones inside—the ones guarding her brothers, ordered to kill Minho, Hongbin, and Siwon at the first sign of her magic.

There was no time to dawdle. But there was also nothing more important than finishing what she'd started—the High Daughter quest she'd been given. Kimoon looked up at her, seeing the dilemma on her face. He sneered, knowing what she would choose.

Not him. Not today. Not while he was the perfect distraction for the guards hurrying to save him. Captain Jia shouted up at her one last time before charging at the approaching men. "Go, Gongju, but do not use your own magic until the princes are safe. I'll draw the soldiers out and distract them."

Mirae could hear men approaching—Keon and Sado, by the sound of their voices. She retreated into the hall, picking a room at random to hide in. This one was a smaller version of Kimoon's study, with a desk and a lit candle. Mirae rushed over and dumped her mother's beads out in the small circle of light, examining her options for magic that wouldn't come from her. She didn't want to use them, but if there was a moment they were required, it was now.

The rooster was missing—she'd given it to Hongbin. The dog, sheep, horse, and rabbit didn't strike her as terribly helpful for getting her out of a tight spot, so she shoved them back into the pouch. The dragon seemed like something she should save for later, so she put it in her pocket. That left the monkey, pig, snake, rat, ox, and tiger. She picked through them, unsure of which one she needed most. She had guesses as to what kinds of abilities they would give her: cleverness, luck, discernment, heightened awareness, inhuman strength, confidence, and courage—all useful for a Sacred Bone royal who was trying to sneak into a dungeon without triggering the execution of her brothers.

Still, Mirae could only stare at the beads, unable to put any of them into her mouth even as she heard Keon's and Sado's footsteps grow closer and closer. The powers of each bead came from her father's life energy. If she used them, she might be stealing years from him in order to save her brothers. And when last she saw him, he didn't seem like he had years to live.

But if she didn't use them, and her father ended up losing all his children in one day, Mirae knew his heart would be shattered forever, leaving him as good as dead.

Someone was running down the hall, throwing open all the doors. Soon, Keon and Sado would rescue Kimoon, and Mirae would never reach her brothers in time to stay their executions. It was now or never.

It was time to choose.

Mirae vowed to give her father her own life energy to replace what she used of his as she picked up the ox bead and put it on her tongue. The powers of the bead made her stumble back almost immediately with vertigo, trembles, goose bumps, and a crashing headache all at once. But the symptoms faded in seconds. As the bead warmed on her tongue, Mirae felt its power swell within her, roping around her muscles and making them bulge.

Once her father-gifted powers had settled into her, Mirae knew she was ready to barrel through anything in her path.

Just then, the door to the room she was hiding in flew open, and Mirae reacted on instinct; she punched her opponent right in the chest with all the strength of an ox, throwing him through the door and into the wall behind him.

When he didn't get up, Mirae stepped past his limp body and hurried down the hall. She paused and ducked when she reached the railing of the giant open staircase leading down to the first floor of the pagoda. She peeked down at the scene below. It seemed as if all the guards in the vicinity had gone outside to battle Captain Jia, just as planned, but how would Mirae find the entrance to the dungeon if it wasn't marked by guards?

Just then, Captain Jia came running into the pagoda, chased by men she was clearly trying to bottleneck at the front door. It was the perfect distraction. Sure that her path was clear, Mirae ran down the steps, prepared to shove the power of the ox into anyone who spotted her. Thankfully, Captain Jia's bright golden axe kept all attention, and danger, focused soundly on her.

Mirae had just reached the bottom of the staircase when she heard a familiar voice echo down to the main level of the pagoda, quieting the clashes and shouts of battle.

"Enough. There's no need for all this violence."

Mirae ducked behind the staircase, hoping she hadn't been seen. After a few seconds, it was clear neither Kimoon nor anyone else had caught sight of her movement.

"Where is the princess?" Kimoon called from the top of the staircase.

"She's hiding upstairs somewhere," said one of the soldiers—Keon, it sounded like.

"Then seal off the prison door. Make sure she never reaches it."

"Yes, Gunju daegam."

"And as for you," he said, likely to Captain Jia. "I don't want to see any more of my men killed. But of course, I can't just let you go. So I have a proposition for you."

Mirae gritted her teeth. Kimoon, king of making deals. But unfortunately for him, Captain Jia wasn't one to compromise. "The only proposition I will accept is one where you let my young masters go before I slaughter you all."

"How about this—you lower your weapon before I let the Netherking's monster out to hunt your princess for itself. You've seen what it can do. "

Captain Jia fell silent. Mirae wanted to rush out and help her friend, but if she did that, she'd never reach the prison unseen.

This was her best chance, here and now. Mirae looked around the first floor of the pagoda, spotting a heavy wooden door ornamented with nothing but iron bars and a large black handle. That had to be the way to the dungeon.

She heard the footsteps of Keon and Sado walking down the stairs, obeying Kimoon's command to seal off the prisoners. It was now or never.

Mirae slipped off her shoes so her socked feet could pad silently across the ornate clay tiles of the first floor toward the door to the dungeon. She twisted the handle, blessedly left unlocked in all the chaos of Captain Jia's escape, and peeked down at the dark steps on the other side, leading to firelight far below. She glanced one last time back toward Captain Jia, who was sneering up at Kimoon's promise to treat his other prisoners fairly if she would but lower her golden axe.

A familiar sound rumbled up to where Mirae stood, pulling her attention back down toward the dungeon. The voice she heard echoed far louder than its usual timbre, only slightly muffled by feet upon feet of stone.

"THIS ROOSTER BEAD IS REALLY ANNOYING, ISN'T IT? BUT IT'S THE ONLY THING KEEPING ME ALIVE RIGHT NOW, SO NO, I WILL NOT SHUT UP. HERE'S TO HOPING MY SISTER CAN HEAR ME BECAUSE RIGHT NOW WOULD BE A *REALLY GOOD TIME* FOR HER TO COME RESCUE ME."

Making her choice, Mirae closed the dungeon door behind her, leaving Captain Jia to fight alone as she rushed down into the darkness on the other side.

The steps were unlit, making it difficult to descend without tripping. Mirae made her way down as quickly as she dared by following the firelight at the bottom and the sound of Hongbin's voice, which had grown earsplittingly loud.

"PERHAPS YOU ARE WONDERING HOW EXACTLY I CAME TO HAVE SO MANY GREEN-TEA LEAVES DOWN MY PANTS. I WOULD TELL YOU, BUT IT'S ALMOST BETTER NOT KNOWING. UNLESS YOU FIND MYSTERIES ANNOYING. IF YOU DO, I'M VERY SORRY BECAUSE THERE IS NOTHING MORE ANNOYING THAN ME WITH A MYSTERY."

Mirae covered her ears as Hongbin continued his incessant babbling, quickly entering the hallway before her. Cell doors lined both walls, though only two of them were closed. Hongbin stood at the front of his, speaking through the grill at the soldier keeping guard, who had his back to Mirae. The man had his hands over his ears, too, but even if he hadn't, he never would have heard her coming over the chaotic ruckus that was Hongbin. At his feet was a naked sword, perhaps drawn to threaten Hongbin, or worse, until Hongbin had opened his mouth and given the guard's hands something more important to do.

Siwon, too, sat in a cell with his hands over his ears. He spotted Mirae and stood, catching Hongbin's attention.

"BUT IF YOU ASK ME, NOTHING'S MORE ANNOYING THAN A SISTER WHO THINK IT'S FUNNY TO HAND YOU A RANDOM BEAD WITHOUT ANY SORT OF EXPL— OH GOOD, YOU FOUND US."

The guard barely registered that Hongbin had stopped talking before Mirae sent the strength of the ox straight into his back. He flew several feet and crumpled to the ground.

Mirae grabbed the keys around the guard's belt and set Hongbin free. He was careful to hug her silently, for her ears' sake. When he pulled away, he pointed at Siwon's cell and mimed opening it with a key.

Mirae turned to Siwon's cell, keys in hand, but stopped when she got closer. There was something different about him here in the dungeon—something she couldn't quite make out in the shadows of his cell, but sent chills down her spine.

"I'm so glad you found us," Siwon said, watching her with eyes shadowed by his loose, unkempt hair. He smiled. "For a second, I thought you were my sister. She always came in the nick of time as well. You actually remind me a lot of her."

Mirae hefted the keys in her hand, not sure what was making her hesitate. Ever since her conversation with Captain Jia by the river, Mirae had promised to trust the captain's instincts as much as her own. But unlike the captain, she'd had no reason to be suspicious of Siwon—until now, and she couldn't put her finger on why.

Still, she needed to act quickly. Captain Jia wouldn't be able to hold off Kimoon's men forever, and Mirae would need help dragging Minho out of the dungeon swiftly and safely. The more friendly hands, the better.

The sounds of battle intensified from above, as something— probably one of Captain Jia's terrifying attacks—shook the ceiling. As if knowing that Mirae was considering leaving him behind, Siwon reached through the bars. "Gongju, I lost my sister because I abandoned her when she needed me most. I swore never to do that again to anyone else, which is why I have never turned my back on you, or Daegun. I know my sister will do you a great kindness in the afterlife if you would think of me as her Minho."

Whatever suspicions Captain Jia had about Siwon, he was telling the truth now. Mirae could feel it. In all the time he'd spent with Mirae, she had only seen a good man who wanted redemption from failing to protect Minho. Who was she to take that from him, when that was what she wanted herself?

Mirae handed Siwon the keys. "Wait here. You'll be safe if you look unsuspecting in your cage. Call out if anyone comes looking for us. Hongbin and I will fetch Minho."

Siwon put the keys on the floor of his cell and sat on them. "Understood. I'll be your lookout. You've saved my life yet again, Gongju. You can count on me to return the favor."

Mirae pulled Hongbin to the far wall of the prison, where an open door led to a secret room of black water basins and a brother who was running out of time.

Chapter
TWENTY-FOUR

The torture room looked the same as it had in Mirae's vision—the same stone floor and stone walls riddled with cracks so deep they couldn't be cleaned. Three basins stood in a line to Mirae's right, filled to the brim with black water that dripped over their edges, making the ground slick with inky pools and smudged footprints.

But only one of the basins had Minho in it, lying facedown.

Mirae knew the risks of touching the black water, but she and Hongbin rushed to Minho anyway, plunging their arms in and pulling him into an upright position.

His eyes were open. At first, he didn't breathe. After a few seconds, his chest rose, and Mirae heard the beat of his heart starting back to life until it matched hers.

Minho was alive. As slippery and heavy as he was, it was difficult to pull their brother from the tub, but Mirae and Hongbin heaved him out and laid him on the floor as gently as possible. Every bit of him and his sokgot was splotchy and stained, from his hairline to his purpled half-moon toenails.

The chest and shoulders of Mirae's borrowed hanbok were stained, too, soaking black water into her skin, but there wasn't time to worry about that. Not when Minho had been lying in the stuff for days.

Mirae scanned the room, looking for anything that would protect Minho from the night chill of the mountain. She gestured toward a cabinet against the far wall and Hongbin scurried over to examine its contents. There was a small array of personal items—robes and satchels confiscated from prisoners who'd come before. Minho's clothes were on the top shelf, which Hongbin reached with a small jump. Together, Mirae and Hongbin got their brother sloppily dressed before hoisting him up between them and heading for the door.

A shadow crossed over the doorway before they reached it, and then, quite suddenly, Siwon was standing there, holding the ring of keys in one hand and the guard's sword in the other. "I can't let you leave, Gongju. Not like this."

Hongbin seemed surprised to see Siwon in their way, but Mirae was not. In the shadow of the doorway, she still couldn't quite make out what had changed about him, warning her of this sudden strange behavior, but she stayed calm. "Move aside, Siwon. We have what we came for."

"Maybe you do, but I don't, and what I came for is the only thing that'll get you out of here alive." Siwon raised the guard's sword. "You need the dark army's commander."

Siwon looked over at the farthest tub. Mirae looked at it, too, and shook her head. "That stuff is the cause of all my troubles. I'm not messing with it."

Siwon pushed past Mirae, making the ox bead inside her stiffen her temporarily enhanced muscles. "Your magic alone isn't going to get us out of here, Gongju. You need her army to stand down."

Mirae heard another crash from above, a sign that Captain Jia was still fighting for her life. "Kimoon's men haven't seen what my magic can do now that they can't threaten to kill my brothers. I'll find a way out, but we have to go now."

Siwon was already beside the second tub, reaching into it with the keys Mirae had trusted him with. "The dark army is a thousand strong and resistant to magic. You'll never make it across Josan if they're hunting you."

"Well, how am I supposed to stop them, Siwon?" she asked, following his movements with narrowed eyes. "And how do you know all this, anyway?"

When Siwon turned his face back to Mirae, it caught the flickering fire set into sconces on the wall, and Mirae finally saw the change in him that had set her on edge. For the first time, she saw the same cold beauty on Siwon that stretched across Kimoon's face—the identical inky flow of Kimoon's locks and Siwon's prison-loose hair.

But most of all, she saw that Siwon's eyes had transformed from near black to a honey brown, matching those of the prince she'd shoved off a balcony, the same man she would someday see on a mountaintop, the so-called Inconstant Son who had had everything taken from him and wanted to make Seolla pay.

Siwon's arms and chest dripped with black, as dark as the Netherking's robes and the cage that constrained him.

So this was the servant boy's true form, unmasked from whatever Ma-eum spells the Netherking had expertly camouflaged him with. Here in the flickering shadows of a dungeon, Mirae saw her companion for what he really was—a liar, and a traitor of noble blood. Siwon turned away from Mirae, who found herself speechless with horror and confusion, and went back to work, fitting the keys into something at the bottom of the tub. A few seconds later, a woman's head rose out of the water.

She'd been folded in half, chained to the bottom of the basin by a large metal collar wrapped around her neck. Her chest heaved like she'd been holding her breath. Unlike Minho, after a moment, she was able to open her eyes and look around.

She paused when she saw Mirae and Hongbin holding Minho between them, then smiled at Siwon as he reached into the water again, unlocking the chains around her wrists. The woman stood and stretched luxuriously, as if every muscle, every tendon ached for immediate attention. She didn't seem to care that she was beautiful and shapely enough to make even Mirae blush and look away from her sheer white dress, her skin as splotchy and stained as Minho's.

Mirae didn't know who this woman was, but she knew enough about black water, and now about Siwon, to distrust her with her life. Mirae raised her free hand, ready to summon a ball of fire. But Siwon stepped between them. "Don't. I told you, she's your only way out of here."

Mirae should have known better than to hesitate for a third time that day, but Hongbin's gasp—heightened by the rooster bead—made her pause and stare, as the woman draped a dripping hand over Siwon's shoulder. Mirae froze with dread.

Siwon didn't shy away from the poison that seeped into his

clothes. He didn't move when the woman's head appeared over his shoulder and kissed his cheek, a black-splotched peck.

"Oh, Siwon," she cooed. "What a good boy you are. I knew you'd make it, whatever your father said. And you've done so much more than expected—just look at these incredible gifts."

She swept a stained arm toward Mirae and her brothers, making it clear that by "incredible gifts," she meant all three of Seolla's Sacred Bone children clinging to each other just a few feet away. The woman smiled and relied on Siwon's steadiness to step out of the basin.

"Hello, Mirae." The woman leaned her head against Siwon's shoulder, drenching his left side in black water. Every time she spoke, more inky liquid came dribbling out of her mouth, tattooing her chin with twin rivers of black. "It's been a while since I bled on you. I just couldn't help myself that night, not when I saw those pins in your hair. The last time I saw them, I nearly drowned in your mother's place."

Mirae stared at the dark pair before her. The woman's ethereal beauty overshadowed even Siwon's. Her hair wasn't as long as the gwisin's, but there was something of her in its likeness. The same build. Similarities hard to miss when they'd both reached for Siwon the same way—like he was family.

Siwon had had a sister who died. Mirae knew who that was now—a gwisin seeking justice alongside the spirits of those who had been sacrificed to create the Netherking's dark army. Someone Siwon had failed to protect as Mirae was failing to protect Minho. The Netherking's daughter, Siwon's sister, had tried to warn Mirae of what was coming by giving her the name of a monster.

Suhee. Not dead by her own hand, as Mirae had assumed from the Netherking's story, but alive. Abandoned by the Seollan queen, she'd found a dark kingdom of her own, and allied herself with a Josan prince to avenge her family. The pearl, the key, was hers.

Siwon was hers, too, it seemed, though he was not cursed as the Netherking was to remain trapped in the Deep. Adopted, then. Another bastard prince of Josan who had found the only people who understood what must have been his intense hatred of Seolla.

"Suhee," Mirae said, slowly leading Hongbin and Minho toward the open door. "We both have people we love here, and the power to destroy each other at our family's expense. Let's not do that."

"Yes, we both have loved ones here," Suhee said, lifting her head from Siwon's shoulder. "But we're going to have to fight over one of them."

Mirae pulled her brothers closer to the door. She kept her hand raised, clenching a hidden fire. "If you or your dark army come anywhere near us, I'll make your husband regret everything he taught me about Sacred Bone Magic."

Suhee laughed like it was a relief to finally let the black water spill out of her freely. "Or maybe you'll find yourself outmatched yet again."

"Please, Gongju," Siwon said. "Lower your arm. We don't need to fight."

"WHAT DO YOU MEAN WE DON'T NEED TO FIGHT?" Hongbin roared with all the power of the rooster bead. "YOU OWE US AN EXPLANATION, SIWON.

WHO ARE YOU, AND WHAT IS THAT . . . THING YOU'VE COME TO RESCUE?"

"Are you referring to me?" Suhee wrung out her hair, pooling black liquid at her feet. "Didn't Kimoon tell you I'm the one keeping your brother alive? His transformation isn't complete, which means he'll die a horrible, painful death if you take him from me."

"We'll figure something out. We don't need you," Mirae said. Suhee clearly didn't know about the vial her husband had given Mirae, or the promise he'd made to bring Minho back to life—not that she'd believe Mirae's word on any of that. Mirae took another step toward the exit, but Suhee merely held out her hand and the door slammed shut.

"Oh, Mirae," Suhee said. "I want Minho alive as much as you do. So much, in fact, that if you give him back, we'll keep this little feud between us. Hongbin is free to go."

"I'M NOT GOING ANY—"

The dungeon door slammed open, cutting Hongbin off. A second later, his rooster voice resounded through the chamber in a terrific shriek, as he was pushed out of the room by an invisible force. The door slammed shut behind him, leaving Mirae alone, clutching an unconscious Minho.

"Like I said." Suhee smiled, her teeth darkening into glossy ebony from the never-ending stream of black water leaking from her mouth. "We can keep this between us. Just hand Minho over."

"Do you really expect me to trade one brother for another?" Mirae set Minho down on the floor so she could raise both arms. No matter what Siwon said, Mirae knew she wasn't getting out of there without a fight. "Let me and my brothers go, and I won't incinerate you where you stand."

"Stop it, both of you." Siwon stepped in front of his mother, looking back and forth between her and Mirae. "We're getting out of here together. We all have what we want."

"You mean the boy she's trying to take from us?" Suhee gestured toward Mirae, her arm deathly pale and bruised with black water. "I did not endure all this horror for nothing. We leave with Minho or not at all. If you love me, Siwon, kill her and take me home."

"No." Siwon shook his head. "She knows that Father is the only one who can turn Minho back. She's heading to the Deep, anyway. We can all just travel there together."

"And do what, frolic in the shallows of Wol Sin Lake like old friends?" Suhee scoffed. "What's gotten into you?"

"It's over, Mother. Or it can be, if you'll listen to me." Siwon reached for Suhee's hand. "Gongju and Father have been talking about his freedom. We don't have to do this anymore."

Suhee turned to Mirae and offered her a mocking bow. "It seems my son has taken a liking to you, which has made him stupid. I'm going to have to do something about that."

"He's telling the truth," Mirae said, lowering her hand slightly. "I made a deal with the Netherking. If we move forward with no treachery between us, I will forgive what has happened in the past. After we fix Minho, no matter what I have or will discover about your plot with Josan, I will do what is right. I swear it."

"Right by whom?" Suhee sneered. "It's very generous of you to be willing to forgive us for the wrongs done to us. Aren't you just a paragon of queenly noblesse?"

"We can argue about this later," Siwon said, hand still stretched out to his mother. "First, let's prove our goodness to each other by escaping hand in hand. I've learned that being kind to your enemies can make them your friends. If it happened once, it can happen again."

"Is that so?" Suhee asked. Even Mirae turned to glare at Siwon's bold words as Suhee seethed, "Have you forgotten how we got here? Are you stupid enough to fall for a Seollan promise after everything I endured?"

"No, Mother. But—"

"You know what we've lost. If you care more about that witch than your own mother, or your sister, then stay where you are and see what happens. Otherwise, put Minho back in his tub until the process is finished."

"You don't want to do that," Mirae said, taking a protective step in front of her unmoving brother. "If you finish corrupting Minho, then you'll lose him forever. Kimoon is the one who will have the power to control my brother, and I have a feeling he won't take kindly to your being released—and claiming Minho as your own—without his permission."

Suhee lowered her head, like she'd just had an idea too good to share. "Oh, Mirae. So bad at seeing through lies that I almost feel sorry for you. Just like the bastard prince. Where do you think this black water came from? Look at me. It's my essence, water from my soul that Minho's been suckling in. That makes him a part of me now. Mine forever."

Mirae looked at the three tubs and the trail of black water between them. In the middle of it all stood Suhee, the ungodly source of Minho's torment. A wide-set mouth that spewed all manner of darkness. "I'll give you one last chance, Mirae. Give me the boy, and I'll let the loud one go free. That is all the kindness I'll give you for bringing my son to me."

"Kindness," Mirae said, "never hurts the innocent. Let Minho go. I will stay."

"The bastard prince and my husband may be intrigued by you, but I know better." Suhee stretched out her neck, lengthening the twin rivers of inky water trailing down into her dress and revealing a dark line sliced across her throat. "You are Noeul's daughter through and through."

"If you really want to break my mother's heart," Mirae said, "then take away her future, just like she did to you. I am her legacy, her everything. Take me, Suhee. Leave my brothers be."

"I will not." There was no hesitation. "Your chance to taste my mercy is over now. I will take him, Mirae, and I will kill you."

"No." Siwon stood in front of his mother, hands raised. "Gongju is misguided and arrogant, but her heart is good. Sol trusted her enough to give her your pearl. I know that working together without violence is what she would have—"

"Do not. Speak of your sister." Suhee raised her hand and Siwon's body rose from the ground, his neck stiff, cuffed by invisible strength. "You swore you would do anything to avenge her. If you cannot keep that promise, then stay out of my way." With a snarl, Suhee tossed her son against the wall—lightly enough that his head didn't crack against stone, but hard enough that all the wind was knocked out of him, leaving him to fall stunned and gasping to the ground.

Mirae raised a hand again, readying it with fire. The Nether-queen may have been corrupted with power Mirae couldn't explain, but she was no match for Sacred Bone Magic. No dark-ness or evil could best the strength of the gods. With her other hand, Mirae dug into her pocket, finding the bead she needed, recognizing it by its ridges and horns.

Before Suhee could turn her magic against Mirae, or Minho, Mirae shoved the dragon bead into her mouth, the one she'd been saving for when all seemed lost. Then she reached into her dress and pulled out the Netherking's vial.

The black water inside was pure, untouched by the dark-ness in Suhee's soul. The other woman's eyes grew wide as she recognized the stuff, but she could only watch, paralyzed with disbelief, as Mirae snuck a sip of the oily, bitter liquid, just as she had back at Noksan. This time, she let it sit on her tongue where it could mix with the dragon bead, turning her Sacred Bone Magic into something stronger than the love in her father's blood. Stronger than the Deep.

Before Suhee could lift a finger, Mirae raised both arms to the sky. This time, she didn't use her persimmon flames or summon a snarling rainbow dragon. Instead, she let the forces on her tongue mingle—more powerful together than they ever were apart.

As the magic surged inside her, Mirae realized that the gods had given her what she needed all along—the formula to dispel all the evil in the peninsula.

Mirae's arms trembled with power. Though Siwon gasped and stared at her, only Suhee seemed to understand what she had done—how the dark and the light were mixing in her blood, black water and opal bead. The eternal state of the moon.

"This ends now," Mirae said, brightening the chamber with the radiant glow that beamed from her skin. "There will be no war or suffering, no coerced liberation for Josan or the Deep. Not like this. And not through you."

Suhee backed away, though she did not flee. "I knew your mother when she was your age. Noeul was turning flowers into gold. Enchanting weapons to sing like sirens. But you? You're just a child playing with fire."

Suhee and Siwon both turned away as Mirae became too bright to look at. "Return to your chains, Suhee. Don't make me punish you for harming my family."

"Punish *me*?" Suhee asked, raising her own arms. "We'll see what *my* family has to say about that."

Mirae could feel him in the room, cold like sudden rain. Suhee's dark side—the man who had corrupted her light. A monster maker, and the final candidate for the Inconstant Son.

His Sacred Bone Magic rose in Mirae's pulse, louder than his lake, drumming like rain filling up a well. Her heart, the Netherking's heart. Every Sacred Bone heart beating in her ear. Mirae could almost see him standing like an illusion beside his wife, the black tips of his crown as long as the drips from her dress.

Mirae lowered her hands to her sides, two powers coursing down each arm. One was pearly white with rainbow glints. The other ran like black veins beneath her skin. Perfectly balanced magic, neither one heavier nor stronger than the other. United by the last High Daughter of the Sacred Bone—the one who would succeed.

When she was at the height of her power, surrounded by a circle of godlike energy that spiraled around her as an infinitely more powerful version of Captain Jia's lotus shield, Mirae smiled to see what she was made of—how beautiful and impenetrable she'd become.

But the gods had allowed Suhee to become powerful as well.

Faster than Mirae could launch her shades of lightning, Suhee shot forward with a scream, carrying the fury of all those years she'd spent in the dark, abandoned, and the pain of all those who had died to get her out.

Only, Suhee didn't bring the full force of her body's rage and hate.

She left most of it behind.

Mirae watched with horror as the line around Suhee's neck explained itself. Her body fell to its knees while her head pulled free, along with her neck and spine, all of which slid wetly out of place, heading straight for Mirae and her arms ringed with light.

A monster that slit throats from the air, a woman with a sharp spine pale as the dragon bead. Her hair and her bones streamed behind her like a mockery of Mirae's white-and-black balance. At the bottom of the tapering, serrated string of discs dangled a pale-pink bean-shaped stomach that sloshed with blood, trailing after Suhee with sprays of red.

When the Netherqueen's rage met Mirae's lightning—a god's might clashing with the ungodly—it cast them both backward, flying, then falling against the wall, which caught them with all the strength of mountain stone.

Chapter
TWENTY-FIVE

Mirae expected the ground to feel cold and slick, but as she came to, the first thing she noticed was a sticky, warm wetness like a slimy halo around her head. It took a moment for the pain to catch up, but when it did, it came with fire and knives.

She couldn't scream. All the breath had been knocked out of her by her fall. The eternal strength of mountain stone had tried to shatter her body, but she'd been cushioned enough by her own ring of magic to stay alive. Alive, but in agony.

Barely breathing, her vision blurring everything in the room together, Mirae stared up at the ceiling. The torchlit stone around her almost looked like the gold walls of her chamber back home. A pale face framed by long black hair materialized above her. The head leaned curiously to one side, just as her mother's used to when soothing Mirae's chills and aches.

But this woman was not her mother. Instead of a starched white collar, she had a long neck of bones; and in place of a rich red hanbok was a red bulb that leaked warm, bloody droplets onto Mirae's stomach. When the monster spoke, black water splattered across Mirae's face.

"I tried to be kind," Suhee said. From the grunts of pain between her words, it was clear that she hadn't escaped their explosive encounter unscathed, either. "Of course, you're just like your mother. You expect to get everything you want, or nothing at all."

Mirae willed her body to move, to do anything. But if any part of her so much as twitched, her eyes rolled back from unspeakable pain.

"You should be grateful." Suhee's face swooped closer, showing off teeth like sharp pearls in her dark mouth. "At least you won't have to watch your brothers die."

Mirae didn't know what was her blood, Suhee's blood, black water, or tears. Everything felt wet and feverishly warm around her, like she'd been submerged in the mountain's magma-rich belly. A devoured morsel that was never going to escape.

"Die well, queenling." Suhee was close enough that Mirae could feel her breath against her neck. "Show your people how it's done."

Mirae closed her eyes, waiting for the jaw-wide bite that would end it all—the pain, the humiliation, and the terror. It was up to others now, the saving of Minho. The council had been right about Mirae's recklessness all along; her mother, too, and Captain Jia. But Mirae hadn't listened to any of them. She never listened. And now everyone she loved was going to die.

Before Mirae could hear the crunch of her own neck being snapped in two, the door to the dungeon slammed open. The sound alone startled Suhee, and Mirae was surprised to see that whatever had entered was so frightening, the Netherqueen retreated entirely, back to the other side of the room.

Mirae shot her eyes to the left, trying to assess the new danger. What she saw shocked her: Captain Jia, limping into the room, dragging her axe. Both had lost their spark—the axe because it was covered in more blood than gold. And Captain Jia because of the deep gash across her chest.

"Gongju. You're alive." Captain Jia spoke haltingly. Out of breath. Out of blood. She saw Minho, slumped on the ground but still breathing. "Alive."

She turned her attention to the monster in the room. Though she raised her axe, wincing with every move, her weapon didn't glow at her touch; her magic was utterly spent. Still, she looked unafraid as she regarded the woman before her. "Kimoon's mudang, I presume. The bastard prince told me I'd have to go through you."

A mudang, indeed. This was the woman whom Mirae's mother had left behind in the Deep. The same creature who had attacked the oracles and destroyed Mirae's Sangsok Ceremony. Suhee the Shaman was even the name Mirae had picked for her disguise in Noksan, unaware how closely her fate would become tied to the woman across from her now.

"Well, Jade Witchling, what are you going to do?" Suhee jeered. "Bore me with a lecture about the virtues of elemental magic?"

Captain Jia clutched her chest, blood blossoming from the wound. "The elements show me your core. Your weakness. Everything."

"And what is my weakness?" Suhee looked past Captain Jia at Hongbin, who had rushed back into the room. He unsuccessfully tried to pull Mirae to her feet. Her lungs felt fractured, useless—her legs even worse. Every part of her he touched burned like dragon fire.

Captain Jia hefted her axe, though her body visibly trembled. "Come and see, mudang."

Suhee turned to Siwon, who'd regained enough breath by now to labor to his feet. "When you're done playing around, grab your black water brother while I deal with this witch."

This time, Siwon hurried to obey.

As Siwon approached, Hongbin grabbed Mirae's ankles and hauled her out of the room.

"Stop," Mirae gasped. "Minho."

Hongbin didn't slow down, instead dragging Mirae down the hallway, back toward the stairwell. "I CAN'T CARRY YOU BOTH."

All Mirae could do was stare as Siwon crouched beside Minho and checked his pulse. He watched her, too, but did nothing to stop Hongbin from taking her. He had what he needed, and Mirae was in no condition to change that.

You must let him die. . . . You must.

Siwon began dragging Minho back toward his basin while Captain Jia stood facing the Netherqueen, bracing for an attack.

The captain wasn't prepared for the screeching head that barreled into her, knocking her axe loose. But as she fell to the floor, her free hand caught hold of the Netherqueen's stomach. It sloshed in her hand like an overripe fruit, spilling its warm juices everywhere.

The Netherqueen strained against her Wonhwa anchor, forced to be gentle lest she rip her own stomach. "Siwon!" she screamed.

He came running, but Captain Jia kicked him backward into the room—hard enough to send him sprawling.

And then, hand over hand, Captain Jia began yanking the Netherqueen out of the sky.

Mirae watched as she, too, was pulled helplessly; each disc, each bone in the Netherqueen's spine became another rung for Captain Jia to climb. Every tug pulled the screeching, disembodied woman closer to the floor until her head was close enough for Captain Jia to grab and wrestle to the ground.

The Netherqueen's vertebrae lashed out, tearing into Captain Jia's stomach and chest, but the captain wrapped her hands around the Netherqueen's bones the way she would grip her own sword. Then, like the Jade Witch she was, she manipulated the elements within her grasp.

The Netherqueen's core was marrow, bone, and tissue. The black water made her powerful, but her weakness was everything else inside her. Like all mortals, her bones were made of dust.

And that's what Captain Jia began turning them back to.

She was too weak to make it happen all at once, but one by one, the Netherqueen's discs and vertebrae disintegrated into puffs of powder that dissipated faster than her screams.

This time, when Siwon came running, he had a sword.

By then, Hongbin had reached the stairwell. Everything hurt, but Mirae let her brother pull her to her feet so she could get a good eyeline on Siwon. She raised her hand against his weapon, heating it as she would an ingot for melting. It was the best she could do from that distance—but it was enough to make him yelp and drop the sword as she collapsed again.

Hongbin caught her.

But not before she got one last glance at Captain Jia. Blood was spurting out of her body as she struggled with the Netherqueen, continuing to methodically turn her bones to dust. The Netherqueen's stomach was still free, bleeding and steaming against the captain's chest.

Mirae refused to be dragged any farther. Ignoring Hongbin's desperate attempts to complete their escape, she raised her hand toward the Netherqueen's bleeding remains.

It was almost impossible to focus, but for once Mirae was determined to follow Captain Jia's example. The Netherqueen's strength was also her weakness. Monster that she was, the Netherqueen was still only as strong as the things that made her—something monsters and humans had in common.

Eyeing the steaming pile of oozing red, Mirae sensed everything Suhee was made of—the pride, the pain, the obsession with revenge. All things that supported the Netherqueen like the bones in her spine. But in the hands of a Daughter of the Sacred Bone, Suhee's dying organ was nothing more than a grape ripe for popping.

Using that image as her guide, Mirae stared at the bloodred fruit and bid it to peel.

In Captain Jia's hands, Suhee's bones were still disappearing one by one, and now her stomach was being sliced into bloodied petals. The Netherqueen arched and whipped what remained of her spine, slicing Captain Jia's chest deeply. Siwon grappled with the wounded captain, squeezing her throat, as the Netherqueen turned to Minho, who sat hunched over like a sightless, broken doll, and screamed, "Kill them!"

When Minho rose, eyes open and heart strong, Mirae's hand fell back to her side as her body, her magic, finally failed her. Minho ignored the deadly brawl between Captain Jia and his friends from the Deep. His eyes were fixed on his siblings in the hallway, though it was clear from the coldness in his gaze that their faces meant nothing to him.

He ran swiftly, just as he had back on the morning of the ceremony. Back then, he'd been trying to outrun Mirae's magic. This time, he was intent on extinguishing it forever.

When Hongbin saw Minho coming, he reached for his brother, only to be grabbed around the neck and shoved into a wall.

"NO, MINHO," he gasped. "GET THE *OTHER GUYS*."

But no matter how loudly Hongbin yelled, Minho only obeyed one voice.

"Kill them," Suhee rasped again. She hovered weakly in the air, just out of Captain Jia's reach. "Kill them, my son."

Minho grabbed Hongbin's shoulders and threw him to the floor. Hongbin tried to struggle back to his feet, but he was no match for the dark water strength in Minho's veins. He lay there gasping, blood matting the back of his head.

Minho turned to Mirae next. She stretched out her hand against him, but her fire never came. She had nothing left to give. The path to freedom lay just behind her, but Mirae slid to the floor, joining Hongbin. "Don't do this, orabeoni," she pleaded. "You've got to break free of her spell. We are the ones you love. You'd never, ever hurt us."

Minho raised his hands, balled into fists. Gentle hands that were poised to pummel what was left of her into a pulp.

"I love you, Minho," Mirae whispered. "I'm sorry for everything, and I forgive you."

She didn't look away. Mirae wanted her last moments to be spent looking at the two brothers she'd failed. She could practically hear the rhythmic thumping of her heart, growing louder and louder until it hit her ears as an actual sound, bringing with it a burst of gold that lodged in Minho's shoulder, hitting him hard enough to hurl him past Mirae and pin him to the stairwell wall.

Mirae blinked in shock and stared down the empty hallway where the sudden sound and light had come from. She saw a proud but teetering silhouette. Captain Jia had saved Mirae one last time with a final heave of her axe. But it had cost her everything.

The golden axe, retrieved and hurled with no thought for herself, had left the captain defenseless against the whipping spine, which finally hit its target dead on. Mirae was unable to scream or move as the tip of the Netherqueen's spine pierced Captain Jia's neck. When Suhee tried to pull out, her bones got stuck in the captain's throat, forcing her to rip free with a jerk that sent the other woman flying backward into the room with the basins. With the last of her strength, Captain Jia curled onto her side to face Mirae across the hall. *Save them*, she mouthed, before her body fell still.

The Netherqueen fell, too. Her bones clattered as they hit the stone floor, twitching in her own dust and blood. She coiled into a ball of long, black hair and spine, shielding her graying stomach. But her voice, shrill and piercing, remained just as strong as before.

"Siwon, put him back in the basin now—before he dies."

Siwon, who had balked at the thought of murder before, did not hesitate at the order to save someone in harm's way. That meant something. It had to. When Siwon ran close enough to retrieve Captain Jia's axe, still pinning Minho to the wall, Mirae grabbed his ankle. He stopped and looked down, witnessing the last of Mirae's strength.

"Please," she said. "Hongbin must live. He must."

She thought she saw Siwon nod, but it was hard to tell as the ring of darkness began closing in. At its center, warped by the fading light, was a pale face. Not Siwon's, or Suhee's. This one wore a black crown. The Netherking's mocking lips said everything he was feeling.

Mirae, Mirae, in my thrall,

Heeding every god who calls.

The Netherking's heartbeat had brought his soul all the way from the abyss to lean over her and gloat, his voice a dark lullaby sending Mirae off into oblivion.

Welcome, welcome, to the Deep.

Welcome, darkest child of all.

Chapter

TWENTY-SIX

Something cold pressed against Mirae's spine while something warm swirled around her legs. There was wetness everywhere, but no more agony. That was good. Mirae didn't think she could take any more pain.

"Pretending to be asleep won't make me go away. Open your eyes, queenling."

Mirae did as she was told. Suhee was back in her body and sitting on the edge of one of the tubs, playing with the water.

As Mirae's eyes became accustomed to the light, she realized she wasn't lying on the floor. She was in the Netherqueen's basin, hands chained to the bottom, the metal shackle around her neck. To her left was Minho's basin. But he wasn't in it.

Hongbin was. Floating facedown.

Mirae pulled against her chains, calling on the rage she was learning to keep close. Rage against the Netherqueen for killing Captain Jia. Rage against herself for letting it happen. Rage for Siwon's lies, wherever he was. Rage for the things Minho would be forced to do, and for how it would break their mother's heart. And rage on behalf of Hongbin, unmoving in the basin beside her.

"I gave you a chance," Suhee reminded her. "I would have let him go, but you were arrogant. You really don't listen to anyone, do you?"

Mirae stopped pulling against the chains. There was no way the Netherqueen had been telling the truth about letting Hongbin leave—he knew too much. This was no time to fall for lies. Mirae had to be smarter than that.

She needed to free Hongbin, whatever it took.

The metal around her wrist had a core, as all things did. A power or a weakness. But Mirae didn't have the patience to find it. She summoned her Sacred Bone Magic instead, calling on it to set her free—to burst the basin and implode the walls. Anything it wanted.

But nothing happened. Mirae tried again, listening for her heartbeat, needing the power it pumped through her body. Why couldn't she find it?

Mirae looked down at the water, chest-high on her body, and remembered how Minho's heart didn't beat, either, when he was under its thrall. The Netherqueen smiled as she watched Mirae struggle. She knew what Mirae wasn't ready to accept.

Without her heartbeat, Sacred Bone Magic was useless. The chains around her could not be broken. The water could not be manipulated. Mirae had been soundly defeated.

"It's a fine invention." The Netherqueen walked over to the far wall where, Mirae realized, Minho stood stoically, looking straight ahead. She wrapped her arms around his waist. "Oh, don't look so upset. If that coil of metal could keep me down, what chance do you have?"

Mirae could only stare—at the water, at Hongbin floating beside her, at Minho streaked with inky stains, wrapped in the arms of his new master.

"I don't understand," she said. "You're from Josan. A woman born without magic. The gods created me to stop a great evil; why can't I stop you?"

Suhee came over and brushed her fingers through Mirae's damp hair. "Because gods die, just like us. I have no doubt they set things in motion a long time ago. But now that they're gone, who's to say things will turn out the way they wanted?"

"They spoke to me," Mirae said. "They brought me here."

"No, queenling." The Netherqueen massaged the top of Mirae's head while collecting her hair into a bunch. "My husband brought you here. And you made it so easy."

"I led Siwon to you," Mirae said, knowing she sounded desperate. "You have to let at least one of my brothers go for that gift."

"No, I don't." The Netherqueen nodded at Hongbin. "He lives because my son said so. Though it would have been better for him if he had died. You really should have killed my husband the moment you saw him, even if it meant riling up entire nations, or losing a brother. But you're not very good at sacrificing, are you? You're not good at anything."

There had to be something Mirae could try. Something she hadn't thought of yet. "Kimoon doesn't want me harmed. Neither does the Josan king. He should be the one deciding what happens to me and to Hongbin."

The Netherqueen laughed and patted Mirae's head. "I forget you've been out for a while. Kimoon and I already had a little chat while I soaked and healed; we've come to terms about what to do with you. He and I have worked too hard to throw this partnership away all because of your meddling. Wars shouldn't be wasted. I know my husband will agree when I explain everything."

"Your husband brought you here, too," Mirae said. "He was willing to risk losing you."

"And yet here I am, rescued, and there you are, begging for mercy," the Netherqueen said. "You know, I'm glad he was right about you. It might take a while to break you, but you'll make a masterpiece of a soldier. Finally, a daughter to be proud of."

"You don't know me," Mirae said, rattling her chains as she strained against them. "I'm not a toy for your petty war. I'm going to get out of here and finish what I started."

"Oh yes, of course. The gods will help you." The Netherqueen yanked Mirae's hair, stretching out her neck. "And while you're waiting for them to crawl out of whatever hole they're hiding in, you'll still be sitting here turning into my creature. Just like Minho. He will soon be leading a glorious army while you steep endlessly, losing your mind."

"What about you?" Mirae asked, her voice strained. "Where will the Netherking put his faithful little monster when he doesn't need her anymore?"

"Oh, I'll be free to visit an old friend. Carting her children behind me—my new family. I'll break her heart the way she broke mine." The Netherqueen smiled. "Don't look at me like that. It could be worse. At least this way, everyone lives. Just like you wanted."

She plunged Mirae's head back into the black water, folding her body in half. Mirae fought against her, but the neck chain clicked into place, locked to the bottom of the basin.

She struggled in vain, looking into pure, thick darkness. Hearing only the horrible thoughts the Netherqueen had put in her head.

Hongbin, gone. Minho, gone. Captain Jia, gone, gone, gone.

And Mirae's magic, too. As gone as the gods. As gone as her queendom would be when the Netherqueen reunited with her husband. Nothing Mirae believed about herself had been true. Not the gods or their promises. All she had now was black water and unbreakable chains.

Mirae would have prayed to her ancestors for help, but it was their legacy that had brought her here, tearing the peninsula apart in ways that peace could never heal. Mirae's mother had made powerful enemies—too powerful for Mirae to defeat.

No. Mirae rested her forehead against her legs, agonizing over all the warnings she'd ignored.

Don't be selfish.

Change nothing but the Inconstant Son.

Failure is not an option.

Let him die.

That one, most of all, she could never have done. Mirae didn't even understand what it meant. Yet that last command had been the most vital. She should have listened to her allies in the present and the future, doing whatever they said, no matter how hard. That was the point of the switches. But if that's what it took to be the gods' champion, letting men die before she was absolutely sure who they were, what did that make her? What did that make the gods?

Mirae hit her arms against the sides of the basin, hoping to shatter it. She struck the sides harder and harder, enough to bruise her arms. She swung her whole body against the tub, trying to topple it. But its walls refused to crack.

Mirae thrashed until every voice in her head told her it was no use. So many people telling her what to do—some from the future, some from the past. But the loudest voice, the most vehement, was her own.

She had failed. Defying the council with this foolhardy rescue attempt had left her with nothing. No brothers, no friends, no protectors. No path, no promises, no gods.

And no magic to bring them all back.

The Netherqueen was right. Mirae hadn't been abandoned. She'd been misled. Brought here not by a god, but by a clever king. She'd been too weak to see through the lies. She, the gods, the oracles, everyone who saw potential in her had been wrong.

Everyone except the Netherking.

The black water was inside her now. Mirae could feel it worming through her veins, filling her lungs with something that didn't work like air. In the next tub over, Hongbin was surely transforming, too, his body changed by the water every second.

Mirae had to get him out.

She struck the basin again and this time, her braid fell loose, releasing something small and black into the water. A bell as empty as she was, except for the silent promise that someday she would fill it to the brim with the one thing she still had: a gods-given power that was hers alone.

Mirae couldn't see the black bell, but she knew its color, the same as the black water around her. The color of every future she'd ever seen. Mirae bowed her head and reached out with her teeth until she found the relic, and biting into the bone-chipping metal rim, she swung her neck to make it ring.

Mirae looked around, having gone from pitch darkness to being swathed in lights and ribbons of explosive color. The gurgling quiet of black water was shattered by music and laughter. The jovial people around her danced with all their hearts, swinging each other around, masked as tigers, dragons, and monkeys. Someone grabbed Mirae and swung her, too, right into their arms.

The person holding her was a man wearing a snake mask, silver-scaled, with fangs hanging over his lips. Mirae could feel something over her face, too. The man, her partner, danced her out of the crowd.

"See? That wasn't so bad," he said. "Don't tell me that wasn't fun."

Mirae looked around through the eye holes of her own mask, catching her breath. Oh, what it was to breathe again, surrounded by life and happiness. She didn't recognize the city she was in—it was no place in Seolla she had ever been to. No festival she had ever thrown. When she looked up and saw the strings of stars hanging from the roofs of all the buildings around them, she realized where she was.

"This is the Festival of Heaven," she said, turning to look at the man with the snake mask. His head bobbed to the beating of the drums. "I'm in the spirit world."

He didn't seem to hear her. "I told you it would be way more exciting up here. You need to lighten up once in a while. Learn to dance when things go a little wrong."

A little? Mirae looked at the happy, glowing spirits around her, beside themselves with joy. Her masked companion plucked a flower out of a passing girl's hair and stuck it in Mirae's, pulling her attention back to him.

Mirae tried to recognize his mouth or chin under the snake mask. Or the timbre of his voice, which was just as concealed by the festival noise as every other part of him. Before Mirae knew what she was doing, her hands flew to his disguise, trying to rip it off.

But his hands were faster. "Whoa, hang on, now! You know we'll get kicked out if anyone realizes we're mere mortals crashing the party."

"Who are you?" Mirae asked, knowing that the panic welling up inside wasn't just for him. "How can you expect me to just dance after everything I've done?"

Mirae's masked companion grabbed her wrists, gently pushing her arms down to her sides. "I'm sorry. I didn't know you'd switched. Tell me where you came from."

As he pulled her away from the crowds down into a quiet alley where children played with frogs and marbles, Mirae told him about the chains, the black water basins, and her brothers, betrayed. He listened, unsurprised, as if he knew the whole story already, or had been there.

But instead of offering any guidance, he continued to walk her away from the noise, the lights, the smells. When the festival was nothing more than a string of lanterns on the horizon and the hum of drums in the distance, they reached a midnight-blue pond, moonlit and gold-spotted with massive, ethereal koi.

Her companion sat on the pond's sandy bank and pulled Mirae down to sit with him. She thought that now, in privacy, he'd pull off his mask and tell her everything he knew. But instead, he removed her mask and held it in his lap. When he spoke, it was gruffly, like he was trying to obscure his voice as much as his face.

"It doesn't matter who I am," he said at last. "I am whomever you end up choosing to keep by your side. That choice will only ever belong to you. All that matters right now is that I'm here for you, exactly as you need me."

Mirae pulled away when the masked man reached for her hand. "If I live long enough to choose you as my companion, then that means I escape the basin. Tell me how."

"Of course you escape." He dropped his hand into his lap. "That's one of the best things about these switches—knowing all the things you're going to survive."

"How do I get out of Kimoon's fortress?" Mirae pressed.

Her companion didn't react to the name. Instead, he looked out across the water. "Right now, you probably feel as if you're lost in the darkest night. The deepest depths."

Mirae nodded. "That's became I am."

"Are you?" He tossed a pebble into the water, sending moonlight rippling across the surface. "You're always telling me there are two sides to every moon. Light and dark, right and wrong, depending on where you're standing."

"Sometimes there is no moon. Sometimes you can't see anything but darkness."

He looked at her, the silver fangs of his snake mask almost grinning. "You're stuck in a tub of water. That's hardly the ocean. You're in chains. That's hardly going to kill you. And your brothers are still alive. That's hardly the end of the world."

Mirae glared at him. "Let's swap places, then, and see how well you do."

He snorted. "Whatever you want, gongjunim. Nothing's quite as scary as you when you're angry with me."

Mirae ignored his last comment but had to admit that he was a little right. She hadn't lost everything. Far from it. There was a way to fix all that was broken, and she was destined—there was that word again—to figure it out. Destined to be at this festival for spirits with a man who, it seemed, had witnessed her rising from the ashes.

But how?

"Mirae, you're not alone," he said. "I'm right there with you. Neither you nor I knew it at the time, but I won't let you down. And you won't let yourself down, either."

"But I don't see any way out. These chains can't be broken."

Her companion picked up her mask and flipped it around, showing Mirae the creature she had chosen to wear. Not an unnamed dragon, but a lamb.

"Not everything in your way has to be destroyed. Not your chains. Not you. Not me. You taught me that when you did the most powerful thing anyone can ever do."

He handed her back the lamb mask. She looked it over—the roundness of its white fur, the gentleness of its black nose, eyes, and smile. It reminded her of the bead her father had used to slay a dragon and retrieve her mother's mind. "You're not talking about magic, are you?"

"I am, in a way." He leaned closer and touched her cheek. This time, she didn't pull away, so he moved his hand down to her heart. "I'm talking about your true power. It works like magic in the darkest of places."

Mirae frowned. "Are you talking about love?"

"You're a Daughter of the Sacred Bone." He smiled. "Matters of the heart are your specialty. You don't just find people across long distances. You can also see their hearts—truly know them across all time and under every moon. None can hide from you. No one is out of reach. But what you do with that power is completely up to you."

Mirae shook her head at the lamb mask. "So what if I can read the Netherqueen's heart? Or Kimoon's, or Siwon's, or the Josan king's? That's not going to unlock my chains."

"Not in the conventional sense, but the gods picked you because of your true power. You will do what no High Daughter, no ancestor, has ever done. You alone are strong enough."

Mirae was as breathless now as she was in the black water, only this time, she didn't feel empty or alone. "Strong enough to do what? Tell me how it ends."

He smiled. "I am telling you. Your heart can defeat anything. So don't be afraid. Don't be angry at the gods, yourself, or me. We are nothing without you. You will show us a better path. The one thing you do know is who we are deep down, and you will find the words that act on us like magic. When we see who you really are, we will never be the same."

Mirae nodded, even as she felt her consciousness returning to that dark and lonely place in which she was imprisoned. But it was all right. Mirae knew she would return to this man, to this moment, someday. She made sure that the last thing she saw of him was the kindness in his smile and the lamb she'd turned him into.

A bit of light to take back into the dark.

Chapter
TWENTY-SEVEN

Mirae didn't return to darkness, but to Kimoon's pale, seething face. His hand gripped her hair, holding her head out of the water.

"What were you thinking?" he fumed. "What on earth made you think that attacking Suhee was better than dealing with me? Look at what your foolishness has done."

Mirae gazed up at Kimoon, at the knife in his hand, then back to him. "What made you think becoming the Netherking's goon was going to save your kingdom?"

Kimoon put the knife against her throat. "I can't decide what would make my father happier—knowing that you're dead or getting to kill you himself."

Mirae looked him in the eye. "So this was your agreement with Suhee? To hand me over to your father, dead or alive? Why do you care what he wants, after everything he's done?"

"Because he speaks for Josan." Kimoon pressed the blade deeper. "We needed that army, but most of all, we needed to control *her*. Everything was fine until you came along. I should have killed you the moment you set foot in my fortress."

A few minutes earlier, the feelings would have been mutual, but now Mirae calmed the rage building in her heart, letting Kimoon say all the words trapped in his.

"Do you know what you've done, Mirae? Do you? You released a monster, and now all the leverage I had against the Netherking is gone. Who knows what he'll do now. His wife and son are outside, preparing to take Minho, the key to this war, out of my hands. You've made me a slave to that vile creature."

"She has a name."

"What?"

Mirae jerked her head away from Kimoon's knife. "Her name is Suhee. She was betrayed by her best friend and left for dead with the evilest man I know. He did things to her. This is not who she was supposed to be. She raised a daughter who had a protector's heart and a son who is capable of showing mercy to enemies. How is that possible if they were raised by a monster, not by a mother with goodness inside her?"

Kimoon stared at Mirae like she was speaking a foreign language. "What are you saying?"

"And then there's you, Kimoon. You barely have any legitimate footing in your family, yet you risked it all to give Minho a chance of coming out of this alive by being tethered to you instead of your father. How could you care about my brother even a little bit and fully believe in this war at the same time? I know you have doubts, Kimoon. I see it in your eyes, clear as day."

Kimoon stared at her, silent. Mirae looked around the room, nodding at the black water, the blood, and the basins. "This is not how you would go about getting justice for your people. You're just doing as you're told. That is the winter in your soul."

Kimoon's eyes narrowed. "Are you pitying me?"

"No." Mirae angled her body so she could face her captor fully. "I'm trying to help you learn from my mistakes. Not everyone who guides you loves you. Not everyone who spurns you hates you. And when you find someone worth caring about, you should protect them with the greatest power you possess."

Kimoon hesitated, as if afraid to ask. "And what is that?"

"The strength to believe in yourself and your calling as a just prince of Josan. But first you have to stop lying to yourself. The greatest gift you can give your kingdom, or Minho, isn't to keep scraps of them alive, but to love and honor the good man you're burying inside yourself. You are your own saving grace—and theirs. That is your true power."

After a long moment, Kimoon removed the knife from Mirae's throat. "Do you really think you can persuade me to let you go like that?"

"I don't need to. I just want to promise you this: when I get out of here, I'm going to give you something no one ever has—a chance to follow your heart. Whatever you choose to do right now, do it for yourself, or that winter in your soul will never end. You'll never become the man you're throwing your soul away to become."

Kimoon was silent for a moment before rising to his feet. "Are those the words of a wily witch or a wise oracle?"

"Neither," Mirae said. "Just me, using the one power I've had all along."

Kimoon looked at the signs of violence splattered around the room. "Everything felt so clear when it was under control. But now—"

"Blood is blood," Mirae said. "Torture is torture. And sons are sons—they always deserve to be loved. There shouldn't be an unbearable price."

Kimoon looked at Mirae's chains and then at his own stained wrists. "How can you possibly see a way out of this? We've made a mess of everything."

"If I can show you your true path, will you walk beside me?" Mirae asked. Several emotions passed over Kimoon's face, though he struggled to keep them under control.

"All right, Mirae. If you make me believe in your power, I'll let you teach me mine."

Mirae nodded and closed her eyes. She wriggled her wrists, brushing the chains against her legs to feel their metal. Kimoon didn't forge these himself, but whoever did intended for them to contain a monster, not a princess. Yet here Mirae was, stuck in the Netherqueen's cage. How were they alike enough to trigger the same enchantment? What darkness did they share?

"The water," Mirae said. "Dump it out."

Kimoon hesitated but then did as she asked. There was a small stopper in the back of the basin. He removed it and stepped back as the black water began seeping out onto the floor, draining away Suhee's essence. Or, as the Netherqueen had called it, water from her soul—the thing that made Minho hers.

Once the level sank below Mirae's ribs, freeing her heart, she hoped the chains would realize that she was not the Netherqueen and release her. When they didn't, she took a deep breath, refusing to lose hope, refusing to let Kimoon see her disappointment. There was a way out. There had to be.

She leaned forward; at least she could feel her heart and magic thrumming back to life as the black water drained away.

Once the chains were free of the water, Mirae examined them, finding their core.

Iron. She could see the metal clearly now. When activated in the armor of the Wonhwa, it gave them inhuman strength, enough to carry a royal palanquin quickly up a mountain. An enchanted iron sword was nearly unbreakable. Mirae hefted the chain to her right, feeling the strength of the metal. Then she pulled on the one around her left wrist. It had been imbued with iron's secondary power—resistance to magic, amplified by the dark water.

One chain was too strong to break with brute strength, the other unbreakable even with magic. Together, joined by the shackle around her neck, they made an impressive cage that not even a Jade Witch would be able to break out of. Even Mirae, a High Daughter, didn't have the strength to pull herself free. She would need something more powerful than magic.

Mirae fell back against the tub. What had the snake-faced man said—that her heart could defeat anything? That her greatest power was love? How would either of those things help her now?

"I told you," Kimoon said quietly. "There's no way out."

Mirae didn't believe that was true. She thought through what little she did know about the black water in her basin—that the Netherqueen's soul had been steeping in it for days, filling it with her essence. And yet Mirae couldn't feel its corruption. It felt no different from the water at Wol Sin Lake. Perhaps that was because she hadn't spent enough time in it, or maybe it was because the black water was doing what it did best.

Instead of corrupting its captive, it sensed Mirae's magic and was drinking her power, amplifying it. Thirsty for something she had and the Netherqueen didn't.

"Actually, leave the water, Kimoon. I need it."

He stuffed the stopper back in place. Her legs were still covered, her purple knees barely peeking out of the black water. Suhee's water. Mirae's water. Infused with the cores of two different hearts.

Perhaps it was time to see which was more powerful.

Mirae studied the water. Dark, wet silk against her arms and feet. Heavy suction where it bloated her clothes. Disrupted only by the metal chains and the walls of the tub.

Mirae plunged deeper than that, trying to figure out the black water's properties and the base of its power. The things she found made her shudder—a dark broth of everything the water had leached from the Netherqueen.

Bitterness against the Seollan queen. Regret for decisions that took her far from home. An insatiable need for more and more magic to keep her loved ones alive. The pain of good deeds that reaped no reward. The eternal hole in her heart that missed her family and friends.

There was also plenty that Mirae had never felt before. The torment of a mother who has lost a child. A wife who had to give more than her body to her husband. A queen who'd seen every one of her subjects die in the Deep, offering themselves to their king and his dark army experiments until she, free to walk the earth, made an alliance with Josan so that their prisoners could be brought to her husband to perfect his army.

And perfect it he did.

The Netherqueen was proud that everything she'd lost would be exacted from her enemies a hundredfold. Her soul screamed for justice. She was not going to have lost her daughter, her kingdom, for nothing.

Because there was something else in all the darkness that the Netherqueen kept close to her heart. Love for the man who had spared her years ago and shown her bursts of warmth that she was forever trying to win back. Love for the boy she'd taken in, who missed her enough to endure great dangers and betray his friends to get her back. Love for that which was fair.

The Netherqueen had a light side hidden in the darkness that created her. And it felt right at home with Mirae, because there were gentle things inside Mirae's essence as well. Compassion for ghosts, courage on dark roads, and companions who hung the moon in her sky.

But there were ugly things, too. Arrogance, naivete, and recklessness that brought the stars in her life crashing down to earth. Brothers who were anchors falling too far to ever come up again. A belief in gods that was turning out to be nothing more than her own disturbing pride.

Mirae accepted it all, the light and the dark within her. None of it was wholly different from the Netherqueen's soul. They were on different paths, yes, desperate at times and power hungry at others. But both loved fiercely. Both had been set on a collision course by the same Seollan queen. Both had been taken in by the Deep. Lied to. Betrayed.

And they both had everything to lose.

There was one other thing swirling in the mix that caught Mirae's attention—an anomalous sliver of soul that the black water was savoring. Something that was Mirae's and Mirae's alone through all time and under every moon. It was more than an essence, more than a taste of her soul or a memory.

Out of every creature roaming the earth, Mirae had risen the highest—higher than the sun rises in the heavens. And she had drunk that which dove as deeply as a queendom's darkest buried secrets. She'd traveled and lived and loved and lost so much on the middling world between the gods and the Deep. Even if she'd only experienced those things in glimpses, the soul she'd switched with had seen them all, and all her memories, those swatches of time, were letters left in her body for the black water to read—a story that could change the world.

The black water felt it all—the old soul that had been within her, the carrier of something more powerful than any magic or despair leached from the Netherqueen, who was powerful in the here and now.

But in Mirae's soul was the legacy of everything that mattered in the future—hope, love, and tenderness that spanned the past, present, and future. She was time's benevolent traveler, a divine warrior with a remedy for the misunderstood and the damaged. The natural enemy to the Inconstant Son, who was filled with hatred and harm. In the end, Mirae's soul would be stronger and brighter than his. The black water, sensing all the power that would eventually bloom out of Mirae's pain, drank deeply from her soul.

It churned around her, as if it couldn't get enough of her vastness. Every drop wanted to have its turn against her skin.

Mirae knew what she needed to do with all the power—her true power—seeping into the basin around her. She raised her head in a prayer to the heavens.

"I have failed you. I ignored the guides you sent my way and named myself your dragon without earning your trust first. I was arrogant, and for that I have cost my loved ones dearly. But still, you granted me one last switch, and that has given me clarity."

Mirae didn't have to open her eyes to feel a presence behind her. Just as she had seen the Netherking's soul standing by Suhee's side, Mirae could sense the blue-robed woman standing just out of sight, watching her with those star-flecked eyes. An oracle who had lived and died so that Mirae's destiny could be fulfilled—the first woman to show Mirae the truth.

Mirae took comfort in the Kun Sunim's presence, speaker for the gods. "I need your help. I do not wish to overrule divine laws, but, in a way, that is what I do—I am an exception for a reason. Not for power, but for a purpose."

Mirae heard Kimoon take a few steps back, as if aware that her magic had returned with a vengeance. But she wouldn't touch a hair on his head—that wasn't what this magic was for. "I ask you to do what I cannot: to let me freely wield what the black water drank from me. If you have not given up on my destiny, if you can still trust me, then let me fully control my gift just this once. When I am free, I will finish your work—this time, the right way."

Mirae opened her eyes and waited for the Kun Sunim to take her prayer to heaven, surrounded by a flock of her ancestors.

When they returned with an answer, Mirae felt it in her bones. Even the black water fell still, waiting for her command.

Every soul in the heavens seemed to be waiting to see what she would do, what freedom Mirae would find with this one final chance.

The black water was rich with her soul. The soul of Seolla's Switcher, who, for a moment, had command of time. If she wanted, she could shoot herself into the future with a thought and see the Inconstant Son's face. Or she could jump into the past to a private moment with her mother and tell her about the Netherking's treachery, equipping Seolla's queen to have his dark army and kingdom destroyed.

But Mirae was a guardian of time, not its master. A lamb treading softly wherever she went. A dragon wise with her strength. The Switcher of Seolla who changed nothing without permission—and the only thing she needed to change in that moment were the chains keeping her from answering the call of the divine.

"I cannot break you in your prime," Mirae said, looking at the iron rings. "You have a long life to live. Instead, I ask you to send me your old and feeble self, from a time when you are ready to return to dust. Will you switch for me, so that we may both escape our looming deaths?"

Mirae held her breath as she waited for the iron rings to respond. A few seconds passed, the room completely silent, as nothing happened. Then Mirae heard Kimoon gasp as the chains suddenly began to change.

What was once unbreakably strong became rusted with red, some of it sprinkling into the black water like tiny droplets of blood. With a few hard pulls, Mirae shattered her chains into red links and dust. As soon as she did the same thing with the shackle around her neck, Mirae's command of time faded, her answered prayer as brief as a shooting star.

But she was free.

Kimoon stared at Mirae as she rose from the basin wearing what remained of her rusted chains like jewelry. He stared at her as he would a queen.

"I made a promise," she said. "You're free to follow your heart now. What kind of man would you like to be?"

Kimoon stared at the ring of keys in his hand. Without a word, he swept over to Hongbin's basin and unlocked his chains.

As soon as Hongbin's head was lifted out of the water, he blustered, "I refuse to wed that chicken. Why would I marry something I love to eat?"

When he saw the man holding his head, he found Kimoon at a loss for words—a problem Hongbin didn't have. "Oh, um," Hongbin began, "you are definitely not a chicken."

"No, I'm not," Kimoon said, releasing him. "Please don't eat me."

Hongbin realized where he was and rose quickly to his feet. Too quickly to do more than slip on the black water. Thankfully, Kimoon was quick to steady him and helped him step gracelessly out of the basin, before Hongbin shoved him to the side and rushed to Mirae.

"Noonim!" Hongbin helped her out as Kimoon had helped him. He gave her a wet hug and spoke quietly, something he hadn't been able to do in some time. "What's the plan? Do we knock Kimoon out and leave him floating?"

"No." Mirae didn't bother speaking quietly. She wanted Kimoon to hear every word. "Our host has had a change of heart."

She and Hongbin looked at Kimoon, who regarded them both for a moment before nodding. "I think the same could be said of you, Gongju mama."

Hongbin looked between them, clearly suspicious of Kimoon's drastic change in tone. "Hearts don't change that quickly."

There was no time to explain the winter in Kimoon's soul, or how Mirae was giving him a chance to change everything he hated about himself. So instead, she touched her brother's cheek. "I switched just a bit ago. I know what I'm doing."

Hongbin touched the shackle around her neck. "Is future Mirae the one who freed you?"

Mirae shook her head. "No, I did it myself."

"Why did she leave you—and me—in here alone? Why didn't she help?"

Mirae looked at Kimoon, remembering the words of the snake-faced man. "Because she didn't need to, and it was important that he watch me free myself. It has changed his path forever."

Hongbin looked between Mirae and Kimoon again, clearly uneasy with how much they were staring at each other. "He's working with the Netherking."

"At one point, so was I."

"He threatened my life."

"And I pushed him off a balcony."

Hongbin was finally speechless. "You what?"

Kimoon shrugged. "I deserved it. But I'm willing to put all that behind us, Gunju, after what I've just seen. Your sister is more powerful than the Netherqueen, yet as kind as Minho. She's the ally I've been waiting for."

Hongbin stepped closer to Mirae, lowering his voice. "His change of heart is either really lucky or extremely fake. Either way, I don't like it."

"He has an army," Mirae said. "And more important, the Netherqueen thinks he's still loyal to her. He will be our means of escape."

Hongbin shook his head. "If there's one thing I've learned the past few days, it's to be very careful about whom we rely on. Are you sure about this, noonim?"

Mirae felt a deep pain burrow into her heart at Hongbin's words. She was the one who'd allowed Siwon to come along, after all, and ignored Captain Jia's warnings over and over again.

Mirae's eyes slid to the floor where her mentor lay, the one person whose instincts she should have trusted completely. Hongbin followed her gaze and put a hand over his mouth. He and Mirae knelt beside their protector, heads bowed with grief that felt heavier than the mountain they stood upon and deeper than any prison below. After a long, teary silence, Mirae wiped her eyes and turned to her brother.

"I'm the Unnamed Dragon, Hongbin. I discern hearts—their truths and their wounds. I can see everyone clearly now, the living and the dead. I will do everything I can to heal us all."

Chapter

TWENTY-EIGHT

Kimoon walked behind Mirae, guiding her across the main level of the pagoda. Keon and Sado approached, stepping over the bodies of men beheaded and gashed by Captain Jia.

"We've prepared the horses and the palanquin," Keon said. "The mudang should be leaving any minute."

Kimoon nodded. "Tell the men to fall back and keep out of sight. Gongju mama and I will deal with Suhee alone."

Keon stared at his prince. "Gunju—"

"I'll be fine." He looked at Mirae. "Won't I?"

"We meet again in the future," she said. "You do not die today."

He nodded. After what he'd seen and already knew about Mirae's switching, visions of the future weren't hard for him to accept. But Keon was another story.

"Gunju daegam, don't forget what she is. Or what the monster will do if—"

"Her name is Suhee, and I will deal with her," Kimoon repeated, gesturing for Mirae to continue past Keon and out the main doors.

Outside, everything was cast in sunset. The sand of the court-yard gleamed like powdered gold, and even the stone of the heavy walls glittered with flecks of warm ruby light.

The sun sat on a distant mountain like the kind of bun that used to sit on Hongbin's head, perfectly round and glossy. The sky was as rosy as his cheeks used to get whenever he talked about his long list of suitors. Now he was recovering from his time in the black water and mourning the loss of a dear friend. Mirae wasn't sure she or Hongbin would ever be able to blush like that ever again.

This time, Mirae didn't approach Suhee with arrogance. She kept her magic tucked away, her hands clasped behind her back. The chains around her wrists clanked as Kimoon steered her in front of him like a prisoner, as though the chains were still intact. He cleared his throat. "I'm afraid there's been a change of plans."

Suhee was kneeling beside the palanquin, helping Siwon set Minho inside. When she heard Kimoon and saw his cargo, she stood and glared at the bastard prince. "What are you doing? She needs to soak for several more days."

Kimoon brought Mirae to a stop. "Surely you don't expect me to cart a Seollan witch and a black water basin across Josan all by myself. In any case, I'm sure my father would like to hear about today's excitement in person. Let's travel to the capital together and give him our report."

Suhee stared at Kimoon as if he'd lost his mind. "Minho's body is ready for the next step. I must take him to the Deep as soon as possible."

Kimoon let go of Mirae's wrists and approached Suhee alone. Pretending she was too weak to support herself without her captor, Mirae began to sway—much less than when she was a shaman, but enough to look drugged and harmless, her hands chained behind her back.

Suhee seemed to buy it, at least believing in the strength of the iron she herself hadn't been able to break out of. She glared at Kimoon. "What's gotten into you? We made a deal."

Kimoon tilted his head. "You know, I still remember the day you came to me just a few months ago, desperate for an ally. Your husband was losing his mind. Your daughter was dead. You had no one else to turn to for help."

Suhee kept her glare fixed on Kimoon. "Except for the first power-hungry bastard I could find."

"Correct," he said, eyes darting over Suhee's face, taking her in as she started to do the same to him. "We were the perfect storm, weren't we? You knew the secret to giving me an army that would help me win my father's respect, and I promised to use it to raze our mutual enemy's queendom to the ground."

"We were perfect *opportunities*," she said. "Nothing more."

"Nothing more?" Kimoon was close enough and Suhee almost distracted enough for what came next. "I've noticed the way you look at me, Suhee. Like I remind you of him—back when he was exciting and kind."

Mirae glanced over at Siwon, who was approaching his mother slowly, protectively. But he wasn't looking at Suhee. He was looking at Mirae and her theatrical sways.

He'd seen them before.

Suhee laughed in Kimoon's face. "Yes, you remind me of him. I'll give you that. But no matter how charming you are, I'm going home to my husband with a royal gift in tow. Don't worry, I'll tell him it's from you, too."

Kimoon was close enough now to cup Suhee's face. "Take this before you go—one last token of what we saw in each other before all we wanted was war."

Suhee neither pushed Kimoon away nor pulled him in. She was mesmerized, staring into his near-golden eyes, feeling the touch of his gentle hands. Lost in some memory—a tender moment she clearly missed with all her heart. Something Mirae had seen in the black water basin.

Siwon, oblivious to his mother's emotions, strode up to Mirae. She'd stopped swaying to watch Kimoon's ruse, glad that both Siwon and his mother were too distracted to notice the bead the Josan prince held between his fingers.

Until he shoved it into Suhee's mouth.

She tried to spit it out, but Kimoon pressed his hands over her face, holding the bead in place long enough for it to do its job.

But he couldn't hold her back for long. Suhee fought him off, sending him sprawling. She spat the bead out in a spray of black water, clutching her throat.

"What did you do?" Suhee seemed more shocked than angry, which meant the bead was working. "What is this?" She was too confused, too disarmed, to pull her spine out of its sheath.

Siwon, however, had no magical bead of calmness holding him back. Kimoon saw him coming and jumped to his feet, pulling out his sword in time to meet Siwon's.

"You shouldn't have done that," Siwon said, pressing hard enough to make Kimoon take a step back. "You've betrayed us for the last time."

"Oh, that's not even remotely true."

The two men pushed away from each other, standing far enough apart that they would be able to block any sudden attacks. But Siwon was soon distracted by Mirae holding up an object, revealing that her iron chains had been broken all along.

The gwisin's pearl was immaculate, even in the fading light of sunset. It caught every shade of the blushing sun and the rising moon. The reflection of Mirae's purple hanbok. The blue glints in Suhee's hair. Beaming with every color around it, the pearl sat cupped in Mirae's palm like a dome of gathering rainbows.

"Where did you get that?" Suhee whispered, trembling despite the sheep bead's calming effect on her body. "I hid it where no one would ever find it."

"Nothing is hidden from me. I've sat in your basin," Mirae said. "I've seen what drove you to become this desperate creature. You were a shaman once. You didn't torture souls—you sent them to their rest. As does your daughter. You know you don't belong in the Deep. It's time to set yourself free and help your daughter find peace."

Suhee stared at the rusted chains dangling from Mirae's wrists, proof that she knew how to break out of the unbreakable—to do the impossible. Then her eyes turned back to the pearl. "You're lying. Sol would never betray me."

Mirae held the pearl higher. "I know how much you love your daughter, and how much she hates *him*. You hate him, too. You have every right to."

"No." Suhee's eyes snapped to Mirae's. "You did something to Sol. You must have."

No one seemed more surprised than Siwon when he interjected, "Actually, Mother, Sol made her own choice. I saw it myself."

His mother glared at him. "Why would she *ever*—"

"Because Sol knew you would wage this war in her name." Siwon took another step closer. Mirae stared at her unexpected ally, letting him speak. "You and Father both want the queen of Seolla to suffer, but Sol is suffering, too."

"That is Noeul's doing. This is all her fault." Suhee tried to snatch the pearl away, but Mirae clutched it to her chest.

"The queen of Seolla visits Sol, you know." Siwon walked close enough to take his mother's hand. "I followed her several times. She's tried everything she can to put Sol's spirit to rest, but only you can do that, Mother. You're the reason she stays."

"I know that," Suhee said, pulling her hand free. "But this war is how we end her suffering. It will free our family. All of us."

"Only if you win." Kimoon held up his sword. "Only if the Netherking means everything he says. Don't you wonder sometimes how he didn't anticipate that you'd be imprisoned by my father? Do you ever suspect he wanted to curb your power before it outgrew his?"

Suhee shut her mouth, locking in both the black water and the dark things she didn't want to say. Mirae held up the pearl, reminding her of her daughter.

"Mother." Siwon rested his hand over the pearl; Mirae let him. "You took me in when both Josan and Seolla betrayed me. You raised me and Sol to be seekers of justice. That's who you were, too . . . until Father's experiments."

Surprised at the vitriol in Siwon's voice when he mentioned the Netherking, Mirae turned to look at him. In his eyes, she saw that he wanted what the snake-faced man had implied was the most powerful thing she could give—forgiveness. For all the lies. For his part in Captain Jia's death. He was here to rescue his mother but wanted nothing to do with her and Kimoon's war. When Mirae nodded, promising him that gift, his face, lit with sunset from behind, began to glow with the starlight she had always seen in him.

Suhee used that moment of distraction to reach between their clasped hands and yank the pearl away. "You really shouldn't play with things you don't understand."

"Mother—"

Before Siwon could grab her or the pearl, Suhee struck him on the head with it, knocking him to the ground. "Your father was right—you're too weak for the Deep. That's why he sent me to do what no one else can."

Mirae and Kimoon backed away as the Netherqueen, her magic far stronger than Mirae had expected, repelled the power of the bead enough to stretch out her neck and unsheathe her spine. Her body fell to its knees, vulnerable, until her body-guard climbed out of the palanquin, moving to tower over her remains.

Minho, the obedient son the Netherqueen always wanted.

Siwon clutched his head, too stunned to rise. But his mother ignored him, facing off against Mirae and Kimoon, her spine swinging like hips as she studied her prey. Her stomach bled healthily, fully restored, apparently, after a quick soak in black water.

When the Netherqueen's spine straightened out like a sword, ready to attack, Mirae summoned a ball of fire in each hand while Kimoon drew his blade.

They weren't fast enough.

The Netherqueen's spine hit Kimoon in the chest, the serrated vertebra slashing through his hanbok, making him gasp and stumble backward.

Mirae shot both fireballs at the Netherqueen's head, but Suhee dodged them easily, and they glanced harmlessly off the stone walls of the fortress. Mirae had more in hand before the first fireballs fizzled out, but she waited to hurl them.

The Netherqueen was quick. Kimoon, with his balance restored, stood back-to-back with Mirae in the center of the courtyard as the Netherqueen circled them, trying to find an opening between Mirae's fire and Kimoon's blade. She laughed as her spine flashed back and forth, grazing Mirae's cheek here, slicing Kimoon's hair there.

Kimoon lunged and struck at the Netherqueen's stomach, nicking the already-seeping organ. The Netherqueen howled and soared out of reach.

Mirae threw her fire, singeing the Netherqueen's hair before asking, "Kimoon, are you ready?"

"Yes," he said. "I'd love to get to the part where she stops shredding my clothes."

"Hongbin?" Mirae said. Though she couldn't see her brother, she felt his presence beside her. "Are you ready?"

"Ready," she heard him say.

She nodded and released the spell that hid him. It had been simple. The sand in the courtyard had inspired the Ma-eum illusion she'd used to disguise him. Combined with the rat bead's stealth, he had been all but invisible while creeping toward the Netherqueen.

She noticed him now, and the jade sword in his hands. But it was too late. Hongbin swung at the Netherqueen before she could even blink, hard enough to lop off her stomach in one blow. Consumed by his rage over Captain Jia's death, Hongbin swung the captain's sword one last time, straight through the Netherqueen's spine.

Suhee hovered for a moment in midair, split, until her bottom half clattered to the ground like a bone-dry snake.

She stared down at herself, too shocked to scream. But then she howled and whipped the rest of her spine at Hongbin, prepared to slash him to pieces. Kimoon pushed him out of the way and stabbed her bleeding stomach, pinning it to the ground.

The Netherqueen screamed and screamed, writhing in the air with half a spine. Hongbin and Kimoon ran over to Mirae. The former handed her Captain Jia's sword. The latter turned to Minho.

"You're going to be all right, I promise," Kimoon said, as he and Hongbin slipped a hand under Minho's arms and pulled him back toward the palanquin.

Which left Mirae to deal with Siwon alone.

He was sitting in the sand, still dazed from his mother's attack and seemingly unsure whom to fight and whom to defend until he saw Mirae lift Captain Jia's sword against his mother's headless, kneeling body.

"No, Gongju." He was on his feet in an instant. "Don't."

Mirae raised a hand as if casting a spell. Siwon flinched, but all she did was point at the Netherqueen's screaming head. "Do you believe there's still good in her?"

He didn't even hesitate. "Yes."

"Then trust me. I'm showing her all the mercy she deserves."

"No, you're murdering her." Siwon drew his dagger. Mirae was no soldier, but she was still shocked at how easily he pushed past her weapon and put the cold metal of his dagger against her neck. "I'm not leaving without her."

Mirae recognized the determination in Siwon's eyes—just as strong as hers had been when she watched Captain Jia die and thought Hongbin would be next. Siwon would kill if he had to. He would do the reckless, selfish thing.

Mirae held still. "There is another way."

"Tell me." Siwon lowered his knife a little. Behind him, Kimoon and Hongbin, finished with Minho, edged closer, but didn't risk coming too near.

Mirae held up the bead that had softened her soul once. "Love. If this doesn't work, then nothing will, and you'll have to accept that."

Siwon studied Mirae's face, looking for a trick of some kind. Finding none, he lowered his dagger. "You would offer me a piece of your father's life to fix my mother?"

"Only if you swear to do what must be done, should the bead have no effect." Mirae still held out the bead, though everything inside her screamed to put it away. She reminded herself, firmly, that she was going to give her father back every bit of life energy that had been taken from him, even if she had to pull it from herself. But for now, compassion had to be extended. It was the only way this vicious cycle would end.

After a moment, Siwon nodded. "Fine."

The Netherqueen used the moment of stillness to speed toward Mirae as fast as a hawk, her teeth sharp like talons. Siwon, putting all his trust in Mirae, in love, moved to stand in his mother's way.

She didn't slow, but she did hide her teeth before barreling into her son. Siwon clasped his mother to his chest as he fell, much as Captain Jia had, leaving Mirae free to shove the dog bead into the gaping neck of the Netherqueen's headless body.

Suhee's throat was hot and gripping—Mirae could feel the heat of the Netherqueen's abandoned organs and blood as she pushed the bead farther into the cavity, planting it between two tendons. When Mirae pulled her hand out, she saw that it was already starting to work.

But not at all like she had expected.

The dog bead had brought Mirae's mother back to herself in the Garden of Queens, restored by her husband's love. But restoration of the mind was different from restoration of the body. Love—real, gentle love—was a part of the Netherqueen that had been cut away, tortured out of her by her husband's need for war. Growing it back now, without being put back together first, was a violence no body could endure.

Siwon watched, horrified, as his mother's eyes rolled back into her head, her spine thrashing against his chest, cutting him mindlessly. Her headless body, too, began to shake. The hole where the bead rested was closing up, healing. Her stomach, even, started to turn blue. Suhee was becoming exactly what she looked like—a woman in pieces.

Siwon held his mother to his chest, not caring how she cut him with bones that were slowly turning rigid, pink marrow oozing out of their chipped ends.

"Kill her, Gongju," he begged. "If she can't be fixed, then please just kill her."

Mirae looked at the jade sword in her hand. Like Suhee, it was no longer what it used to be. In Captain Jia's hands, it was a shield. In Mirae's, it was an act of war that the Deep would never forgive. Mirae lifted the sword over her head and struck the Netherqueen's body with everything she had.

As soon as the sword hit flesh, it glowed, slicing through the Netherqueen's shoulder and lodging in her heart. Sparking, searing, smoking everything it touched except for Mirae's hand.

The sword glowed a sickly green, like something venomous, before Mirae could yank it out of the Netherqueen's chest and let it fall to the ground. The headless corpse in front of her toppled over, and the Netherqueen's head fell still.

Hongbin was beside Mirae in an instant, wrapping his arms around her. Kimoon retrieved the pearl and stuck it in his pocket, all the while eyeing the Netherqueen's motionless corpse warily.

But Mirae looked only at Siwon. He was staring at his mother's spine, coiled like a snake in his arms. Her white bones surrounded her motionless head like a pale version of her husband's crown.

"You had no choice," Hongbin said, seeing where Mirae was looking. She couldn't see Siwon's face, but she didn't need to. She knew his heart, and she knew what it felt like to lose someone she'd do anything to protect—even someone unspeakably mutilated by evil.

Mirae pulled away from Hongbin. "Kimoon, go inside and ready your men. They have a big decision to make."

Kimoon gave a short bow, one between equals, before doing as he was told. He looked back once, something unreadable flashing over his face. But it left as quickly as he did.

Mirae reached into her pocket and pulled out the blue stone she'd retrieved from Kimoon's office. Hongbin frowned at the seong-suk. "What are you going to do with that?"

"Everything that happened today is our ancestors' fault." Mirae hefted the stone. "It's time they fixed the things they've broken."

Mirae turned and hurled the blue seong-suk against the wall behind her. When it shattered, the blast radius of the Deep Deceiver's soul knocked everyone to the ground.

When Mirae opened her eyes, a milky-blue woman was crouched over her, wearing the crown of Seolla. She had one hand on Mirae's brow. Realizing the Deep Deceiver was right in front of her, Mirae sat up and bowed to the apparition.

"Why did you shatter my stone?" There was no warmth to speak of in the icy soul, and the look the Deep Deceiver gave Mirae seemed especially cold.

"I didn't know how else to wake you, and I didn't have time to figure out anything else," Mirae said. "There's something I need you to do for me, as quickly as possible."

The Deep Deceiver frowned but said nothing. Mirae pointed at the Netherqueen's bones. "I need you to trap her soul, like you did your own. I want you to save her."

The Deep Deceiver rose to her ghostly feet. "I did not lock my soul away for centuries as an act of mercy. I preserved myself to tell you that I should have been crueler. Compassion for monsters is a mistake. I am here to tell you how I came to know that."

"You can do that after—"

"Thanks to you shattering my stone, my soul only has a few minutes left in this world." The Deep Deceiver moved to cut off Mirae's view of the Netherqueen's corpse. "I will not waste them so that you can act like the fool I was. The only thing I came here to discuss is your mission. You must prepare for war against the Inconstant Son."

Mirae lifted her chin. "Well, Suhee is not the Inconstant Son. She was corrupted because you failed to stop him. You might even have created him with your cage. And you need to make that right. Save her, and I will listen to everything you have to say."

The Deep Deceiver gritted her milky teeth. "I will not spend my precious minutes on—"

"Save her," Mirae demanded, her dark eyes boring into the spirit's. "Only then will I listen."

The Deep Deceiver looked as if she'd rather disappear entirely than face the indignity of obeying. But after a few seconds, she knelt beside Suhee's headless body. Mirae placed the black bell over Suhee's stomach while the Deep Deceiver closed her ghostly eyes.

Mirae watched, breathless, as black mist seeped out of Suhee's body. Its swirls circled the bell, melting together onto its surface like shadowy paint. When every last tendril of ebony haze lay gleaming on the bell's dark metal, the Deep Deceiver opened her eyes and handed it back to Mirae, no longer matte, but glazed with Suhee's soul.

The Deep Deceiver scowled at Mirae's look of relief. "I'm ashamed at how little we've learned in the centuries we've been battling the Inconstant Son. You are woefully unprepared for everything to come. I was supposed to change that, but instead, you wasted my powers on—" She gestured at the bell. "There's only one way to end the terrors of the Deep, and it looks nothing like mercy. Your naivete horrifies me."

Mirae was horrified, too—at how similar her ancestor's words sounded to the Netherqueen's tortured tirade. "Isn't there something you wanted to tell me?"

"Yes, and I'll keep this next part simple enough for even you to understand. First, don't ever believe the Inconstant Son can be reasoned with, or changed. He is evil, and he can only be stopped by your most violent side. You must not take pity on him as I did."

Mirae nodded at the Deep Deceiver's warning. "How do I kill him?"

"It doesn't matter how as long as you do it without hesitation." The Deep Deceiver reached out as if to touch Mirae's hand, though her fingers passed right through Mirae's body. She was beginning to fade. "No matter the heartbreak, no matter the injustice or the unbearable suffering, do not fight this war with your heart. I refused to be a monster, and that has doomed us all. Heed this, if nothing else—we despise the callously cruel until they're on our side. They are not broken, those who can embrace both the light and the dark. After all, if the gods' hands are not clean, their servants' can't be, either."

The Deep Deceiver rose to her feet and bowed. Then she walked right through Mirae, becoming blue mist on the other side that never took form again.

Chapter

TWENTY-NINE

Mirae helped Hongbin inside the palanquin, where he sat beside his brother. Minho was unmoving, staring at something no one else could see, but Hongbin declared that he was determined to talk his brother's ear off the whole way home to help him "remember all the things he has to come back for."

Once Minho and Hongbin were settled, Mirae found Siwon still standing over his mother, as unmoving as Minho. He stared at the pile of bones and the black hair streaming out of them like blood.

Mirae walked over to him, her steps quiet out of respect. "Where will you go now?"

For a split second, Siwon glanced over at Kimoon, who had returned with his soldiers. "I don't know."

Mirae studied Siwon's face—really studied it. Now that neither his face nor Kimoon's was contorted with rage, pain, or secrets that they were desperate to hide, she finally saw it. There was a definite resemblance in the shape of their jaw, the height of their cheeks. Their eyes were the same shade of honey brown, lighter than Mirae's. Mirae had never met the Josan king, but she had a feeling he was the source of their likeness.

"You have royal blood," Mirae said, "don't you?"

Siwon looked away and nodded. "Kimoon's mother was a favorite of the king's—a concubine. Mine was a seamstress. She would have been killed if she told the truth about how she got pregnant. So she was forced to leave her home."

Mirae hung her head sadly. "Where did she go?"

"The only people who would take her in were bandits, though she was careful to always remind me that I was better than a life of crime. I was of royal blood, and someday I would be a prince. But then one day our gang tried to rob a merchant caravan, not realizing it was transporting True Bone royals, protected by Wonhwa guards in disguise."

"Your mother was killed in battle," Mirae said, understanding his hatred of Seolla.

He nodded. "I was lucky. I escaped and grew up to be as strong and . . . handsome as my mother. I used that to get several different positions at the palace. I thought maybe if I made my way up Josan's complex social circles, my father would be willing to recognize me. I just wanted to get close enough to try."

"But then you met Suhee."

He nodded. "I knew her as a myth. The court shaman who appeared out of nowhere one day, and then disappeared years later. When she returned once again, she spoke to the dowager queen about Josan finally getting its revenge on the queen of Seolla. The dowager queen thought Shaman Suhee had gone mad. Things went badly and Shaman Suhee . . . lost her temper. I was just a passerby, but I ended up being the lone survivor and witness to what she did."

"Why didn't she kill you?"

"I guess she saw how young I was and took pity on me. Instead of ripping me to shreds, she abducted me. But she was kind. She earned my trust in little ways. A lot like you."

Mirae frowned at the comparison. "How could you trust someone who murdered people right in front of you?"

He hesitated. "Honestly, I thought her arrival was auspicious. I thought maybe this was my mother looking out for me. Because she promised that she would always be with me, and that someday . . ."

"You would become a prince." Mirae put a hand on his shoulder. "I can't say I wouldn't have seen things the same way, if I was a child in your shoes."

Siwon nodded. "I wanted to make my mother proud, but she was gone when I felt lost in life, and Suhee wasn't."

Mirae turned Siwon to face her. "I want to offer you the same thing I promised your brother. Whatever you've had to do in the past, you're free now. Go and be the man you want to be. You'll always have a home with my brothers and me, if you so choose."

Before Siwon could speak, Kimoon walked up to Mirae. "I'm sorry to interrupt, but I've done as you asked, Gongju mama, and my men wish to accompany us to Seolla. They have sworn to help you hunt down every member of the dark army and cut them down."

Mirae nodded. "Then let's take care of Minho so we can be off."

"Are you sure you don't want me to bring some of the black water from his basin?" Kimoon asked. "There's plenty left, and he may need it."

Mirae shook her head, pulling out the Netherking's vial. "I don't want him absorbing any more of the Netherqueen's essence. This stuff is untainted, fresh from Wol Sin Lake. I've even used some of it myself. I'm hoping its purity will let Minho be his own master again."

Mirae and Kimoon walked back toward the palanquin, leaving Siwon to his considerations. Mirae crawled inside the palanquin as soon as she reached it and, with Hongbin's help, tipped Minho's head back. With bated breath, she carefully poured half of the black water that remained in the Netherking's vial into her older brother's mouth.

At first, Minho didn't swallow, merely holding the dark liquid in his mouth like tea in a cup. But as it started to trickle down his throat, he erupted into gags and coughs, clutching his neck.

"Ugh. That stuff is *vile*," he said. But his look of disgust quickly changed to one of confusion and then surprise as Mirae and Hongbin strangled him with hugs. "What is this?" he wheezed.

"Just a brother and a sister saving a colossal idiot," Hongbin said. "From now on, you're never allowed to go anywhere without us."

"Or anywhere, period," Mirae said, squeezing Minho even harder. "You must be a homebound hermit until we say otherwise."

"May I at least be a hermit who can breathe?" Minho asked, gasping for air when they finally let him go. He looked around the palanquin. "Where in the gods' names are we?"

"Hongbin will tell you everything," Mirae said, shooting her younger brother a look. They'd already agreed that Minho shouldn't be told what had happened to Captain Jia. Not like this. Mirae was going to tell him about the captain's sacrifice when the time was right. "I believe Hongbin said something earlier about talking your ear off."

Mirae gave her brother one last squeeze before moving back outside so that her siblings could sit comfortably. But she couldn't help but peer back in on them through the window, her heart warm at the sight of them safely together.

"At last," Hongbin said, settling next to his brother and leaning his head against Minho's shoulder. "We get to engage in our favorite pastime. I talk, you listen."

Minho chuckled. "You know, for some reason, I feel like I've missed that. Strange."

Hongbin wrapped his arms around Minho. "Not strange. It's wonderful."

Mirae smiled and left them alone to catch up. Eight of Kimoon's men raised the palanquin onto their shoulders and began the laborious descent down the mountain. When Kimoon came to stand beside Mirae, watching it leave, she said, "You know, I could give your men a little something to help them carry their burden."

"It's not polite to call princes a burden," Kimoon said. "At least, that's true of your brothers. Me, you may call whatever you like."

An Inconstant Son. Perhaps someday a snake-faced lover. Mirae shook her head. "I'll just call you friend."

Kimoon smiled. "Well, friend, I have a feeling neither of our parents will approve of the decisions we've made today. Except for the part where you pushed me off a balcony. My father will like that bit very much."

"Well, whatever we end up telling them, let's agree to continue what we've started."

Kimoon nodded and followed his men down the hill. "Yes. Whatever that is."

Mirae looked back to see Siwon taking fistfuls of sand and dusting them over his mother. Mirae strode back over to him and took his elbow. "You should tell Kimoon who you are."

Siwon pulled away. "No. I don't want to live in any more palaces. Before I can decide who I really am, there's something I need to do."

Mirae brushed the sand out of Siwon's palm and replaced it with the black bell, a relic coated with Suhee's soul, making it now safe to the touch. "Hold on to this until we part ways. It will help you say goodbye."

Siwon clasped the bell and pressed it to his chest. He nodded his thanks and followed Mirae down the darkening mountain path.

They made camp just outside the green fields of Noksan. Mirae slept back-to-back with Minho for warmth while Hongbin slept on his other side. Although Kimoon had guards on watch, every once in a while, Mirae would wake with a start and expect to find Captain Jia sitting calmly by the fire, keeping them safe. But then Mirae would remember the sacrifice that had been made in order for her to have this warm back pressed against hers.

Dawn came too soon, and Mirae was forced to return to her feet, trailing after the palanquin so that her brothers could rest. Hongbin was doing well, but the only thing that had any effect on Minho was the rest of the black water in the Netherking's vial. After drinking it, he fell asleep, and the remaining black in his veins began to fade away.

Mirae made sure to check on him often, not just for his own good, but to break up the monotony of the journey. As she walked, Mirae also took the time to use her Sacred Bone connection with her mother to check on her, and was surprised to find the queen roused, no longer under the Netherking's spell. Mirae wasn't sure how, or why, her mother had miraculously recovered, nor did she ask. She wasn't ready to speak to her mother through Sacred Bone Magic, not after everything she'd learned about the woman who had raised her. Still, Mirae knew she needed to prepare for their inevitable reunion. From the glimpse Mirae caught while soul-walking, her mother was preparing a caravan to meet them at the Seollan border.

Despite her trepidation, Mirae was still relieved at the sight of the Wonhwa guards and her recovered mother standing like a wall of might at the barrier between the two nations.

Her mother, without hesitation, embraced Mirae as soon as she crossed under the opalescent barrier. It wasn't just the way her mother held her lovingly that made Mirae realize how much she had missed her stoic strength. It was also the way she smelled, of ginseng and persimmons. Mirae would have never let go if she hadn't heard her mother gasp at the sight of Minho.

The palanquin had been set down carefully at the border. Kimoon and his men stayed back, as did Siwon, but Hongbin pulled Minho to his feet and joined the family embrace.

When their mother finally pulled away and took a moment to look at their guests, she walked up to the Josan–Seolla line and held out her hands. Kimoon took them and bowed to the queen he'd been raised to hate.

"Your Majesty," he said. "It's an honor to finally meet you."

Mirae's mother held his hands tightly. "I assume you had something to do with the safe return of my children."

Kimoon looked as if he wasn't quite sure how to tell her the truth about his involvement with her son's abduction, but Minho walked over and put one hand on Kimoon's shoulder and the other on his mother's, standing with one foot on either side of the border. "Kimoon did his best to make sure I stayed alive."

"And he helped us escape," Mirae added. "In a way, he's been our secret ally all along."

Mirae's mother nodded but eyed the prince critically. "When you see your father, I hope you'll carry a message for me."

"Actually," Mirae said, "I thought Kimoon might stay here. If he wants to. I think we all know how he'll be repaid for his kindness if he returns to the Josan capital."

Mirae's mother was silent for a moment. Then she gestured to Kimoon's men. "Just him. I won't have our lands invaded."

"They're loyal to me, not to my father," Kimoon said. "If anything, their punishment will be worse than mine, and they are ready to swear their fealty to Seolla."

This time, the queen's silence lasted even longer. "Fine. But you will stay just until we figure something else out. I have a long list of rules you'll need to follow."

Kimoon bowed again. "Your grace is immeasurable."

She gestured for him and his men to cross over alongside her sons. The men from Josan were met by stony-faced Wonhwa; they weren't the only ones who realized their captain had not returned.

When they were alone, Mirae's mother took her hand. "Jia didn't survive?"

Mirae shook her head. "Father?"

Her mother looked away. "He hasn't woken up. I'm not sure he ever will."

Mirae pulled out her mother's beads. "Will these help?"

Her mother gave a start, then nodded. "I'm so sorry, Mirae. For the lies, the secrets . . . for *everything*."

They were both silent for a moment, each unsure how to say what they were feeling—how to blame, forgive, and console each other. But her mother spoke first, cupping Mirae's face.

"If I had been even half as brave as you, Josan and Seolla would be running festivals, not starting wars, and Hongbin would be expanding his ever-growing list of suitors."

Mirae placed her hands over her mother's. "Captain Jia said to never talk about the list."

Her mother smiled sadly. "Well, we should always listen to Jia."

She patted Mirae's cheek before sweeping her sons away to join the caravan. Mirae found herself alone with Siwon, and turned to him one last time. He grabbed Mirae's hand and put the black bell in her palm. "What will you do with her?"

"Why don't you stay and help me figure it out?"

Siwon shook his head. "I can't. Don't worry, I'll behave myself."

"Well, you were raised by bandits, so I'm not going to hold my breath on that."

"I suppose trouble is in my blood." Siwon smiled and looked away. "I'll be all right."

"Is there anything I can do?" Mirae asked as he turned to leave.

He paused. "More than you already have? You showed me kindness. Forgiveness. You turned the tides of an ugly battle and even uglier hearts. It's the most powerful thing I've ever seen. And I'm pretty sure I'll never be the same."

Mirae watched Siwon walk away, hearing words from a masked man in the future echoing after him long after he was gone.

It took a few days for Mirae to catch Minho alone. Constantly surrounded by healers and guards, he was barely allowed any space to breathe.

Thankfully, during that time, no retaliatory attack came from Josan. Kimoon was never disavowed by his father— perhaps in an effort to buy Kimoon's silence, or perhaps to make it seem as if he'd been *asked* to abandon his duties and move to Seolla. It was the only show of power the Josan king had left, and it probably didn't hurt that the people of Seolla responded so positively to it. It was almost impossible not to like Kimoon when he wanted to win someone—or even entire villages—over.

One night, on her way home from a day trip to Geumju to visit and thank Jisoo and Yoonhee, Mirae saw palace women leaving Minho's room and thought she might try to see if he was alone. She walked past his guards, who bowed respectfully, just as they used to when she was crown princess.

When she entered Minho's chamber, he welcomed her with a sad smile. "At last, someone who isn't going to bully me into healing faster than I am able."

Mirae sat on the floor beside her brother's sleeping mat. It wasn't just the black water he was having difficulty healing from. The news of Captain Jia's death had hit him hard. He never talked about it, even when Mirae offered in private, but she knew he was suffering.

Mirae put on a smile for him. "Yes, your life is so difficult. People constantly fawning over you, making you eat delicious food."

Minho chuckled softly. "Hey, there should be *some* perks to being king."

Mirae laughed and nodded in agreement. She plucked a few grapes from the tray of food in front of her brother, stalling for a moment before asking, "So, how are you doing, oreobani? Aside from being poked and prodded and never having a moment alone to yourself."

Minho stared at the wall, as if lost in thought. "I feel strange. Like there's still a hint of the Netherqueen inside me—a piece of her that wants me to do things that I would never, ever . . . it's hard to explain."

"I'm sure it is." Mirae took his hands. "But you're home now. You're safe. Soon, you'll even be king, so you won't have to listen to anyone but me, your extraordinarily wise and enchanting high counselor. Self-appointed, of course."

Minho gave her a smile—a real one, this time. "You might have to fight Hongbin for that ridiculous title."

Mirae smiled back. "Don't worry, I've got a title for him, too."

"Will he hate it?"

"Very much."

Minho laughed. After a moment of companionable silence, he squeezed Mirae's hand. "Are you sure about this? Is abdication what you really want?"

Mirae nodded. "I have a destiny as the Switcher of Seolla. The Inconstant Son is still out there. I feel him working in the darkness, hatching a new plan to destroy the peninsula. Wherever I am, danger will always follow. So for now, I am entrusting the well-being of Seolla to you while I figure out what the gods will have me do next."

"Well, since Mother is still very alive and doing much better now that the cage has been doubly fortified, I'll have plenty of time to learn about being a ruler before anything needs to be entrusted to me. Though maybe it's about time we shook things up around here. Maybe we men can start doing a little more than we've been previously allowed."

"You better, or else I'll come back here and whip you into shape."

Minho smiled. "We'll see about that. I won't always be your gentle older brother, you know. People change, sometimes forever."

"Not you. You will always be the best man I know." Mirae gave Minho one more hug and left him to his dinner.

Chapter

THIRTY

That night, when Mirae closed her eyes to sleep, she determined once and for all to root out whichever shadow in the Deep the Netherking was sulking in. The first few nights after her return, Mirae had let the man be. Then she'd sent out soft probes with their Sacred Bone connection, but he had refused to respond to her summons. Now it was time Mirae faced the enemy she'd thwarted and showed him what kind of High Daughter she really was.

Mirae found her way to the Deep easily in her soul-walking state and let herself inside. She found the Netherking sitting in the mint-green light of the moon spot glistening above, eyes closed in meditation.

"Queenling," he murmured, loath to leave his trance. "Why are you disturbing me?"

Mirae sat across from her old nemesis, hands resting lightly on her knees. "Because we have a deal, and I'm here to keep my promise."

The Netherking didn't open his eyes. "Come back tomorrow. I'm busy."

Mirae breathed deeply as if joining him in his meditation. "I saved Suhee's life, you know. And Siwon's. I'm a woman you can trust to keep her word."

A brief hint of a sneer twitched the corner of the Netherking's mouth. "Have you asked my wife how she likes her tiny new prison?"

Mirae refused to rise to the Netherking's bait. "Didn't you want to tell me the truth about my ancestors? Tonight is your chance. I'm here to listen, as agreed."

Finally, the Netherking opened his eyes, black from his pupils all the way to his lids. "Didn't the Deep Deceiver tell you what I would say, when you shattered her soul stone?"

Mirae stared into the Netherking's ebony eyes, fighting back her unease. "We didn't talk much. She was too busy saving Suhee."

The Netherking stared back at Mirae with those pure black orbs, wide and unblinking. "So the truth about the cage can only be acquired through me. An interesting choice."

"If you have anything to say, do it now," Mirae said, regretting her decision to visit her enemy. "The next time you see me won't be on friendly terms."

"If you insist, queenling." As the Netherking's unblinking eyes bored into Mirae's, the skin around them started to flush. "What do you know of the Deep Deceiver?"

Mirae answered quickly, with all the ease of a memorized text. "She was the second High Daughter, the greatest Jade Witch Seolla has ever known. She ended a civil war bloodlessly through her command of the elements. Afterward, her soul was preserved for the day when she would be needed again as Seolla's savior."

"A savior?" The red around the Netherking's eyes branched into crimson veins, a frightening sight that made Mirae scoot backward. "Do you know why there was civil war in Seolla?"

Mirae shook her head and told herself to stand her ground. Whatever the Netherking was doing, she would not be intimidated. He was trapped, soundly beaten. "That story is a myth hidden by time, but I've come to believe that it was a war fought between Sacred Bone Daughters and the magic-adept men who rallied to the Inconstant Son. I think he was your progenitor, whose sins you're paying for."

The skin around the Netherking's eyes purpled, becoming bruises streaked with bloodred veins. "And how was all that 'civil unrest' resolved by the woman you call a savior?"

Mirae looked around at the answer she sat inside of. "She cast all dissenters, the ancestors of your people, into this cage, showing them mercy that she now regrets. I imagine the tradition of putting a mark on all magic-adept men would have resumed with greater urgency as well."

"Oh, she did more than that, queenling. So much more."

Mirae scooted back from the Netherking as the walls of the Deep began to shake, and the Netherking turned his mottled face up to the moon spot shivering overhead. "This isn't any mere cage, queenling. It's a well of magic that's about to run dry."

Mirae jumped to her feet, her heart pounding as fast as the Netherking's. What did he mean, this was a well of magic, and how could it possibly be nearing its end? Mirae's mother had refortified the cage with Mirae's help. There was no way for any man to simply leave such a prison.

The Netherking's eyes widened as the flesh of his face seemed to shrivel, bulging the black orbs staring out of his skull. The moon spot above him darkened as the giant, warted green hand writhed its way to the top of the lake.

Forgetting she was just a sleepwalking soul, Mirae reached for the Netherking, desperate to shake him out of whatever terrifying trance he was under. But as soon as her flesh touched his, the Netherking's black eyes snapped to hers, and his jaw unhinged, widening his now impossibly large mouth as black water erupted from inside his belly, creating an inky torrent that barreled into Mirae with enough force to send her soul soaring back where it belonged.

Mirae woke with a start, hearing a panicked call ringing out in the middle of the night. Words she never wanted to hear again.

Minho was missing.

Mirae sat up and put a hand to her neck, finding her pulse. She closed her eyes and followed the link between herself and her brother. His heartbeat was strong. Loud enough for her to see where he had gone.

Then it disappeared.

Mirae ran out to the palace courtyard wearing only her night-dress. She hurtled past the gates, past the gathering search party, and into the surrounding forest.

Mirae waited for no one as she took the familiar path to the Garden of Queens, through the shadowy trees and their spiderweb illusions.

Using her magic to travel with the speed of a gwisin, Mirae sped through the dark portal and onto the path of gritted bones.

When Mirae finally reached Wol Sin Lake, she dispelled her magic abruptly and stood, exhausted, on the brink of the bone-white shore. Though she was weak and shivering in the icy dark, Mirae stepped into the lake, looking for Minho.

This was where she'd heard his heartbeat last.

A giant moon glowed at the center of the black water, broken by ripples that looked like crooked smiles. Together, the pale moon spot and the inky water it rested upon formed a wide, all-knowing eye that stared up at the heavens. Both seemed to watch Mirae approach. She stared back—and when the giant eye blinked, Mirae froze.

In an instant, the moon spot was shattered. Minho was treading water at its center, up to his chest in black water. The moon glowed around him like a broken egg, bright as a fallen star.

Mirae wanted to go to him, but the Netherking's giant, bodiless hand was in front of her, its fingers slowly uncurling, revealing what lay hidden in its palm.

A fresh vial of black water and a dark crown of bones.

Everything the Netherking would need to start over.

Minho took a deep breath, like he found the cold water refreshing, savoring the ice in the air. "It's so beautiful out here," he said. "More beautiful than I could have imagined."

"Minho," Mirae said, knowing it wasn't her brother she was talking to. "You're still in there. Don't let him do this to you."

Minho turned around. "You know, queenling, I can never thank you enough for proving me right about you at every turn. As soon as our powers clashed in the garden, I knew you were the missing piece to my plan."

"How is this possible?" Mirae asked through chattering teeth.

Minho stepped toward her, skirting the green hand until he came close enough for Mirae to feel the feverish heat emanating from his body, keeping him warm in the water. Minho picked up the vial and tapped it. "You were wrong about the black water I gave you. It wasn't pure."

By now, Mirae's heart was beating loudly enough for the three of them. Three Sacred Bone heirs in the lake, sharing a pulse. A Switcher and the Inconstant Son reborn, tethered like the light and dark halves of the moon. Mirae tried to summon fire in her palms, but the black water seemed to freeze everything inside her, bound to the Netherking's will. And despite it all, the man in front of her was still Minho.

You must let him die . . . You must.

"What did you do to the black water I gave him?" Mirae choked out.

Minho smiled. "Let's just say I've been sitting in it for a while. You know, steeping it with all the essences that are me."

"But I used it, and I was fine."

"That's because I allowed you to be."

Mirae shut her eyes. She couldn't look at Minho's sneering face, at the horrors she'd forced down his throat.

The Netherking smiled with Minho's lips and cupped Mirae's face almost tenderly. "As you said, you drank some of it, too. If I wanted, I could take you instead."

"Do it." Mirae grabbed her brother's hands, pressing them to her face. "Take me. I'm willing."

The Netherking laughed. "I know when I'm outmatched, and you, Switcher, cannot be controlled. Minho has had practice being a good boy. You, on the other hand, were very right when you said you were made to destroy me. You've proven that a hundred times over. Which makes you the kind of enemy I really can't allow to remain alive."

With that, the Netherking retrieved his crown from the giant hand and plunged its long, sharp tips into Mirae's chest, staining her nightdress with blood that pooled into the shape of a moon.

Mirae stumbled back, amazed her wounds didn't hurt more. But she was too cold to feel the warm blood leaving her. And there was something else that hurt more than anything.

"Minho." She sank to her knees, chest-deep in black water. Something she'd experienced before, but not by her brother's hand.

"That's right," the Netherking soothed. "That's my new name. My new life. I finally get to see this golden Seolla I've heard so much about, and I'll very much enjoy making it mine."

"Please," Mirae said, staring at the crown sticking out of her chest. "Take me instead. I'll be obedient. I promise."

The Netherking patted her head. "I had such plans for you, until you turned out to be the Switcher of Seolla. You're too dangerous now. I need to be absolutely sure I won't fail. That's what makes Minho perfect."

There was blood in her mouth. Mirae coughed it up, letting it dribble like the Netherqueen's black water as she fumbled for the secret pocket in her nightdress, made so she could keep her ancestors' relics with her always.

"Oh, and I wouldn't recommend reaching out to your mother with the final beats of your heart. If you give me away, you really won't like who pays for your mistakes this time."

The Netherking caught Mirae as she pitched forward, laying her gently in the water, facedown. Then he pushed her under, summoning his hand to do the rest as he waded to shore.

The warted green hand crushed Mirae against the floor of the lake, as heavy as a dozen anchors. The spikes of the crown drove deeper into her chest, making her scream where no one could hear. But Mirae's other hand was still free, clutching the jade dagger of the Silver Star, first High Daughter of Seolla.

Everyone who was supposed to stop this had failed—including Mirae. But she wasn't the same girl who'd been manipulated in the Deep. The Netherking feared she was nothing but a thorn in his side; she would show him just how right he was.

Greener than the Netherking's hand, the dagger began to glow. When it was hot enough to make the water around it boil, Mirae stabbed the apparition holding her down.

She felt it lift, her body surging forward as the hand swept away, leaving waves in its wake. Mirae stayed underwater, aimlessly floating, knowing the black water wasn't going to be useful to her until the Netherking left. Once he did, he wouldn't be in control of it anymore. It would rally to the Switcher in its belly. Hungry for a taste of her.

Just like before.

Mirae knew the instant the black water recognized her as its new master. Much as it had in the Netherqueen's basin, it swirled around her, eager to taste the soul of a woman who had crossed through time. It ate what it could, becoming a part of her. It drank from her essence, her timelessness, more powerful than anything in the Netherqueen's soul.

More powerful than the Netherqueen's husband's, too.

In his hands, black water could corrupt. It could transform. Build an army. Raze a queendom. But in Mirae's, it was endless, full of possibility. As long as it was fed, it would be her ally, storing her divine power in the depths of its belly, casting whatever she wanted.

Most important, black water could heal anything it touched.

As soon as she felt her wounds scarring over, Mirae burst out of the water and charged the shore, summoning the rage of her ancestors boiling in the blood that no longer spilled from her chest. Hotter than any fury she had ever felt. Stronger than any hand that dared to hold down a Daughter of the Sacred Bone.

The Netherking raised his arms, summoning seaweed to catch Mirae's ankles, rocks to trip her, but Mirae remembered well how the Netherking's wife had shrieked and took to eating men from the air. She, too, rose up into the Seollan sky, where the pale moon could make the black water drip from her like gems.

The Netherking stared up at Mirae as he would a false god. "How is this possible?"

As if in answer to his question, the ghost pearl, unbidden, rose out of Mirae's pocket. Mirae watched, stunned at its starlike beauty, as it floated in front of her face. It rose above her head, hovering like a weightless crown—her own personal moon.

The Netherking grew paler than the pearl, staring at something behind Mirae. She turned in the air and saw that she was not alone. Sol hovered just behind Mirae like a bright reflection. A starry shadow with unresolved rage. She'd brought her army of gwisin with her; they stood together, facing the man who had mutilated them. A pale army to rival his dark one.

"No," he whispered. "You can't betray me."

Whether he was talking to Mirae, the gwisin, or his daughter's pearl, all three descended upon him. The black water rose like a floor to meet Mirae's feet, carrying her forward faster than she could fly.

When Mirae came crashing back to earth, prepared to break the bones and the beautiful, precious body that held two kings, the magic in her palm ignited like blazing stars. The Netherking's magic flocked to him, too, as if the lightless void between galaxies had been summoned to whirl about his body. The domed shields Mirae and the Netherking created flew at each other like two halves of the same moon, destined to meet. Destined to destroy each other.

When their universes clashed, the might of the gods met their match in the man who Mirae knew was never meant to be—her enemy, the Inconstant Son. And their collision left the Deep quaking for hours to the lake-loud beating of their hearts.

ACKNOWLEDGMENTS

First and foremost I want to recognize and thank my incredible mentors Roseanne A. Brown and Swati Teerdhala. I was ready to shelve this book and all my dreams of being a published author until these fantastic women took me under their wing. I am eternally indebted to them. Team Tigerwraiths forever!

Next I wish to thank my rockstar agent, Holly, for being an exceptional advocate and champion. I'm in awe of her sagacity, empathy, and near-magical ability to keep my chin up.

I am also thankful to my editor, Alice, for loving Mirae's story and helping me draw out the heart of it. I've never mind-melded with anyone over my books so easily. We make a good team! I would also like to extend sincere thanks to the rest of my team at HarperTeen. You're all superstars, and I cannot thank you enough for all you do. Additionally, I'd like to express my appreciation to Keurim for her keen and perceptive notes, and to Priscilla Kim, my incredibly talented cover artist, for bringing Mirae to life. Seeing such a determined and stunningly rendered Korean princess on a book cover brings such joy to my inner teenage self.

Next I'd like to thank Amanda, the first person to read my initial draft in its entirety. You encouraged me to complete a manuscript that changed my life. I'd also like to thank my early critique partners (a.k.a. the Writers of Wonder). To Meghan, Cassy, Crystal, and Chelsea, I'm more grateful than you know for your friendship and support. Brooke and Alex, thanks for all the check-ins and for reminding me to celebrate every step of the way. Thank you, June, for your wisdom and for being a listening ear. Writing can be such a lonely business.

I'd like to give a special shout-out to Tesia Tsai for all the writing sprees, treats, and motivation. You kept me sane and creative. I don't know where I'd be without you. I also want to give special thanks to Na-Young for sharing in all my joys and giving me a room of my own to write in when I needed one. To Aaron, my wonderful husband and cheerleader, how can I ever thank you for filling my days with laughter, kindness, and happiness? I love you "mostest in the universe!"

Lastly, I owe a great debt to the writing teachers of my youth, Mrs. Warren and Mrs. Young, for believing in me, and for their predictions, which I wanted to come true. I'd also like to give heartfelt thanks to Gerald Morris, Megan Whalen Turner, Clare B. Dunkle, and John Flanagan for writing back to me all those years ago. I took your advice, and it has made all the difference.

Of course I owe a big thanks to my readers and all the relentlessly beautiful lights in the world.

사랑으로,

Lena